The B

Alex Gerlis is the author of the acclaimed Spies series of four Second World War espionage thrillers which are noted for their detailed research and intricate plots and feature two great adversaries: the British spymaster Edgar and his Soviet counterpart Viktor. The television/film rights for *The Best of Our Spies* have been bought by a major production company.

Born in Lincolnshire, Alex was a BBC journalist for nearly 30 years. He lives in west London with his wife and family and three black cats, a breed which makes cameo appearances in his books. He's a lifelong supporter of Grimsby Town, which has provided some preparation for the highs and lows of writing novels. When asked if he has worked in the field of espionage he declines to answer in the hope some people may think he has.

Also by Alex Gerlis

Spy Masters

The Best of Our Spies
The Swiss Spy
Vienna Spies
The Berlin Spies

The Richard Prince Thrillers

Prince of Spies
Sea of Spies
Ring of Spies
End of Spies

ALEX GERLIS

THE BEST OF OUR SPIES

CANELO
US

San Diego, California

 Canelo US
An imprint of Printers Row Publishing Group
9717 Pacific Heights Blvd, San Diego, CA 92121
www.canelobooksus.com

Printers Row Publishing Group is a division of Readerlink Distribution
Services, LLC. Canelo US is a registered trademark of Readerlink
Distribution Services, LLC.

This edition originally published in the United Kingdom in 2020 by
Canelo.

Published in partnership with Canelo.

Correspondence regarding the content of this book should be sent to Canelo
US, Editorial Department, at the above address. Author inquiries should be
sent to Canelo, Unit 9, 5th Floor, Cargo Works, 1–2 Hatfields, London SE1
9PG, United Kingdom, www.canelo.co.

Publisher: Peter Norton • Associate Publisher: Ana Parker
Art Director: Charles McStravick
Senior Developmental Editor: April Graham
Production Team: Beno Chan, Julie Greene, Rusty von Dyl

Library of Congress Control Number: 2022934238

ISBN: 978-1-6672-0229-7

Printed in India

26 25 24 23 22   1 2 3 4 5

Chapter 1

Northern France, May 1940

The first time they saw German troops was around eight hours after they had left Amiens.

Fear had swept through the twenty of them, mostly strangers who had silently come together by happening to be on the same road at the same time and moving in the same direction. '*Don't head north,*' they had been warned in Amiens. '*You're walking into a battle.*'

Some of the original group had heeded that advice and stayed in the town. A dozen of them had carried on. They were refugees now, so they kept moving. It had quickly become a habit, they couldn't stop themselves.

A tall, stooped man called Marcel had assumed the role of leader and guide. He was a dentist, from Chartres, he told them. The rest of the group nodded and were happy to follow him.

Marcel decided that the main road would be too dangerous, so they dropped down to follow the path of the Somme, passing through the small villages that hugged the river as it twisted through Picardy. The villages were unnaturally silent, apart from the angry barking of dogs taking turns to escort them through their territory. Anxious villagers peered from behind partially drawn curtains or half-closed shutters.

Occasionally, a child would venture out to stare at them, but would quickly be called home by an urgent shout. Some villagers would come out and offer them water and a little food, but were relieved to see them move on. Refugees meant war and no one wanted the war to linger in their village. In a couple of the places, one or two more refugees joined them. No one asked to join, no one was refused. They just tagged along, swelling their numbers.

On the outskirts of the village of Ailly-sur-Somme a middle-aged couple came out from their cottage and offered the group water and fruit. They sat on the grass verge while the couple appeared to be arguing quietly in their doorway. And that was when they called her out.

'Madame, please can we have a word with you?'

She was sitting nearest to the house, but was not sure that they meant her. She looked around in case they were addressing someone else.

'Please, could we speak with you?' the man asked again.

She walked slowly over to the doorway. Maybe they had taken pity on her and were going to offer a meal. Or a bed. She smiled at the couple. Behind them, in the gloom of the hallway, she could make out a pair of piercing eyes.

'Madame. You seem to be a very decent lady. Please help us.' The man sounded desperate. 'A lady passed through the village last week.'

There was a pause.

'From Paris,' his wife added.

'Yes, she was from Paris. She said that she had to find somewhere in the area to hide and she asked us to look after her daughter. She promised she would be back for her in a day or two. She said she would pay us then. She promised to be generous. But that was a week ago. We cannot look after the girl any longer. The Germans could arrive any day now. You must take her!'

She looked around. The group were getting up now, preparing to move on.

'Why me?' she asked.

'Because you look decent and maybe if you are from a city you'll understand her ways. Are you from a city?'

She nodded, which they took as some kind of assent. The woman ushered the girl from inside the cottage. She looked no more than six years old, with dark eyes and long curly hair. She was dressed in a well-made blue coat and her shoes were smart and polished. A pale brown leather satchel hung across her shoulders.

'Her name is Sylvie,' the man said. His wife took Sylvie's hand and placed it in the woman's.

'But what about when her mother returns?'

The wife was already retreating into the dark interior of the cottage.

'Are you coming?' It was Marcel, calling out to her as he started to lead the group off. His voice sounded almost jolly as if they were on a weekend ramble.

The man leaned towards her, speaking directly into her ear so that the little girl could not hear. 'She won't be back,' he said. He glanced round at the girl and lowered his voice. 'They're Jews. You must take her.'

With that, he quickly followed his wife into the cottage and slammed the door behind them.

She hesitated on the doorstep, still holding the little girl's hand. She could hear the door being bolted. She knocked on the door two or three times, but there was no response.

She thought of trying to go round to the rear of the cottage, but she was losing sight of her group now. Sylvie was still holding her hand, glancing up at her anxiously. She knelt down to speak to the little girl.

'Are you all right?' She tried to sound reassuring. Sylvie nodded.

'Do you want to come with me?'

The little girl nodded again and muttered 'Yes.'

This is the last thing I need. She thought of leaving her there, on the doorstep. They'll have to take her back in. She paused. *I need to decide quickly. Maybe as far as the town, there'll be somewhere she can go there.*

By the time they had walked down the path and started to follow the group, the shutters in the cottage had been closed.

It was as they left the next village that they came across the Germans. They emerged from behind the trees one by one, with their grey uniforms, black boots and oddly shaped helmets, not saying a word. Slowly, they circled the group, which had come to a halt, too frightened to move. The German soldiers moved into position like pieces on a chessboard. They waved their machine guns to herd the group into the middle of the road.

She was terrified. *They are going to shoot us.* The little girl clutched her hand.

She breathed in and out deeply. Remember the training they gave you, she told herself:

When you are in a potentially dangerous situation, do not try to be anonymous.

Never look away, or at the ground. Do not avoid eye contact.

If you are in a group or a crowd, avoid standing in the middle, which is where they would expect you to hide.

If you fear that you are about to be found out, resist the temptation to own up. It is a fair assumption that the person questioning you or searching you will miss the obvious.

She heard some shouting from behind the trees and over the shoulder of the soldier nearest to her she spotted two officers emerging. One of them was speaking loudly in bad French.

'We are going to search you and then you can move on. Are any of you carrying weapons?'

Everyone around her was shaking their head. She noticed that Sylvie shook hers too.

He waited a while in case anyone might change their minds.

'Are there any Jews in this group?'

There was silence. People glanced suspiciously at those stood around them. At the word '*Jews*' the little girl's hand had tightened its grip on hers with a strength she could not have imagined. She looked down and saw that Sylvie had her head bowed and appeared to be sobbing. She realised the extent of her predicament. If they caught her looking after a Jewish child, she would have no excuses.

'My men will come and search you now. I am sure that you will all co-operate.'

Too late.

The soldiers spread the group out along the road and began searching people. Marcel was close to her and was searched before her. The soldier searching him gestured to him to remove his wristwatch. Marcel started to protest, until one of the officers walked over. He smiled, looked at the watch that had been passed to him, nodded approvingly and slipped it into his jacket pocket. Along the line, members of the group were being relieved of possessions: watches, pieces of jewellery and even a bottle of cognac.

The soldier who came to search her appeared to be in his teens. His hands shook as he took her identity card. She noticed that his lips moved silently as he tried to read what it said. One of the officers appeared behind him and took the identity card.

'You've come a long way.' He handed her identity card back to her. She nodded.

'Is this your sister?' He was staring intently at the little girl.

She gave the faintest of nods.

'She is your sister, then?'

She hesitated. She had not said anything yet. She could do so now. They wouldn't harm a child. The little girl now placed her other hand round her wrist, stroking her forearm as she did so.

4

'Yes. She is my sister.' She had replied in German, speaking quietly and hoping that no one else in the group heard her. Trying to appear as relaxed as possible, she smiled sweetly at the officer who was probably in his mid-twenties, the same age as her. She threw her head back, allowing her long hair to settle over her shoulders.

If you are an attractive woman – at that point the instructor had been looking directly at her, along with the rest of them – *do not hesitate to use your charms on men.*

The officer raised his eyebrows approvingly and nodded.

'And where did you learn to speak German?'

'At school.'

'A good school then. And does your sister have an identity card?'

It was too late. She should have realised this would happen. *Does he suspect something? She doesn't look anything like me. Her complexion is so much darker.* She had lost the chance to tell them the truth.

'She lost it.'

'Where?'

'In Amiens. A Gypsy stole it from her.'

The officer nodded knowingly. He understood. *What do you expect? Gypsies. Don't we warn people about them? Thieves. Almost as bad as the Jews. Almost.*

He lowered himself down on his haunches so that he was at eye level with the little girl.

'And what is your name?'

There was a pause. The little girl peered up at her for approval. She nodded and smiled.

Tell him.

'Sylvie.'

'Sylvie is a nice name. Sylvie what?'

'Sylvie.'

'What is your surname – your full name?'

'Sylvie.'

'So, your name is "Sylvie Sylvie"?' The officer was beginning to sound exasperated. Sylvie was whimpering.

'I'm sorry, sir. She is frightened. It's the guns. She's never seen any before.'

'Well, she'd better get used to them, hadn't she?' The officer was standing up now. Not satisfied.

5

From the east there was a series of explosions followed by an exchange of rifle fire.

The officer hesitated. He wanted to continue with the interrogation, but the other officer was shouting out urgent instructions to the soldiers.

'All right, move on,' he said to her.

It was only when the soldiers disappeared back into the woods and the group moved on that she realised how petrified she was. Her heart was ramming against her ribs and cold sweat was running down her back. The little girl walked on obediently beside her, but she could feel and see her body trembling.

As the group walked slowly along the road, she realised that she was stroking Sylvie's hair, her trembling hand cupping the child's cheeks, wiping away the tears with her thumb.

Not for the first time and certainly not for the last, she had surprised herself.

–

They had walked for another hour. Marcel had dropped back at one stage and sidled up to her.

'And where did she come from?' He gestured at Sylvie, who was still clutching her hand.

'The couple who gave us water and fruit outside their cottage. The last village but one. They made me take her.'

'You realise…?'

'Of course I do!'

'Aren't you taking a bit of a risk?'

'Aren't we all?'

Marcel had spotted a forest ahead of them and said that the deeper they got into it, the safer they'd be. But, as she had begun to realise was the case in the countryside, distances were hard to judge and the forest was not quite as near as it had seemed and by the time they found a clearing, everyone was exhausted.

That night she found herself with Sylvie on the edge of the group, resting next to an old man and his wife. While the rest of the group slept the old man had given her his blanket, assuring her he was not cold. Sylvie was curled up alongside her under the blanket, fast asleep.

The old man had also given her the last of his water. He was not thirsty, he assured her. The moonlight poked through the canopy of the forest, the tops of some of the trees swaying very gently despite the apparent absence of any breeze. The old man moved closer to her and spoke quietly: he and his wife had lost both their sons at Verdun and had prayed they would never see another war. He had tried to lead a decent life. He went to church, he paid his taxes, he had never voted for the communists. He had worked on the railways, but was now retired. They could not stand the thought of being in Paris when it was occupied, so now they were heading to the town where his wife's sister lived, he explained. It was bound to be peaceful there.

'You look so much like our daughter,' he said, patting her affectionately on the wrist. 'You have the same slim figure, the same beautiful long, dark hair, the same dark eyes. When my wife and I saw you for the first time yesterday – we both remarked on that!'

'Where does your daughter live?'

The old man said nothing, but his eyes moistened as he held his hand over hers.

The old man was kind, but there was something about him that unsettled her. As she lay down on the cold earth, a familiar yet unwelcome companion descended upon her. The memory. The old man alongside, she realised, reminded her of her father. He too worked on the railways. The same dark eyes that couldn't hide the suffering. The same awkwardness. The reason why she was here now.

She had tried so hard to forget her father, but now the dark memories were stirred, she knew she would be troubled for the rest of the night.

She slept in short, unsatisfactory bursts, as she always did when her father came back to her. At one stage she woke with a start, aware that she must have cried out in her sleep. She looked round and noticed the old man's eyes, glinting in the moonlight, staring at her. When she awoke in the morning she felt stiff and cold. As the group moved off, she fell in with the old man and his wife, but the kindness of the previous night had gone and he ignored her.

–

'Come closer.'

It was later that afternoon and the group had paused at the edge of the forest, through which they had been walking all day. The old man, who was calling out to her, was now slumped at the base of the tree

7

and had aged ten years in the past ten minutes. His legs were twisted under him and his skin was as grey as the bark he was resting against. His wife knelt by his side, anxiously gripping his right arm with both her hands. He held his other arm out towards her, fingers urgently beckoning her to him.

'Come here,' he called out. His voice was rasping and angry. The rest of the group were moving off, leaving just her and Sylvie with the old man and his wife.

She looked down the forest path, where the rest of the group were now disappearing beyond the sunbeams. They knew that there was nothing they could do for the man and they were anxious to try and reach the town before nightfall. She could just make out Marcel, his short walking stick waving high above his head to encourage them along.

'Leave him,' Marcel had said. 'I warned everyone not to drink from the ponds. This water can be like a poison. He took the risk. We must move on.'

She hesitated. If she lost contact with the group she could be stranded in the forest, but she had made the mistake of stopping to help when the man collapsed and it would seem odd if she abandoned him now.

She knelt down by his side. Around the tree was a carpet of bracken; green, brown and silver. His lips were turning blue and spittle flecked with blood was dribbling down the sides of his mouth. His eyes were heavily bloodshot and his breathing was painfully slow. He did not have long to go. She recognised the signs. She would soon be able to rejoin the group.

'Closer.' His voice was now little more than a harsh whisper.

With a shaking hand he pulled her head towards his. His breath was hot and smelled foul.

'I heard you last night,' he said. She pulled back, a puzzled look on her face.

He nodded, pulling her back towards him, glancing at his wife as he did so, checking that she could not hear. 'I heard you cry out,' he whispered. 'I heard what you said.'

He waited to regain his breath, his whole body heaving as he did so. His reddened eyes blazed with fury.

'This victory will be your greatest defeat.'

8

Later that afternoon she realised how soon you became inured to the sights and the smells of war. They had a tendency to creep up on you, allowing time for the mind to prepare itself for what it was about to experience. But not the *sounds*. The sounds of war might have been no more shocking, but they had a tendency to arrive without warning, imposing themselves in the most brutal manner. You were never prepared for them.

So it was on that dusty afternoon at the end of May, where the Picardy countryside had begun to give hints of a nearby but unseen sea, and where a small group of French civilians desperately trying to flee the war now found that they had walked right into it.

It took a few seconds for her and most of the others in the column to realise that the cracking sound a hundred yards or so ahead of them had been a gunshot. Maybe it was the shock of the strange metallic noise, that seemed to echo in such an undulating manner in every direction; more likely it was the fact that it was the first time most of them had ever heard a gunshot. In a split second, she reassembled in her mind what she had just seen and heard. Moments earlier, the tall figure of Marcel had been remonstrating with the German officer. She could barely make out what he had been saying, although she did hear the word 'civilians' more than once, as he pointed in their direction with his walking stick. Then there was the cracking noise and now Marcel lay still on the ground, the dusty, light-grey surface of the road turning a dark colour beneath him.

A wave of fear rolled through the small group that had been held up beyond the makeshift German checkpoint where the shooting had taken place. '*I know the area*,' Marcel had told them. '*I can handle the Germans*.'

Apart from the woman with four children, and three elderly couples, the group was mainly women on their own. All fools, she thought. All allowing themselves to be herded like cattle. All part of the reason why France had become what it was.

She knew that she had made a terrible mistake. She could have headed in any direction, other than east. That would have been suicide. When she looked at where she had ended up now, she might as well have gone east. She realised now that, of course, south would have been best. Due west would have been safe too; not as safe as the south, but better. But to have come north was a disaster.

9

It was not as if she had been following the crowds. Half of France had been on the move and each person seemed to be heading in a different direction. She had made up her mind when she left home that she would head north, and it wasn't in her nature to change her mind. She had tried a few weeks ago and this was why she was in so much trouble now. It was crazy though. She had passed through Abbeville when she was a girl, on the way to the coast for the only happy family holiday that she could remember. It had been an idyllic day, no more than a few hours respite on a long journey, but for some reason this was where she had decided to head.

The German officer walked over to the man on the ground, the pistol still in his hand. With his boot he rolled the body over onto its back and then nodded to two of his men. They picked a leg each and dragged the corpse to the ditch by the side of the road. A long red smear appeared on it where his body had been. The officer inspected his boot and wiped it clean on the grass verge.

One of the soldiers came over to the group and spoke to them slowly in bad French. They were to come forward one by one, he shouted. They were to show their identity cards to the officer who had shot the man, and after they had been searched, they would be allowed to carry on into the town.

The light had not started to fade yet and beyond the checkpoint she could see the outskirts of the town quite clearly. Plumes of dark smoke hung all over the town, all of them remarkably straight and narrow, as if the town lay beneath a forest of pine trees.

She couldn't risk the checkpoint. Not with this identity card. The first Germans they had encountered had not paid much attention to people's identities. They had seemed more intent on finding what loot they could lay their hands on. This checkpoint seemed to be more thorough. She had known that she would have to find another identity, and assumed she would get the opportunity in the town. She had not counted on coming across the Germans so early; no one had. The last news she had heard was that the Germans had not yet reached Calais. That was what Marcel had told them, and now his feet were sticking out of the ditch in front of them, his blood now turning black on the surface of the road.

She edged towards the rear of the column, looking around her as she did so. She spotted her opportunity. The soldiers were distracted by dealing with the mother and her four children, all of whom were crying. No one was watching the group. She leaned over to Sylvie, who was still clutching her by the waist, and whispered that she was going to the toilet in the field. She would be back in a minute. The little girl's eyes filled with tears. Reluctantly, she reached in her pocket and took out the bar of chocolate. It was the last of the bars that had filled her coat pockets and it was all she had left to eat. She pressed it into Sylvie's palm, noticing that the chocolate was soft and had begun to melt.

'If you are a good girl and keep very quiet, you can have all of this!' She was trying hard to sound as gentle as possible. She looked around. No one was looking at her. Towards the front of the column she saw the smartly dressed lady in her mid-thirties who had introduced herself as a lawyer from Paris, headed for the family home in Normandy.

'You see that nice lady there? The one with the smart brown coat? She will look after you. But don't worry, I will be back soon.'

Still crouching down, she edged towards the ditch and then through a narrow gap in the hedge. The corn was high in the field, and not far away was a large wood, which seemed to taper as it spread towards the town. She waited for a moment. She was certain that the Germans had not counted how many there were in their group and hopefully would not realise that one person had crept away. If they did come and look for her now, she was near enough to the hedge to be able to persuade them that she was just relieving herself.

It looked as if she had landed in an Impressionist painting: the golden yellow of the corn, the blue of the sky unbroken by cloud, and ahead the dark green of the wood. A timely breeze had picked up and the corn was swaying slowly. It would disguise her moving through it to the wood. If she could make it there she would have a good chance of reaching the town under the cover of the trees and the fading light.

Chapter 2

It is what comes in the wake of an invading army that is the true measure of a conquest.

The tanks and crack troops of the Panzer Group that entered the small town of Abbeville in the last week of May 1940 were quickly followed by the Wehrmacht, the regular troops with their grey uniforms and a sense of mild inferiority which they happily took out on their new subjects. And then came the camp followers: the cooks, the medics, the prostitutes and the officials. Especially the officials. It was as if the German Reich had been meticulously collecting minor officials for years and storing them in a cellar in Bavaria in the expectation that, come the conquest of Europe, they would have an army of them to promote beyond their natural station and help ensure the efficiency of any occupation.

And it was one of these minor officials, who now clearly regarded himself as anything but minor, who was to be her undoing.

She had entered the town the night before, waiting for a black blanket to drape over the Picardy countryside before she felt it was safe enough to leave the cover of the wood and crawl into the first row of ruins. From there she had worked her way through the outskirts, crossing debris-strewn roads and hurrying down streets where no building had been left unscathed. As a church bell struck ten, she had climbed into the attic above a row of abandoned shops and found a room where the window was more or less intact and there was large, dusty sofa. As the adrenaline of the escape from the checkpoint ebbed away she realised how hungry she was. Her last proper meal had been in a farmhouse the other side of Arras and since then she had managed on overpriced bread, and fruit she had taken from obliging orchards. She had been saving the bar of chocolate for an emergency. Keeping the little girl quiet had been that emergency.

In the corner of the room was a filthy sink, with a long crack running diagonally through it. The single tap, high above the sink, was stiff to turn and when she managed to release it there was a shudder and a hiss, but no water. She had last drunk water in one of the villages they had passed through the day before. Now, her throat was dry and she felt lightheaded. Not long before they arrived at the checkpoint outside Abbeville they had walked through a small forest, dotted with *étangs*. Marcel warned people against drinking the water and she knew that he was right: the surface of the little lake was still and scummy, but the old man who had given her the last of his water the night before insisted on drinking from an *étang*. They had barely walked for another five minutes before he became violently sick.

His face appeared in her dreams that night, but only fleetingly, although she couldn't get his last words out of her mind: 'This victory will be your greatest defeat.'

She dreaded to think what she must have said in her sleep to cause him to say that, but it was a good thing that he had decided to drink from the *étang*.

She dreamt a series of confused dreams that all seemed to end with her trying to catch a train or a bus that was always pulling away just as she reached it. In the final dream she found herself hiding in a warm bakery, the smell of freshly baked baguettes overwhelming.

She woke to find two boys standing in the doorway staring at her. She had no idea how old they were: certainly not teenagers, yet not so young that they could be described as children. But what mattered was what they had in their arms: baguettes, two each. The smell of them had already filled the room.

'What do you want?' she asked sharply.

'Somewhere to stay.' It was the older boy, probably thirteen now that she thought about it, thinking back to her days on the children's ward. He was trying to sound confident, but he was trembling. 'Is this your place?'

Outside she could hear the sound of the shop doors being wrenched open and then slammed shut, followed by shouting in German. 'They've gone, they're not around here,' one of the soldiers was saying.

'Are they after you?'

The younger boy nodded. He looked terrified. 'We took some food. A patrol spotted us so we ran away. They didn't see us come in here. I promise you.'

13

'You can stay,' she said, 'but let me see what food you've got.'

They laid it out on the filthy table in the middle of the room. The two baguettes, a large round cheese with a thick yellow rind and not much of an aroma, and a long, thick smoked sausage.

'Do you have anything to drink?'

The younger boy glanced nervously at the older one who nodded. He pulled a flask from an inside coat pocket.

'It's water,' he said, 'it's all we have left.' He grudgingly handed the flask over to her.

She drank all of the water in the flask in one go and then looked at the two boys.

'I'll take a baguette and half of the cheese and sausage. Then you can stay. It's your rent. Keep quiet and stay away from the windows. Understand?'

The boys nodded. They had risked their lives for this food and now had given half of it away, but they had no alternative. Crouched on the floor, shoulder to shoulder, they sat in silence, eating while sunlight swept into the room, picking out the dust and the cobwebs. The boys were exhausted and by noon had fallen asleep.

She stayed on the sofa, the remains of the bread and her share of the cheese and the sausage carefully stashed in her bag, which she clutched to her chest. By early afternoon, she had a plan. She would head for the hospital. It was the natural place for her to go. They would probably welcome her and, apart from anything else, there she would have a good chance of finding a new identity.

She left the boys asleep. She thought about taking the remains of the sausage that was poking out of the older boy's side pocket, but he was stirring and she thought better of it.

There were plenty of grey-uniformed Germans in the streets, but they weren't stopping anyone, as far as she could tell. In the distance, there was the muffled sound of artillery fire and the occasional roar of aircraft. Outside a bombed church she noticed a queue forming, which she instinctively joined. She still had some cash and, if this was a chance to buy something while her money was worth anything, she did not want to let it pass. The people in the queue were talking quietly. The Allies were trying to retake the town, she heard someone say. An attack was imminent. God would save them. It was only when she reached the front of the queue that she realised she had been wasting her time. A young priest was sitting on a chair in the porch of the church taking confession, his cassock gently blowing around his shoulders in the wind. She turned to leave, but thought that would only bring unwanted attention, so she allowed him to bless her and mutter a prayer she didn't bother to listen to.

As she moved away there was a roar of artillery, much nearer now. Two old men were discussing it.

'It's coming in this direction,' said one.

The other shook his head: 'No, it's being fired from the town.'

It hardly seemed to matter as far as she was concerned. She had no idea of which side she was meant to be on anyway.

She headed towards the centre of the town. The first bridge that she came to was intact and she joined the throng of people hurrying across the Somme. It was only when she was halfway over the bridge that she found she had been sucked into a queue, with German soldiers marshalling people into rows. This was nothing like the checkpoint outside the town, manned by just one or two easily distracted soldiers. This was a proper checkpoint. The civilians were being funnelled into one of four rows, each row guarded by half a dozen soldiers with their machine guns drawn. At the end of each row was a trestle table, where a black-uniformed SS officer sat alongside a Wehrmacht officer. Behind the trestle tables was another row of tables, laden with paperwork and manned by anxious officials. The officers at the first table were passing the identity cards they were checking to the men at the second row of tables.

There was nothing she could do. She had walked into a trap and there was simply no prospect of her being able to slip away from it. She edged along the queue, taking care to breathe slowly, look calm and, above all, avoid drawing attention to herself.

After all, why would they be interested in her? She tried to reassure herself. She had a good cover story: '*I am a nurse, heading for the hospital, ready to volunteer my services.*' Why was she in this part of the country, so far from home? She would smile, she would always smile. Her best smile. '*I was frightened. Isn't everyone? I joined other people escaping the fighting and thought I would head for somewhere quiet. I made a mistake.*' Then she would smile again.

She realised she was being ridiculous anyway. She was worrying far too much. It was hard to imagine that with everything they had on their minds, the Germans would remember anything about her. A foolish promise she had made in a rash and impetuous moment. It had been an exciting proposal they had made two years ago in Paris and one that was not hard to agree to after the wine, the flattery and the charm. The training in Bavaria. '*Go home and wait there,*' they had told her. '*We'll come and find you when we need you. Lead a normal life. Go to work, go home, and don't talk about politics to anyone. Just make sure you are where we know you are.*' She was not important. In the great scheme of things, she was barely even a pawn. Surely it would be weeks, months even, before they remembered about her, and by then she would be beyond their grasp.

'*Carte d'identité… Carte d'identité!*'

The soldier next to the SS man behind the trestle table was shouting at her and a sentry was pushing her roughly in the side. She had reached the front of the queue.

She fumbled in her bag and found her identity card, only just remembering to smile as she placed it carefully on the rough wooden surface. The SS man looked at the card and handed it to the soldier next to him, who spoke to her in hesitant French.

'Where are you heading?'

'The hospital. You can see that I'm a nurse. I'm going to volunteer to—'

He cut her short. 'Why are you in this town? You have travelled a long way.'

She shrugged and smiled again. 'I used to come to this area for my holidays when I was a child. I thought it would be safe. I didn't realise…'

The SS officer looked carefully at her and then at her identity card. He was turning it slowly. She noticed that his fingers were immaculately manicured, his nails quite perfect. He looked once more at the card and passed it to the table behind him.

It was then that she noticed that the men in civilian clothes behind that table were checking the cards against lists. What if her name was on one of the lists? She was being ridiculous again, but it did make her realise that getting a new identity was an absolute priority. By whatever means, she would make sure…

Something was wrong.

She sensed it before she saw it.

She could not tell which of the officials had been looking at her card, but one of them had called over a man in a long raincoat who was standing behind the table, and together they were looking at an

16

identity card and checking it against the list. Another man, also dressed in a long raincoat was called over and he too looked at the card and then at the list. The three men nodded and she was sure that at least one of them glanced in her direction. She tried to look as relaxed as possible, but her heart was crashing against her chest. She turned round, but it was impossible. There were soldiers every side of her. Maybe if she pretended to faint, or to—

'Please…' One of the men in long raincoats had appeared at her side and was holding her firmly by the elbow.

'We need to do some more checks. Please come with me.'

–

'You are sure that you have told me everything?'

The Gestapo officer who had brought her to the Hôtel de Ville from the checkpoint had stopped circling her chair and now stood directly in front of her, his arms folded tight against his chest and looking genuinely confused. He had removed his raincoat and his hat and looked no more than thirty. His French was excellent, so she abandoned her attempts at speaking in her much less fluent German.

'I told you. I was recruited in Paris two years ago. I have been trained. My instructions were to stay where I was, but I left a week ago when the police became suspicious of me.'

'In what way?'

'What do you mean?'

He was beginning to look exasperated now. This was the third time they had been through the same set of questions. She sensed that he was primed for resistance, that he was only really at ease when interrogating people who refused to co-operate. That was what he was trained for, not someone apparently going out of their way to co-operate. He seemed uncomfortable in the face of such co-operation. She drew a deep breath, trying hard not to look put-out at having to repeat herself.

'What I mean is that I was worried that the police were interested in me. I told you, one of the nurses at the hospital said that someone had been asking her about me, whether I was ever involved in politics, that kind of thing.'

'And the name of this nurse?' He was sitting at the desk now, his pencil poised.

'Thérèse.'

He looked at her, saying nothing but raising his eyebrows, the very faintest hint of a smile appearing on his face. She knew what he was after.

'I cannot remember her surname. We weren't in the same department. I just knew her as Thérèse. In any case, that was not the only thing. I was followed home from work on more than one occasion and there always seemed to be a *gendarme* in our road. They never used to be there all the time. The day before I left, there was a car parked opposite with three men in it. I am certain they were police. That is why I decided to go. I couldn't risk staying.'

He looked unconvinced, but said nothing, tapping his pencil on the pad in front of him. They were on the top floor of the Hôtel de Ville, in a small room, with the noise seeping in along with the sunlight through the closed shutters.

There was a knock on the door and a soldier came in, handing over a small envelope. The Gestapo officer opened it, read it quickly and put the note back inside the envelope. He nodded at her. *Carry on.*

'I know that my orders had been to stay at home and act normally and I would be contacted, but I panicked. Maybe I was wrong, I don't know, but I was convinced they were after me. What use would I have been then? So that is why I escaped. I was not running away. I used my own identity, didn't I? If I was running away, surely I would have changed that?'

He nodded. Against his better judgement, it was hard to disbelieve her. Of course, he would have liked nothing better than for her to say nothing. He could cope with defiance, but he was unsure how to deal with this.

'And tell me about your recruitment in Paris.'

'Again?'

'Yes, please.'

'I met Herr Lange at the German Embassy there in February 1938. He arranged for my training in Germany. He gave me my instructions. The last I heard from him was that I was to wait for him.'

'Where was the Embassy?'

'Pardon?' It was the first time that he had asked this question. 'I cannot remember the exact address.'

He looked pleased, as if he had discovered a chink in her defence. 'You cannot remember the address. I see. Where was it near?'

'The river.'

He snorted and got up from behind the desk and came to stand in front of her. He placed his hands on his hips and leaned over her.

'*Everywhere* in Paris is near the river. You will have to do better than that.'

'It was near a station, the Gare d'Orsay – I remember that. And the National Assembly was nearby, of course.'

'Of course.' He was beginning to look disappointed. He had quite perked up at the prospect of having an excuse to hit her.

'I remember now. It was in the Rue de Lille. That's where it was!'

He nodded and returned to his desk, gathering up his papers and kicking the chair back under the desk.

'Well, you won't have to wait very long now. Herr Lange is on his way.'

-

He arrived in the middle of the following afternoon. He was shorter than she remembered, but with the same broad shoulders and thick, swept-back hair. He walked smartly into the room, accompanied by the Gestapo officer. He removed a beige raincoat to reveal a well-cut suit. Ignoring her, he neatly folded his raincoat, looked around for a coat-hook which he couldn't find and draped his coat over the back of the chair behind the desk.

The Gestapo officer was hovering in the doorway, keen to remain part of the proceedings. Lange continued to ignore both of them while he checked that the window was locked and the shutters closed.

'Thank you,' he said to the officer, who was still showing no signs of leaving.

After a moment he took the hint and turned sharply out of the door.

Lange waited until the echo of the officer's footsteps had long disappeared before going to the doorway, glancing up and down the corridor and then locking the door.

Only then did he acknowledge her, with a courteous nod of his head that was almost a bow, as he pulled a chair over and carefully positioned it directly in front of her. He sat very still, saying nothing. During the silence that followed, she realised that she could no longer hear any artillery fire. He carefully arranged his shirt cuffs so that just an inch of them emerged from his jacket sleeves. His cufflinks appeared to have a green jewel in them. He gestured at the door.

'He's angry that he never had to lay a finger on you. The Gestapo feel they have failed unless they have managed to hurt someone.'

'I never gave him cause to.'

'Apparently not.' There was a pause as he looked carefully through a typed document. 'Things have not gone exactly according to plan, have they?'

She shook her head. Two years ago, it had seemed such a good idea. She had continued to feel committed and enthusiastic until just a few weeks ago. Then the reality of what it could mean started to hit her. Perhaps, in her heart of hearts, she had never expected anything to come of it. Maybe, like a teenage crush, it had been just a passing fancy. But war had brought with it a fear that she never imagined could cut so deep. So no, things had not gone according to plan. She shrugged as if the matter was not that important and spoke in a soft voice.

'I've told him already. I was frightened. I thought the police were after me. I didn't want to get caught. That's why I left the city. Look, you know that the French authorities evacuated most of the population of the city last September. I'd only been allowed to remain because of my job. I felt isolated. I don't know what I was thinking, but I was afraid.'

'And you have not been having any second thoughts… any doubts about your mission?'

'Of course not, absolutely.' She was aware that she had replied perhaps too fast. But she could hardly tell the truth. *Of course I've had my doubts. Every night for the past few months I've gone to sleep with them and woken up to them.*

'You must not worry. It is perfectly natural to have doubts, even to be afraid. Everyone experiences that fear, they would probably not be taking their role seriously if they did not feel like that. What matters is that you overcome this fear and that you realise that doubt is a luxury you simply cannot afford.'

He leaned closer to her, his soft voice dropping slightly. He reminded her of the young priest in the porch of the church the previous day. He was so close that she could smell a strong tobacco on his breath and his hands, held together as if in prayer, lightly touched her wrist.

'Because you know, Ginette, you passed the point where you could change your mind a long time ago. The day you first came to see me, from then on, you were on our side. In our world, indecision is a luxury not open to us. Remember, you did not apply to become a waitress in a bistro. This is not the same as working in a shop. It is a vocation that you have taken on – for life.'

'I understand that, I...'

He was leaning even closer now, speaking so quietly that she had to lean towards him to hear anything. She picked up the scent of cologne on his face. He was almost whispering directly into her ear.

'And let me warn you. You have no alternative but to do everything we ask. We will always have people watching you. We will know everything that you are doing. They are there to protect you, but also to protect our interests. You know how important you are to us because we had you on that list, didn't we? The minute you arrive there you will be implicated so your only option is to do what we say. I think that you understand the consequences if you don't.'

She nodded that she understood and, with an enormous effort, she managed a smile that she hoped did not look forced.

'Of course. I was frightened, I was not acting rationally.'

He pulled away from her, leaning back in his chair.

'So you keep saying.' He straightened his suit, flicking a speck of dirt from the sleeve. 'I cannot pretend that this has not been an... inconvenience. When we tried to contact you last week, we were most angry to find you had gone. You know that your instructions were to stay put and we would find you. I know that I said it might be months before we would contact you, but I also said it could be any time. You should have stayed where you were. We have no evidence that the police were after you. I must say, when we put your name on the list of people who were to be detained, I did not expect that we would actually find you. I thought you would have changed your identity. If you were truly attempting to escape from us you would have at least travelled under a different name, so I am inclined to believe you. So, you must not worry. In fact, things have actually worked out rather well. You have headed in the right direction, without realising it. We will be able to take good advantage of the situation.'

She felt a slight sense of relief. She was trapped, of course, but the truth was that she could have ended up in worse traps. At least now she was in the hands of the Abwehr rather than the Gestapo.

'And your mother. How is your mother?'

The slight sense of relief disappeared. She started to speak, but he interrupted before she could begin.

'She was very worried when we visited her the other week. Out of her mind with worrying about you, so I am told. But don't worry. We will keep an eye on her.'

I have no doubt you will, she thought.

Her fear must have shown, because he patted her knee, speaking almost reassuringly. His hand stayed on her knee longer than it needed to.

'What you must realise is that in the world you are now in… which *we* are in,' – his hand moved between the two of them, so as to emphasise their common endeavour – 'in this world you can never be quite sure of where you belong or of who you belong to. You will move from shadow to shadow and you will soon understand that you can never be sure of who you really are. The only advice I can give you is that once you start out on this journey, as you have, keep going in the same direction. Do not hesitate, do not waver. Keep going. Do you understand?'

Without waiting for her reply he went round the chair behind the desk and picked up his briefcase. He deposited it on top of the desk and pulled out a sheaf of papers, placing them in a neat pile.

'Here,' he patted the pile of papers, 'we have your new life. Your new identity, everything. We had, of course, been hoping to have longer to prepare you, but as we are learning – in war, things happen in such an unpredictable way.'

He removed his suit jacket and rolled up his sleeves. He was ready to start work.

'We need to move fast. We will remain here for another twenty-four hours and then we will head east along the coast. I need time to brief you, and you have to learn your new identity. Ideally we would have more than twenty-four hours in which to do this but an unexpected opportunity has presented itself and we would be foolish not to take advantage of it.'

She felt sick. Although Lange was as charming as when she first met him, this did not compensate for the fact that the plan he had outlined two years ago – and which had been refined and worked on since then – was actually going to be put into action. She was not sure that she had ever believed that would happen. There was nothing she could do now. She could not run any more.

'You say we head east. Where are we going?'

Lange reached into his briefcase and pulled out a map, which he proceeded to unfold. He spread it out on the floor in front of her and pointed to a port to the north east of Abbeville.

'Here. Dunkirk.'

Chapter 3

London, April 1941

Tucked away in a small road south of Wandsworth Bridge, to the west of Clapham Common and close enough to Lavender Hill and Trinity Road to catch the hum of wartime traffic, lay the Royal Victoria Patriotic School. It had been two years since its pupils had been evacuated to Wales and the handsome greenstone building now served an entirely different purpose. It was now the home of the London Reception Centre, its hospitable name belying its true role. Following the fall of France and after Dunkirk, 150,000 refugees from Europe had escaped to the United Kingdom. They were screened at reception centres around London and the very small minority whose stories did not quite match up, became the guests of the London Reception Centre to face the MI5 interrogators.

And so it was in the Royal Victoria Patriotic School, early on an unseasonably dull and chilly April morning, that two guards unlocked one of the windowless cells in the south courtyard and its inmate had a brief glimpse of light for the first time in nearly ten hours. Familiar now with the routine, he obligingly held out his hands to be handcuffed and waited while the blindfold was placed around his eyes.

And then the brisk walk. Hurried along by the guards' hands on each elbow, he could anticipate when each turn was to be made, when steps were to be climbed or, more often, descended, carpeted corridors to be walked down and doorways to be entered. They came into the room that he assumed must be in the basement of the main building, though he could not be sure, in the same way that he could no longer be sure how long he had been there, or even which day it was.

He was guided into the room and placed in front of a chair. Only then was the blindfold removed, along with the handcuffs. He stood still, dazed and disoriented, blinking in the yellowish light that hung low just in front of him. Due to his slightly stooped posture, he appeared even shorter than he was. His most noticeable features were his long arms, which hung limply by his sides, the fingers nervously playing with the cuffs of what appeared to be a cardigan specially knitted for him, but without much affection. He could still not get out of his mind something he had overheard the guards saying on his first night here. One pair of guards was handing over to another pair and they were chatting, clearly assuming that the Belgian was asleep.

'And what's he like then, Bert, this Belgian?'

'Pathetic-looking little chap, Alan. Rat-like without the cunning.'

That had really upset him. Now one of the guards was pushing him down into the chair and then both guards moved behind him, just beyond his line of sight. He blinked again to adjust his eyes to the dimly lit room, taking in the long table ahead of him, behind which sat two men.

So started the Belgian's fourteenth interrogation in what he estimated could not be more than one week. As he had done throughout, he endeavoured to adopt the plausible manner to be expected of an innocent yet aggrieved man.

The older of the two men in front of him was the only one who ever addressed him directly. He was distinguished-looking, possibly in his fifties. The Belgian assumed from the way he spoke Flemish that he was Dutch, although he could not be sure. He was also fluent in French and English, though he had only used the former on one occasion on the first day and then it had no hint of Walloon to it. The Dutchman only had an ashtray in front of him, no notes nor even a pen. He chain-smoked and would occasionally offer the Belgian a cigarette, which he always declined. Most of the interrogation was carried out in English, not least for the benefit of the man who sat to the Dutchman's right and who never directly addressed him. The Englishman appeared to be in his forties and constantly referred to the notebooks and files spread out in front of him, in a manner which the Belgian found disconcerting, which he guessed was the idea. There were two things that the Belgian did notice about the Englishman: his height and his face that never betrayed any flicker of emotion. If you stared hard at the Englishman, with his haircut very marginally longer than the military regulation cut most people around him seemed to have, then you'd realise that he was a good-looking man, the Belgian

25

thought. But look away from him even for a second and you would be hard pressed to recall any detail about his face. The interrogation would be punctuated from time to time by the Englishman shaking his head, or sighing, or stopping the questions to go into discussion with the Dutchman, with their heads turned away from the Belgian.

As the questioning started today, the Belgian noticed a different tone to the Dutchman's voice. He assumed it was another ruse, but he certainly sounded more confident – even slightly jolly. The Belgian concentrated on his breathing. He concentrated on trying to remember what he had been taught:

Breathe in and out deeply, speak slowly and think before you answer any question – even the easy ones – so that they will never be alerted by a change in your manner. Stick to your story. Believe in your story. That way, they will have to believe you.

If they haven't got anything to hit you with after a week, then all they will have is what you tell them. The longer you hold out, the safer you will be.

'Good morning, Vermeulen,' said the Dutchman. 'Permit me to sum up where we have got to.' The Englishman was staring at him without blinking.

'You entered England in May 1940 following the fall of Dunkirk. You were initially screened at our reception centre in Crystal Palace, where you received security clearance. You then found accommodation at a bedsit in Acton in west London, where you have lived ever since. You have worked in a variety of semi-skilled occupations, although you are, of course, a qualified lawyer in your native Belgium.'

The Belgian nodded.

'You have led a blameless life, Mr Vermeulen, is that not true?'

The Belgian nodded again, slowly, trying to gather his thoughts. He was sure that for the very first time, he could make out the trace of a smile on the Dutchman's face. The Englishman leaned forward.

'But, Mr Vermeulen, I don't need you to reassure us of that. We know it ourselves! And shall I tell you why?'

Vermeulen had no time to respond.

'You see, we have been watching you very carefully ever since you left Crystal Palace. You never received a genuine security clearance there, as you thought you did. We had been – how do they say here – expecting the pleasure of your company even before you left Belgium. Shall I tell you why?'

The Belgian found himself nodding, although his instinct told him he should not respond to a question like that.

'You are one of life's pathetic creatures.' He repeated that sentence in Flemish. The Belgian was shocked and feared he was showing it. Until now, the Dutchman had always been proper, even polite in his manner and his tone.

'Look at you, Vermeulen. How old are you? Forty-three? You look ten years older. Your skin is so pale that it looks as if you have never been in the fresh air. And it appears that a decent meal is not a habit of yours. You've never married and, as far as we can gather, you had no social life. Who would want to marry *you*, Vermeulen? Do you even *like* women, Vermeulen? Who would want to be *your* friend?'

Vermeulen felt tears swell in his eyes. Never in his life had he heard such personal remarks like these, at least not in such a direct way. He always assumed that those people in the office in Brussels made them, but that would be behind his back. And his neighbours. Even some of the people at the church. He must stay calm. This was a ruse. He had been warned about it. It was proof that they had nothing on him, he tried to reassure himself. What was it the instructor had said? *Don't react to abuse. It will be a sign that they have nothing on you.*

'You spent your time either at work, or at church, or in your small apartment playing with your radio and your gramophone. You applied to join the Free Belgian Forces when you arrived in this country, but, of course, you knew you would be turned down. You are a weak man; you are not an example of the Aryan race which you so aspire to, are you? And this story about you being a lawyer? You were a clerk at a law firm in Brussels – and not even a very good clerk. You had not been promoted in years and, of course, you blamed the Jewish partners for that, didn't you? The German Sixth Army hadn't even taken their boots off after they entered Brussels on the seventeenth of May last year before you were knocking at General von Reichenau's door volunteering your services. And what did you have in mind? Probably being a very senior clerk, with other clerks working for you. You would spend your time denouncing Jews and socialists, assisting the Nazis in their occupation of your country and, for the first time in your miserable little life, becoming someone important. But you made one mistake.'

There was a long pause. He had had no idea that the Dutchman had been aware of some of the things he was saying now.

'The mistake was to let your new masters know that you speak fluent English – probably your only real talent, Mr Vermeulen. We know that your employers had sent you over here for a while in the early 1930s to work in the office of their London associates, did they not? So when the Germans discovered that Arnold Vermeulen is not just an eager collaborator who understands radios, but also speaks excellent English and is familiar with London, they realised that you have a perfect role to play here in London!'

Vermeulen decided now to deploy the one card he had left, though he had to admit it was a creased and low-value one. The last thing the instructor had ever said to him: '*If you sense things going wrong in an interrogation, give them something. Admit to a failing, own up to a minor deceit.*' There was an outside chance that it might work, but his confidence was not strong. His voice was shaking; he knew that he sounded too eager to please.

'It is true, sir. I lied about being a lawyer. I felt ashamed that I had never had better qualifications and I thought that if people believed I was a lawyer in Belgium then they would give me a role here that would better suit my skills. My employers in Brussels had never given me a chance. They always promoted their young family friends but never me. And the radios? It was to listen to music. Is that a crime?'

'So, as we say: we were expecting you.' Again, the Dutchman had ignored Vermeulen's answer.

'You had made enough noise in the Nazi headquarters when you first turned up there to bring attention to yourself. Did it really not occur to you that we may have our own people there? And we knew what your role would be. You were not going to be doing any spying yourself. True to your vocation as a clerk, your role would be to be the conduit through which the intelligence gained by a more active German spy would be passed back to the Nazis. In other words, you would not do any actual spying yourself, but you would pass on the information of an agent who did. Perhaps someone not able to send their own messages. At this point, Mr Vermeulen, would you care to comment?'

'I am not a German spy, sir, that is a ridiculous accusation; I keep telling you that I am an innocent refugee—'

'That's right, an innocent refugee who only wishes to assist in the liberation of his country from Nazi occupation. Very admirable I am sure; we have heard it for the past week. We are very familiar with

28

your story, Mr Vermeulen. But let me continue. Our information was that you would be what we call a "sleeper". For a period of time, you would do nothing. You arrived in this country without a radio, so we knew that only when your agent was ready to pass on information would you collect the radio from where it had been hidden. Until then you would lead, as I said, a blameless life. But then you would receive a signal that would let you know that your life as an active Nazi agent was to begin. Our understanding is that this signal would come from your agent once they had information that they wished to be transmitted to your masters. Do you wish to comment at this stage?'

The Belgian shook his head. 'It simply is not true…'

'Two weeks ago we followed you to Oxford. You were using all the old tricks to check that you were not being followed, but you were not very subtle about it. For instance, you took five different bus journeys while in Oxford and constantly looked behind you. That is how an amateur behaves. We believe that the purpose of your visit to Oxford was to collect the radio transmitter that had been hidden in that area. Of course, once you had the transmitter, we would arrest you and with such concrete evidence you would be persuaded to tell us the truth.'

'I tell you this is not true. I visited Oxford to see the sights and the—'

'—"and the architecture" which is your "special interest". Yes, I have heard that all week, Mr Vermeulen. You keep telling us. Let me continue. Our plan went wrong, did it not?'

The Englishman to the left of the Dutchman coughed and nodded.

'You are clearly a very nervous man, Mr Vermeulen. Obviously you are nervous now. That is understandable. You are being interrogated. But I think that your general disposition is a nervous one, is it not? Because what happens in Oxford when you are about, we believe, to collect your transmitter? You are sick. Not in a discreet manner. You did not find a toilet or a quiet alleyway. You were sick in the street, drawing attention to yourself. And as we all know, one of the people who came over to see what the fuss was all about was an enthusiastic member of the local police force, who decided to question you. When he asked for your papers, for some reason he was not satisfied and decided to take you to the police station so that he could check them out further. Maybe it was your nervous manner that made him suspect something, I don't know. My guess was it was because you are foreign and the British police are always suspicious of foreigners. So our plans – that is, *your* plan and *our* plan – were ruined by that overzealous police officer. If he had minded his own business, I believe you would have led us to the radio transmitter. So, once again, where is that transmitter, Mr Vermeulen?'

'There is no transmitter, I assure you. I don't know what you are talking about.'

'Now we come to the interesting developments. A radio transmitter is very important if you are to send your messages. That is obvious, as I am sure you know, Mr Vermeulen. But what is also important is the code in which you were going to send that message. And it is in connection with that, that we have some news for you today.'

The Dutchman lit another cigarette. A thin mist of grey-brown smoke now hung between the Belgian and his questioner. The Englishman leaned back in his chair, his gaze remained fixed on the Belgian, but his features faded as he moved out of the light.

'You will appreciate that once you were arrested in Oxford, we were able to search your room in Acton. You kept it very neat, Mr Vermeulen. You lead a simple life. You do not have many possessions and we were able to examine everything that you own very thoroughly. It is something that I specialise in. And until last night, we found nothing incriminating.'

He repeated the last sentence in Flemish.

Another pause. The Belgian was now feeling sick. '*Until last night,*' the Dutchman had said. What did he mean by that? He wondered whether to say anything now or whether this was another of the tricks that the Dutchman used.

'You are a religious man, are you not, Mr Vermeulen?'

The Belgian found himself nodding.

The Dutchman reached for a briefcase on the floor behind him and produced a much-used leather-bound book. The Belgian could feel his breathing quicken. He could not imagine that they could not hear it.

'*The Holy Bible.* Flemish version. Very devout. We found it by your bedside. I read your Bible very carefully, Mr Vermeulen. I must admit that it was the first time I have done so in many years. And then I spotted something, Mr Vermeulen. Little pinpricks that had been made under the first letter of the first sentence of some chapters. Very deliberate marks. They are not mistakes. And they only appear under the first letter of the first sentence of a chapter, nowhere else. And there we have it. Your code! You would transmit the chapter numbers and your controllers would understand from the collection of chapter numbers you had selected and the order in which you sent them, what the message is. It is clever, but it was not clever enough. So, you see, we have our proof.' He banged the Bible down on the table.

For the first time, the Belgian could say nothing. He did not know how to respond. He had been assured that it would be impossible for anyone to spot the marks in the Bible. He could not understand how the Dutchman had spotted them. Even he had trouble finding them and he knew they were there. He had nowhere to go.

The Dutchman now dropped his more conversational style and spoke in a firm manner in the Belgian's native Flemish.

'Vermeulen. Since the war started I have interrogated ten men who turned out to be Nazi spies. I would estimate that in half of the cases, the evidence against them was not as strong as it is with you. Eight of those men have been executed. The current interval between being found guilty of espionage in a court of law and execution is around five weeks. Do you want to ask me a question?'

The Belgian's shoulders sagged. He was terrified. It was taking all of his efforts to try to show no emotion, but he had no doubt that he was failing.

'Shall I help you with the question, Vermeulen? What you should really want to know now is what happened to the two spies who were not executed. Shall I tell you?' The Dutchman had reverted to English. His tone was markedly less aggressive. It was almost friendly.

Vermeulen nodded.

'They came to work for us. To carry on sending information to the Germans, but this time, the wrong information. Now, you would not actually do that yourself. But, of course, we do need your co-operation. We need it to locate the transmitter, to find the correct frequency and the times they would expect to hear from you and the correct use of the codes. We need you for all of that. And no tricks, no tiny changes to procedure that would alert the Germans to the fact that you have been captured. We would soon spot that, and that would be your death sentence.

'Can you imagine what it is like, Vermeulen, to be told one day that your final appeal against execution has been turned down and that you will die the next morning? Can you imagine how it feels to have to get through the rest of the day and then through that night? Who will you write to Vermeulen... anyone? Would you still believe enough to be able to pray? And then as you see the sun start to rise through the cell window, you will be alert to every sound, but even then, you will not hear them until they are in the cell. I've witnessed the execution of some of my spies. It is not a pleasant sight. The look of fear on a man's face as his hands are bound stays with you forever. If I close my eyes now, I can picture them, desperately looking round for someone to comfort them, for just a smile. They know then that – whatever drove them to be Nazi agents – it wasn't worth it. The distance from the cell to the gallows is very short, but I promise you it will be the longest walk of your life. And then they will strap your feet and place a black hood over your head and that will last another lifetime. Only you will know the muffled fear as you feel your hot breath close to you and the struggle to breathe as you wait for the trapdoor to open.'

The Dutchman paused while he lit another cigarette and the haze between the two of them thickened. For the first time, the Belgian could detect the very slightest trace of a smile on the Englishman's face, before it faded as he leaned back into the shadows again. The Belgian was sure he was on the verge of losing all physical control. Nothing that the instructors had told him had prepared him for this moment.

The Dutchman was in no hurry to continue as he carefully examined the end of his cigarette from different angles, before placing it again between his lips and inhaling deeply. He stared again at the Belgian. He could see it in his eyes now. There was a moment when their eyes told him it was over. It was usually quite sudden, the realisation that they knew the game was up. Often, this look of doom appeared before the man realised it himself. With a quiet satisfaction, he spoke again.

'So, what I need to know, Mr Vermeulen, is whether you wish to join the eight agents in unmarked graves under the walls of a British prison, or whether you want to join the two whose necks are still intact?'

Vermeulen was sobbing now, so much so that it was some time before he could speak properly. They were enormous sobs of sheer fear.

'You see, Vermeulen, I think the Germans see you as a clerk, nothing more than that. I think your role is to help another agent.

Someone more important, perhaps. I could be wrong, but that is my guess. Am I right?'

The Belgian fought hard to control his breathing before he was able to speak.

'I was never a Nazi, sir, I was fooled. There has been a misunderstanding, sir. I wanted to help Belgium. This is all such a relief, to be able to tell you the truth and to be able to help you.'

He was pleading now, his arms stretched out towards the two men in front of him. He did not know whether to be terrified or relieved. He was shaking and his voice quavering.

'I did not hate the Jews. Mendelssohn is one of my favourite composers. And my dentist – he is a Jew. I promise you, I never supplied any information to the Germans. I promise you, sir. I always intended that the minute the agent tried to give me information here, I would contact the authorities. You have my word.'

He was sobbing now, the tears streaking down the pale face, the bad skin. The Dutchman was used to seeing men fight for their life. It was his job to reduce them to this state. You break them down until they are more compliant than a baby. Then you can do what you want with them. No matter how many times he had seen it happen, it was no less edifying.

For the first time that morning – if it was morning – he stood up and walked round the table and towards the Belgian. His disposition was now friendly. He put one arm on his shoulder and spoke quietly to him in Flemish.

'What's his name, Arnold? The agent. What is he called?'

'I don't know the word in English... pie... it's a bird...' Vermeulen was speaking between loud sobs, struggling to catch his breath as he did so. He was desperate to finish the sentence, as if his life depended upon it.

'Magpie,' said the Dutchman. '*Une pie* means magpie in French.'

'One for sorrow.' It was the Englishman, speaking out loud for the first time.

'...and he's not a man. It's a woman.' The Belgian's voice had an eager tone to it now. He wanted to show he was doing all he could to help.

After that, the Belgian who had been so taciturn over the past week barely stopped talking for the next two days.

Chapter 4

London, May 1941

Late in the afternoon of Thursday, 1st May, five men gathered in a sun-filled room in a large house just behind Ham Common in south west London. The first hint of summer hung in the air and under a cloudless sky the day remained warm. The windows were firmly shut and barred, as they always were, meaning that silence prevailed as the men entered the room that was far larger than needed, but was the most secure room in a very secure building.

The Dutchman and the Englishman sat side-by-side, as three other men followed them into the room and arranged themselves opposite them.

A noticeably large man sank into the chair opposite the Dutchman and the Englishman, with the other two men flanking him. As with many men of his build, he moved in a careful and surprisingly dainty manner. He spoke first, addressing the man to his left.

'Jean-Louis, can I introduce Colonel Visser and Captain Edgar to you? Colonel Visser has spent most his career with your own *Deuxième Bureau* and also his own native Dutch Intelligence. He is now our chief interrogator at the London Reception Centre up in Clapham which I told you about the other day. He is our best source of new recruits. Captain Edgar is one of my top case officers here at MI5. Colonel Visser, Captain Edgar, Jean-Louis is here to represent the interests of the French Government in exile.' He nodded at the Dutchman and the Englishman in turn as he rearranged the notebook on his lap. 'Another success, I take it?'

Both men began to speak at the same time. With a generous gesture of his arm, the Dutchman allowed Captain Edgar to continue.

'Indeed, sir. Another triumph for Colonel Visser if I might say. Quite masterful. The Belgian was a miserable wretch, but he held out

34

on us for far longer than anyone could have expected. That damned policeman in Oxford. We were quite possibly yards and even minutes away from catching Vermeulen red-handed with the transmitter. Then Vermeulen goes and throws up in the street, the policeman arrests Vermeulen and the whole operation is up the spout. Without the bloody transmitter, if you'll excuse my language, we had nothing on Vermeulen. Tricky job we had on our hands.'

'You see, Professor Newby,' Colonel Visser was speaking now, cutting across Captain Edgar and directly addressing the large man in front of them, 'he had been well-trained. To a point. They always are well-trained; the Germans know what they are doing. But what matters is where that point is. Vermeulen knew that we had no evidence on him and his confidence increased as the interrogation went on – and not without reason. Without the transmitter we had a Belgian national who had been living openly in this country for just under a year and who had no contact with the enemy in that time. All of his possessions had been checked when he entered this country and they had been cleared then. He had no reason to suspect that we had anything on him now. He had enough wit about him to do as they had told him. I come across it all of the time. "Stick to your story. If they have anything against you, you will know soon enough." You can almost see their lips moving as they repeat that to themselves.'

The Dutchman cleared his throat. He desperately wanted a cigarette but he had been warned of the professor's aversion to them.

'They even used a classic Abwehr technique by deliberately building a flaw into his story. The idea is that we think we have spotted something against him, but he is prepared for that and eventually owns up to it and then it appears not to be so important. In his case, it was pretending to be a lawyer. We made him admit that he was just a clerk. He claims that this was his opportunity to be somebody, that no harm was intended, and we are then meant to think that maybe he is not really a spy after all, just a fool.'

The Dutchman could feel the packet of Players Navy Cut getting heavier in his shirt pocket.

'So, a week into the interrogation he must have felt confident. And as he felt more confident, the more anxious I became. I was certain that he must have brought something incriminating with him into England. The transmitter would have come separately in a parachute drop or by some other route and then been cached for him, but

35

he would have carried some kind of codebook in with him. It was impossible that he could be so clean. Our information from Brussels was so good that we knew he was an agent. So I went through all of his possessions myself. Every night after the interrogations, I went through everything, even though my men had already searched everything twice over. The Bible was the last item I looked at. It was clever. The pinpricks did not begin until halfway into Exodus and I believe that I only spotted the first one because I still had my desk lamp on as the sun rose through the window, and that combination of light somehow picked out the marks. Divine providence.'

That reference did not appear to be appreciated by the professor of theology who sat opposite him.

'There we have it. We confronted him with this evidence, and then it really was just a matter of time.'

'Will he work for us then?'

'Oh yes indeed, Professor.' Captain Edgar was speaking now. His tall frame leaning forward in the low chair, edging him closer to the other three and placing him in front of Colonel Visser.

'Colonel Visser's description of a judicial execution was masterful. It certainly did the trick. I thought Vermeulen was going to pass out there and then. Good job the chap doesn't have a weak heart.'

Professor Newby continued looking at Captain Edgar for some time after he had finished. He turned to the Frenchman on his left.

'Jean-Louis. We are called the "twenty committee" because of the two Roman numerals, XX. They represent the words double cross, hence the two Xs, which also signify twenty in Latin as I am sure you are aware. *Vingt.* Our role in the Double Cross Committee or "twenty committee" as you may sometimes hear it referred to, is to identify German spies whom we can turn into double agents. In other words, we find them and then persuade them to work for us. Colonel Visser is our best source of new recruits. So what I need to know from Colonel Visser and Captain Edgar is whether we can turn Arnold Vermeulen.'

Captain Edgar spoke first. 'You can turn Arnold Vermeulen in any direction you want, Professor. Left, right, upside down, inside out. You name it. He's yours to do what you want with.'

'Do you share this assessment, Colonel Visser?'

There was a hesitation from the Dutchman, who was weighing his words in marked contrast to Captain Edgar's enthusiasm. 'Indeed, Professor. But I would have a significant concern.'

'Which is?'

'Which is that, in himself, Vermeulen is only of secondary interest. There is very little that we can get directly from him. He has not been involved in any espionage since his arrival in this country. His only real interest to us is as a way of getting to the primary agent, whom he refers to by the code name Magpie. We must do nothing that would jeopardise our chances of getting hold of her. To do that, we have to handle Vermeulen very carefully.'

'What kind of a chap is he?'

'He is, as Captain Edgar says and as is all too obvious to any observer, a weak and pathetic individual. He is a loner. A small man, consumed and possibly motivated by resentment and envy and prejudice. He saw the German conquest of Belgium as an ideal opportunity to be someone for perhaps the first time in his life. However, we must not make the mistake of underestimating him. This man is not a complete fool, as much as we would like to think so. He has his strengths. Apart from his fluency in English and his ability with radios, he has a certain stubbornness, he has a commitment.'

'By which you mean what, Colonel?' This was the man to the Professor's right who, up to this point, had been busy taking notes.

'Despite what we think of him, he still volunteered to help the Germans. Maybe he did not envisage risking his life as a spy in this country, but he was still motivated by some kind of an ideological commitment to the Nazi cause. We have to trust him if we are to get our *entrée* to Magpie. She is our real aim. And I am not sure how far we can trust Arnold Vermeulen.'

Colonel Visser gestured towards Captain Edgar on his right. 'We have done well to obtain a confession from Vermeulen. But without Magpie, it will mean nothing.'

'What do we know about Magpie?' This was the Frenchman to the left of the professor.

'We know Magpie is important,' said Edgar. 'We know she is a woman and that she is French. Other than that, we know nothing. Nothing.'

'Narrows it down somewhat,' said the professor. The others smiled briefly. There was a long silence. The sun had dropped now, but the room was still too warm and perfectly quiet. Professor Newby was the first to speak.

'Correct me if I am wrong, Jean-Louis, but was there not a mass exodus of population after the Germans conquered France?'

Jean-Louis spoke in a resigned manner, lowering his head, which less-kind observers than those in the room might have imagined was shame. 'The population of France is forty million. We estimate that up to a quarter of the population left their homes around the time of the German invasion. The population of Paris was three million before the Germans marched in on 14th June. Less than a million were still there when they actually arrived. Cities like Chartres, where my wife's family is from, like Troyes and like Évreux in Normandy, they just emptied.'

'A picture of chaos, you see,' said the professor. 'Utter chaos. A quarter of the bloody population on the road, no civil order, tens of thousands of French refugees end up over here, and for the Germans to slip one or two agents in among them… well, it was the easiest thing in the world, and Visser has indeed caught some of them. Apologies Jean-Louis, but you get my meaning. We are searching for a needle in the proverbial haystack.'

'How do you propose we find her, Visser?' asked the Frenchman.

At this point, both Visser and Edgar smiled and eased back in their chairs.

'Oh, we know how to find her all right.' Edgar was smiling and removing a map from his jacket pocket.

'You see,' Visser added as Captain Edgar got up and spread the map out on a table near the door, 'Arnold Vermeulen has been a good deal more helpful than I think we may have given him credit for.'

-

The following day began particularly early for Arnold Vermeulen. He had been alone in his cell at the Royal Victoria Patriotic School since his interrogation had ended the previous day. Apart from the guards checking on him twice an hour, sometimes more, he had been alone with his thoughts.

At first, he had felt a sense of utter relief: that the constant interrogations were over; that they had promised to spare his life in exchange for him agreeing to work for them, and relief that his war was over. He had never meant it to go this far. He just wanted to show those Jews that they could not run things their way anymore. In his worst nightmares, he could never have imagined that the Nazis would ask him to become an active spy for them. In England. It was a ridiculous notion. His health was not up to it. He had spent the past year waiting for a knock on the door.

The sense of relief had allowed him to have his first proper sleep since arriving here, but it had been a brief one. He woke up drenched in sweat and overwhelmed by terrible thoughts. What if it was not true? What if they had deceived him? Could it be a trick? He spent the next couple of hours reassuring himself that without Magpie, he was useless to them – and he was the only person who could give them Magpie. He relaxed and even managed to eat all of the stew they brought him early in the evening, along with bread that didn't taste like bread, and a dry pudding. This time he fell into a truly deep sleep, which he remained in until the cell door burst open at five in the morning.

The small cell, with its pervading smell of new concrete, was filled with two guards, two other men wearing a different military uniform, and the tall Englishman who had sat in on all of the interrogations. He spoke.

'Get up, Vermeulen, we are moving you.'

The Belgian stood in the centre of the cell. Two of the guards had moved behind him. One of the men in the uniforms he had not seen before threw some clothes on the bed.

'Get undressed and put those on.'

Vermeulen was dazed. He looked around the cell, smiling in the forlorn hope that one person in the cell would return his smile. Slowly, he started to remove his own clothes, which he had fallen asleep in, and which were the ones he had been allowed to wear since his arrest, after they had examined them. He removed the cardigan that his mother had knitted for him a year before she died, the shirt, and the trousers from which they had already removed the belt. He stood there in his underpants, vest and socks, shivering in fear and the cold of the early morning.

'Carry on.'

Vermeulen peeled off the socks, hoping no one would notice the holes in the heels and then the vest, his spindly legs, small pot-belly, hairless chest and pock-marked shoulders exposed.

'Everything.'

Vermeulen could not remember the last time anyone had seen him naked. He felt totally humiliated. He turned round hoping for some privacy, but the guards behind could see him now. He was sure that one of them was grinning at him. He removed his underpants and tried to put on the new trousers as fast as possible in one movement, but only succeeded in slipping on the bed and exposing himself to everyone in the cell, so prolonging the embarrassment. He could feel tears welling up in his eyes again, his humiliation complete.

He stood in front of the men in the doorway, in the rough grey trousers and matching shirt and clog-like shoes without any socks. The guards handcuffed his arms behind his back and the Englishman spoke in an almost casual manner.

'Things did not work out as we had expected them to, Vermeulen. We are going to have to deal with you in a different way. Follow me.'

With that, the whimpering Vermeulen was virtually dragged out of his cell, across the courtyard – all of which he was seeing for the first time as he was without a blindfold, which he knew must be an ominous sign – and hauled into the back of a black van. He was placed on a small wooden bench which went along the side of the van, with the two men in the new uniform on each side of him.

They drove for well over an hour. At the very start of the journey he had asked his new guards where he was being taken, but the reply of '*Not a word*,' was accompanied by him being pushed back on the bench. Not in an aggressive manner, but it did mean that his handcuffed arms were pinioned against the side of the van and that hurt. He knew what was happening. They had fooled him. The English were not supposed to act like this. They were going to torture him now and he had nothing more to tell them. He had told them everything he knew. 'We are going to have to deal with you in a different way,' the Englishman had said. He spent the rest of the journey imagining every way in which they were going to deal with him, and each way was worse than the one he had thought of previously.

By the time they arrived at their destination, daylight had taken hold. The van had stopped outside enormous gates and Vermeulen was led round to the main entrance. The sign said 'Wormwood Scrubs' and Vermeulen recognised the prison from the bus. He lived just two or three miles from here, and for a while he had had a job in the hospital next door. A small side-gate half-opened and the tall Englishman walked ahead of them. His long gait meant that the guards had to hurry Vermeulen along to keep up.

They stopped at a guardhouse, where forms were quickly exchanged, quiet words spoken and shackles attached to his ankles. They continued their progress through the prison, accompanied now by two armed guards in front and two more behind, as far as he could make out. He was able to walk in the shackles, but not without considerable noise and some discomfort as they chafed against the rough material of his trousers. Down a long corridor with barred windows along one side, through a double set of locked doors and into an enormous room, which felt like an empty factory. In the gloom Vermeulen could make out no distinguishing features, although there appeared to be some large machinery against a far wall. The small group marched across the rough concrete floor to the centre of room, their footsteps and Vermeulen's chains echoing against the distant walls. As they reached the centre, the tall Englishman turned abruptly and walked towards the Belgian.

He had a pistol in his right hand, which he slowly raised, holding the barrel against Vermeulen's temple. The Belgian struggled, but the two guards had little trouble in holding him steady.

'You are of no use to us now, Vermeulen. The truth is that we do not trust you. You have reached the end of the road.'

There was silence in the room, broken only by Vermeulen's panicked breathing and the echoing sound of the safety catch being released. The Englishman waited. The Belgian's eyes were wide open, as was his mouth. No sound came out. Vermeulen slumped to the floor.

The Englishman circled the body, prodding it once with his shoe before turning to the guards.

'Take him away.'

-

When Captain Edgar came to visit Arnold Vermeulen later that morning, he found the Belgian lying on the metal bed, curled into a foetal position. When he saw Edgar enter the room he instinctively moved away from him, so that by the time the door shut he had forced himself into the back of the bed, against the corner of the two walls. They were alone.

'Please relax, Vermeulen.' The Englishman spoke in a quiet voice, but Vermeulen had no trouble hearing it.

'Didn't quite go to plan before, sorry about that.' He gave the impression of not being very sorry at all. He drew up a chair close to the bed, very close to Vermeulen. The Belgian was unable to get any further away from Edgar. 'Plan was to pull the trigger, you would just hear an empty click and realise that the pistol was not loaded. I would then tell you this is what would happen to you if you did not do exactly as we ask of you. Any tricks, anything less than total co-operation and that would be your fate. Except, of course, next time the pistol would be loaded. Only thing, we didn't count on you fainting down there, which is why I am making this little speech now.'

Vermeulen nodded eagerly.

'I just wanted you to realise quite how serious we are. You told us on Wednesday that you have met Magpie once. So she knows who you are. That means that without you, we cannot get to Magpie. So you are working for us now. And that means no tricks, no using the secret warning signals that you no doubt have agreed, nothing clever. When you start your transmissions, you do it by the book. If you use any device like a warning word to let them know that you've been turned, we will find out. Just do everything that we ask of you. If you don't, you now know exactly what the consequences will be.'

The Englishman stood up, looking around the room as he did so. 'Bit grim in here. This was where you were going to be staying, but instead we have decided to move you back to your bedsit in Acton. We're pretty certain that no one has been around there looking for you, so the story will be that you went to visit a friend in the north. Don't worry, for the first time in a long while, Vermeulen, you are not going to be on your own. You will have company. Your landlady has very obligingly made arrangements for my men to occupy the other three bedsits in the house. She thinks you are an important engineer and three colleagues are moving in.'

The Englishman slapped his hand a bit too hard on Vermeulen's leg and the Belgian jumped. 'So you see, Vermeulen, for the first time in your life, someone thinks you are important! Now get ready, we've got a busy couple of days.' To all intents and purposes the Englishman could have been describing the plans for the weekend to an old friend up from the country.

'Today we need to go to Oxford, don't we? Pick up the transmitter. And on Sunday… we go for a walk in the park.'

At ten minutes to eleven on the first Sunday that May, a woman in her mid-twenties emerged from Ealing Common tube station in west London. She had taken care to dress in a manner designed to attract minimum attention. Her slim figure and long legs were concealed by a slightly larger than necessary raincoat that was closer to shabby than smart, but only just. Her long dark hair was covered by a plain woollen scarf. She came out of the station and turned right, taking care to walk neither too fast nor too slowly. Everything about her was calculated to ensure that she blended in. She was grateful for the opportunity for fresh air that the short walk would afford her. A journey that she could have comfortably done in three quarters of an hour had actually begun more than three hours ago in central London. Since then, she had taken a circuitous route. Walking, buses, different tube lines, waiting at stations and then crossing to other lines. Only when she was absolutely sure that there was no chance she could have been followed, did she begin the final phase of the journey that had brought her to her intended destination.

A few hundred yards from the station, on the other side of the main road, was a narrow strip of parkland. Park was perhaps too grand a word. 'Gardens' it was called, but it seemed more like a wide strip of grass to her, buffeted between a narrow road behind and the main road. The gardens were actually split in two, bisected by a broad avenue.

To anyone watching her, her pace had not changed, but she had slowed down very slightly, enough to be able to look carefully into the larger of the two small strips of park. He was there, as he had been a fortnight ago when she first met him, and as he had been on every other alternate Sunday for the few weeks before that. On those previous occasions she had not actually gone into the park but had walked past it to satisfy herself that he would be there when she needed him.

She noticed that the little man was sitting on the bench furthest away from the station. Next to him, he had placed his newspaper, and on top of the newspaper sat his hat. He had signalled that it was safe to meet. If he was wearing his hat, but with the newspaper on the bench next to him, that would mean come back in half an hour as he was not certain all was clear. If he was wearing his hat and reading his newspaper, it was not safe to meet and she would calmly continue her walk.

The woman entered the small park and casually approached the bench. No one else was in the park; there never seemed to be anyone. It was not the kind of place where anyone would want to sit down for too long, not even the English.

'Is this seat free?' She spoke in English.

'Yes, of course, please let me remove my newspaper.' The final check. 'I am reserving this for a friend' would have been a warning, but by then it would have probably been too late. Vermeulen had done all that they had asked of him and Magpie had flown safely into his nest. He knew that at least half a dozen men were watching him, but since Friday he had been quite clear in his mind. He would do whatever they asked.

Satisfied that it was safe, the woman spoke in French.

'You have the transmitter now?' She was looking ahead of her as she talked. She was relaxed, but her dark eyes were darting left and right as she spoke, taking in everything around her. Vermeulen had felt a surge of desire when he first saw her. He knew that a woman like this would not even think about him, but even to be sitting next to her made his heart race.

She had to repeat the question.

'Yes, I collected it soon after we met two weeks ago.'

'No problems?'

'None. It had been well hidden. It is in good working order.'

'Good. You can send your first transmission then.'

'And what shall I tell them?'

'That I am well, and I am working on the main plan. I hope to have news soon. That's all. They are to be patient.'

-

Three days later, Captain Edgar returned to the large house on Ham Common. This time, Professor Newby was on his own, in a study on the top floor, behind an enormous desk, gazing out of the window and all but shielded from view by a wall of files piled up in front of him. He stood up when Edgar entered the room and pointed him towards the two armchairs on either side of an unlit fireplace.

'More success, I gather from your message?'

'Indeed, sir.' Edgar noticed that the professor was pouring two very large measures from an ornate decanter. From bitter experience he knew that this would be a very dry sherry, dry to the extent of being barely palatable. The first time he had met Newby, the professor had subjected him to an unnecessarily long story about how he had brought a dozen bottles of this sherry over from Spain before the war. At the time, Edgar had thought better of affecting anything other than pleasure at drinking it. Now Newby treated him as a fellow connoisseur.

'Let us drink to it while you tell me.'

Edgar allowed the merest hint of the sherry to touch his lips before he spoke.

'As agreed, we gave Vermeulen a bit of a scare on Friday. Made it bloody clear to him what would happen if he didn't play ball. Then we made a fuss of him, gave him a hot bath and a decent meal and even some wine and a clean set of clothes, though he does seem to have a strange attachment to this filthy cardigan he insists on wearing. Took him down to Oxford first thing the next morning and found the transmitter straight away. Wrapped in an oilskin inside a suitcase, which was also wrapped in an oilskin. That had been carefully stashed in the rafters of a disused boatyard. Probably been there best part of a year, hard to tell. Clever though. All Vermeulen would have had to do was climb the remains of a metal ladder attached to the wall, pull the package out with a boathook that was left there, remove the outer oilskin and then you have a man with a case. Nothing too unusual about it at all. Would be nice to get our hands on the chap who put the transmitter there, but I suppose we shouldn't be greedy.'

'Does the radio work?'

'Oh yes. Have to hand it to the Germans, sir. Superb bit of machinery. Our chaps have had a look at it, given it a bit of a clean-up, but works like clockwork, if that's the correct phrase. Say what you like about them, sir, but they're bloody impressive engineers.'

'And has the obliging Mr Vermeulen had occasion to use the transmitter yet?'

'He made his first transmission on Sunday evening. That is his protocol, he tells us. To go to the park every other Sunday at a quarter to eleven and if Magpie has anything for him, she turns up at eleven. Appears the poor chap has been religiously turning up at the park every Sunday since he arrived here, terrified at getting it wrong. That was his downfall, of course; he had become such a stickler for routine that the moment he changed it, when he went to Oxford, we realised

45

something was up. So, Magpie first turns up two weeks ago, tells him she is ready for her first message to be sent back to their bosses and he's to retrieve the transmitter, which he tries to do the following Sunday – the day we caught him. Luckily, we had matters neatly tied up in time for our new friend to be dutifully sat on his park bench in time for her arrival the next Sunday. As I say, he made his transmission that night. Tuned in at the appointed time, used the Bible code and told his bosses that Magpie was now active, and to expect to hear from her soon. Germans replied back that they were surprised it had taken so long, but to wish her luck.'

'Did Vermeulen behave during the transmission?'

'Yes. We had a couple of our most experienced radio chaps watching over him. They know what to look for. Selection of frequency, speed of his keying, any deliberate mistakes – anything that would suggest he was trying to surreptitiously let the Germans know that he has been compromised. As far as they can tell, he was as good as gold.'

'And how did the meeting itself go?'

'Just as Vermeulen said it would. Bang on eleven o'clock, woman turns up the main road opposite the park. Vermeulen has been sat there for fifteen minutes, all his signals on green. We've got the place well covered, of course, but keep well back. Over she comes. They have a little chat. She leaves ten minutes later.'

'And you were able to follow her?'

'Only just. Very smart lady she is, very smart. She was a textbook example of how to do it. If we hadn't put a tail of seven people on her, we wouldn't have made it. She went to Ealing Common Station and then spent the next two hours on a tour of London. Thought we'd lost her at one stage on the Strand heading towards Fleet Street but then one of our chaps spotted her on a bus going in the opposite direction. It stopped at a red light and he managed to get on. She got off in Northumberland Avenue and then walked down the Embankment, across Westminster Bridge and into St Thomas's Hospital. Magpie, Professor, turns out to be a nurse.'

'And does this nurse have a name?'

'Indeed she does. Nathalie Mercier. Aged twenty-six. From Paris. Arrived in England second of June last year. Story was that she had been treating French soldiers and was scared of what the Germans would do to her. As far as we can tell, she was certainly working in a field hospital in Dunkirk at the time of the evacuation, so nothing suspicious about her. Cleared at Balham at the end of June.'

'Is she a genuine nurse?'

'Indeed. Met her matron. They think she is wonderful. Very competent and quite beautiful, I must tell you, sir. Slim figure, long legs and long dark hair. Her eyes are jet-black, quite the most beautiful ones I have ever seen. Patients adore her, especially the chaps.'

'Naturally. And what did matron say?'

'This is where it is most fortuitous, sir. Contacted matron and said "We need to see you on a matter of national security, please say nothing to anyone," usual routine. When I arrive, I say it is in connection with Nathalie Mercier – we knew her name from when we followed her into the nurses' quarters. "Ah," says Matron. "It must be about her transfer request." Appears that the beautiful Nathalie has applied to be transferred to a military hospital. Not fussy which one, any one would do it seems, though she would prefer to be in the London area. She said she felt she wanted to give something back after France's defeat, do her bit for the Allied cause. Matron believes it, of course, which is convenient for us because we have a ready-made cover story about why we're interested in her.'

'Which presumably is the reason why she was now ready to make contact with the Germans. So you said…?'

'Yes, of course! I was indeed here to check her out as to whether she can get security clearance to work in a military hospital. No need after all to resort to the rather complicated tale I had prepared for Matron about needing to check over some paperwork. Matron would be sorry to lose her, but quite understands.'

Professor Newby sat still, holding his sherry glass in front of him with both hands, gently turning the glass and watching the slow movement of the drink. Edgar's sherry remained untouched.

'This has the makings of something most interesting, Captain Edgar. In the fullness of time we will grant Nurse Mercier her request. Until then, we have her exactly where we want her.'

Chapter 5

Surrey, August 1933

Owen Quinn had spent the summer of 1933 watching and playing as much cricket as he could manage, and also watching his grandfather die at a hospital in Guildford.

He was still a few months short of his sixteenth birthday, unaware that these few weeks would mark his transition from childhood to adulthood.

The summer had started very promisingly. His grandfather's illness, that no one discussed, meant that he was able to use his grandfather's ticket for the Test Match against the West Indies at the Oval. The ticket allowed entry every day, although the match ended early on the third day thanks to the English bowler, Marriott, taking eleven West Indies wickets. Quinn had spent the rest of the day exploring the heart of London. He had walked down Whitehall to the Houses of Parliament. He had stood outside 10 Downing Street and Buckingham Palace, and had even gone into some of the shops in Oxford Street. He had sat by a small lake in St James's Park eating his cheese and pickle sandwiches, before walking back to Waterloo Station to catch a train home in a carriage full of businessmen and civil servants. He could not have imagined being happier.

Cricket was still his passion. In the past year he had become taller and his slender figure had filled out enough for him to become a useful, quick bowler and careful batsman in the summer, and a quick defender in the winter. His grandfather had taken to coaching him and came to watch him when he could. After one game, when Owen had taken four wickets and scored a match-winning forty-three his grandfather had briefly placed an arm round his shoulder as they walked to the car. 'You played like a proper Yorkshire man then.' Owen knew it was meant as the ultimate compliment.

But other passions were creeping in, though Quinn was too naive at the time to recognise them for what they were. He was in the top French class at his grammar school and towards the end of term their teacher, grateful for such a responsive group of students, took the enthusiastic class to London to see a French film that he told them all of France was talking about. Feeling at the height of sophistication and allowed to wear their own clothes, the small group of boys travelled up from Surrey in the company of Mr Bennett who, despite his impeccable English accent which even extended to when he spoke French, still insisted on being addressed as Monsieur Bennett.

The film was *Boudu sauvé des eaux*. It was a witty comedy about a businessman who saved a tramp, and the effect that the tramp subsequently had on the businessman's family. Monsieur Bennett told the boys that Jean Renoir was a very important director, but on the journey back to Surrey it was the actresses that he could not get out of his mind. It was not just their beauty. It was the style and sophistication that he had never observed in anyone in England. At night, he began to dream of them. Accepting that they were unlikely to reciprocate his interest, however fluent in French he might become, he began to return the waves and greetings of the girl across the road, who was the same age as him and went to the girls' grammar school. He started to time his leaving the house at the same time as she left hers so that they could walk to the bus stop together. Sometimes in the evening they would stand and talk outside one of their neat semi-detached houses. They even went for walks in the park. Towards the end of that summer, he started to allow his arm to brush against hers, and on some nights she would move hers away only slowly. *If only*, he thought, *she was French*.

Owen Quinn was close to his grandfather, who had moved down from Yorkshire in search of work. He did not share the same middle-class reserve as the rest of his family. He remembered the scandalised silence in the family when his grandfather had announced that he was no longer going to church every Sunday. When his parents had asked him why he was no longer going, his grandfather asked them to give him one good reason why he should. His parents exchanged low glances, but could not come up with a satisfactory reason. Owen decided then that when it was up to him, he would not go to church either.

He was someone who the young Owen could talk openly to, so when he was moved into hospital that July, Owen visited him most days. Owen's grandmother and mother and aunt visited every day, but their visits comprised them sitting still by the bed, handbags tightly clutched on their laps, punctuating the silence with 'How are you feeling, Arthur?' or 'Is there anything that we can get you?' They would huddle together in the corridor outside his room, whispering and hoping that Owen would not see them dab their eyes.

He took to visiting his grandfather on his own and they would talk openly, though his grandfather was losing the ability to talk at any length. One day he remarked to his grandfather that it didn't seem like he was getting better. He immediately regretted saying this, but his grandfather placed his hand on top of Owen's hand. He told him he was the first person to acknowledge this and how much he appreciated it. They sat there, hand-in-hand, until his mother and grandmother arrived.

On a baking Thursday at the end of August, when the grass was beginning to turn brown, he again found himself alone with his grandfather, who was having trouble breathing now and barely ate. His skin seemed to have changed colour and was pulled tight across his face and arms. It was early afternoon and the sunbeams were darting into the room through the large window, catching a storm of specks of floating dust as they did so.

His grandfather was drifting in and out of sleep, his uneaten lunch on a tray at the side of the bed, the smell of cabbage, boiled potato and beef stew pervading the room. Owen had moved over to the window, looking down at life going on as normal below and wondering how that could be. His grandfather spoke and Owen moved over to the bed.

'Tell me, Owen. What do you want to do when you are older?'

'Play cricket for England, I suppose.'

They both smiled.

'I'd probably like to do something with my geography or my French. In fact, I think I would even like to marry a beautiful French-woman!'

Owen smiled as he had expected his grandfather to do – and he did, but only very briefly. He held Owen's hand tight.

'Be careful what you wish for.'

He then fell asleep. Owen thought he would have to ask his grand-father what he meant by that later. But then his grandmother arrived with his parents and his uncle and aunt, and Owen was ushered out of the room. He went home on his own. His grandfather died that night. He could never get out of his mind his grandfather's last words to him.

Be careful what you wish for.

Crete, 22nd May 1941

The German attack on Crete had been raging for days and it was evident that the Allied grip on the island was slipping. The night before, the Germans had captured Maleme airfield. They were now able to land troops and all the supplies they needed, as well as having a base for their Stuka dive-bombers. It was these planes that had launched wave after wave of attacks on the British naval ships that had been helping to defend the island. The fall of Crete was now just a matter of time.

The eight-hundred-man crew of HMS *Gloucester* were exhausted. Alongside HMS *Fiji* they were trying to rescue survivors from the destroyer HMS *Greyhound*, but were coming under constant German attack. The RAF had withdrawn their air cover. Only half a dozen planes remained on the Greek island and rather than sacrificing them, they had been sent to Egypt. The reputation of the cruiser, known as *The Fighting G*, meant little now. More waves of Stuka dive-bombers came and HMS *Fiji* was fatally hit. HMS *Gloucester* was running out of ammunition and defenceless when another Stuka attack came in.

Lieutenant Owen Quinn had no idea how long he had been in the water. As he slipped in and out of consciousness, he could not even be sure that he *was* in the water. There was more flotsam and debris and bodies around him than water, and any water that he could make out was black and thick with oil or stained red with blood.

He was twenty-three and too young to die. He had been in the Royal Navy for eighteen months. He had just finished his degree in geography at London University when he'd joined up and his interest in the weather, tides, coastlines and beaches had been put to good effect. He had been commissioned as a navigation officer and was having 'a good war'. He found the action they had been involved in – and there had been plenty of that – exhilarating and he feared nothing. He never thought he would die. Until now.

He lost his grip on the oil-stained plank of wood that had been keeping him afloat, but was pulled back to safety by a man who looked like one of the stewards from the officers' mess.

The steward was still wearing a white jacket, but the oil stains made it look like a black and white striped football shirt. Quinn tried to speak to the man, but his throat was too dry and there was a vicious taste of oil and salt in his mouth.

He thought he could make out a lifeboat in front of him, weaving its way through the wreckage to haul any survivors aboard. Quinn tried to swim towards it, but he could not move one of his legs and his back was in agony.

Again, he slipped below the surface and again he was hauled back by the steward dragging him up by his collar. The lifeboat was gone now. He was resigned to his fate, but without any sense of acceptance. No life flashed before him. The steward who had twice saved his life, and whose name he now remembered was Travers, let out a groan. A bloody froth bubbled from his mouth and he slipped off the plank and smoothly into the sea. Less than a minute later, behind him he heard the clank of oars and a cry of 'Here's one!' as a lifebelt tied to a rope was thrown just in front of him.

His greatest wish was for a drink of water and then to be rescued and it was about to happen.

Be careful what you wish for.

Chapter 6

Hertfordshire, November 1941

The country road was narrow and potholed and the ambulance appeared to have been specially chosen for its lack of suspension. The driver was under the impression that, after weeks at sea in a hospital ship, what an injured Royal Navy officer would most appreciate was a constant stream of jolly chatter. There were a few feeble jokes, a long story about how his wife was not coping with rationing – 'They ought to take a person's weight into account, sir' – and an account of how his mother was convinced she had seen a German spy in her church – 'He was staring at her, sir' – but for some reason the authorities had not been interested. For most of the journey from Southampton he had sustained this commentary through the small window behind his left shoulder. He had to slightly turn around as he did so and each time he did that, the ambulance lurched a bit too much for Owen Quinn's liking.

As they drove around London the driver shared with Quinn his own insight into how the war could be won – 'We need to bomb the hell out of them, sir, if you'll excuse the language, sir.' Just north of London, the nurse in the back did manage to persuade the driver to keep quiet for a while as the patient was trying to sleep. The driver then went onto a series of smaller roads. 'We'll be there soon, sir,' had been his refrain for the past hour and now the road felt like a dirt track and every movement jarred his back and leg. After a while the ambulance slowed down almost to a halt and made a sharp left turn.

'Here we are, sir. Calcotte Grange.'

The road surface for the next half a mile was surprisingly smooth.

Calcotte Grange had been many things in its one-hundred-year history. It lay in open countryside north of St Albans in Hertfordshire and was built by the family after whom it was named. They had

53

made their fortune in India and were keen to display it. As a result, everything about the house was larger than necessary. There were far more rooms than they needed and those rooms were bigger than required. The drive was longer and wider than many of the local roads and many of the side buildings and outhouses had no real purpose whatsoever and had been empty since they were built.

But what they possessed in wealth, the Calcottes lacked in sensitivity. Misinterpreting the lack of any obvious signs of gratitude or even admiration from their neighbours, they assumed this was because the house was not impressive enough. As a result they embarked upon a second phase of utterly unnecessary building. At the centre of this was a chapel. Characteristically, the chapel dwarfed the local church. Locals called it Calcotte Cathedral.

The family's lack of judgement became their downfall. A lack of funds prevented the completion of the chapel and forced the sale of the property before the turn of the century. Calcotte Grange became a girls' school before being converted into a nursing home for recuperating officers in 1916. After the war, it remained a nursing home and in 1940 reverted to its military use, becoming a hospital for Royal Navy officers.

The Royal Navy had cause to be grateful for the Calcottes' unintended munificence. The large rooms had become small wards and at last the building that had been intended as the chapel was completed, though by now it had become a physiotherapy centre. The purpose of Calcotte Grange was to treat officers who no longer needed acute care. For most of the patients, the hospital was where they were sent to recover, with the hope that they would soon be fit enough to resume active service.

It was to Calcotte Grange that Lieutenant Owen Quinn was brought in November 1941, six months to the day from when HMS *Gloucester* had been sunk. His memories of the hours and days after his rescue were a series of blurred photographs rather than a clear film. The precious drink of water just after he was hauled into the lifeboat, the excruciating agony of his back and leg, the perilous transfer to the rescue ship and then the morphine and the oblivion until they reached Alexandria.

He had since been told that for a couple of days he was touch and go. He had lost a lot of blood and there were concerns that his wounds had been infected in the filthy water. But, at the age of twenty-three, he had youth on his side and after a delirious first week he was on a very slow road to recovery. He had suffered disc damage to his back and broken his right femur, but the doctors assured him he would be back at sea within a year. Three operations later he was on a hospital ship back to England and Calcotte Grange.

He had arrived at Calcotte Grange at night and awoke on his first morning to find his parents sitting nervously at his bedside. His father was still wearing his coat, scarf and gloves. His mother had adopted the same pose as she had at her father's bedside: anxiously clutching her handbag to her lap. She allowed herself a brief display of emotion and gave her son a peck on his cheek. Her eyelashes were moist as they brushed his cheekbone. His father became uncharacteristically jolly. His conversation fluctuated between detailed accounts of cricket matches from that summer and the tedious story of how the local council had allowed him a whole two days off to come and visit his son. They remained for two hours and, confident that their only child would live, left, promising to return before Christmas.

Quinn quickly settled into the routine of the hospital. He was in a ward with three other men. One never spoke more than three or four words at a time, preferring to lean on the windowsill and stare out over the open Hertfordshire countryside. He had been in the Arctic convoys. The other two were lieutenant commanders. One had also been wounded in the Mediterranean and had been in the same hospital as Quinn in Alexandria, and there was no detail of his injuries or indeed the man's naval career of which Quinn or the other patients were left unaware. The other had been injured while supervising the loading of his ship in Devonport, which he didn't talk about very much. He spent much of his time reading Dickens.

On his second day, he had a series of consultations. He was examined by the senior medical officer and the senior physiotherapist. They studied his file and concurred with the doctors in Alexandria: he would be back at sea sometime in 1942. '*Absolutely no reason why not.*'

The physiotherapy routine was brutal and he had to go through it every day, apart from Sunday, but by the New Year he no longer needed the wheelchair and his aim was to walk without the aid of sticks by Easter.

The senior medical officer, Dr Farrow, was a kindly man who had worked in a field hospital on the Western Front in the Great War and then returned to general practice in Norfolk. He should have retired in 1940, but the war had prevented that. He had a permanent air of weariness about him.

At the beginning of January, Dr Farrow received a visit from three men, two senior Royal Navy officers and a tall man in a dark coat who never gave his name but said he was involved in intelligence planning. The two Navy officers were clearly there to make Dr Farrow understand that the visit was sanctioned by the Navy. It was the tall man in the dark coat who did all of the talking.

He wanted details of all the patients in Calcotte Grange: their names, ranks, ages, injuries and prognoses. Dr Farrow started to explain that this was irregular, that there were ethical considerations, but he was told firmly by one of the Navy officers that this was official business and his co-operation was required. '*All the ethics have been taken care of, Farrow,*' he was assured. He was unsure what that meant, but was too tired to argue.

Dr Farrow went through the sixty-three patients currently in Calcotte Grange. The tall man clearly had something in mind. Those with more serious injuries who were unlikely to recover for some time were eliminated, as were those over the age of forty or above the rank of lieutenant commander. They were soon down to thirteen names.

'Forgot. One more criterion. Any of these chaps married?'

Farrow looked at their details again. The list was reduced to eight.

'All right, let's have their files out, need to see a bit more detail.'

The Navy officers then looked at the files one by one, muttering to each other as they did so. Three more came out. Five remained.

The tall man studied the names carefully.

'What does Broadhurst do?'

'Gunnery officer,' replied one of the Navy men.

The tall man shook his head and handed the file back to Dr Farrow.

'And Bevan?'

One of the Navy men peered over the tall man's shoulder and then consulted a list of his own.

'Engineer. Same as Stewart here,' pointing to another file.

Again he shook his head and handed the files back to Dr Farrow. Three files were spread out in front of him now. He was studying their photographs. He pulled one file out.

'He seems right.'

Farrow lifted his glasses as he looked at the file.

'Yes, Beresford. Good chap. Had a rough time of it though. Having a few sessions with the psychiatrist.'

More shaking of the head. Two remaining.

'This chap. How old?'

'I think you will find that he is twenty-four.'

'Bit on the young side, but looks the part. And what does he do?'

'Navigation officer.' It was one of the Navy men again, looking through the file. 'Well thought of. Something of an expert on tides and coastlines. Even studied that sort of thing at university. Didn't know you could do that. Certainly not in my day.'

The tall man read through the file again.

'Looks like he is expecting to go back to sea.'

'Indeed,' said Dr Farrow. 'He is most keen to do so and we ought to have him ready by the end of the summer. No reason why not. Strong chap. Young and played plenty of sport. Always helps.'

'And if he was not going back to sea, when could he be out of here?'

'Well, there is no reason why he shouldn't go back to sea...'

'If he were to be based in London. No active service. Behind a desk, that type of thing. When would he be ready for that?'

'Well, he is almost there now, but a couple more months should do it.'

Silence in the room apart from the ticking of a large clock on the wall and nervous coughing of one of the officers. The tall man was reading the file carefully and nodding his head approvingly as he did so.

'He's our man. Has to be. Fits the part perfectly. I need him ready by the middle of April.'

Dr Farrow started to say something, but one of the Navy officers held up his hand to stop him.

The tall man stood and the other three people in the room did likewise.

'Lieutenant Owen Quinn. He's our man. One other thing, Dr Farrow. A new nurse will be joining you next week.'

–

Nathalie Mercier arrived at Calcotte Grange in the second week of January and for the first two weeks she was on night shifts, as was customary for new nurses. She was due to start work in the physio-therapy department by the end of January, but the night shifts gave her some time before then to find out what she could about all the patients.

There were only sixty or so patients in the hospital and when all was silent and still in the early hours of the morning she had the opportunity she had been looking for to study their files. As a new nurse, she was based in the same office as the night sister, which also happened to be the office where the patients' files were kept. They were locked away in a cabinet, but the sister had shown her where the key was, in case of emergency only.

Between the hours of one and three in the morning, not very much happened around her or anywhere else in the hospital. The sister on duty would leave the wards at one 'to do her paperwork' and would return at three, red-eyed, slightly unsteady and smelling of cheap sherry. There were two other nurses on duty, each in separate offices in different parts of the hospital, looking after around twenty patients each. Nurse Mercier removed four or five files at a time, relocked the cabinet and studied the files carefully. It was risky and she had not touched any files on the first two nights, instead observing the patterns of what went on around her. The office was at the end of a long corridor and any movement on the stone-tiled floor reverberated with the efficiency of an alarm system. She knew she would have to be both very unlucky and careless to be caught with the files.

When she started to look at the files after the second night, the information that she found in them was useful – some of it very useful. As well as their medical histories, they were full of detail about the patients' previous postings, how and where they had been injured and, in some cases, where they were due to be posted after being released from Calcotte Grange. She made careful notes. It was all information that would be well received. At long last, she was playing her part.

It was not until her fifth night shift that she came to the 'P/Q' drawer and found his file. She recognised him from the photograph attached to the front of it. She remembered having seen him asleep on the ward on her first night. He was no more than a boy really, quite presentable in an English kind of way, with his fair hair and unblemished, pale skin. But it was a note at the front of his file that really caught her attention. It was written and signed by Dr Farrow. 'No return to active service,' he had scrawled. 'Transfer to

Naval Intelligence requested. Approved after satisfactory completion of physio and final medical. Intelligence wants him by April. Top secret project. Tell Quinn of new posting in March. Delicate situation, Quinn anxious to get back to sea. Will be unhappy but Intelligence insist. Big role for him. Farrow.'

She read his file in detail. She read it again the next night and found it hard to believe what she had stumbled across. They would be delighted with this. More than delighted, in fact. It was a real opportunity. She had to be careful, but she also had to make the most of it. She checked him on her ward rounds. He looked innocent laying there fast asleep, his fair hair splayed out across the bleached-white pillow, mouth slightly open to reveal a perfect set of white teeth, and his pyjama top unbuttoned. She gently pulled the top sheet back over him and tucked it in. He stirred very slightly and turned onto his side, his hair falling over his eyes as he did so.

She knew what she had to do. There was no question about it. She looked around the ward. It could have been far worse, the one in the bed opposite was overweight and had bad skin and the two by the window were in their forties and looked it.

She carefully brushed his hair away from his eyes and he stirred, turning over to his other side.

–

It was towards the end of January that the lieutenant commander who had been injured in Devonport came back from his own physiotherapy session one day with a twinkle in his eye.

'You'll enjoy your next session, Quinn. They've laid on quite a treat for us.'

He had forgotten that remark by the time he arrived at physiotherapy the next morning, but now she was walking towards him through the long hall. Past the parallel bars, across the mats and with a smile, tying her flowing dark hair as she walked. She had dark eyes that had seemed alight even from the other end of the room. By the time she appeared in front of him he was quite transfixed. She was wearing a uniform that appeared to be halfway between a nurse's and a physiotherapist's. The uniform was predominantly white and pulled in tightly around her waist with a wide belt, to accentuate her already slim figure. She was above average height; her legs were long and slim.

'Lieutenant Quinn? I am your new physiotherapy nurse. My name is Nurse Mercier.'

Quinn stood still without uttering a word. He was trying hard to compose himself. She had walked out of a French film.

'*Avec plaisir*,' he replied, trying to sound as nonchalant as possible.

'*Ainsi, vous parlez français?*' she asked.

Quinn panicked. His French was good enough to hold a decent conversation, or at least the first part of one, but that would be in normal circumstances and these were not normal circumstances.

'*Un peu*,' came out making him sound unwell. 'I do speak a bit, but I am sure that your English is much better than my French.'

'Nonsense! I will help to make you better and I will help you to speak better French, and you will help me to speak better English. *D'accord?*'

'*D'accord.*'

Which was how Owen Quinn's life came to change forever.

His treatment was still supervised by the physiotherapists, but now Nurse Mercier was with him throughout all of his sessions. She was responsible for overseeing all of his treatment. He realised it was in his imagination, but he liked to think that her face lit up when he hobbled into the room and that she seemed to give him that much more attention than her other patients.

When he was practicing walking on the mats without sticks, she would be right behind him, her hands gently holding him at the top of his thighs. He had to concentrate hard on keeping his balance, which was difficult with her hands gripping the side of his thighs, sometimes seeming to slip an inch or two round to the front. He began to spend more time in the downstairs lounge, where he knew she would go and spend her morning or afternoon break. Invariably she would come over and sit with him and they would talk. She now called him 'Owen' rather than 'Lieutenant Quinn' and he began to call her 'Nathalie', certainly when no one else was in earshot.

She would ask him about his life and what plans they had for him once he left Calcotte Grange, and she would tell him about her life in France. She talked of her strict upbringing as an only child in Paris and of how her parents had died within a few months of each other when she was in her late teens. She spoke of how she became an army nurse and ended up in Dunkirk and managed to scramble onto one of the last boats back to Britain.

At the beginning of February, Quinn was moved into one of the side rooms. These tended to be reserved for the more senior officers, or those with the most serious injuries, so Quinn was surprised that one was being offered to him rather than to a more senior officer, but he did not complain. He assumed that it was because he had already been in the hospital for three months.

He told Nathalie about his new room at their next session and she began to visit him there at the end of the day. It was not unusual for the physiotherapists or their assistants to visit the patients on their wards, especially if they had a difficult session that day.

Nathalie's visits became nightly. At first, they were brief, sometimes she would just stand inside the partially closed doorway and wish him a good night and correct his pronunciation. Other times she would sit by his bed, talking of how she had no one in France and of how nursing was now her life. She would untie her hair, shaking her head to allow it to fall by the side of her face and would turn slightly away from him. Once or twice when this happened, he caught a glimpse of her jet-black eyes, moist like pools of water.

One evening he was telling her of how he hoped to go back to sea soon, how it seemed right to do so. He was not terribly close to his parents and, of course, he was not married, so he did not really have to worry about someone left behind.

Nathalie gazed at him as he spoke and then looked down towards the bed. Without looking up she spoke quietly.

'Tu n'es pas seul maintenant.' You are not alone now.

Her fingernail was gently tracing circles on his forearm, the fair hairs on his arm picked out against the bright red of her nail varnish. He stopped talking and she brushed her fingers down his arm. The room was so quiet that Quinn could feel a buzzing in his ear. Their fingertips touched and hands intertwined. Maybe it lasted a second, possibly longer, but for Quinn it was a lifetime. That was the first night that she kissed his lips as she left. It was not a kiss that lingered, but as she kissed him she placed a hand on his shoulder and he could taste her warm breath.

The following day he did not have any physiotherapy and did not go down to the lounge. He was confused. He knew he had fallen desperately in love with Nathalie, but was sure that it was unrequited and that she was just being kind to him. If he was honest with himself he knew that he was not bad looking, but Nathalie was a beautiful woman who was not only his nurse, but also two years older than him. He felt embarrassed at having a schoolboy crush at his age. Although the hospital seemed relaxed about allowing the patients – who were officers after all – and the medical staff to mix socially, having a friendly chat over a cup of tea was probably the limit of what they had in mind. A relationship was quite another thing.

The next day Nathalie was not in the room when he went down for the physiotherapy. He was supervised for the whole session by the senior physiotherapist and for a time he was aware that the senior medical officer and a couple of uniformed naval officers were watching him, which was not altogether unusual. Often when a patient was being considered for release back to active service he would be carefully assessed as he went through his paces.

That afternoon he sat in the lounge for an hour either side of the afternoon break, but there was no sign of Nathalie. He decided that she had realised herself that perhaps she had crossed a boundary the other night and had gone elsewhere. Or, perhaps, it was his fault. Two nights ago she had assured him he was not alone. He should have told her then that she wasn't either. Why had he missed that opportunity, to tell her that he cared for her? Why had he not held her when she kissed him, pulling her closer to him and promising never to let go. He was desolate, chiding himself for his response which she must have seen as him not caring.

That night he lay in the bath in the private bathroom attached to his side room. Nurse Slade, the large nurse who always reeked of tobacco, had helped him into the bath. He was careful to remove the towel only when she had left. She would give him twenty minutes and then knock on the door before entering, allowing him time to put the towel back in place before she helped him out of the bath.

He liked to lie in the bath with the harsh overhead light turned off. Enough light seeped in from his bedroom for him to see what he was doing, but he found lying in the warm water, in the half-light, was relaxing.

He had only been in the bath for five minutes when there was a gentle tap at the half open door. It was far too early for Nurse Slade and, in any case, her taps at the door tended not to be gentle. He had enough time to grab the towel and cover himself when the door from the bedroom opened. Silhouetted in the doorway was an unmistakable figure. Nathalie entered, leaving the door from the bedroom fully ajar, so the bathroom was now flooded with light.

He started to speak, but she placed her forefinger over her mouth. *Silence.*

'I told Nurse Slade I needed to see you and would help you out of the bath. The door is locked.' She was speaking very softly.

And with that Nathalie helped him out of the bath, removing his towel as she did so. He stood quite naked in front of her, the first time he had ever been like that with a woman, the water dripping fast and heavy from his body. He began to breathe deeply and opened his mouth to speak. She smiled, shook her head, placing her forefinger in front of his lips and then allowing it to move inside his mouth. *No need to speak.* She was staring directly into his eyes. In the half-light, her eyes were even darker and brighter than he had imagined.

'It is all right. Don't worry. I told you, the door is locked.' She was speaking in no more than a whisper, her face just a few inches from his. '*Nous avons seulement quinze minutes.*' Just fifteen minutes.

As she spoke she was releasing her belt and unbuttoning her white uniform. She stood as naked as he was before him but, even before that, he had already begun to respond. She moved towards him so that their bodies were now touching. She reached out, her hand sliding down his bare back and then round to the front, setting fire to every inch of his flesh as she did so. She led him towards the bedroom.

'*Venez.*'

The next fifteen minutes were everything that Owen Quinn had ever dreamed of and more.

Be careful what you wish for.

Chapter 7

March 1942

At the beginning of March, two weeks after Nathalie had come into his bathroom and his life, Quinn awoke from an early evening doze to find a tall man in a dark coat and wearing a trilby with a wide brim sitting very still in the chair in the corner of the room.

The two men stared at each other for quite a few seconds before the tall man broke the silence.

'Captain Edgar. Not your lot. Army.'

More silence before Edgar pointed to Quinn's bedside table where there was a bottle of very good malt whisky. Quinn raised his eyebrows.

'Don't worry. Officially sanctioned. Understand you prefer it to rum.' He smiled at his own joke. Quinn could not remember when he had last drunk whisky, other than in his dreams.

'Chaps here tell me that you should be out of here soon, Quinn.' The man was speaking quietly. He had taken his hat off and was turning it carefully in his hands as he did so, first clockwise, then anti-clockwise, as if checking for imperfections. Despite speaking quietly, his voice managed to fill the room. He had no discernible accent, certainly not public school. Not quite officer class, Quinn thought. Maybe even the very slightest trace of an educated northern accent, but he really couldn't place it.

'Yes, sir. I am hoping to return to active service as soon as possible.'

'Not on the cards, I'm afraid.' Captain Edgar was shaking his head. 'I'm told that they don't think you're up to it. Back not strong enough. Leg still playing up.'

Quinn was fully awake now, quite stunned. 'But when I got here they told me I would be back at sea this year!'

'Well, Quinn, the best laid plans of mice and men...'

Quinn could feel himself getting angry and upset.

'But surely this is something that the doctors would—?'

Captain Edgar held up his hat to stop Quinn speaking.

'But we do have a plan that will appeal to you, Quinn. You are going to come and work for us.'

'Us?'

Edgar waved his hat, as if batting away the question.

'All will be revealed. We are quite impressed with what you have to offer, Quinn. Bright chap. You are a navigation officer, aren't you, Quinn?'

'Yes, sir.'

'Specialising in the weather and coastlines, that type of thing?'

Quinn nodded.

'Splendid. Just what we're looking for. Couldn't find a better man. You are going to meet one of our chaps soon. Archibald. He'll tell you all then. Welcome onboard.'

As he arose to leave the room, Edgar paused in the closed doorway, his head above the doorframe.

'Just one thing, Quinn. Your nurse. Nathalie Mercier.'

Quinn felt himself turning bright red. He started to speak.

'Gather you've got rather... sweet on her.'

Quinn started to speak again, but Edgar continued.

'And her with you, I gather. No need to explain. Understand and all that. Pretty woman, perfectly natural. Bit... irregular in this kind of place, but she assures us that you both... feel... the same way about each other.'

'Yes, sir, if I can...'

Edgar shook his head as he stood up.

'No need to explain, Quinn. She'll be able to go with you. Just make sure you do the decent thing.'

The next day, he was called in to see Dr Farrow, who confirmed what Captain Edgar had told him.

Dr Farrow was clearly uneasy about having to impart such bad news and for the whole time that he spoke to Quinn, he determinedly stared at the chewed pencil he was twisting in fingers.

He tried hard to convince Quinn, while managing to sound somewhat less than convinced himself.

Leg healing nicely... but back not really holding up terribly well, not made the progress we had expected... not your fault... one of those things... too risky

65

to let you go back to sea... know we told you we hoped to get you back to active service, but not really worked out... very sorry... accept we were possibly too optimistic... know just how disappointed you must be... look on the bright side... Intelligence chaps picked you out... big job, important etc. etc.

And that was that. As far as Quinn was concerned, he couldn't very well argue with the Royal Navy and the doctors. He was not going back to sea. He had somehow ended up in Intelligence and he had no idea why or how.

-

There are parts of south-eastern England that are so flat that at certain times of the year the harsh winds flying in from the Russian steppes manage to do so unhindered. The last week in March 1942 was one such time. In the morning, the day would be calm and there would be enough sun for those patients who were up to it to be able to gather on the vast terrace at the front of the house that the Calcottes had so thoughtfully provided.

By noon the wind would start to pick up and within minutes it would be whipping around the turrets, terraces and out-buildings of Calcotte Grange. Even the most hardy of the Navy officers would be driven indoors, with inevitable talk of 'battening down the hatches'.

On the last Thursday of March, a group of patients were in the lounge, looking out over the sweeping drive and watching the arrival of a long black car. Owen Quinn was one of that group, more anxious to see the outcome than the others. He had been warned to be ready for a visitor that day and the visitor was in the car, delayed by sheep. He had been waiting for his visitor since Captain Edgar had turned up in his room a month previously.

The car pulled up in front of the main entrance and Quinn watched the driver open the rear passenger door. The man who had got out was above average height and wearing Royal Navy uniform. One of the Navy officers who Quinn had seen around the hospital from time to time was there to salute him and lead him into the building.

It was another half an hour before Quinn was summoned into the presence of a surprisingly elderly looking man, who stood up slowly as Quinn entered the room, stiffly walked over to him, returned Quinn's salute and shook his hand in a formal manner before leading him over to two chairs by the window.

They were in a small room overlooking the back of Calcotte Grange. The gardens behind the house had not been as manicured as those at the front and the area closest to the house was now a large vegetable garden. Wooden fences had been erected around the vegetables to keep the sheep out and one of the gardeners was repairing part of the fence as they looked out. The muffled echoes of a mallet striking the wooden posts were the only sound until the elder man finally spoke.

'Captain John Archibald. Royal Navy most of my life. Tried to retire a few years ago, we'd bought a lovely place in Lincolnshire. Between Boston and the sea. Do you know the area?'

Quinn shook his head.

'Very quiet. My wife had been dreaming of a place like that for years and I promised her that when I left the Navy we would find somewhere like it. Cannot see a soul from where we are, but there's a splendid village just down the lane. Everything you need. Pub, shop, post office, church – in that order. Village green has a phone box next to the war memorial, but otherwise it is perfect. We'd been there a year when this war started and they hauled me back. Saw plenty of activity in my time, Jutland you know. But after the Great War I'd moved over to Naval Intelligence and I suppose that is why they wanted me back. And that is why I am here now.'

Captain Archibald was looking out of the window. Owen noticed his hands, which were enormous with thick fingers and had the appearance of the hands of a labourer. The hammering had stopped and the gardener was trying to lead a stray sheep away from the vegetables.

'I know you wanted to go back to sea and that's splendid. But the doctors here are not sure you're totally up to it. In any case, we have a much bigger job for you – greater good and all that. I work in Naval Intelligence, as I mentioned. I need people like you. You're a bright chap. Plenty of people like doing the exciting stuff, but I understand you're a bit of a wizard with maps and charts. Is that true?'

Quinn hesitated.

'Well… yes, sir. I did a degree in geography at London University. Coasts, sandbanks, meteorology – that's what I was interested in. So when I joined up in November '39, specialising in navigation was right up my street. I read maps for pleasure in the same way that other people read books.'

'Well, it is good to have you onboard, Quinn.'

Quinn noticed that while this was not a command, it was certainly not a question either. At no stage in the conversation had it been anything other than assumed that Quinn would be joining Archibald.

'But I had been hoping to return to sea, sir. The doctor said that—'

'The doctor may have thought that was possible a few months ago but he clearly does not think so now. This is why we would like you to join us.'

'And there really is no alternative?'

'To not being at sea? I am sure there are plenty of desk jobs at the Admiralty, but let me tell you, we have chaps queuing up to join Naval Intelligence.'

'I am pleased to be joining you, sir. If it really is out of the question for me to go back to sea, that is.'

'Good chap. The doctors tell me that you will be out of here in a couple of weeks. Is that right?'

'So I understand, sir. I am walking well now. Still a bit of pain, but I'll be glad to get out of here and doing a job of work.'

'That's the spirit, Quinn. I know you wanted to get back to sea and I understand that. But you need to understand that you are going to be playing a vital role in the war effort. There will be times when it doesn't seem like it. You will just think that you are pushing pieces of paper around. None of us knows how long this damn show is going to last, but it will not be until it is all over that you will have any idea of the part you've played. One other matter, Quinn: I understand that you have recently become engaged.'

'Indeed, sir. All rather sudden… not that we *have* to get married, please don't misunderstand. But when Captain Edgar came to see me earlier this month it was clear that he was aware of our… of our relationship. I didn't want Nurse Mercier – Nathalie – to get into any kind of trouble and Captain Edgar had urged me to do the decent thing so I proposed. And blow me down, sir, she accepted! I'm the happiest man in the world. She is the most beautiful woman and I love her very much.'

The hammering had resumed outside the window. Captain Archibald started to speak, hesitated, stopped and then spoke.

'I was going to say, Quinn, that your private life is none of my concern, but, of course, that is untrue. Everything you do, everything about you will be my concern once you start working in my unit. But just be careful. Love is a wonderful thing, but it does have a habit of getting in the way of things. Try to keep your feet on the ground. They're discharging you from here on Friday, the tenth of April. You start with us at Lincoln House in Duke Street at nine o'clock on Monday, the thirteenth of April. Lucky for us.'

Chapter 8

London, 1942

His wedding had not been quite as Owen Quinn had envisaged, which was hardly surprising as he had never really given much thought to getting married other than assuming that one day he would. Much more to the point, it was certainly not as Marjorie and William Quinn had ever imagined their son's wedding would be.

Over the years, Marjorie Quinn especially had frequently imagined her only child's wedding, even planned some details of it. It would, of course, be a day to remember. Their friends and some relations would all be invited and impressed. The sun would shine, the church would look perfect, the flowers would be immaculately arranged and no detail would be disregarded. It would be the height of taste and would inevitably mark their ascendancy in their middle-class community in Surrey. Ideally, the bride would be from their area and certainly from a similar background. She would be attractive and intelligent though, of course, without any unhealthy modern tendencies towards independence.

Marjorie Quinn did recognise that the war could affect her plans, but had reckoned on her son simply delaying marriage until a year or two after the war. Her cousin's daughter had married an American and that had been most upsetting, but then that side of the family were from Yorkshire.

But to marry a Frenchwoman, with no family – and a nurse, which was almost trade… it had all been too awful for Marjorie to contemplate. William had agreed at first but had soon changed his tune when he first met the girl. It was hard to deny that she was… *attractive*, one had to acknowledge that. But Owen had known her for just a matter of weeks when they became engaged *and* he was a patient of hers. It all seemed too hasty and not a little improper. She wondered whether the whole business may have been the result of any of the medication that Owen was on.

She certainly never imagined that the first time she would meet her son's bride-to-be would be when they were actually engaged. In a way, she blamed herself. They ought to have visited Owen more often after he was taken to Calcotte Grange. But the journey from Surrey involved a series of trains that took forever and the trains tended to be crowded with soldiers, many of whom were not British.

As soon as they heard of the engagement in late March they had come up. William's brother had managed to get hold of some extra petrol coupons and they were able to use his Ford Anglia. On the journey up, they had agreed that they would take Owen aside and do their best to talk him out of it. He had always been such an *impetuous* boy. William said it was because he was an only child.

The day was a disaster from the start; at least it was from Marjorie Quinn's point of view. As soon as they arrived at Calcotte Grange, Owen and the girl piled into the car and they headed off to what she had to admit was a most agreeable tea-room, where they had a small area to themselves by a roaring fire. William could hardly take his eyes off this Nathalie from the moment he first saw her. The girl and Owen actually *held hands* the whole time and even *kissed* in front of them. She drank tea without milk and smoked constantly. She ignored most of Marjorie's carefully rehearsed and very polite questions about her life in Paris and kept asking for amusing stories about Owen as a boy.

The one positive aspect of the whole sorry situation was that at least Owen was not going back to sea, which she had never been happy about. She did like the sound of the new job in London. It seemed important, although Owen insisted that he was not allowed to tell her anything about it.

The young lovers arrived in London in April. The Navy found them a tiny flat in Pimlico, from where you could hear the trains at Victoria Station on a still night. They also put in a good word to allow Nathalie to return to her old hospital, St Thomas's. She would live in the nurses' home until their wedding in June.

That took place in a grim church in Chelsea. The vicar had a streaming cold but no handkerchief and, for some unaccountable reason, was unable to pronounce 'Owen' properly. He was so slow in both speech and movement that the ceremony felt more funereal than matrimonial. It rained for the duration of the wedding and for some time after. Marjorie and William had invited a dozen friends and a similar number of relatives. Owen had invited the two or three chums from school whom he had been able to contact, along with another Navy officer from his new office. Nathalie had brought along three other nurses, none of whom she seemed to know particularly well, but who all spent most of the ceremony dabbing their eyes.

And that was it. Barely thirty of them in a damp and dimly lit church that could accommodate at least ten times that number. Marjorie Quinn did turn round at one stage during the ceremony and spotted a tall man in the very back row, well into the shadows. He was wearing a dark coat and his face was obscured by a wide-brimmed trilby. She did wonder whether he was one of the Yorkshire relatives – they were the kind of people who would not remove their hats in a church – but when she next turned round the tall man was no longer there. She decided he was simply a passer-by seeking refuge from the rain.

And so, on a wet day in June 1942, Owen Quinn, aged twenty-four, married a Frenchwoman two years older than himself.

–

Now it was September and Owen Quinn was surprised at the ease with which he had taken both to his new role in Naval Intelligence and to married life.

The Navy had been what he considered to be surprisingly helpful in finding them the flat in Alderney Street in Pimlico. He really had not realised that they went to that kind of trouble. It was a tiny flat, he had to admit that. The kitchen was little more than a galley and the small lounge which led off it had to accommodate two enormous old armchairs, a pair of rickety side tables and a stained dining table. The narrow bathroom was always draughty, but having spent eighteen months at sea and the best part of a year in hospital, Quinn had no problem with the flat – unlike his new wife.

It was an improvement on the nurses' home, but for Nathalie, the bedroom was the only room that she was happy with. Somehow they had managed to get the double bed that his parents bought them into it and from then on the bedroom became the focal point of their home life.

It was hard to predict Nathalie's shifts at St Thomas's. Sometimes it would be long days, occasionally a week of nights, which he hated.

Weekends were difficult to plan. She did seem to work more Sundays than not, which he could not really understand but she promised him that she was not being asked to do any more than her fair share. She assured him that working more Sundays meant she was not required to work so many nights. Her Sundays at work did mean that he could go down to Surrey for lunch with his parents.

There was a war on after all, and at least they were together. She more than made up for it in their time together. On the occasions when he found himself alone in the flat becoming maudlin, he would remind himself of how his life had changed in little more than a year. Clinging to the plank of wood in the sea off Crete, he had thought his life was over. Now, not only was he alive but he was married to a woman he loved and who had previously existed only in his dreams. His life, he had to admit to himself, was as near perfect as he could have wished it to be.

Be careful what you wish for, he very occasionally reminded himself. But he would chuckle when he did so. He now seemed to have what he had always wished for and there really did not appear to be anything he had to be careful about.

On the rare days when neither of them was working they would go for long walks. She liked to explore London. Owen had lived in the capital as a student, but Nathalie brought a totally different eye to it.

She would spot sights that he had walked past many times but never seen. She would be thrilled at the names of little streets, delighted at a small shop only selling buttons, or appalled at the food shops which she said were disgusting. He would remind her that there was a war on, but she insisted that the food shops and the steamy cafés they would sit and drink in were proof that the English did not care about food.

They would walk along and Nathalie would always look up. Her long hair would drop further down her back, resting sensuously in that spot halfway down it which he would always caress before they fell asleep. She would marvel at the tops of the buildings and the strange creatures carved into them or protruding from the walls.

They would be arm in arm and she would tell him long stories, some amusing, most sad, about life at the hospital. And against his better judgement, he would find himself drawn into telling her about his work. Nothing serious, of course: he knew that he was not allowed to do that. But the titbits about daily office life and the people who

73

inhabited it seemed to amuse her and there seemed to be no harm in that. She would laugh loudly and pull herself closer to him. They would kiss and Owen would notice the looks, some disapproving, and many more admiring, of passers-by.

It would be on the occasions like this that he would feel able to again broach the subject of her life in France. He had assumed that once they were married, he would find out more about her, but he realised that he still really knew very little. He was curious about what school she went to, what hospital she had trained in, what boyfriends she had had, and about any extended family.

Nathalie was never rude and would always appear to answer his questions but, by the end of these conversations, he would realise that she had said nothing of any significance. The hospital '*was a very large one, but you know what these Paris hospitals are like*' – which he did not. '*But you never tell me about your girlfriends!*' '*There are uncles, aunts and cousins, but we are not a close family. You are my family now.*' He would ask these questions again in bed, after they had made love and were lying face to face on the pillow, stroking each other's arms. She should have been at her most open then, but the answers would be the same and with a whispered '*Ça suffit*' she would let him know that was enough. The conversation would end.

He was not intending to pry, but he felt that he did not really know his wife and all he wanted was to be part of her life. He imagined that when the war was over they would spend time in Paris. They would stroll through the *Rive Gauche*, stopping to look at the second-hand bookstalls and the artists on the Left Bank. They would walk into agreeable bars at any time of the day and he would drink cognac. They would stop at the Café des Deux Magots in Place St Germain des Prés, drink proper coffee and hope to catch the intellectual discussions around them. If they had enough money they could even dine at Fouquet's on the Champs Élysées.

He attributed her reticence to a remark she had made one Saturday afternoon in late July when they were walking back towards Pimlico by the river. Maybe he did not appreciate enough what it meant to have to flee your country. It had been a perfect day, warm with a steady breeze and they had walked past the Houses of Parliament, crossed Westminster Bridge, by St Thomas's, along the south bank before crossing over Chelsea Bridge, heading back towards Pimlico. On Grosvenor Road there was a small group of soldiers coming towards them. As they came closer, he realised they were Free French and greeted them with a '*Bonjour! Ma femme est française.*' But Nathalie seemed shy and uncommunicative and after the briefest of pauses she moved him along, explaining that they needed to get home. As they moved away from the soldiers, he asked why. She was silent for a few seconds as they continued walking and when she lifted her head to speak her eyes had turned into those moist, dark shining pools.

'It is no longer *my* France. My France has been taken from me.'

And there was the café. It was an incident that bothered him at the time but which he allowed to slip from his mind after her apology.

It was a Thursday afternoon in August and he had finished work early. Nathalie met him in Piccadilly Circus and they walked down Haymarket towards Trafalgar Square. It began to rain in the way that it does in an English summer: a few drops without apparent warning and then a sudden and heavy downpour. Nathalie was wearing high heels and a summer dress. She was not dressed for the rain. They dived into a small corner café and sat against the wall at the end of a long Formica table. The rain had caused her dress to cling against her figure and Owen removed his jacket to drape over his wife's shoulders. Within minutes the café filled up and a family of four squeezed onto their table.

It was evident from their initial enquiry – '*Are these seats free?*' – that they were French and Owen happily introduced themselves. It ought, he thought, to have been a perfect encounter for Nathalie. '*From Paris. The 7th arrondissement. Near Les Invalides.*' The few sentences that Nathalie uttered were short to the point of being curt. The parents were in their early forties, the two boys in their early teens. They had come to London in early 1940. The father spoke to them in hushed tones as the boys flicked their straws at each other.

'I travelled a lot to Germany for business during the 1930s. I could see how...' He paused and then muttered to his wife in French.

'Dangerous,' she said.

'...dangerous it would be for us,' he continued. 'We are fortunate in having family in London. We could not risk remaining in Paris. We cannot imagining—'

'Imagine,' she corrected him.

'...imagine what is happening there now to our family and our friends. We were so lucky to escape.'

Owen looked quizzical.

'Where you involved in politics?'

Before the man could answer Nathalie, who had spent most of the time looking at the pepper pot she was fiddling with on the table, spoke.

'They're Jews, Owen. Can't you tell?'

Owen was taken aback. No, he had not been able to tell. These were the first Jews he could recall meeting. But what had really taken him aback was Nathalie's tone. She had been quiet throughout what he thought was a pleasant and even fortuitous meeting. But her tone and her manner bordered on rudeness.

Before he could say anything else, Nathalie was standing up.

'We had better leave now, Owen.'

The downpour had not abated. If anything, it was even heavier.

'Are you sure?' He knew that, if there was one thing she hated, it was getting wet.

But she was already pushing her way through. The family all had to get up to make way for them. Outside, she did not wait for him as he tried to leave in a more polite manner. He had to trot to catch her up.

'What was all that about, Nathalie?'

'What was what about?' She was walking fast, despite her high heels. Her arms folded tightly across her as if that might keep her dry.

'Why did we have to leave so suddenly? It must have seemed rude.'

She stopped and turned at him.

'You English are so concerned about manners and doing the right thing. That is all you think about. I did not want to be with those people. We were on our own. Why did they have to come and sit there and interrupt us.'

'Nathalie!'

'They're always like that, thinking they can push in and take things over as if they own the place.'

Owen was genuinely confused. They were walking next to each other now, the rain still heavy.

'Who are "they", Nathalie? I don't know what you mean.'

She paused to look at him.

'You're lucky then.'

They didn't speak again until they were back in Pimlico.

Later that night she apologised. She realised she must have been rude. She had sat with two people as they died that morning in the hospital and she was upset. Sometimes being reminded of France made her even more upset and that must have been the reason for her behaviour in the café.

-

Duke Street ran from Piccadilly to the north and Pall Mall to the south. Lincoln House was about halfway down and on the eastern side of the street. It was a block down from Fortnum and Mason – where Owen Quinn occasionally wandered into the Special Officers' Department but never bought anything. A few doors along was the Chequers Tavern, a small pub which was reputed to have been the first one built in the city after the Great Fire. It was not, Owen was informed on his first day, regarded as a suitable place for officers to drink. He never found out why.

Lincoln House was a seven-storey building, more than eighty years old and difficult to distinguish from the other buildings in an otherwise elegant street. It had dutifully served some of the less exciting parts of the insurance industry until it was requisitioned by the Government in 1940. The attraction was its sheer ordinariness and anonymity. On more than one occasion, even after he had been working there for months, Quinn had found himself walking past the gloomy entrance, with its dark brown doors and grey metal shutters, with the words 'Lincoln House' picked in fading gold characters painted on a filthy strip of glass above the door. The entrance was tucked against an art gallery that rarely seemed to open and always had the same miserable, dark landscape in the window. The building was narrower than most of the others in the street, but not so much that it stood out. The white façade had weathered over the years and the exposure to London grime and rain gave the exterior a mottled effect. Now the building housed a series of offices, all of which fulfilled some security- or intelligence-related purpose. The entrance led along the length of the art gallery to a reception area and guardroom at the back. From there was a main stairwell, on one side of the building, with a door leading off it at each floor to small suites of offices. When he first went to work on the sixth floor of Lincoln House, Quinn had been told that the higher the floor, the more sensitive the work being handled there. He was not sure if this was true, but like so much of the gossip that passed for information in wartime, he did not take it too seriously – but did find a place for it somewhere in his memory.

The very first thing that Quinn asked Captain Archibald when he arrived at Lincoln House on Monday, 13th April, was the name of the unit. Who was he working for? What was it called? What should he tell people?

It had seemed a reasonable question, not one that he would have expected Archibald to hesitate at answering for quite as long as he did.

'That's a jolly good question, Quinn. We don't really have a name. We are part of Naval Intelligence and we handle Special Projects. You'll have your security briefing later today, but the easiest thing is not to discuss anything with anyone. You work for the Royal Navy, you're stuck behind a desk – that is as much as people need to know. It's all that I've told my wife for the last twenty-five years. Best advice I can offer is that you should give the impression to people that your job is a bit boring, that you are slightly embarrassed to be doing something as menial as this. Keep it simple. That way, they will soon lose interest. Let me show you round.'

There was not much to see. The whole suite of offices looked as if it had been recently decorated. The smell of fresh paint was evident and, that morning, boxes and charts were still being brought into the office. The central office area had a large chart table in the middle, with maps and charts stacked against it. Around the room were grey filing cabinets that were being filled by a small, well-built woman called Mary. Along the floor were what were now becoming stacks of boxes, many of which seemed to be filled with photographs.

'Time to meet the whole crew,' said Archibald. Apart from Mary, there were two other women in the office. Agnes sat in one of three side offices and told Quinn quite clearly that she *ran* the office. She was probably in her late fifties, possibly even older. Her grey hair was pulled into a tight bun and her spectacles were perched on the end of her nose. Whenever she spoke to someone, she lifted her head slightly higher than they would expect so that she could see them through her glasses. And there was Rosemary. English Rose, he thought. The kind of girl he always imagined he would end up with until his dreams had come true. He knew Rose's type; he had grown up with them. From somewhere in the middle class, somewhere in the Home Counties and somewhere between presentable and plain. Rose was in her late twenties, as far as he could tell, and had it not been for the war would have expected to have been married by now. Rose took security very seriously; it seemed to give her a sense of importance that she had never expected to have. Rose's role was to type up reports and letters.

There were two other men in the office. There was Porter, who was never referred to as anything other than Porter. He didn't wear any uniform and was stone deaf.

'Atlantic convoys,' Archibald told him, by way of explanation. Quinn had to assume that Porter had lost his hearing in an Atlantic convoy, but he never pushed the matter. He was not sure whether Porter had been Royal Navy or Merchant Navy. He suspected the latter. In so far as there was any communication with Porter, it was done by writing notes. But there was no call for too much communication. Porter's role was to manage the maps and the charts. To get out the ones that Quinn needed, put away those that he had finished with and collect new ones.

And Riley. He was never quite sure what Riley's role was, even though he and Quinn did share one of the three side offices. As far as he could tell, he provided some kind of a filter for Quinn, looking at paperwork before it came to him and checking whatever Quinn produced and Rose had typed. Riley only had one arm and the empty sleeve was pinned to the side of his jacket. No matter how hot it was – and at times it was very hot in the office – Riley always kept his jacket on.

They were not what Quinn would have described as a merry bunch. It did strike Quinn as slightly odd that the group responsible for Special Intelligence Projects comprised an elderly captain brought out of retirement and who did not seem to be in the best of health, an injured lieutenant, one deaf man, a man with one arm, and the three women. But a week into his new role, Archibald did mention that they were not the only unit in Naval Intelligence handling Special Projects, so he did not think about it again.

Quinn soon fell into a routine. A project could last a day, or a month, or longer. Captain Archibald would call Quinn and Riley into his office and outline the project and Quinn would then have Rose type a note for Porter detailing what maps and charts he required. They would all be planned naval operations and Quinn was required to put together a detailed brief on routes, coastlines, sandbanks and the like. It was work that he was good at and that he enjoyed. He just wished that he was at sea doing it.

His first project came in May. He had arrived in the office one morning and was called straight in by Archibald, who was sitting behind his desk.

79

'Arctic convoys.'

For a moment, Archibald said no more. Quinn wondered whether he was being sent on an Arctic convoy. A shudder of fear followed by excitement went through him.

'What the convoys are carrying into Murmansk and Archangel is keeping the Soviet Union in the war. But as the weather improves, they are sailing into waters where night never falls. It makes attacks on them too easy. The Luftwaffe and the U-Boats are sinking too many ships.

'We need the Soviets to tie the Germans up on the Eastern Front. They can only do that if we can ensure that they are properly supplied. If the supplies don't get through, the Red Army could collapse. And if that happens…'

Archibald was spreading out a large map of the Soviet Union on the chart table as he spoke.

'…then the war's over on the Eastern Front. That will make life somewhat tricky for us. Can't let it happen. Molotov is coming to London in the next week or two. He needs to be assured that we have all of this in hand. We're losing too many ships at the moment.'

Archibald had been indicating the depth of the German advance into the Soviet Union. His pencil was perilously close to Moscow. As he continued, he was straightening out a chart of the Barents Sea, placing it over the map of the Soviet Union.

'So, this is what you need to concentrate on, Quinn. Best route for getting the convoys safely into these ports.' He was pointing at Murmansk, and Archangel just below it.

'Best routes, how much sunlight there's going to be on any given day, sandbanks, any other ports we could nip into. That type of thing. Beauty of our little outfit is that we have time to think, come up with options if you like. Good luck. Remember that Riley is here to help you.'

Quinn immersed himself in the Arctic routes. He researched the weather, the amount of daylight, possible new routes, ports that some of the ships with smaller draughts may be able to dart into if they had to. Porter was forever bringing in new charts and maps, stacking used ones and rearranging the ones on the table. English Rose typed patriotically and Riley read everything he wrote. Captain Archibald seemed pleased. Quinn found the work interesting without being taxing.

At the beginning of August, Owen and Nathalie Quinn had a week's holiday. They stayed with his parents in Surrey for two days and then borrowed his father's car and – thanks to more petrol coupons obtained by his uncle – drove to Devon for their first holiday together.

He was back at work on Monday, 10th August. He was the first to arrive in the office apart from Archibald, whose presence in the office seemed to be ubiquitous. He was standing at the chart table when Quinn came in.

'Morning Quinn. I hope you are refreshed after your holiday. You are going to need to be.'

He indicated for Quinn to join him at the table. On it was a map of the English Channel, showing the southern coast of England and part of the northern coast of France.

'Here is our next project, Quinn.'

Archibald was bouncing his pencil up and down on a point on the map between Le Havre and Calais.

'Dieppe.'

Chapter 9

Berlin, November 1942

The man in the German Navy uniform pausing at the top of the steps of the SS headquarters looked much older than his fifty years. He rubbed his hands and buttoned his greatcoat before removing a black leather glove from each of the pockets. It was late in the afternoon of the last Monday in November and the arms of a true Prussian winter had started to wrap themselves around Berlin a few weeks previously, their grip tightening by the day. This had been one of those days when it felt as if the sun had not appeared at all. He had heard stories about the conditions on the Eastern Front which made him shiver in more ways than one. At least in the city you had some refuge from the cold.

He was not pleased. He had arrived back in Berlin that morning after a weekend in Rome arguing with incompetent Italians, and he had spent the past hour here in Prinz-Albrecht-Strasse arguing with the SS. In truth, he was not so much arguing with the SS as being shouted at by them. '*You don't share your intelligence with us,*' they told him. '*We never know what you lot are up to. You have people working for you that we don't trust. What's this about a Jew working for you in Madrid? If only the Führer knew, he would take a most dim view.*' And so on. He had heard it all before. It was how the SS operated. They'd shout, they'd scream and intimidate you and eventually you'd give in, or at least appear to. *Give me the Italians any day*, he thought. *As stupid as they are, at least they are not Nazis.*

If he had been able to see Himmler, that would not have been too bad. He did listen, sometimes. But the Reichsführer-SS was with Hitler in Berchtesgaden, as usual. He never liked to leave him on his own in Bavaria for too long. So he had spent the afternoon with idiots, who he knew hated him and who he knew had designs on his organisation.

He finished buttoning his greatcoat. As he climbed down the steps of the SS headquarters, he felt a sense of relief. The irony was that the former school of Industrial Arts and Crafts was one of the most handsome buildings in the city. But he knew what went on in Prinz-Albrecht-Strasse now. It was not exactly a state secret. The SS wanted people to know how they tortured their prisoners and the sense of terror seemed to radiate from the building like radio waves. He had always told his men not to forget that they were an *intelligence* organisation. '*There is nothing especially clever or intelligent,*' he would say, '*about using electrodes – as long as you get the wiring right. People would say anything just to get you to stop. But if you want quality intelligence, you use your brain.*'

He paused on the pavement and straightened his Navy cap. At least he would be able to go home now and have a proper rest. His wife was away and he could enjoy the solitude. One of the joys of living by the Wansee was the silence that lay across the surface of the lake like a shroud. You could cloak yourself in it.

Jürgen came out of the car and walked round to him. He smiled. He had worked hard to surround himself with men he trusted and Jürgen was one of those. They were hard to find now. Most young officers had joined the Nazi Party and once they did that, whatever their motives, you could not trust them.

'Sir. I'm afraid you need to return to Tirpitz Ufer. Colonel Preuss insists that it is most urgent. He wanted me to come and tell you in person. He did not want a message sent while you were in there.' There was a noticeable distrust in the younger man's nod at the building. He nodded. If Preuss said it was urgent, then it was urgent.

The car turned right into Wilhelm Strasse and then right again into Anhalter Strasse.

The man in the back of the car stared out at a Berlin that was at the same time so familiar and yet so strange. At the end of the third full year of the war the city was a cauldron of contradictions. This once liberal city was now at the heart of the German Reich. The majority of the population had happily gone along with this, but there were days when some of the four million Berliners thought they could still detect a whiff of pre-war decadence in the air. Most would shake their heads and dismiss it as an illusion. A very few would dare to see it as a sign of hope. But like everyone else, they kept quiet. It did not pay to even think too much.

They were now driving along the north bank of the Landwehr Kanal and into Tirpitz Ufer. It was like that in the regime too, the man in the back of the car thought. Contradictions and paranoia seeped into every ministry and organisation in the city, fuelled by the Führer himself. Adolf Hitler trusted no one. He would not allow any organisation to become a centre of power and therefore a threat to him. So at every level and for every function, more than one organisation would exist and inevitably they would be in conflict at worst, or an uneasy alliance at best, with a rival body. Hitler's thinking was simple and over the years it had proven to be highly effective: you don't need to worry about an organisation if someone else is doing that for you.

The car drove past the Bendlerblock, the headquarters of the Wehrmacht and pulled up outside number 76–78. It was the headquarters of the Abwehr.

The Abwehr was one of the complex patchwork of organisations operating in the area of intelligence and security. As Hitler intended, they each kept a check on the other. The *Schutzstaffel* – the SS – was perhaps the best known and most feared, although that was an honour closely contested by the secret police, the *Geheime Staatpolizei*, better known as the Gestapo. Then there was the *Sicherheitsdienst* – the security service, known as the SD.

The Abwehr was the military intelligence arm of the German Army, the Wehrmacht. The head of the Abwehr reported to the OKW, the High Command of the Wehrmacht. The man climbing out of the back of the car, going into the four-storey building and returning the eager salutes of the guards had been the head of the Abwehr since 1935. Admiral Wilhelm Canaris.

Canaris headed for the lift and his office on the fourth floor, but Jürgen touched his elbow and steered him away from it. 'Preuss thinks that we should meet in the Map Room.'

They headed down the stairs into the basement, past the rooms where the cipher clerks and radio monitors were sat in serried ranks, past the small armoury and then to a door on their right. Canaris used a key on his chain to unlock one of the locks; Jürgen did likewise with the other.

They were now in a narrow, dimly lit corridor that reminded Canaris of the submarines he had commanded in the Great War. It was only possible to walk in single file and there was a subtle but discernible sense of walking down an incline.

The corridor twisted slowly to the left and the gap between floor and ceiling narrowed. Both men removed their caps. The echo of the two men's boots reverberated around them, giving the illusion that there were people marching ahead of them. The corridor came to a dead end. A small flight of three metal steps, the width of the corridor, was in front of them. At the foot of the steps were two armed SS soldiers.

They parted to allow the two men up the steps. As they approached the top, a heavy door swung open. It was half a yard thick and heavily padded. No sooner had they entered than the door swung shut. It had taken the effort of two men to close it. The room was brightly lit and circular, with padded walls and ceiling. There were maps around the walls, but the room was dominated by a small circular table, around which were arranged six chairs.

Four of them had been occupied by men who stood up as Canaris and Jürgen entered the room. Canaris knew three of them very well and acknowledged them by their first names and a nod of the head.

'Hans' was Generalmajor Hans Oster. Canaris had appointed him as his deputy and Oster also headed the Abwehr's *Abteilung Z*, or Central Division, which had overall control of all the other parts of the Abwehr.

The other 'Hans' was Colonel Hans Preuss, who headed Abwehr I, which was responsible for Foreign Intelligence.

'Reinhard' was Major Reinhard Schmidt, one of Preuss's senior officers.

Like the other two, Canaris trusted him implicitly and like the other two – as with Canaris himself and Jürgen – he was not a member of the Nazi Party.

The fourth man he did not know, but he imagined that he must be the reason they had gathered in the Map Room. The very name of the room was euphemistic. It was a room that very few people in Tirpitz Ufer headquarters even knew existed. The room was completely soundproof and surrounded by enough gadgets to ensure that nothing said in it could be picked up, electronically or otherwise. For an outsider to be brought to the room was most unusual and a measure of the gravity of what was about to transpire.

All six men sat down and Preuss began talking. 'Admiral Canaris, I am sorry to bring you here at such short notice. This is Georg Lange.

He works for us in Paris and is responsible for the recruitment and the running of a number of agents.'

Canaris nodded at him.

'I have seen your name in reports, Lange. Good work,' he acknowledged.

Lange was short, but well built, giving the impression that he kept fit. His thick fair hair was slicked back and he was wearing a smart suit, which Canaris guessed was French. He was playing nervously with his watch strap.

'You can trust Georg, sir.' As in most of the corridors and offices of Berlin, as throughout Germany, people had learned to speak in code. A conversation could take four or five times longer than it needed to, because of the necessity to ensure that the person you were speaking to shared your own point of view. You wouldn't ask a friend whether they were experiencing any food shortages, which would be far too direct. But you might ask them whether they had a family lunch on Sundays, their reply might be along the lines '*Not every week*' and eventually both parties would feel able to admit that they did not have enough food.

So Preuss's 'You can trust Georg, sir' was his way of saying that the man was not a Party member.

The colonel continued.

'Georg was already working in our Embassy well before June 1940, sir. He recruited a number of agents and as you are aware, sir, we have had mixed fortunes with them. I will let Georg take up the story.'

'Thank you, sir.' Georg sounded unusually confident, in the circumstances. Canaris placed his accent from the Frankfurt area.

'We recruited an agent in 1938, sir. We had very high hopes for her. We gave her the code name Magpie… *Elster*. She was very committed to the German cause and is a most beautiful woman. Very intelligent, very quick to learn and a good temperament. The story of how I found her is very interesting. In fact, she—'

'That is for another day, Lange. Continue with the matter under discussion please,' said Preuss.

'No,' said the Admiral. 'I want to hear how you found her.'

'The point is, sir, I didn't really find her. She found us. She turned up at the Embassy in Paris. She spoke reasonable English and is also a nurse, so her cover story more or less wrote itself. We managed to slip her over to England during the Dunkirk evacuation. We were fortunate that she panicked, as half of France did, and headed north. So instead of losing her we were able to pick her up in Picardy, in a town called Abbeville. Most convenient for Dunkirk, as I say.'

'Can we trust her then?' asked Canaris. 'If she fled, that is. Presumably her instructions were to wait until you contacted her – standard procedure?'

'I am certain we can trust her, sir. Her story was credible. She believed that the French police were after her. She was travelling under her own identity. She is sharp enough that if she had been fleeing from us, she would have used another identity. Then we would never have found her.

'The plan for her was to get to England and find work in a hospital and when the time was right, apply for a transfer to a military hospital and then supply us with information. We felt that this would be a good source of steady information. She would be able to find out about casualties, what units had been posted where and where people were going to be sent when they were released from the hospital. It would be good information to have – not top grade, but it would all be very useful.

'We did have a concern about her ability to get the information back to us, so we gave her a radio man. He is a Belgian who could not wait to lick our arses the minute we rolled into Brussels. When we found out that he had a passion for radios and could speak good English, we decided to make use of him. We gave him the code name Sparrow. It is a small and common bird in England; we felt it was an appropriate name.

'So, Magpie travelled to England in June 1940. For a year, we hear nothing of her. We had told her to take her time, not to rush, but we did not expect it to be that long. Then at the end of April last year, we get our first contact.

'To be honest, sir, it was nothing much. She wanted us to know that she was working as a nurse at St Thomas's Hospital in the centre of London and that she had applied for a transfer to a military hospital. She was hopeful. Apparently she had heard that there was a shortage of nurses who could work in the area of physiotherapy. She had told them that she trained to work in physiotherapy in France.

'For a few months, nothing happened. She kept in touch with Sparrow. Every Sunday he goes to a park on his way back from church and when she has something to report, she goes to meet him there.

They bump into each other in the park. Apparently, that is a very English pastime. Then in January, she hears she is to be transferred to a military hospital. It is called…'

Georg put on a pair of reading glasses and read from his notebook.

'…Calcotte Grange. It is in the countryside, just north of London. Not a big hospital, but a specialist place where Royal Navy officers are sent to recover. Apparently the aim of the hospital is to get them fit as soon as possible so that they return to active service and fight your former navy comrades, Admiral.'

Canaris nodded: *please carry on.*

'So they have a big physiotherapy unit and Magpie is well suited. We are in business. The only problem is that it makes it difficult for her to contact Sparrow, but she can take some Sundays off, so when she has information to pass on, she is able to take a day trip to London. Not a perfect solution, but in the circumstances, a safe one.

'We start to get some good information. Not top class, but decent. You know the kind of thing: what ships are where, casualties, how well ships are equipped. Useful information on the convoys and especially on what they think of the weaponry on the ships: what guns jam, what they rate, what they dislike. No information that is going to change the war, but it all helps to build up a bigger picture and can fill in gaps in our knowledge. It has all been gratefully received by the different recipients we have sent it to – especially, of course, the Navy.'

Jürgen collected a jug of water from a table at the back of the room and poured six glasses. Georg drank gratefully from his before continuing. Canaris knew full well that everything Georg had said so far was very routine. It was the kind of information that normally would not come anywhere near him. He gestured for the man from Paris to continue.

'Then…' he was allowing a dramatic pause, during which he sipped carefully from his glass, his hands very slightly shaking '…a young Royal Navy officer falls in love with Magpie!'

Canaris nodded for him to continue. He would forgive the dramatic telling of the story if he found it justified.

'Of course, we knew that with such a beautiful woman… that men would be attracted to her. That was part of her attraction – to us! And Magpie was not a naive woman. She was experienced with men, shall we say. But this officer was different.

'He is two years younger than her and only a lieutenant. The relationship is no coincidence, Admiral. Magpie had surpassed herself. She managed to gain access to all of the patient records in the hospital and she discovered from a note in his file that this young lieutenant was due to be transferred to Naval Intelligence when he was released. On a "top secret project" according to a note on his file. Even he was not aware of it at the time, he was hoping to go back to sea. It also seems, according to his file, that he specialises in navigation and his ability to analyse coastlines and sandbanks is very highly regarded. So she put herself in a position to encourage the relationship, you might say. If you met her, Admiral, you would not be surprised that a healthy young man so eagerly took the bait.'

The silence hummed around the already very silent room. No one in it was in any doubt of the significance of what Georg was saying; least of all Georg himself, who seemed to have grown in stature as he spoke and now had a certain smugness about him as he continued.

'Magpie decided to reciprocate this officer's interest in her. She—'

'I presume we know his name?'

'Yes, sir. Quinn. Owen Quinn. Not easy to pronounce. Magpie allowed herself to be attracted to this man. She allowed him to fall in love with her and she allowed their affair to become… fully consummated, shall we say. Events then moved very fast. She feared that he would be discharged from the hospital and that he would then disappear. He would go and work in Intelligence; she would have no way of keeping in contact with him.

'Then something remarkable happened.' Lange paused again while he sipped from his glass. 'Quinn proposed to Magpie! And she, I do not need to add, accepted.'

'They allowed him to do that?' This was Oster speaking.

Major Schmidt spoke now.

'Remember, sir, that Magpie would have received security clearance to go to this hospital in the first place. She applied for a transfer to a military hospital around March, April 1941 and the transfer came through in January. Nine months. Presumably they used that time to check her out.'

'And also,' said Georg, 'she was clean when she came to England. Nothing incriminating on her whatsoever. That was the job of Sparrow. Let him carry the risk for her. She had no radio, no code-book, nothing. To all intents and purpose, she was exactly what she appeared to be: a French nurse.'

89

'I still find it remarkable,' said Generalmajor Oster, 'that within what seems like days of their meeting as nurse and patient, they are apparently sleeping with each other and then weeks later get married. Are we certain about this, Lange?'

'But as Lange has told us, Generalmajor, Magpie was clean. There would be absolutely no reason for the British to suspect her,' said Schmidt. 'Lange has done a good job. She had an excellent cover story and he took the very wise precaution of sending her over clean.'

'Gentlemen. Can we not argue, please. I know you find it remarkable Oster, but we need to remember this: we spend our time thinking as intelligence officers. It is our job to be suspicious of everything, all of the time. Not everyone else is like that, as we know. The British would see this girl as having had full security clearance and would hardly be surprised at a young man falling in love with her. Please continue, Lange.' Canaris was no longer tired. The Italians and the SS were a distant memory, a quiet night by the Wansee a distant hope.

'The Royal Navy are obviously a very romantic service, Admiral. They did agree to the marriage. Quinn moved to London in April and started his new job. Magpie returned to her old job at St Thomas's Hospital and in June they married and now Magpie is Mrs Quinn.'

'To live happily ever after,' said Generalmajor Oster, shaking his head.

Major Schmidt now took over.

'Thank you, Georg. Your work is of the highest quality that the service expects.' There were murmurs of agreement around the table.

'Admiral. Magpie is proving to be an outstanding agent. We are only getting small bits of information so far, but what we are receiving is top quality. We have every reason to expect that in the future, we will get more information. The lieutenant tells his wife very little, but as the months have gone on he does tell her more. She knows to take it very slowly, not to show too much interest in his work.'

'So, what do we know?'

'His unit is commanded by a captain…' Schmidt was looking through a file in front of him, searching for the name. 'Archibald. John Archibald. Saw active service in the—'

'…Battle of Jutland.' Canaris finished the sentence for him. 'I know of Archibald. Outstanding captain. Injured but continued to fight.'

'We know for a fact that this Captain Archibald worked in Royal Navy Intelligence after the war. Came out of retirement in 1940. We know that Quinn has been working on planning routes for the Arctic convoys, but we only found out about that after he finished that work. We did not get much, but what we did get was all accurate.'

'The big news,' said Preuss, taking over now from Schmidt, 'is that Quinn worked on the Dieppe raid in August. We got a whisper that he was working on something big, no details, but afterwards Quinn told Magpie that he was heavily involved in the planning. Did a lot of the work on the landings, had to put together a report of the coastline and the weather. Apparently, he was very upset afterwards. What were the figures? Six thousand Canadian and British troops went over? One thousand killed, two thousand taken prisoner, I think. No wonder he was upset.

'It is evident that he is working at the highest levels of Naval Intelligence. The projects that he works on are the most important ones. If we are very lucky, Admiral, it can only be a matter of time before the Navy puts Quinn onto working on the Second Front. All of our intelligence, as you know, tells us the invasion of northern Europe is the priority for the Allies. All their planning effort is going into it. Magpie could not be in a better place.'

Canaris got up slowly and paced around the room, deep in thought. The news from the east was bad. The Russians – aided by their great ally, the winter – were now not only holding the German advance but beginning to repel it in places. This meant that an Allied invasion somewhere in mainland Europe was increasingly likely. It was the big obsession among the planners here in Berlin and in German Army headquarters throughout Europe. When would the British and their allies launch an invasion of mainland Europe – and where would that be? To have someone in the position that Magpie was seemed, to Canaris, to be almost too good to be true.

'Is Sparrow functioning normally?' he asked.

'All his transmissions are in order. He has two or three opportunities in each transmission to let us know if he has been compromised, but he is as clean as a whistle, as they say. We would know if he wasn't,' replied Lange.

'And no one else knows about Magpie. Not the SD, no one?'

'No one, sir,' said Schmidt.

'Let's make sure that it stays that way. Excellent work, Lange.'

Chapter 10

Against his better judgement, Owen Quinn had to admit – if only to himself – that he was enjoying his work. The truth was that if he was now given the option of going back to sea, he would hesitate. It would be a dilemma, whereas back at the beginning of 1942 there would have been no question that he would rather go back to sea on active service.

It was not just that he was living with the woman he loved in what were, considering that there was a war on, close to idyllic circumstances. It was also that, as he became busier and more involved, the more interesting and stimulating he found the work. Dieppe had been a blow, of course. Not that he had blamed himself, and Archibald insisted that nothing he had done had helped contribute to the disaster. But no one wants to be involved in an operation where half the men who go out on a mission don't return.

But if it was a setback, then it was one that seemed to act as a spur for the work of the small team on the sixth floor of Lincoln House. Their brief was to identify possible landing places for the Allies by studying the sweep of the northern coast of Europe, from the Bay of Biscay in the west to the Westerschelde that marked the Belgian–Dutch border in the east. Quinn could spend a week looking at a single port or one beach that, to be honest, he would not recommend attempting with a rowing boat in peacetime and perfect weather conditions. But they all needed to be looked at, if only to be eliminated.

Porter was forever bringing in new charts and maps and Quinn was spending less time in the small office he shared with Riley and more time at the large chart table, poring over the sheets in front of him. At times he would have Porter on one side of the table like an assistant at an operation, pulling off one map, replacing it with another or going to find another one stacked only-he-knew-where on the map shelves that had recently been installed. On occasions he would have English Rose – which, of course, was a name he never called her to her face – stand dutifully by the table as he dictated notes and observations on what he was looking at, and she would take them down in shorthand before typing them up. He would then amend the report. Riley, inevitably, would check it and Rose would type up the final version.

By June 1943 the work had taken on a different dimension altogether.

Most days he would leave work by six o'clock. If Nathalie was on a night shift he would leave a bit earlier, the incentive being that if he could get home before six she would still be in bed, where he would give in to her entreaties to join him with no resistance whatsoever. But if Nathalie was on a late shift which meant she would not be home until midnight, he was in the habit of staying late at Lincoln House. He preferred to absorb himself in his maps and charts without Rose fussing around him, without Riley's ubiquitous presence and without Porter forever trying to be helpful, but all too often getting in the way.

Archibald tended to leave the office by five o'clock in the afternoon. One evening in June, Quinn was deeply absorbed in a study of Quiberville *plage* in Normandy. The charts were particularly reliable as a resistance cell in that area had managed to obtain up-to-date copies from the Mayor's office in Quiberville itself and they had found their way to London courtesy of a returning RAF Lysander. They were especially good-quality; beach gradients, distances from shoreline at different tides. Gold dust. He was struggling a bit with the text on the chart. If *rampe* meant an upward gradient, as he seemed to remember it did, then he guessed that *pente* was a downward gradient. No point in guessing though. If only Nathalie was allowed to help him, it would save so much time. It was not exactly a word he could casually introduce into their everyday conversation. Now he would have to ask Riley to get it translated, which was an unnecessarily cumbersome process. Perhaps he could raise the matter of being able to use Nathalie for some translation again with Archibald.

'Late watch, Quinn?'

He had been so engrossed in the chart that he hadn't noticed that Captain Archibald had appeared behind him. Despite the warm evening, he was wearing his Navy greatcoat, which he was now unbuttoning. The large wall clock on the left showed it was just after seven thirty. The one next to it showed it was an hour later in Quiberville *plage*.

'Useful?' Captain Archibald was looking at the chart.

'Very useful, sir. Part of that batch that the RAF brought back last month. Much more detail than we have had before. My French is not totally up to it though. Need to get some translations done. All these charts we're getting in from France are ideal, just what we need. But obviously the text on them is all in French. The translation is slowing down the whole process. There's an example here. I do need to know what *pente* means. I think it signifies a downward gradient, but I have to be sure. There's another one here – *peu profond*.'

'Well,' said Archibald, tapping a large dictionary on the desk, 'I'm sure it's all in here.'

'To an extent, sir, but it sometimes needs more of an understanding of the *context* for the words to make sense. We need to be one hundred per cent certain, as I'm sure you'd expect.'

'Ever thought of asking your wife?'

'Of course not, sir. I never discuss my work with her.'

Archibald was nodding his head in a pensive manner, as if something was occurring to him.

'Well, you're absolutely right not to ask her. Makes sense at one level: it would certainly be convenient. But not really on, I'm afraid. Essential that you keep this work and your private life completely separate. What I will do is find a decent translator for you though, someone to come in here. Anyway, I'd hoped I would catch you while no one was around. My office?'

Archibald had an ability to frame an order so as to make it sound like a reasonable question. Quinn followed him into his office.

Archibald eased himself into his chair and gestured for Quinn to do likewise on the one on the other side of the desk.

'You are not in a hurry, are you, Quinn?'

Not that it would not matter if he was. It was Archibald's way of saying this is going to take some time. Quinn shook his head.

'As you know, General Morgan was appointed as Chief of Staff to the Supreme Allied Commander in March. Three months ago. He's really got his foot on the accelerator now. His brief is to plan cross-Channel operations. That means the Second Front, the liberation of Europe. I've seen the brief. There is not much room for doubt as to what they're after. Morgan has got to plan for a full-scale assault against the Continent. Now they did want him to look into the possibility of that being this year, but he had ruled it out pretty quick. Out of the question. But they insist it will have to be in 1944. Churchill, Stalin and Roosevelt are promising that to each other, so it's hardly for Morgan to refuse. The only question is – when – and where?

'Morgan has pulled a group of senior officers together to plan it and I am on that group. About fifty of us altogether, British and American. Free French are being kept out of it. Churchill insists, doesn't trust them. De Gaulle will be furious when he finds out. We're called COSSAC: nothing to do with Russians on horseback, comes from Morgan's title, Chief of Staff to the Supreme Allied Commander. Explains why I'm not here all the time.'

'The area that I am most involved in is where the landings will take place, which is where you come in. Come over here.'

The whole of one side wall of Archibald's office was taken up with a large map showing the southern coast of England and the northern coast of France and Belgium, up to and just beyond the Dutch border. Archibald had moved over to stand in front of the map. Quinn joined him.

'There are a number of factors we have to take into account. Perhaps the most important is that once we get over here,' he was holding the pencil delicately between his thick fingers, waving it in the air over France, 'then we've only just begun. There will be plenty of fighting to come and we must not lose sight of the fact that the objective is Germany. Of course, we want to liberate occupied Europe, but Germany is the key. So, the nearer we can land to Germany, the less fighting there will be on the way there. Which rules out…' his pencil was now waving above Brittany and the Cotentin peninsula around Cherbourg '…this area. Too far away.

'There are two factors we need to take in to account before deciding where to land, as you know. Many other subsidiary considerations, of course. But they will all stem from the main two. Fancy having a guess?'

Quinn was rubbing his chin with his right hand, a frown across his forehead.

'I would say distance from the British coast, sir.'

'Ten out of ten, Quinn. Distance from the British coast.' Archibald's pencil was now somewhat unnecessarily hanging over Hampshire. As a Navy man, Quinn was aware of the location of the British coast.

'Normandy is a hundred miles away. Too far, perhaps. Calais, twenty-five miles. Ideal. Belgium, getting further away again. Remember, we need to ship an army across the Channel. Morgan is talking about twenty-four Allied divisions, so the shorter the crossing, the more chance we have got of not being spotted en route and the less chance of something going wrong. The chaps have to get ashore in the landing craft and then come out fighting. Being army chaps, many of them will get seasick, so the shorter the journey, the better the state they will be in to face the bullets at the other end. Don't forget too, we need air cover. Range of a Spitfire, Quinn?'

'One-seventy-five, one-eighty, sir?'

'One hundred and fifty miles. Important figure to remember, that. Need to fly over there and back and have plenty of fuel to be of some use in keeping the Luftwaffe at bay while they are over there.

'So the favoured location is here… round the Pas de Calais.' The pencil was now drawing an imaginary circle around Calais and where the coastline dropped south, just to the west of it.

'Perfect distance. Of course, the Germans will be expecting us there, which is why they've got von Salmuth's Fifteenth Army in that area with five Panzer divisions to support him. If we go west of the River Orne, here…' Archibald's pencil pointed at Ouistreham at the mouth of the Orne and then glided left over the Calvados Coast: Lion sur Mer, St Aubin sur Mer, Arromanches, Port en Bessin, '…then we come up against the Seventh Army. General Dollman. Not in the same league as the Fifteenth and he's only got one Panzer division backing him up.

'So there is a temptation to head for the area that is not as well defended. But then even if we went to Normandy because it is defended by the weaker army, the Germans will send reinforcements over there quickly enough, so we would not hold that advantage for very long.'

Archibald stepped back from the map in a surprisingly sprightly manner.

'Would you care to guess the second important factor, Quinn?'

The younger man hesitated. There were so many considerations.

'I suppose it would be where do we land – on a beach, or a port?'

'Good. As you know, it is not just the troops we have got to land. There're the tanks, vehicles – all the supplies. So a port would be the obvious place – but if we learned one lesson from Dieppe, as you know, it is that attacking a well-defended port is just too risky. All the aerial reconnaissance photos we're getting in show just what we're up against and the resistance is telling us the same too. All the ports would be death traps. Too well defended and heavily mined.

'The solution then would appear to be a beach landing. Tricky, of course. You still have to land an army and get them and all their equipment off the beach in more or less one piece. And it is not as if the Germans have not defended the beaches. As you know, they're mined, boobytrapped – and there are plenty of bunkers and gun emplacements. Rommel has done a good job, but he has had three thousand miles of coastline to worry about. Even he cannot defend every stretch of beach in northern France. The beaches have to be our best bet. There'll be a chink in his armour somewhere. Our job is to find it.'

There was a long pause. Archibald was standing in front of the map, about a yard away from it. His arms were folded and his pencil was sticking out, waving in the air like a conductor's baton during a particularly sombre piece of music. He moved closer, until he was stood just inches from the map. Quinn moved in with him.

'Come here, Quinn. Lots of pros and cons, as you can see. Do we go for north west France?' He was tapping the Normandy coast again. 'Longer route, further from Germany, but not as well defended. Or do we go for the north east?' The pencil was now hovering somewhere south of Calais. 'Better defended, but shorter crossing and, of course, puts us much nearer Germany.

'But then it is also where the Germans will be expecting us. They have the same maps as we do, after all. But if we are going to plan a successful invasion, a decision needs to be made as to where we are going and COSSAC has made its decision. This is where the Second Front will be, Quinn, between here…' Archibald's pencil was resting on Boulogne sur Mer. As he continued to speak, the pencil followed the coast down as it fell south west. '…and here.' His pencil had rested in the Baie de Somme.

'Ever been to the Bay of the Somme, Quinn?'

'No, sir.'

'Beautiful place. Full of wildlife. Quite stunning. Hope we don't ruin it, but I expect we will.'

Another long pause.

'So that is where it will be. Between Boulogne and the Bay of the Somme. We need to decide the best stretch of beach to go for. Morgan's preference seems to be here... avoid the cliffs between Cap d'Alprech and Équihen-Plage,' he was indicating a point just below Boulogne, 'but no further south than Le Touquet. It's a seven-mile stretch.'

His pencil rested on the small town of Plage de Ste Cécile.

'But we need to keep our options open. Still need to check out the whole coast down to the Bay of the Somme, another twenty miles or so. But concentrate on this top area.'

'So, this is now your job, Quinn. By the time you've finished, you are going to know every inch of that stretch of coastline. You will get to know every grain of sand. It's about seven miles, but you will see it in your sleep and as you walk along the streets here in London. We need to know about the beach gradients, whether the sand can take tanks and our heavy armour. We need to know about tide, about unusual currents. We need to be aware of every sandbank, every rock. We need to know that even if a beach is ideal to land on, what are the exit routes like? We need to know what the weather is like. In short, Quinn, we need to know everything – and then a bit more.'

Quinn was not sure whether he was meant to say anything. He realised that everything that they had been working on up to now had been leading to this. The work had felt at times that it lacked focus, he felt like a sportsman who had been warming up for the big event. In the course of the past hour, he had been told the location of the Second Front, the biggest secret of the war.

'Come with me, Quinn.'

Archibald walked out into the central office area.

'You're not alone in this, you know. Plenty of units like this working on the planning across London. But we have something to help us.' Archibald was unlocking a large metal filing cabinet. There was a central lock and then each of the three large drawers had a lock.

'Do you remember after Dunkirk the BBC broadcast an appeal for people to send in anything they had on the northern European coast? We were after whatever they had, maps, holiday guides, postcards, photographs.'

Quinn nodded. He remembered the fuss his mother made about sending in some dog-eared postcards her sister had sent from her

French holidays. She had asked Owen to see what he could do to ensure they would be returned to her.

'Thought we'd get a few thousand. Millions of them came in. Literally millions, Quinn. I'm told that people have been driven quite crazy sorting them all out, but they've done that now. And here...' he was pointing at the now unlocked filing cabinet '...are the fruits of their labours. All the material sent in to do with that stretch of coastline. A surprising amount.'

They both stared at the cabinet, daunted by what lay in it.

'And there are more, they'll be brought in over the next few days. My guess, Quinn, is that perhaps no more than two, perhaps three per cent of all that will be of any use. But that two or three per cent will be invaluable. Look at this picture here.'

It was a snapshot of a boy and a girl standing against a wall, self-consciously close to each other, their faces partially obscured by ice creams. Archibald turned the photograph over and read the caption.

'Ian and Wendy. Le Touquet. August 1937.' Now this is exactly the kind of thing that we need. Someone in Intelligence followed this up. Contacted the parents. Sure enough, they had measured the height of Ian and Wendy every birthday, so we know how tall they both are in August 1937 – four foot nine and four foot six it says here – and from that we can get a very good idea of how high that wall is. And because we can pinpoint it thanks to this sign next to it, we know that at this point, our boys would need to get over a wall that is approximately four foot high.

'I think that you are going to be very busy, Quinn.'

–

It was not in Owen Quinn's nature to be anything other than optimistic. 'You're a glass-half-full man,' his grandfather had often remarked. He was always of a most positive disposition. But an event at the end of June did give him cause to wonder.

It was a balmy summer evening and he was enjoying the stroll home through St James's Park. Nathalie was working late at the hospital and he was in no hurry. He had just entered the park when he heard his name being called. He turned round to see a large figure in RAF uniform running across the road to catch up with him.

'Quinn. I refuse to believe it! You're alive!'

'Well, I was this morning when I last looked in the mirror!'

'It's me, Linwood. Remember?' He had removed his RAF officer's cap.

'Of course, Linwood. Good God. Didn't realise you were in the RAF. I had no idea what you were doing.'

'Don't think I've seen you since we left university, eh? Joined up in '39. Didn't fancy your lot, tendency towards seasickness. Army sounded a bit dull and flying just up my street.'

'Battle of Britain?'

Linwood shook his head. 'Bomber Command. Giving them a taste of their own medicine. Now what about you. Last I heard, you were dead. Drowned at sea?'

'Almost, Linwood. Not quite though. Was on HMS *Gloucester* when it was sunk off Crete in '41. Damn-near didn't make it. Don't remember an awful lot, to be honest. Spent months in a hospital back here. Not fit enough for active service, apparently, but serving behind a desk. You understand.'

'Of course I do, old chap. Glad to see you alive. Look, I've got to go back up to Lincolnshire tonight – getting a lift. Fancy a drink first? Bit of catching up to do.'

The pub in Victoria was emptying of civil servants and they found a quiet table at the back. Linwood negotiated his way over, doing his best not to spill the beer.

'Like navigating through German flak, eh? There you are, Quinn. Pint of best mild. Does you the world of good. Now then, tell me everything.'

'Not an awful lot to say I'm afraid, Linwood. Don't really keep in touch with many of the chaps from university. Joined the Navy, as you know. I am married though.'

'Congratulations!' Linwood had stood up to reach over the table and warmly shake his hand, spilling some of the beer in the process. 'You're a dark horse, aren't you? Never had you down as much of a ladies' man. Now, tell me all about her.'

'Well, what can I say? She's French, came over at the time of Dunkirk. And she's a nurse. She was working at the hospital in the country that I was sent to when I came back here – that's where we met.'

'What does she look like, Quinn?'

'Well, perhaps not for me to say, but…'

'Come on old chap, if *you* can't say what she looks like then who on earth can!'

'What I mean is, I don't want to appear boastful, Linwood, but she is rather beautiful. At least I think so.'

Linwood moved his large frame and fleshy face across the table. He was looking very interested. 'Description please, Quinn.'

Quinn blushed. 'Super figure, lovely long hair, remarkable eyes.'

'Too good to be true, Quinn. Refuse to believe you. Got a photograph?'

'I do actually,' he said, taking his wallet out of his top pocket. He passed over a small photograph somewhat sheepishly. 'Here we are.'

Linwood went silent and studied the photograph carefully from different angles. He turned it over. *Owen, all my love – amour – Nathalie xxx.*

'Quinn – she's beautiful. Totally beautiful. You were telling the truth.' Linwood was speaking in almost reverential tones now. 'How on earth did a chap like you…?'

'A chap like me what?' Quinn was slightly offended.

'No, no, no – don't take it like that. Just that when we were at university you were the fairly quiet type. Would never in a month of Sundays have thought…'

Linwood couldn't say much more. He just waved the photograph, before looking at it closely again. *Would never have thought that a chap like you would end up with a girl like her.* That's what he means to say, thought Quinn. I sometimes wonder that myself, if I'm honest.

'And is it true what they say about French girls?' Linwood was looking quite flushed now.

'What is it that they say about French girls, Linwood?'

His friend leaned towards him and lowered his voice.

'Oh, come on, Quinn! You know. Great lovers and all that. No inhibitions.'

'Linwood! You're talking about my wife!' Quinn had defused any tension by laughing.

'Does she have any sisters over here or friends? If so, I insist on meeting them next time I'm on leave. Tell me everything!'

'Not a lot more to say, actually. Told you most of it.'

'Where is she from?'

'Somewhere in Paris, not exactly sure.'

'And family? What about them?'

'Look, Linwood. Don't mean to be rude, but I've learned not to ask. It's different with the war. She's had to leave her own country and that's not easy. I suppose I need to be sensitive, can't ask too many questions.'

'Don't get upset, old chap. Just seems a bit… odd that you know so little about her.'

'Well, as I say, that's the war for you.'

'Understand,' said Linwood, though Quinn had the feeling that he didn't really.

They left the pub soon after, Quinn to go home and Linwood to head back to Lincolnshire. They exchanged addresses and promised to keep in touch.

For the rest of that evening he was unsettled by his encounter with Linwood.

Despite what he had said, in his heart of hearts he knew that it was odd that he knew so little about his wife.

He was determined to find out more. He needed to be more assertive – Nathalie herself had told him that.

The opportunity came the following evening. Nathalie had not been at work and when he arrived back at the flat she was walking around wearing nothing but his dressing gown. The front was open and she was smiling. An hour later, after they had finished making love for the third time, they both lay in bed, exhausted and happy. Nathalie had managed to get hold of a bottle of French wine which was meant to be very good and it now lay empty on their bedside table. Empty bodies, empty wine bottle. He felt decadent and totally relaxed.

Nathalie lay on her back naked, staring at the ceiling. Owen rolled over onto his side and leaned over her. With his finger, he gently traced a pattern across her breasts. Her black eyes swivelled from the ceiling, locked into his and she smiled.

Carpe diem.

'I want to know more about you, Nathalie.' The question sounded awkward and even his speaking seemed to have broken a perfect mood. Her eyes frowned very slightly and the smile subsided.

'What do you want to know, Owen? I've told you everything. I'm a boring person. Do you want me to be more exciting? Shall I tell you that I am secret agent who arrived here by parachute? That I am a descendant of Napoleon? Ask me whatever questions you want. Go on.'

There was a pause. Linwood's observation that he seemed to know little about her had struck a chord; he didn't know a lot about her. Try as he might, there were times when he felt that he had absolutely no idea of what she was really like. But he had no idea what questions to ask. He smiled and kissed her cheek and she took hold of that hand that had stopped tracing patterns on her breasts and started it again.

Chapter 11

London, July 1943

A fortnight after Archibald had told him about the secret invasion plans for the Pas de Calais, Owen Quinn and Nathalie were invited to dinner by Archibald.

'Mrs Archibald is on one of her rare visits from Lincolnshire and I thought it would be a good idea: we've invited two other couples. Melrose is Army, but a perfectly decent chap. Work with him at COSSAC though you don't know that, of course. And Hardisty is at the Air Ministry. Wife's French, so that ought to be jolly for your wife. Strictly nothing about work, of course.'

Nathalie, who had recently begun to complain that London was a boring city, was nonetheless not enthusiastic about the invitation.

'My English will not be good enough,' she said as they ate their supper the evening that her husband told her about the dinner.

'Your English is almost fluent, darling.'

'Almost?' She sounded angry.

'Well, yes. "Almost fluent" is not a criticism – it actually means that your English is excellent. You will have no problem in taking part in the conversation, I assure you.'

'They will all talk about work.'

'We are not allowed to talk about work.'

'Why?'

'I have explained that to you, darling. What I do is secret. I am just not allowed to discuss it. Same reason as I can never tell you anything. The same will apply to everyone else there.'

'But what is that word you use to describe how you find your work? Sounds like "tea"?'

'"Tedious" do you mean?'

'Yes. So if your work is so tedious, how can it be so secret?'

'That is how it is.'

'So it will be very boring. I suppose we will have to talk about the weather.'

'Quite possibly. And cats.'

'Why cats?'

'It's a joke, Nathalie. An English joke. You say that the English talk about the weather. Well, the other great English topic of conversation is their pets.'

'But we do not have any pets. We can be sure we will not talk about food. No one is interested in food in this country. In France, there would be riots if we had to eat the kind of food you are happy to eat in England.'

Nathalie was toying with the remains of the casserole that she had cooked. Owen was finishing his second helping while she had hardly eaten at all. With his mouth full he gestured towards his plate and gave a thumbs up sign. 'But this is good!'

'That is my point, Owen. You are satisfied with this. The meat is tough and you cannot buy the proper herbs anyway. You English think that pepper and salt is all you need. I am ashamed of this meal, even though I had to smile very sweetly at the butcher to persuade him to give me a tiny bit more of what you call meat here. Even then, it is not what I call a proper casserole. It's mostly carrots.'

-

The dinner took place in Archibald's club, which was round the corner from Lincoln House, in St James's Street. Quinn had worn his best uniform to work and Nathalie met him outside there at seven, looking ravishing. She was not allowed beyond reception, but Quinn basked in the approving looks of the guards when he went down to meet her.

She linked her arm into his, her fingers squeezing the inside of his elbow and her shoulder nestling against him. They strolled into Jermyn Street where she promised to buy him a suit when they were rich and into St James's Street, turning left, crossing the road and walking the twenty yards or so to Archibald's club.

Quinn had to agree that the dinner was hard work. You could blame the food (Brown Windsor soup, an oddly greyish beef in a thick, dark sauce, followed by apple pie) on wartime, but the conversation was somewhat stilted. And this was despite the wine, which was a very decent Côtes du Rhône.

Hardisty, it turned out, had met his wife in Paris before the war, when he had been an air attaché at the Embassy, so he was fluent in French. For much of the meal they had to listen to Melrose's wife, the extent of whose wartime deprivation seemed to be some minor problems with domestic staff. Captain Archibald and his wife talked about their life in Lincolnshire, while for much of the time Hardisty's wife and Nathalie were speaking in French.

At first, Nathalie had been solicitous enough in finding out which part of Paris Madame Hardisty was from.

'The 8th arrondissement – off the Boulevard Haussmann. And you?'

'Oh, we moved around. Usually south of the 14th.' Madame Hardisty smiled politely, clear now that it was most unlikely that their paths had ever crossed.

She was answering all their questions politely enough, but did not sustain any conversation.

It was a balmy July evening, so they walked back to Pimlico.

'Did you enjoy the evening?'

'It was fine.'

'Did you get on with Madame Hardisty?'

'She was fine. But you know, we are from very different... societies. She is a different kind of person to me. You have to learn to understand this, Owen. This kind of person, they live in a very different kind of France. The France they expect to find after the war is very different to mine.'

Quinn wanted to ask her just what she meant, but Nathalie had a way of shutting down a conversation when she wished it to go no further. By now they had turned into Alderney Street and he had more important things on his mind.

–

Two days after the dinner there was a minor disaster in Lincoln House. In response to Quinn's demands for some help with translation, Archibald had found an elderly, retired French teacher with what he described as an admirably high level of security clearance. As far as Quinn could gather, the main criterion for her high level of security clearance was the fact that both of her brothers had fought in the Great War.

So two or three days a week Miss Lean would slowly make her way to the office where she would sit at a desk and, with the aid of a large dictionary that she brought with her in a basket, laboriously translate.

The minor disaster came with a message one morning that Miss Lean had slipped on her way to work and broken both of her ankles. She would not be returning. Miss Lean was replaced by a Frenchwoman in her late thirties who was physically stronger than Miss Lean (it would have been difficult to be otherwise), but emotionally fragile.

She only had to look at a postcard from France, or a photograph or even a map, for her to burst into tears. After just one week, Archibald had to agree that her psychological state was not conducive with working in such a sensitive environment.

'What are we meant to do?' Quinn asked Archibald. 'We need all these translations done and until then, it's just holding us up.'

They were in Archibald's office. Quinn was clutching a pile of papers that needed translating, which he had brought in for added impact. Archibald was thinking quietly, drumming his long fingers on the desk in front of him. After a while, Archibald nodded quietly to himself.

'There is a possible solution, Quinn. Not one that I am terribly happy with, but one that may work. I know that this was mentioned a few weeks ago, but now it seems that your wife...' he had put his glasses on now and was looking at a sheet of paper '...did indeed have a higher level of clearance than we had at first realised when she moved to Calcotte Grange. What we've done is check her out a bit more and we can move her clearance up another notch or two so that she has the right level to help you out with some of this. Help you shift all this stuff. You're going to be inundated with material, aren't you?'

Quinn nodded in agreement.

'No reason then for you not to take the odd low level stuff home, work over the weekend, peace and quiet, that kind of thing. And with so much in French, to be able to ask her will save a lot of time. Obviously, we keep it all hush-hush and she doesn't need to see any more than she has to. Nothing top secret, you understand. She can't know about the context of what you may ask her, but the odd word here and there – no harm in that. She doesn't need to know what all this is about and I certainly don't mean go tell her where landings are going to be, eh!'

Quinn was surprised, but agreed that it did indeed sound reasonable. It was certainly going to make life that little bit easier. Recently

Nathalie had been going on about how he told her nothing about what he did and she was wondering whether that meant he didn't love her.

-

RAF Scampton
Lincolnshire

Dear Owen Quinn,

My name is Andy Wood and I was a close colleague and friend of Flying Officer Anthony (Tony) Linwood. It is with deep regret that I am writing to inform you that Tony is listed as missing, presumed dead, after his Lancaster was lost in action in an air raid over Hamburg last month. Tony was a loyal and brave member of 617 Squadron and is sorely missed by everyone here at RAF Scampton.

I gave Tony a lift back to Lincolnshire the same night that he bumped into you in St James's Park and I know how thrilled he was to have met up with you again. He was in very good spirits that night and I am sure that is in large measure due to having met up with you. He was full of admiration for you and said what a lucky man you are. Sadly, the raid in which he was killed took place just the night after you and he met.

I am sorry for the delay in writing to you with this appalling news, but I only recently found your address among his papers.

Yours truly,
(Flight Lieutenant) Andy Wood

-

Owen's parents arrived in London on the last Sunday in July for a much-heralded and long-planned visit. He and Nathalie had bickered all morning as they prepared for his parents' arrival. Nathalie sat on the bed painting her nails: 'It is not often that I have a Sunday off,' she complained, 'and when I do, I'd rather not spend it with your mother. She reminds me of the sisters at the hospital – always critical, always checking on what I'm doing.'

But you're not doing a lot, Owen thought as he moved the furniture round in the tiny lounge. He had somehow managed to shift one of the enormous armchairs into their bedroom, which meant that they could open out the table and squeeze the four of them around it, even if that did mean him having to sit on the arm of the remaining armchair. He had little doubt that his mother would strongly disapprove of that.

'Shall I tell you how long I had to queue for the chicken?' the voice in the bedroom asked.

'You've already told me, Nathalie. Two hours.'

'Two hours.'

'Well, it does smell absolutely delicious, darling. I honestly can't remember the last time I had chicken. Must have been in the New Year at my parents'. They'll be thrilled. You can't beat roast chicken.'

She appeared in the doorway of the bedroom to inspect the rearrangement of the lounge. She was wearing his dressing gown; tantalisingly partly open at the front, revealing that she was wearing nothing underneath. Her hands were held out in front of her, the fingers spreadeagled and slowly waving as she tried to dry her nails.

'It's only just a chicken. In France it would have been living on a farm for very old chickens. Even French foxes would have the sense to ignore it. And where are you going to sit?'

'For heaven's sake, just stop it!' he shouted.

'Pardon?' She looked genuinely taken aback.

'Just leave it will you. Please stop complaining about everything. I am entitled to have my parents round and for them to have something decent to eat. I know this country is not France but I think it has been pretty decent to you. How would you like to be back in France now, with all those bloody Nazis around?' He stepped back, shocked at his own outburst.

'Owen,' she said, smiling sweetly and allowing the dressing gown to slip from her shoulders and to the floor. 'You've never spoken to me like that before. Come here…'

'Hang on, you do realise that the curtains are open and…'

She stepped back into the bedroom, where the curtains were drawn.

'And what?'

He put down the cutlery. He could lay the table later, after he had peeled the potatoes. He was inside the bedroom, his shirt already off when the doorbell rang.

'So we had to stick to the A3 even though…'

'William, I am sure Owen and Nathalie do not want to hear all about our journey today. It is not as if we had to fight our way past the Germans!'

Marjorie Quinn shrieked at her own joke and her husband and son laughed politely, while her daughter-in-law looked confused.

'Well, I must say, Nathalie, that it is a real treat to have chicken. Delicious. Cordon – what is it you call it in France?' asked her father-in-law.

'They call it cordon bleu, William, though I would not have thought that this is cordon bleu. Personally, I prefer my chicken to be roasted for rather longer, but then you probably have not had much experience recently, have you, Nathalie? Owen dear, do you really need to be sitting at the dining table on the edge of an armchair?'

'Mother, please!'

'Please what, Owen?'

His mother, father and wife had all stopped eating and were looking at him.

'Mother… this is my home and my wife… please do stop going on.'

The ensuing silence was broken ten minutes later by Marjorie Quinn's much diminished voice.

'I was only saying…' she said softly.

Her husband patted her on the wrist. 'Probably best not to say anything dear…'

They left soon after lunch: their journey that morning having been so difficult they didn't want to leave it too late.

Once they had returned to the flat after seeing his parents off, Nathalie led him straight into the bedroom.

An hour later she planted an arm firmly across his chest as he tried to get up from the bed.

'But we need to clear up.'

'Your reward hasn't finished, Owen. Why are you looking so puzzled?'

'Reward for what?'

'That you're not a boy any longer, are you?' She was brushing the long fair hair away from his damp brow, combing it back with her long fingers. 'The way you spoke to me this morning, the way you spoke to your mother... you are learning to stand up for yourself. I think I like it.'

An hour later, Owen was to be found happily tidying up the flat and merrily whistling as he washed up the dishes.

Nathalie soaked in a tepid bath for longer than she normally would have done. Life is so confusing, she thought. Everything starts off by being confused. And then you realise what you have to do and you go and do it and everything becomes clearer. And then, things get in the way. Events. People. Places. Emotions become involved, even if you don't intend them to or even want them to. So you end up being confused again.

Chapter 12

London, November 1943

'Well, all I can say is that this is most irregular. Most irregular.'

'But Leigh, everything you chaps do is most irregular!'

'I simply cannot imagine what Selbourne thought he was playing at, agreeing to this nonsense.'

Major Edgar stood up, his tall frame blocking out some of the sunlight as he did so. He was not averse to using his considerable height to help bring his influence to bear on a situation and he needed to use all of his influence now in what was a very tense situation. His recent promotion had added to his sense of confidence.

There was silence in the room. They were in the Baker Street headquarters of the Special Operations Executive, the SOE. Outside, there was a steady hum of traffic. Inside, a small ornate clock on Leigh's desk was ticking in what appeared to be an erratic manner. The clock reminded Edgar of Leigh: ornate and erratic, and from an earlier era.

Edgar was becoming exasperated. The small man he was now towering over reminded him of an ineffectual country vicar, with a high-pitched, whiny voice to match. Edgar did not understand why they picked these academics from the Oxbridge colleges where they had spent most of their lives and assumed that, because they were an authority on a medieval French poet no one had heard of, they would therefore fit naturally into the upper echelons of British Intelligence.

'The 3rd Earl of Selbourne is the Minister for Economic Warfare, Dr Leigh. He is responsible for your organisation. He has agreed to this operation.'

'I am quite aware of who Selbourne is, Edgar. No doubt Churchill twisted his arm. But it does not stop this being most irregular.'

Edgar was having to exercise considerable restraint. Leigh had used the word irregular in nearly every sentence for the past ten minutes.

His face was a bright red and his hands a pallid white as they gripped the arms of his chair.

Edgar had some sympathy for Leigh. His job could not be an easy one. The SOE had been set up in July 1940 as part of the Secret Intelligence Service, or MI6. Its remit was to work behind the lines in occupied Europe, carrying out acts of sabotage and secret warfare. Its main role was to work with resistance groups. Much of its work was done through country groups. Edgar was aware that, as far as France was concerned, it was typically complicated. There were two groups. RF Section worked with the Gaullist faction. F Section was the independent country section for France. Dr Clarence Leigh's role was to liaise with both RF and F Sections on behalf of the head of SOE. Edgar assumed that he used medieval French poetry to help resolve disputes. Or start them.

'Dr Leigh. I do acknowledge that there is a historic rivalry between our two organisations, but surely you must understand the absolute importance of this mission.'

Major Edgar believed passionately that the mission of the London Controlling Section for which he worked was of paramount import-ance. The LCS had been set up by Winston Churchill in June 1942 to plan deception operations against the enemy, and its overriding priority now was the invasion of Europe, which was planned for 1944. The invasion was fraught with risk, but one way of helping it to succeed was by persuading the Germans that the invasion was going to take place somewhere else. Edgar was the case officer responsible for handling three German agents to work on behalf of this deception. Two of them were doing so willingly, having agreed to become double agents. The most important one was not aware of the crucial role they were currently playing. It was in connection with that agent that Major Edgar was enduring a most uncomfortable afternoon with Dr Leigh.

'And you absolutely insist that there is no other way?'

The first chink was appearing in Leigh's armour. His resigned tone sounded as if he was addressing a student who was handing in an essay late.

'No. If there was, I can assure you we would have gone down that route.'

'Very well then. I'll speak to Newby at F Section. Best work with them if you don't want de Gaulle to catch wind of this.'

'Thank you very much, Clarence. I have no doubt that Winston will be most pleased to hear of a new era of co-operation between our two organisations.'

Leigh snorted. 'But one thing that I do need to make very clear, Edgar. This is a most irregular business. In everything we do in SOE, security is of absolute paramount importance, as I am sure you appreciate. For us to be asked to train a German spy in our methods and then send him over to France puts our own security at risk. It could jeopardise our whole operation. Therefore, we will have to train him at a different location than we normally use and bring new people in to do the training. We will have to incur considerable costs in the process. I do expect your people to pay for this.'

'Of course,' said Edgar. It was a small price to pay.

'Very well, then. I shall see Newby this afternoon and inform him of the situation. You ought to be able to see him tomorrow, certainly in the next few days. Are you now able to give me any details about this agent? What code name does he go by?'

Edgar was already putting on his large, dark coat.

'Goes by the code name of Magpie. And he is a she.'

'Oh!' It was a long, high-pitched and slightly surprised 'oh'. Before the war, Clarence Leigh had inhabited a world where women were little more than bit-part players and it still came as a surprise to him that they were involved at all in the world of espionage.

–

It was a bitter November night. Autumn had finally surrendered to winter and a thick, yellow-stained fog had draped itself across the city, tightening its grip with every laboured breath. Owen would have happily stayed in the warmth of the office or gone straight home, but he had arranged to meet Nathalie at the hospital so that he could walk her to their flat. When he left Duke Street, it had been not much more than a heavy mist, but with each footstep it became increasingly dense so that by the time he reached Victoria Embankment he could barely see a yard ahead. It reminded him of being at sea: the speed at which a mist would roll in before visibility was no more than a few yards and all eyes on the bridge would be on him as they sailed into the unknown. His pace slowed down to little more than a crawl as he felt his way along the wall, its surface clammy. Below him, Quinn could hear the river, the water lapping hard against the bank and the bridge ahead. The sound of the river was muffled by the thick fog and had an unfamiliar echo.

To all intents and purposes, it felt as if he was the last person left in London. No other soul was about until a policeman in his dark cape briefly came into view and then disappeared, his torch doing no more than emphasising the thick swirl of the smog. Ahead of him, he could hear the sentries outside the Palace of Westminster marching up and down, their hobnail boots scraping on the pavement, but they remained invisible. The bitter, sulphuric taste of the smog crept down his throat and he began to feel nauseous. His eyes were stinging. The air was filled with menace. The cold stone of the wall gave way and he realised that he had reached the north side of Westminster Bridge. By holding the luminous dial of his watch close to his face he could see that it was twenty past eight. He had promised to meet Nathalie outside the hospital at eight o'clock and he knew that she'd be concerned, even allowing for the fog. She was prone to impatience. Although St Thomas's was just on the south side of the bridge, it would take him another ten minutes at least to get there. He hoped she would understand, but feared that her impatience might get the better of her.

He felt a surge of optimism. He always felt like that when he knew he was about to see his wife. He'd been married for a few months before he realised what was happening, before he recognised that when he wasn't with her he was bereft and when he was with her he was whole, complete.

Owen hesitated. For some reason, he was fearful of crossing the bridge, his progress inhibited by trepidation. And he sensed that it was not the fog. From his time at sea he was well used to moving in the dark, trusting his sense of navigation. He hesitated for a good five minutes, during which time the fog very slightly lifted, but as it did so there was a sharp drop in temperature. He pulled the brim of his Navy cap low over his face and, turning up the collar of his coat, set out into the void. Progress was noticeably easier. Visibility was now as much as three or even four yards. As he approached what he took to be the middle of the bridge a woman came into view, walking on the other side of it and in the opposite direction to him. Her hands were thrust deep into her coat pockets and her head, around which was a tightly wrapped scarf, was looking down at the ground ahead of her. Owen paused. He could not take his eyes off her: a stranger, yet achingly familiar. As she came abreast of him he moved into the road so as to get a better view and as he did so, he realised that it could be Nathalie.

But there was something so unfamiliar about her that he hesitated in calling her name, settling instead for an uncertain 'Hello?'

She looked up and in the very brief moment before she recognised her husband beneath his cap and raised collar, he saw her as he had never seen her before. Her face appeared different: softer, more relaxed and, above all, unguarded. If time had stood still at that exact moment and he had been forced to use one word to describe how she looked different, it would have been that one. Unguarded. Then, as she realised it was him, her face instantly arranged itself into a more familiar look. The face hardened very slightly – and then she smiled and almost skipped over to him, before pecking him on the cheek and then moving her warm mouth to his.

'Why are you so late, Owen? I thought you weren't coming. I decided to make my own way home.'

'Haven't you noticed the fog, darling?'

Her kiss was moist against the side of his mouth. 'I'm pleased you came, Owen. You're so…' She hesitated, struggling to find the right word '…dependable.'

And with that, arm in arm, they walked back to Pimlico. Well before they arrived back at the flat, he had allowed the confused image on the bridge to fade from his memory. In years to come he would often recall that encounter on the bridge and wonder about exactly what he had seen in her expression. If he had thought about it for longer at the time, with the memory of exactly what had happened and of just what he had seen still fresh in his mind, then he would have come to the conclusion that she looked as if she was wearing a mask. But what he could not tell was whether she was wearing that mask before she saw him, or after.

-

Portman Square was a brief walk from the SOE headquarters in Baker Street and it was in a mews house just behind the square that F Section of the SOE was based. F Section looked after SOE operations in France and its primary role was to work with the French resistance.

Major Edgar had to admit that, while he was not quite sure what he was expecting, it was certainly something a bit more substantial and imposing than a pleasant mews house occupied by fewer than ten people. A woman in her mid-thirties with a vague, central European accent that he could not place led him up a series of narrow staircases to the top floor. They moved along an uneven corridor into what he assumed was a section of the adjoining house. They were now in a room converted out of the attic. A large skylight ensured that, despite the November gloom, the room was bathed in light.

Behind a small desk a man in civilian clothes was on the phone.

'*Oui, Philippe. Bien sûr, bien sûr. Je comprends. D'accord. A bientôt.*'

He put the phone down and came over to greet Edgar. The woman had closed the door, remaining in the room.

'Good to meet you, Edgar. Newby. Tony Newby. Major Newby if you're interested in that kind of thing. Everyone seems to be a major these days, eh?'

'Hope you were impressed by the French. Pretty much the extent of it, I'm afraid. Rely on the likes of Nicole here. I've learned that if you keep saying *d'accord*, folks think you know what you are talking about, eh?'

Very quickly, Edgar realised that although this bonhomie was in welcome contrast to Leigh's petulance, it almost certainly masked a strong character. Edgar could see Newby's eyes summing him up and his brain playing with him. This was a man who had already sent more than three hundred agents into occupied France and was now being asked to send one more. A German spy.

'Dr Leigh has told me what you chaps are after, but how about if I hear it from the horse's mouth, eh? *Bouche de cheval* – is that correct, Nicole?'

'To an extent, sir. I would try *on l'appris de source sûre.*'

'Thank you,' said Edgar. 'I do realise that this is somewhat... irregular, but I hope you will understand that the circumstances are extenuating ones.

'In 1941 we identified a previously undetected Nazi agent. She had entered the country in 1940, after Dunkirk, but kept her nose clean for the best part of a year. She came into our sights thanks to a Belgian whom we'd been watching ever since he came into the country. We turned him, which led to her. As you've no doubt been told, her code name is Magpie. Magpie is a French nurse and by all accounts a very good one. I ought to add that she is also a most beautiful woman.'

Newby indicated his approval with one long, slow nod.

'Magpie was working at a hospital in central London when we came across her. By a sheer stroke of luck, it so happened that she had recently applied for a transfer to a military hospital, which made some sense. Plenty of decent intelligence to be picked up in that kind environment if you think about it. Morale, where people have been based, where they are being sent, casualties, what equipment works, what doesn't... all useful stuff to the Germans.

'We decided to keep her where she was for the time being. Keep an eye on her, but have her up our sleeves. Sure enough, it all worked out a treat. We thought that if we were clever and lucky, we could put her much closer to Allied intelligence than either she or the Germans could have hoped. Plan was fairly simple: send her to a hospital for recovering Navy officers, ensure that one of the patients she just happens to be looking after is due to be moved into Naval Intelligence when he is discharged from hospital. So we ensure that she has access to the files and that one of the files has a note that a particular officer is indeed due to be transferred to Naval Intelligence when he is released. Lots of references to "top secret" et cetera – you get the picture. Perfect opportunity for her. As we hoped, she starts to get particularly friendly with this young officer. He, of course, thinks she is the most wonderful woman he has ever seen – no young chap in his right mind and his position wouldn't think that. We move the young man into his own room, pretty much put the two of them into bed with each other. He's then told "no, you are not going back to sea, not up to it. Important job for you in Naval Intelligence. Oh and by the way, we know what is going on with you and the nurse so if you want to make a decent woman of her..." Not exactly a whirlwind romance, Major, but worked a treat.'

'And he... is totally unaware?' Major Newby had started to speak.

'Not the foggiest idea. Can't stress this strongly enough, Newby. He has no idea whatsoever who she is. He is unaware of what is going on. Thinks this beautiful Frenchwoman who is two years older than him has fallen in love with him. He is like the cat that got the cream – gallons of the stuff, in fact. Still is, actually.

'By the end of June '42 we've got them happily married and settled into a little flat we found for them in Pimlico. Put one of our chaps next door just in case. His bedroom is behind theirs and apparently he does not get a lot of sleep. Our man is ensconced in an office of Naval Intelligence that we have especially set up round the corner from St

James's Square. We keep it all very lovey-dovey for the best part of a year. We know that she is picking up bits and pieces from his work and is passing all this back to Paris. All useful stuff to them, but fairly low-level. They like what they get, but tell her to play a waiting game. Quinn's telling her a bit more than he strictly should be doing, but by and large he is being a bit more of a good boy than we had hoped he would be, to be frank.

'In June this year we move things up a gear. COSSAC, as you know, is planning the invasion of Europe and we in the London Controlling Section are supposed to be coming up with a really watertight deception plan. We've got two or three double agents in place already and the message we are trying to get across to the Germans is that the invasion will be in the Pas de Calais. Absolutely essential that the Germans get a consistent message from different sources. They must all complement each other. Needs to come together like a jigsaw.

'We move things up a gear with Quinn. Until then, he had not been working on terribly high-profile stuff – idea was to ease him in. Now we let him into the world of invasion planning. The Allied landings, he is told, are going to be in the Pas de Calais and that is what he is going to be working on. Oh – and we upgrade her security clearance, so that he is able to take some stuff home, that kind of thing. Intended to get him to drop his guard a bit and it works a treat. He starts taking home maps, charts, the whole bloody lot, if you'll excuse my language. She's sending it all back to Paris, Abwehr lapping it up, pleading for more.'

Edgar paused and stared up through the skylight, through which the sky had already turned a shade of grey. He was coming to the difficult part.

'The deception is absolutely vital if Operation Overlord is to succeed. We are talking about landing tens of thousands of men, tanks, armour, equipment and supplies on the beaches of Normandy. It would be tricky enough in friendly conditions. But with the beaches being mined and defended, with all the hazards of the long sea crossing and the extended lines of supply – it is a very risky operation, to say the least. So if we can convince the Germans that the invasion is going to be much further to the east, then at least that will tie up some of their defences.

'From what the boys at Bletchley are telling us they're picking up from Ultra, the Abwehr are totally buying what Magpie is telling them.

Alongside everything else we are doing on the deception front, they are convinced that the Second Front will come through the Pas de Calais.

'But there is another part of this deception operation. We don't just want the Germans to think *before* D-Day that it is the Pas de Calais. We don't want them to realise *on* D-Day that they've been tricked and then shift everything into Normandy. If that is the case, then this whole operation would only have bought us a day or two's grace and to be honest, that may not be enough. We need to persuade them *even on* D-Day – and for as long as possible after it – that Normandy is a feint, that the real invasion will take place a couple of weeks later in the Pas de Calais. That way, we tie up the Fifteenth Army and all of its Panzer divisions hundreds of miles from where they can hurt us.

'Which is where you come in, Newby. We think that the best way to persuade the Germans not only that the Pas de Calais is the target but also that Normandy will be a feint is to send Magpie over there as one of your agents. In other words, actually have her there in the Pas de Calais.'

Major Newby nodded his head in an approving manner that surprised Edgar. For a moment, he appeared to be lost in thought.

'This sounds rather interesting, Edgar. However, the way we work is to link our agents up with French resistance groups. I am not sure how I can justify exposing them to danger.'

'We have thought that through. We would want to send her out around two months or so before the planned invasion. For those two months, that group ought to be the safest resistance cell in the whole of France. The Germans won't want to touch them, they will want Magpie to stay active for as long as possible. As soon as she becomes inactive then we'll need to get the message to them, but it is a risk. I accept that – but if things work out, we ought to be able to warn them.'

'And is she aware that she could be recruited to the SOE?'

'No. It all hinges on whether you think that you can pull it off.'

'I think we can. Do you agree, Nicole? We train our agents at Wanborough Manor initially. Those that get through the three weeks there are sent to Beaulieu in the New Forest. We'll obviously have to keep her well away from these places. Can't risk her meeting other agents or even too many of our own people. We'll have to take over a country house we have never used before and are never likely to use again and get some army boys to help us with a few weeks' training. We can fly her in by Lysander, not having to train her on how to use a parachute will save time. Any idea where you want to send her in the Pas de Calais?'

'Around Boulogne.'

'Nicole?'

'The FTP is very active around there. There are some small cells that are very quiet. It's deliberate while we wait for D-Day; the idea is only to activate them when we need them. We could certainly find one to send her to – as long as we can be sure that we can get a warning to them the minute they are in danger. You'll understand that we could not possibly be associated with a plan that deliberately sacrifices any of our units. We must be satisfied that they will have some protection.' It was the first time Nicole had spoken at any length. He still could not place her accent, which was certainly not French. In the strange half-world in which he now lived, he knew better than to ask.

'And do we know her true identity?'

'No. She calls herself Nathalie Mercier, which is not her real name. Of course, now she is known as Nathalie Quinn. She says she is from Paris, but we rather doubt that. She did meet the French wife of a colleague, who said she did not think she had a Parisian accent. Of course, it is all rather tricky to check these things out nowadays.'

'Well,' said Nicole, 'we are going to need to give her a new identity anyway. By the time we have finished with her, she will not be sure who she is.'

'I would not be so sure about that,' said Edgar. 'So I can rely on you to call her in?'

Newby escorted Edgar downstairs. Together they stood in the mews courtyard, the cobblestones feeling incongruous in the midst of the busy city. Newby was filling his pipe with tobacco.

'Nicole rather rules that place for me. Quite brilliant. She can't abide smoke though, so I have to sneak out. I'll get her to look after Magpie. One question though, Edgar.'

'What is that?'

'Your chap Quinn is going to be devastated when he finds out that you chaps have married him off to a Nazi agent, isn't he?'

Edgar moved to the other side of Newby to avoid the cloud of tobacco smoke drifting towards him. He pondered the question as if it was one that until now had never occurred to him.

'I imagine he will, but I daresay that he will get over it.'

Chapter 13

December 1943

Nathalie Quinn had been hiding in the ditch beside the railway track for over an hour. Face down in the wet gravel; flecks of sharp stone pitting her face. The damp shrub that she had uprooted earlier from the hedgerow behind her was covering her, but the moisture was now beginning to work through her clothing. When she had set out two hours previously, the night seemed surprisingly warm for the time of the year, and the moon bright enough for her to find her way across the fields.

But now the chill of the December night air was eating through her and she was regretting not taking the extra sweater that she had been offered just before she set out. Enough cloud had drifted over the vast sky to obscure the moon and cast pitch darkness all around. She was grateful for that now. The last half mile before the railway line had been the most perilous. She had waited in the copse at the top of the hill for ten minutes, checking that there was no movement below. She then crept down, making sure she kept in the cover of the trees where possible. At the bottom of the hill she hid behind a high hedge for just long enough to catch her breath and check that the road was clear.

This is where they'll get me. There's a bend in the road. They'll be waiting behind that bend and come out once I start to cross the road.

But you could wait all night and still not be certain there was nothing there, so she crawled through the small gap, scratching her face in the process, then dashed across the road and jumped over the ditch into the field on the other side.

She had slipped as she landed in the field, covering herself in the chalky mud and slightly spraining her wrist – '*merde*'. But at least she was clear. She had decided beforehand that the road was the riskiest part of the journey and now that was behind her. She had a choice now: either take the shortest route by going diagonally across the field, but risk being seen in the open, or take the long route by using the cover of the hedgerow along the perimeter. Crouched in the mud, she looked up at the sky. The moon was quite obscured now by the cloud. She would risk going across the field. '*Time is never on your side,*' they had told her.

At the other side of the field she came to the mesh wire fence at the top of the railway embankment, exactly where she had been told it would be. She waited for five minutes, just in case there were any patrols on the line below. The wire was difficult to cut, much thicker than she had expected and the wet steel caused her cutters to slip. Her hands were freezing cold. She had to cut through the wire in a dozen places to make a big enough hole for her to climb through. She then tied the wire back to the fence. It would be easy enough to spot close up, but from a distance it would look like the fence was intact. She threw the shrub she had collected into the ditch and slid down into it. She covered herself as best she could and waited.

Now it was gone midnight. In the past hour she had counted the two trains she had been told to expect. Her whole body shook as the trains rushed by, just inches from her. They moved these trains in the dead of night, so that the chances of anyone spotting the amount of tanks and the equipment they were moving were minimised. Any minute now, the third one was due. If what they told her was correct, then it would be an empty train with just three carriages. She had been trained to recognise the differences in noise. After the third train, there would be exactly six minutes before the target train was due. Six minutes to emerge from her cover, make sure that the track was clear, lay the charge and be at least at the other side of the wire fence and behind the hedge when the train came past and she pressed the detonator. She would then have to rely on the confusion to give her enough time to make it back up the hill to safety.

Six minutes. Three hundred and sixty seconds. When she first started, it had taken her twice that long to set the charge.

The third train came past, travelling more slowly than the previous two. She waited until the sound of it had stopped reverberating along the track before pushing her cover away, realising just how cramped and uncomfortable she had been. She had ended up in a foetal position and she was now having trouble straightening her knees. She crawled along the side of the track – *'Keep as low as possible, all the time… they will be looking for something with two legs, not four'* – the shingle cutting into her. She rolled over onto her back and from inside her coat pulled out the explosives. With her hand, she scooped out enough gravel under the track to bury it. She connected the wire, covered the explosives with the gravel and crawled back to the ditch. She attached the wire to the detonator and then scrambled up the siding, digging her long nails into the cold earth to help her up the embankment. *Untie the hole in the fence, pass the detonator through, climb through the hole, tie it up again and move along the hedge.* As she started to do that, she could hear the low rumble in the distance of the train. She had done everything well within the six minutes. There was now maybe a minute in which to get as far as possible from the track. Crawling now on her feet and one hand, the other clutching the detonator, she moved far enough along the hedge, stopped, and started to wind-up the machine. She was covered in mud and her lungs ached. Her left hand was bleeding. She was breathing hard and could feel the sound of her heartbeat crashing in her ears. Surely, if anyone was close by, they would be able to hear her. The train was closer now. Through the gap in the hedge she could see it approaching the point where she would press the charge. *One, two, three…*

An empty click. The train passed. And now the lights were shining on her. Not just torch lights as she had expected, but large searchlights, so she could see nothing and all she could hear was the shouting. The night had turned to day.

She was hauled up by her elbows, not too roughly, and a man wearing a thick jumper and a beret was standing in front of her.

'Not bad. Better than yesterday, but not yet good enough.'

He handed her a flask of hot, sweet tea.

From the trackside, a man shouted up.

'It's fine. A decent connection. Well concealed.'

The man in the beret leaned over the hedge.

'And it would have gone off?'

'Oh yes.'

He turned to her and nodded approvingly.

'You want to know your main mistake? You had clearly decided before you set out that the road was the most dangerous part of your journey. Do you know why that was a mistake?'

She shook her head, sipping the hot tea.

'It is a mistake because *every* part of your journey is the most dangerous part. Remember that. If you decide that one part is the most dangerous, then inevitably you will be a tiny bit more relaxed in other parts, which is what happened in this field. You took the easy route across the field, even though you had enough time. You were exposed for too long. We spotted you then. And you took too long with the fence. I told you to take gloves. But you did well with laying the explosives and you were well-hidden in the ditch. We will try again tomorrow. Now, you will want a bath, no?' His sharp Provençal accent cut through the thin night air.

Nathalie brushed herself down. She knew she had done well. The man with the beret was a hard taskmaster and 'not bad' actually meant 'very good'. She was almost there. She was exhausted. There would be a car waiting at the road and she would soon be back at the house, where a hot bath and a clean bed waited.

The small group trudged back through the quiet north Lincolnshire night.

–

Christmas in London.

The man in the beret had informed her in the farmhouse when they finished the debrief late one night.

'You'll be driven to London this Friday – that's Christmas Eve. You'll be brought back here on the Wednesday. After Boxing Day.'

'And how will I be able to let my husband know I'm coming?'

'He'll be told. A condition of you being allowed home is that you avoid seeing anyone you know, apart from your husband, of course. It's too risky. Your husband knows that. He's told his parents he is on duty over Christmas and can't leave London.'

She nodded; it would be best not to show too much of a reaction.

'Do you have many friends?'

'A few – not really though. I'm friendly with some of the nurses at the hospital and Owen sometimes sees people he was at sea or at school with when they're in London, but no…'

'Keep it that way. One misjudged remark to one person could undo everything and we can't risk that. Just keep yourselves to yourselves.'

'I understand. What will you be doing for Christmas?' she asked him, trying to break through his ever-present coldness.

He carried on folding up a map. 'You don't need to know that,' he snapped, as cold as ever.

She had been subjected to mock interrogations for most of the past two days and she doubted whether the real thing could be much worse. Her cheek still smarted from where he had struck her earlier that evening, but that had been the least of her humiliations.

The previous day she had been blindfolded, driven around in a car for what she thought must have been at least an hour before being dragged into a building. A male voice that she could not recall having heard before spoke to her.

'I am going to give you a code word. Under no circumstances must you reveal this code word to anyone. Do you understand?'

She nodded.

'The code word is "ploughshares". Please repeat it to me.'

'Ploughshares.'

'And again.'

'Ploughshares.'

'That is the last time you utter that word. Understand?'

She nodded again.

'Do you understand?'

'Yes,' she replied.

She was led down some steps and into a room where the blindfold was removed.

The room was cold, windowless and harshly lit. She assumed that it was a cellar, certainly the ceiling seemed to be lower than normal. There was a damp, fusty smell. She was alone in it apart from a tall woman who was wearing a dark woollen coat. When she spoke, which was not until some time had passed, it was in French, with a distinctive Marseilles accent.

'I am very experienced. Eventually I will persuade you to reveal the code word. It will not reflect badly upon you if you let me have it now. It will show judgement.'

Nathalie raised her eyebrows and laughed. 'Really? Do you think I am stupid?'

'Some of the methods I will use are not pleasant I can assure you. What does it matter if you tell me now or later?'

It matters a lot, she thought. Everything I've been taught, both here and in Germany.

Hold out for as long as possible.

Give others a chance to escape. That is what they'll be looking for.
Even one hour can make a difference.

'You know I won't tell you.'

Focus on something else. Maybe an object in the room, or an activity you remember like a bike ride or visiting an exhibition.

Listen carefully to their questions. They will reveal how much they don't know.

Use delaying tactics: ask them to repeat a question or have a coughing fit.

Try to avoid losing your temper, no matter what the provocation.

Do not appear shocked at anything they say or do, no matter how upsetting.

'Remove your clothes.'

'Pardon?' She knew from the tone of her voice that she sounded shocked, which she knew she was not meant to do.

'I said, remove your clothes.'

The woman was holding a large cane, the kind normally seen in gardens. She decided to think about the Tuileries Gardens in Paris which she had visited the day she first went to the German Embassy. Nathalie removed her cardigan and shoes and pulled her dress over her head, taking care to brush her hair back into place with her hands. The stockings followed. The cold bit into her now. The floor was uneven concrete, covered in sharp bits of grit.

'Everything.'

The cane was being waved menacingly in front of her. She removed the rest of her underwear.

'Legs apart, put your hands behind your back.'

The woman went behind her and tied up her hands.

For what must have been an hour the woman walked in circles around her: sometimes very close, other times further away. Every so often she would ask:

'Are you ready to tell me yet?'

Nathalie would not reply.

Another hour. One more hour, they'll be happy with that.
Once you go beyond an hour, every minute is a bonus.
Buy time, it is your most precious commodity.

The sound of heavy footsteps could be heard coming towards the room and then men's voices outside the door.

'Shall I let them in or do you want to tell me? It's very easy, either for you to tell me or for me to let them in.'

One word, what does it matter?

In any case, surely she would not bring the men into the room. There had to be limits. She'd been subjected to something like this in Germany and even they hadn't gone that far. One of the instructors had felt her breasts during a mock interrogation. But she was fully clothed then. He seemed more embarrassed than she was. He even apologised afterwards.

The woman walked over, towering above her. She held the top of the cane under her chin. It was rough and nicked her chin.

'You tell me the code and they don't come in and you can get dressed. You have held out for longer than we expected. We will be pleased.'

Nathalie was on the verge of breaking. Nervously she shook her head.

'Are you sure?' The woman looked surprised.

The woman drew the tip of the cane down her neck, between her breasts and between her legs, holding it there. She could feel tears welling in her eyes and her face and neck reddening. The nick on her chin had started to bleed and she could feel a trickle of blood running down her neck.

'One last chance? I don't want to have to bring them in. Please tell me.'

Nathalie spat at her in the face.

The woman did not flinch. No expression crossed her face as a small line of spit rolled down her left cheek. She leaned close to Nathalie and whispered in her ear.

'They are not good men, you know. They can be animals. I never expected we'd have to bring them in. The code word?'

She stepped back, waiting for Nathalie to spit again. Still no response.

'Come in,' she called out. Nathalie could detect a nervous reluctance in her voice.

Two men she had never seen before entered the room. One of them much younger than her, the other much older. She had to stand there while they circled her, speaking in a language she did not recognise.

Until then the room had been chilly and she had been shivering. Now she was burning hot and could feel the perspiration trickling down her back. The men were inspecting her as if she was an animal at market and they, prospective buyers.

'Tell me the word and they will leave now.' The woman sounded exasperated, even unsettled. Nathalie stayed silent.

'Shall I leave you on your own with them or do you want to tell me the code word?'

Nathalie said nothing, defiant but also too terrified to speak. She could feel a leather-gloved hand run down the length of her back, move over her bound hands and rest at the base of her spine. The young man stood inches in front of her, slowly looking her up and down – more down than up – a cold smile on his face as he slowly licked his lips. He placed a cold hand on her chin, lifted it up and with the other hand ran his fingers through her hair. She could feel the rough hem of his coat brushing against the inside of her thigh.

The older man now had both of his hands against the back of her thighs, very slowly moving them to the inside of her legs and upwards. She could feel his breath, hot and damp against the back of her neck. Behind the young man, she could see the woman, who was beginning to look agitated.

If he moves his hands any higher up, I'm telling her the code word. This is impossible.

The gloved hands lingered at the very top of her thighs. The younger man was now standing directly against her, their bodies touching. His face was so close to hers that it was impossible for her to focus properly on him. She could feel the shape of his body.

'Don't tell her,' he whispered. 'I don't want you to tell her the code word. I am enjoying this.' He stepped back an inch or two to allow enough space for his ice-cold hands to run up and down the front of her body, his sharp fingernails scratching her.

'The code word?' The woman had moved to the rear of the room, as if she didn't want to see too much of what was going on. Her voice appeared to be shaking.

The younger man smiled and shook his head. 'Don't tell her,' he whispered again.

She said nothing.

His hands were now cupping her breasts. She was close to breaking point.

'Even…' she started to speak.

'Even what?' said the woman.

She hesitated. '*Even the Germans don't behave like this,*' was what she had been about to say.

'Even… if this goes on for another day, I won't say anything.'

The older man had now placed his gloved hands round her neck. At first, the touch was very light and he was almost stroking her. But very slowly, the grip tightened. At the same time, the younger man had taken her nipples between his bony fingers; playing with them at first and then pinching them hard. She could feel the tears streaming down her cheeks.

It is perfectly possible to withstand physical torture, they had told her.

You will be amazed at how much pain the human body can withstand.

The important thing to remember is that it is not in their interests to harm you. You will be of no use to them then.

She wasn't so sure, but it was at this point that she realised: the British would surely not expect someone like me to be able to withstand all this? If it goes on any longer then they will surely start to get suspicious. They will wonder how I was able to withstand all this.

'Ploughshares!' she spat the word out and at the same time drove her knee sharply into the younger man's groin. He crumpled to floor in agony, while the older man tightened his grip on her neck, so that he was almost choking her.

'Stop!' the woman cried out. 'It's over. Go now.'

The older man reluctantly released his grip.

The younger man slowly hauled himself up, one hand clutching his groin.

She had moved a few paces away from him now, but he lashed out at her with his fist, which she just managed to avoid.

'I said, stop!' shouted the woman. 'Enough,' she said to the men. 'You can leave now.'

The younger one in front of her looked disappointed. The older one allowed his hands to move down from her neck and brush against her breasts, holding them there for a moment.

'I said, that's enough. Go!' The woman sounded angry.

As the men left the room, she turned to Nathalie, avoiding looking at her directly. She looked shaken.

'We did not expect you to last that long. You did well. Get dressed now.'

Once she was dressed the man in the beret came into the room to put the blindfold back on.

She reckoned that having held out so well in the interrogations was the reason she was being allowed home for Christmas.

She had been dropped off at the flat in the early afternoon of Christmas Eve. Owen, she had been told, would be home by four.

It was a strange sensation, arriving home at a place that she had never truly regarded as such. The flat was still and cold, if anything it felt colder inside than out. She walked around the empty rooms, not even bothering to put the lights on. She glanced at the noisy kitchen clock. Ten to two. Another two hours before he's home. And that sensation again, the unaccountable feeling of actually looking forward to seeing Owen that had taken her by surprise when she first felt it, and which surprised and disconcerted her now.

In the lounge she picked up their wedding photo from a shelf. When she'd first seen it, she thought they looked like two strangers, randomly placed next to each other. Owen seemed to be standing in the light, his face beaming proudly. She was very slightly in the shadow and just that bit further away from him than you would expect.

In the photograph he looked little more than a teenager, young even for his years. But next to the wedding photograph was one that she hadn't seen before, taken in Hyde Park as the leaves of autumn swirled around them. A passing Canadian officer had obligingly taken the picture and there they were: faces pressed together, both smiling, both in the light. No longer strangers.

Is it me who has changed – or him?

She carried on walking around the flat.

Just visiting, she thought. Just passing through. Always, just passing through.

The place was meticulous, as she would have expected. Owen was always tidier than her. In the bedroom she noticed her slippers neatly arranged at the foot of the bed. She kicked off her shoes, the sound of them clattering against the skirting board echoing through the flat. Still wearing her coat, she slumped into an armchair.

It was only then that she realised quite how exhausted she was. The past two months had taken her by surprise. As it was, she had been busy enough with the quantity of information that Owen was bringing home. He thought he was being careful: arriving home that much earlier and then sitting at the table with his maps and charts while she cooked dinner. It was so easy to come behind him, kiss him on the neck, playfully cover his eyes with her hands and look at the chart. You could learn a lot that way. Occasionally he would ask her help with a word or phrase, never telling her what it was to do with, but she would look at it with far more attention than it needed so that she could take in as much information as possible. It might just be the odd word, but it all counted and the messages that she was getting back from that horrible little Belgian told her that the people in Paris were delighted.

And then, in November, Owen had come home to say that Captain Archibald wanted her to meet a lady. So the three of them went to a hotel behind Marylebone High Street where they were joined by a lady who spoke fluent French, but was not French. She had never worked out where she came from.

They were sat in a small annexe of the lounge, out of earshot of anyone else. The lady introduced herself as Nicole and gestured for Nathalie to join her on her sofa.

'We think that you can be of help to us,' the lady had said. 'Would you be willing to help in the cause of the liberation of France by returning there? It would not be without danger.'

Nathalie looked towards Owen, who smiled and nodded his head. She remembered that he looked terrified.

The woman continued to speak very fast and very softly in an educated accent. 'Because of the nature of his work, your husband is aware of our interest. It is important that he knows what is going on, to an extent. You would have his support, but it has to be your decision. We would train you and then you would be flown to France. You would work with your countrymen out there.

'If you indicate your agreement now, Nathalie, then we will proceed. If not, then this meeting has never taken place. But we do need to know now.'

And that was that. Would she be interested? She had looked towards Owen, who appeared overwhelmed. She asked him what he thought and he said nothing, but nodded weakly.

Just a week later she was somewhere in Lincolnshire. She actually had no idea where she was, and couldn't even be certain that it was Lincolnshire. She had feigned sleep as they drove up the Great North Road and after some three hours noticed the dark mass of a cathedral rising high in the distance, after which the car headed east. Not long after that a coach passed them going in the other direction with 'Lincoln' on its destination board. At that point Nicole had drawn the curtains in the back of the car ('*so you can get some rest*') and they arrived at the destination an hour later. From the position of the moon and the stars, she could tell that they had continued north east, so she was assuming she was still in Lincolnshire. The Germans had made her study enough of those wretched maps of the United Kingdom for her to have a reasonable sense of where she was.

Apart from the instructors, she was the only one in the isolated farmhouse. The house was set at the bottom of a large hill and surrounded by woods. It was quiet, apart from the constant drone of planes, especially at night. From what she could make out, they were mostly bombers – Lancasters as far as she could tell, dozens of them at a time, flying low and south.

The only other company in the area appeared to be starlings. Thousands of them. During the day they would gather in a dark mass in the trees, staring down at her as if they alone knew the truth. At dusk they would fly around silently, but if anything disturbed them then the sound would be deafening.

The dining room in the farmhouse had been converted into a classroom, with a blackboard on top of a large pine dresser. Upstairs there were three bedrooms. In a cupboard in the bathroom she had found newspaper lining the shelves where the sheets and towels were kept. They were copies of the *Lincolnshire Echo* from December 1942. She could not be sure if they had been left there deliberately to confuse her, or if they were an oversight. If it was the latter, it was a bad mistake.

Nicole slept in one of the bedrooms and one of the other instructors, who always wore a beret and never a coat, in the other. His name was Claude. As far as she could tell, the other instructors who would turn up for a day or two at a time would sleep downstairs. There would always be at least two of them there.

The training divided into three main parts. Firstly, there was instruction on how to use the radio transmitter. She knew she would be hopeless at that, but she could hardly tell them that the Abwehr had so despaired of her inability to use the transmitter and master codes that they had lumbered her with that ghastly Belgian. This time the instructors were more patient and she made some progress.

Then there was the explosives training. Considering that she had trouble lighting the gas on their cooker in London, Nathalie surprised herself at how she was able to cope with the explosives. What she was meant to do with them once in France was another matter. She could hardly blow up a railway track. She also had weapons training. The American Sten Mark 3 was one she seemed to excel at, and she got used to carrying the Webley revolver at all times.

The final part of her training was the hardest. Going over her cover story again and again. Knowing everything about her new self. How to conceal her true identity. What to do if captured – *hold out for as long as you can, but at least twenty-four hours. That will give your comrades a chance to escape.* How to arrange a rendezvous – *in as busy a place as possible.* What to do if the person you are meeting is not there – *keep walking at the same pace, don't come back to the same place.* And so on. It was all rather familiar. This was the only time when she felt truly compromised. She needed to have every sense primed to ensure that she let nothing slip. '*I've never had any training like this before,*' she had to keep reminding herself. '*I must make deliberate mistakes. I am an innocent nurse who had just been recruited to the SOE.*'

She must have dozed off, because she was woken with a start by the call of '*Darling*' as the front door of the flat opened.

Owen walked into the lounge, carrying a large box which he put on the table before rushing over to her.

Normally so talkative and enthusiastic, Owen said very little that long Christmas weekend. He seemed to be happy just to have her with him. They didn't leave the flat at all on the Saturday, Sunday or the Monday. It was cold and wet and they both seemed to be happy to stay in, dozing in their armchairs and listening to the gramophone. The box he had brought in with him was a hamper courtesy of Captain Archibald and contained enough food and drink to keep them replete as well as banish all thoughts of rationing from their mind. Their neighbour, Roger, could be heard in the flat next door. He was a civil servant who had invited them round the previous Christmas, but neither she nor Owen felt obliged to return the invitation. Apart from him, the rest of the house appeared to be empty for most of the weekend.

Nathalie found she was catching up on lost sleep; invariably she would awaken to find Owen staring at her, as if he'd been checking she was still breathing. And when she did emerge from her slumber, she'd smile at him and then he would come over and sit on the side of her armchair and stroke her hair, or cup her chin in his hand and pull her head towards his.

Owen never asked, not once, about where she had been or what she had been through. She assumed he must know something, but she had to resist the temptation to tell him.

He ought to know.

He ought to know, she thought, why she had recoiled when they were making love the first night she was back and he ran his fingers through her hair as he liked to do and as she liked him to do. But now it reminded her of the young man in the interrogation, running his cold hands through her hair. After they'd made love that night he was stroking her breasts when he suddenly stopped. He'd noticed that her nipples were reddened and slightly bruised.

I'll tell him. Then he'll realise.

But in the end she told an unconvincing tale about getting trapped as she climbed over a gate and no more was said about it.

He ought to know why she wanted to sleep with the bedside light on. She could not fall asleep otherwise, fearing she was still blindfolded.

The weather turned mild on the Tuesday, the day before she was due to return. In the afternoon they went for a long walk, both lost in their thoughts. Owen was as withdrawn as he had been throughout Christmas. It was so uncharacteristic, she thought. Normally he was bursting with enthusiasm and had so much to tell her. Now he seemed happy just to be with her and with little to say. She was exhausted. The journey that Georg Lange had told her she had irreversibly set out on would continue. She would give anything for it to stop.

They must have walked for hours because it had turned dark without either of them noticing the city in blackout. They were in a small road in Chelsea, a single light above a shop which, despite the blackout, was throwing out a surprising amount of light around the dark buildings, picking out windows and doorways, bricks glistening. The light caught the shape of a tall dog sitting silently at the kerb. Its dark eyes reflected the light and its head turned slowly, watching them as they walked towards a pub they had spotted at the end of the road.

The inside of the pub was dim, bathed in a yellow light and silent. A cloud of brown tobacco smoke hung just under the ceiling. Two old men were sitting alone at either end of the bar, looking suspiciously at them and at each other. The benches around the sides of the small room were occupied by half a dozen people sat on their own, all occupied in their thoughts. The only noise came from a table which an army corporal shared with two women: both noticeably older than him and wearing too much cheap make-up.

'You're just trying to get us drunk, aren't you?' one of them admonished, as she knocked back another glass of what appeared to be gin.

At the next table sat an old lady, her large handbag on it. She was swirling around the contents of her drink, an improbably short cigarette unlit in her mouth.

Owen and Nathalie sat at the only other table, which was so rocky that they had to hold on to the top to keep it still. Despite this, their drinks still slopped onto the surface.

'I'm sorry about this,' he said to her.

'Sorry about what?'

'This place. Not very grand.'

'It's fine, Owen. Don't worry. I quite like it actually.'

'Like it! I thought you hated this kind of thing?'

'What kind of thing?'

'Pubs, the English way of life – that kind of thing.'

She smiled, pulling little rivers out of the pool of beer that had spilled on their table. 'Maybe I'm beginning to get to like English things then.'

He leaned over, taking both of her hands in his.

'And does that include me?'

She leaned towards him and kissed him, to the raucous cheers of the table next to them.

Lincolnshire, January 1944

She was back in a ditch in Lincolnshire, covered in leaves, waiting for the dog to find her so that she could get back to the cold house and have a bath.

It was the end of January, the ground was frozen solid and the moon was bright. Tonight they had given her a large, weighted knapsack that she had to carry across the fields and the ditches. She had to set up the transmitter and send a brief message and then wait for the reply. She then had to scale a wall that was more than six feet high and break into a locked shed before laying explosives under a bridge over an icy stream.

She had done all that and then found somewhere to hide, all as instructed. She knew that as long as it took at least ten minutes for them to find her after she had left the bridge then she would have passed. More than twenty minutes had already passed when a large hand reached down into the ditch and hauled her up. Claude, the man with the beret, patted her on the shoulder.

'You are ready,' was all he said. There was still no warmth in his voice or his manner.

The woman was standing behind him. '*Très bien.*'

She had expected a bit more ceremony, a bit more elation but perhaps they were as exhausted as she was.

Back at the farmhouse the bathwater was only lukewarm and the bed felt cold. In a matter of weeks maybe, she could be back in France. She had expected to return in very different circumstances.

Tomorrow she would be back in London, with Owen. Her over-whelming thought as she drifted off to sleep was how surprised she was that she found herself actually looking forward to being back with her husband. The cold does strange things to you.

Chapter 14

The chauffeur knew to check with his passenger before this particular journey.

'Short route or long route, sir?'

Admiral Canaris looked at his watch. He preferred the long route. Anything to put off arriving in that wretched building. A pleasant drive through the Tiergarten would take the edge off his nerves. But the one thing you did not risk doing was keep them waiting. People had been shot for less.

'Better go the short way, Karl.'

The long black Mercedes-Benz Tourenwagen pulled away from the Abwehr headquarters in Tirpitz Ufer and then turned left into Potsdamer Strasse, where they slowed down for the first checkpoint. The SS guards peered into the back of the car, clicked synchronised '*Sieg Heil*'s and waved them through. Then into Potsdamer Platz, where they took the second exit into Hermann Goering Strasse. Canaris smiled. Their arrogance means they can't even see the irony of naming a wide road after a fat man. Moments later they came to the security barrier at the entrance into Voss Strasse. More peering into the back of the car, a check on a clipboard, a word with the driver about where to park, a '*Sieg Heil*' or two and they were through.

Canaris never ceased to be both amazed and appalled at the same time by this building. When it opened in January 1939 the myth was that Speer had built it in a year. *Imagine, how wonderful we are! This magnificent building, constructed in just one year!* Canaris knew it had taken two years, but he also knew better than to contradict people in matters like this. As he was fond of saying, people had been shot for less.

He climbed the dozen steps into the front, high-columned entrance, choosing to walk through the middle of it. In the main reception area he had to wait behind a fat SS general who was complaining that his driver was not waiting for him. He informed the woman behind the desk that he had arrived and sat down to wait for his escort, doing his best to avoid making eye contact with Heinrich Müller, who was on his way out of the building. The last thing he wanted now was to have to make small talk with the head of the Gestapo. The Bavarian was a small man with a thin face. It went without saying that Canaris did not trust him. What made it worse was that Canaris rated Müller's abilities. He was not someone to underestimate. But look at him: that was the problem with Germany these days. The country run by sergeants and corporals. People with no class.

Out of the corner of his eye he noticed that Müller was now walking towards him. This was going to be difficult. Just in time, a tall, young and appropriately blond and blue-eyed SS-Obersturmführer appeared next to Canaris. They exchanged '*Sieg Heil*'s – one more enthusiastic than the other – and set off together. Admiral Canaris always thought of Daniel at this moment. He realised that Old Testament prophets were not people that immediately came to mind in this building out of all places, but he had an acute sense of being in the lion's den.

The young SS-Obersturmführer was walking fast and Canaris was having to concentrate on keeping pace with him. Through the central courtyard and past the ridiculous statues of naked young men and towards the central part of the building.

They were now entering the heart of the *Reichskanzlei*, the Reich Chancellery. The office of Adolf Hitler.

Sentries were posted every few paces now and the corridors and the rooms off them were increasingly ornate. The SS-Obersturmführer's jackboots were echoing around off the walls. Still they continued walking, the marbled floors reflecting the light from the small windows, magnificent crests adorning the walls. It was an extraordinary building, he thought. You had to hand it to Speer. He had managed to design a building that both impressed and intimidated those who entered it. The long walk was deliberate. You were left in no doubt as to the importance of where you were heading.

The SS-Obersturmführer wheeled right, leading Canaris into a stunning reception room. He clicked his heels and gestured towards one of the chairs arranged around an unlit fireplace. He then stood at ease on the inside of the door.

Canaris had a moment to reflect and to wonder. When you were summoned to the Reich Chancellery, you could never be quite sure what it was about. It was difficult to predict. Canaris had been good at it up to now, but he was growing weary at trying to stay one step ahead of trouble.

If he was lucky, it would be about Hitler's current obsession: where the Allies would land in northern Europe – and when. At least he could tell him what he wanted to hear. He had been discussing it with Oster that morning:

'What matters is not what the Abwehr thinks, but what the Führer thinks. That stubborn bastard made up his mind months ago that the Allies would invade through the Pas de Calais. All that we have done is tell him what he wants to hear. He still believes that he is the great military strategist.'

As long as the Führer remains convinced about the Pas de Calais, then the sooner this damned war might be over, he thought.

His thoughts were interrupted by the arrival in the room of Martin Bormann. Canaris groaned inwardly, while outwardly greeting him. Hitler's Private Secretary was always rude. He never treated Canaris with respect. A few minutes somewhere near a trench thirty years ago and these clerks now thought they were important enough to be running Germany.

'Just you, Canaris?'

'Just me, Bormann.'

'Uhm. I thought you would have others with you. Are you sure no one will be joining you?'

'I am sure.'

'Very well, follow me.'

Canaris followed Bormann, with the SS-Obersturmführer following him. Through an internal door, down a short, narrow corridor, past two sentries and into an inner office. What struck him most whenever he came in here was the sheer height of the room. The magnificent, brown marble walls were as tall as a house, leading up to a splendid panelled ceiling. Having spent so long in submarines, Canaris felt lost in a room like this.

The three of them walked in single file across the long carpet. Four chairs were arranged around a large, low desk.

Bormann sat in one of the chairs and gestured for Canaris to sit in another.

'He wants me to assess your intelligence reports, Canaris. Everyone's telling him different things. He doesn't *like* you, but he respects the Abwehr.'

'And you Bormann?'

'I neither like you nor respect the Abwehr, Canaris. But I am here to do what the Führer says. Essentially, he is looking for good news. He doesn't get much of that these days. Russia, North Africa – it's all terrible. His obsession this week is with the Second Front. That is all he's talking about. Come over here.'

Canaris followed Bormann to a large table covered in maps and charts. A large map was spread out on top of the table showing the northern coast of France and the southern coast of England.

'He is obsessed with the Allies attempting to land again in northern Europe. He thinks he knows best, don't forget that. He certainly doesn't trust his generals. Look what happened when they tried to land in Dieppe. And now they will have to land a whole army, not just six thousand men. The outcome of the war will depend on whether the Allied invasion of northern Europe succeeds or not, Canaris.

'If they fail, then they will not be able to try again for years – and by then we will have re-equipped the army, the Luftwaffe will have new and better aircraft and the navy will be stronger. And while we do that, we will be able to move enough divisions away from western Europe to sort out the Russians in the east. But it all depends on making sure that their invasion fails. And the best way of doing that is by ensuring that we are ready for them when they land. What the Führer wants to know is, where do you think they will land?'

'I believe it will be in this area.' Canaris was pointing to the Pas de Calais, south of Boulogne.

'And tell me why?'

'Because it puts them nearer to Germany, because there are more places to land, because the sea crossing is shorter, because the terrain is easier and because they will have more air cover. According to Goering, the RAF have been mounting more raids over the past few weeks over the Pas de Calais than over any other part of northern France. Von Rundstedt and Rommel are trying to defend the whole of the northern coast, spreading our forces out too thinly. I believe we should concentrate our defence on the Pas de Calais. At least von Rundstedt has kept the Fifteenth Army in the Pas de Calais and most of the Panzer Group is there.'

'And what makes you so certain?'

'Our intelligence. As you know, we have at least two agents operating inside Britain – the Pole and the Spaniard. Both are extremely reliable and the message we are getting back from them is a consistent one: the Allies will invade in the Pas de Calais. They are operating quite independently of each other, of course, but they both report that General Patton's First US Army is based here in Kent, ideally placed for the short sea crossing. The landing craft are all in Dover and Folkestone. And I am pleased to report another important development which you can convey to the Führer.'

Bormann raised his eyebrows and stepped back half a pace from the table.

'I am pleased to report that we have another very well-placed agent. Her code name is Magpie. She has been in England since 1940 but has only really been active since 1942, when she entered into a relationship with a Royal Navy intelligence officer. In the past few months, the quality of material we have been getting from her has been quite outstanding – and it all points to the invasion being in the Pas de Calais. It is intelligence of the very highest quality, which corroborates all our other intelligence. And today I can report a very significant development.'

Bormann's full attention was now focussed on Canaris. He nodded towards him. *Carry on.*

'At the end of last year the British Special Operations Executive recruited Magpie. Because of her training with them, we have heard very little from her in recent months. The contact has been very intermittent. But we do know that they were training her to work with the French resistance in the area where the invasion would take place. Her role would be to ensure that the resistance group was prepared for the invasion. She has now completed her training. She will be flying to France soon.'

'And do you know where?'

'No,' he said, dismissively, allowing a pause for Bormann to reflect on his question. 'Of course, they are not to going to tell her where she is going. We will only find out when she arrives. But I anticipate here.' He pointed at the map. 'Somewhere round… here. In the Pas de Calais. Just south of Boulogne.'

Bormann nodded approvingly.

'So,' he said, gathering his papers and picking up his gloves, signalling the briefing was over, 'I shall be able to tell the Führer what he wants to hear. He'll appreciate that.'

Canaris smiled and bowed towards Bormann, gesturing for him to leave the room first.

Bormann stopped in the doorway and stepped close to Canaris.

'You had better be right, Canaris. Remember, I don't like you and I don't trust you.'

As he left the Chancellery, Canaris felt that, on balance, he was pleased he had resisted the temptation to describe the feeling as mutual.

Chapter 15

England, 20th April 1944

The door of the dark brown Humber slammed shut and even before she had a chance to wave goodbye and blow a kiss, as she knew would be expected of her, the car had accelerated down the road. Nathalie's last view of her husband was of a blurred but forlorn figure, stepping from the kerb into the road to keep the car in view even as its tail lights disappeared into the night.

Quinn stepped back onto the pavement and Captain Archibald walked over to him from where he had been standing in the entrance of the pretty, wisteria-covered safe house in Holland Park where Nathalie had stayed for almost three months. Sensitive to the mood, the older man said nothing for a while, bouncing slowly on his heels.

'Chin up, Quinn. Expect you'll see her soon enough. Could be just a few weeks the way things are going.'

Quinn walked ahead of Archibald, not wanting him to see the tears that, despite himself, now filled his eyes and were beginning to roll down his cheeks. He intended to say something suitable in reply to show that he agreed, but could not find any words. Archibald clearly sensed the situation.

'Tell you what, Quinn. Why don't you take yourself for a walk round the block? Clear your head. You can stay here tonight and take the day off tomorrow. That will give you a long weekend. As long as you're out of the house by nine o'clock tomorrow morning. Need to get the place ready for when we hand it back to the owners.'

So Quinn went for a long walk, circumnavigating Holland Park. He hadn't known the area before Nathalie was moved here when she had returned from her training at the end of January.

'Best steer clear of Alderney Street,' they had said. 'Don't want anyone asking awkward questions. This place is safer. She'll stay here until it's time to move on.'

They had had no idea how long she would be in the safe house; it could have been a few days, a few weeks, a few months. In the end, it had been three long months.

She was allowed out on her own during the day and he was permitted to visit her and even stay over some nights, though there was always someone else in the house which he found awkward. Whenever he awoke during the night, which was often, he would invariably catch her with her dark eyes open and staring into the matching darkness.

There were so many things that needed to be said, but their relationship had slipped into a kind of silence. If anything, that made things somewhat easier: Nathalie had always seemed to prefer the quiet and didn't feel the need to fill the void with conversation as Owen did. Although she was evidently nervous, she also seemed more relaxed with Owen, more prone to physical contact than before. Now, she would frequently hold his hand, or stroke his face, cupping her hand under his chin as she did so and holding it there for a while. If he ever tried to broach the subject of her going away, she would remind him that she could not discuss it. '*You ought to know better, Owen.*'

For a while he had allowed himself to imagine that Nathalie might not be sent away after all. Maybe they had changed their minds, perhaps she had not performed as well as they had hoped when she had gone away for training, possibly they were having second thoughts about her. She was certainly spending far longer than he had expected in the safe house. From the little he could gather, she spent most of her time in the house learning her cover story and practising her radio skills, but in recent weeks there seemed to be less of that and much more waiting around.

But deep down, he knew it was a forlorn hope, and by the second month of April Nathalie's movements had become far more restricted. She was no longer allowed out of the house on her own and Owen was no longer allowed to stay the night. It was clear that her departure was imminent.

Owen was still allowed to visit her after work, but he could not stay for more than an hour. He would find that, by the time he arrived, Nathalie had already eaten and was sitting in the small lounge, and he would join her on the sofa where they would talk awkwardly. Neither of them could talk about work and there was precious little else that they could discuss within the earshot of one of Nathalie's minders, who would inevitably be hovering in the kitchen. If they ever dropped their voices, the minder would come closer.

It wouldn't be long before he would be told that the car was ready to take him back to Pimlico and he would leave, not quite sure when he would see her again.

On the third Monday of April, Owen arrived at the safe house in Holland Park just after six thirty to find Nathalie waiting for him in the small entrance hall, wearing a light raincoat and clutching her handbag. Captain Archibald emerged from the lounge.

'Thought you two deserved a night out. It's a lovely evening so I suggest you stroll up to Notting Hill and find somewhere to eat there. Back by eight thirty please, at the latest.'

So they strolled up to Notting Hill. Owen kept glancing behind him as they set out.

'You won't spot them, Owen.'

'Spot who?'

'Who you're looking for. Of course, they're following us. You don't think they'd let us out all on our own, do you? They watch me like a hawk now.'

Owen put his arm round his wife's waist and pulled her closer to him. She responded by placing an arm across his shoulders and slightly inclining her head towards his.

'They'll be four of them. North, south, east and west. And we won't have the faintest idea who they are.'

'Well, that's good, isn't it?' said Owen.

She shrugged, as if she had never really thought about it like that.

'It will be any day now, you know that, don't you, Owen?'

He nodded. 'I know I shouldn't ask you this, but I don't suppose you have any idea at all of where you're going, do you? Do you know what you are meant to be doing when you get there?'

She pulled sharply away from him, their arms disentangling as she did so.

'Owen! You know that you can't ask me that.'

They were in Notting Hill Gate now, and at the end of a little alley by the side of a cinema, next door to a sweet shop, they found a pretty fish and chip restaurant called Geales, where they were shown to a table on the first floor in an area where there were just three other tables, two of which were occupied.

Despite her disdain for English food, Nathalie attacked a large piece of cod as if she hadn't eaten for a week. Owen could not remember the last time he had eaten such a large and tasty haddock.

By the time she had finished eating, Nathalie appeared slightly more relaxed. A smartly dressed couple in their sixties had taken the table next to them, so they spoke quietly, struggling to hear each other's voices.

Nathalie was holding a chip in her hand, toying with it as she spoke.

'You have to learn to accept things, you know, Owen.' She still pronounced his name as if it were two words.

'I'm not sure what you mean.'

'Like the people following us, whom we don't see. The two people who've just sat down at the next table. They're watching us. Nothing is what it seems. It's the war. People do things in war... because of the war... that they wouldn't do otherwise. That is what you have to accept. That war changes everything and when it ends, only then can you judge things properly.'

Owen was not altogether sure what she meant, but she had put the chip down now and was holding his hand, her fingers interlinked with his as she leaned over the table and kissed him on the lips. It was just gone eight o'clock and they knew that they couldn't be late, so they paid the bill and made their way back to Holland Park.

The night that Nathalie left, Archibald had arranged for a car to bring Quinn to the house from work. He was there by six o'clock. Although no one said as much, it was clear that she was going that night. Conversation had not been easy. He did not want her to go, but knew he could not allude to that. Nathalie was clearly nervous: she was physically sick more than once, but there was a steely determination in her. 'My duty' was the only thing she ever said when the much-avoided subject of her return to France crept to the surface. Owen did not need telling that the window for an Allied landing in northern Europe was a narrow one, between mid-Spring and mid-Summer. He realised that her mission to France must be linked to the Allied invasion.

At seven o'clock that night the woman called Nicole turned up at the house and took Nathalie into the small lounge. Archibald arrived and took Quinn in the kitchen.

'It's tonight, Quinn, I'm sure you've realised that by now. She'll leave in about two hours' time. You'll have a chance to say goodbye, but do keep it... what I mean is, don't make it difficult for her. She's got a long night ahead of her.'

So he hadn't made it difficult. He had actually been terribly good about it.

'See you soon. Take care. I love you,' he said when he was sure they were out of anyone's earshot. As the car arrived, a quick embrace picked out by the dipped headlights of a passing car, a final '*Whatever happens, you must know that I will always love you,*' whispered in her ear, so quietly that he couldn't be sure she heard. She said nothing, but smiled, her hand brushing his face, her fingers lingering on his lips. Her warm mouth pressed on his cheek and now he was walking quickly past the smart homes, with their white façades and their perfectly arranged flora, and along the sweeping avenues.

The tears had stopped now, but had been replaced by a sense of foreboding.

Owen Quinn wondered whether he would ever see his wife ever again.

—

Nicole had drawn the curtains in the car as soon as it set off, so again Nathalie had no idea in which direction they were heading. It was of no importance. She was heading for France, which was all that mattered.

The way she felt at that moment was about all she could be certain of. She could not really be certain of who she was. There was her real identity. Then there was Nathalie Mercier, who had come over from France in 1940. There was Nathalie Quinn who had married Owen Quinn in 1942. Then there was Magpie, for the Germans, and her new code name for the British, Rider. And her new French identity, Geraldine Leclerc. Six identities. Tonight she had become Geraldine Leclerc.

She could certainly forget about Nathalie Mercier and Nathalie Quinn; she would have no need for them again.

She did not have a watch. Everything she would be taking with her to France would be given to her later that night. She sensed that they had driven for the best part of two hours when the car pulled off the road and drove for some time over an increasingly bumpy track before pulling to a halt.

The car had pulled up close to the door of a long, single-storey building. There was a full moon, but it only showed an empty rural landscape. Trees and hedgerows on the horizon, and the smell of earth in the air. She followed Nicole into the building and into a sparsely furnished room, with a long table in the middle and chairs set against one wall. The wall at the far end had a door set into it. The windows were painted black.

On the table were clothes and various documents. Nicole stood behind the table facing Geraldine.

'Your flight to France leaves in one hour. You must prepare now. Please remove all of your clothing. All of your jewellery, everything.'

Geraldine undressed slowly, with Nicole watching her.

'You must understand, this could save your life. If you have anything on you that could not have come from France, or would reveal your true identity – that could cause you to be arrested by the Germans.'

Geraldine stood for a brief moment in her underwear before Nicole nodded for her to carry on. Her bra and knickers joined the small pile of clothes that had appeared behind her. Nicole handed her a large dressing gown.

'Put the jewellery in here.' Nicole had pushed a small box across the table for her. She removed everything, including her engagement and wedding rings.

'There is one more thing I have to do. I am sorry. Please come here.'

She walked over to Nicole. As she did so, she could hear the roar of an aircraft apparently landing near to the building. The older woman looked at her watch, nodded and produced a large pair of scissors. She pointed to a chair.

'Sit down. I need to cut your hair.'

'Please, not too short.'

'Your hair will draw attention to you as it is now. It is very long and very beautiful. You need to look as anonymous as possible.'

A few minutes later the floor around her was covered in locks of her hair. That which remained was now above her shoulders. She could not remember when it was last so short.

'Try to wear it pulled back at all times anyway. That way it will look different to your photograph. It helps if your hair is a bit different from the photo anyway. That way any Germans looking at your identity card will concentrate on the photo rather than any other detail on the card. They expect a woman to change her hair style. Now. You take a shower. Use this towel and this soap and shampoo. They are French, you probably remember them. You will even smell French when you land.' The very faintest hint of a quickly-fading smile.

The shower was in a small bathroom behind the main room. After her shower, she dressed in the items that Nicole handed her one by one. The labels showed that every single one of them was from France. The few spare clothes that were going into her knapsack were shown to her before they were packed, along with a few other items like a watch, toiletries and a torch. The Webley Mark 3 revolver she had used in Lincolnshire was there too, along with plenty of ammunition.

'You will wear these.' They were the spectacles they had made her wear when her photo was taken. An optician had come to the house in Holland Park to test her eyes and found that she could do with weak lenses anyway. The frames were thick and scratched, with a bit of tape holding part of them together. They made her look older. She glanced in the mirror that Nicole held in front of her. She was a different woman now. And not one she could imagine having much in common with.

'We are nearly ready.' For the second time that evening there was something close to a smile from Nicole. 'The paperwork now.'

She handed her the all-important *carte d'identité*, the identity card.

Nom: Leclerc.

Prenom: Geraldine.

Profession: ouvrière.

She had been born on 14th January 1914. She was a thirty-year-old factory worker from Arras. She felt like one.

Some money and few ration coupons. A letter from a friend working in Toulouse – '...*they treat us well and the weather is wonderful*'. An article torn from a magazine about fashion for the summer of 1944. And two creased photographs, of her new parents – '*avec notre amour*' – and of the brother and sister she never had – *Henri, dix ans. Juliette, sept ans*.

And that was it. Her new life stuffed into a knapsack and the pockets of her jacket.

Nicole left the room for a moment and returned with a tray, which she put on the table in front of Geraldine. One cheese sandwich, a hardboiled egg, one apple and a glass of milk. The last supper, which she didn't feel like eating.

A very plain-looking thirty-year-old factory worker from Arras was now ready to return to France.

–

Flight Lieutenant Tony Taylor of 161 Squadron of the Royal Air Force had long since given up on being confused, although tonight he was finding that harder than usual. '*In this line of work, you'd be confused every minute of every day if you stopped to think about it, so best not to think about it*' had been the helpful advice proffered when he joined the squadron eighteen months previously.

The squadron certainly made a change from flying freight in the Far East and worrying about what the Japs would do to him if he ever bailed out. His new squadron was based at RAF Tempsford in Bedfordshire. Closer to home, none of those bloody flies and a nice mix of work. Most of it was flying Whitleys on parachute drops, which suited his talents for navigation.

But when there was a full moon, out came the Lysanders, like Count Dracula. *Funny aircraft, really*. Single engine on the nose, high wing over the top of the cockpit and a strong, fixed undercarriage, attached to the wing by two improbably large struts. It had started out life as a reconnaissance plane, but they soon realised that the fixed undercarriage and general performance of the plane meant that it was ideal for landing on rough terrain, fields being a speciality, which was why they needed a full moon. *Farmland tends not to come with its own landing lights* Tony Taylor liked to joke. The Lysander had a cruising speed of one hundred and sixty-five miles an hour but could land and, crucially, take off at just eighty miles an hour. Good aircraft, thought Taylor, though you wouldn't know it to look at it. 'Reliable' was the word he'd use to describe it – and it needed to be, for what it was being used for.

They specialised in landing agents and equipment in France. The Spy Taxi, they sometimes called them, which was funny really, as his brother had driven taxis in London before the war. *No tips from these passengers, though* was another of his jokes. You could get a couple of the people and some equipment in the back, fly over to France, land in a field, drop them off, possibly bring someone back with you, and be home in time for breakfast. A few times he had brought back RAF pilots who had been shot down and hidden by the resistance, which was always nice. Good to have them back. The agents, he knew nothing about. You weren't really meant to talk to them – not that you could above the roar of the engine anyway – or even look at them properly.

There was too much to think about anyway. You had to plot your route across the Channel and then look out for the landing strip. Check they were flashing the correct Morse code signal and then come in to land. Watch out for the trees and the telegraph wires. An L-shaped flare path would have been lit on the ground. Land, turn round ready to take off again and offload the passengers and any supplies. A ladder was fixed to the left hand side of the fuselage to make things easier. Ideally, you'd be back in the air again within three or four minutes, the engine running the whole time.

They always took off from RAF Tangmere near Chichester. It was normally a fighter base, but it was right on the coast, so extended the range of the plane. The Lysander had a normal range of six hundred miles, but this could be extended to nine hundred with an extra fuel tank.

That afternoon he'd flown down from Tempsford to Tangmere as usual and waited for his instructions. Met report promised a nice clear night across the Channel and over most of France, so that was good. At four o'clock he got the call.

'You're flying just south of Boulogne, so no need for the extra fuel tank, you can take some more supplies instead.'

'Fine.'

'Oh – and you're not flying from here. There's a small airstrip about fifteen miles inland from here. Hardly ever used. Want you to fly there when it's dark, pick up a couple of passengers and off you go again.'

'Talk about a taxi service.'

Which is why Flight Lieutenant Tony Taylor was confused. They must have a very good reason for not wanting to fly from Tangmere.

He'd been on the ground for half an hour. A small truck had brought out some of the supplies, which he helped to load. Two long cylinder-like containers, which usually carried weapons and ammunition, and four smaller cases, one of which was a radio transmitter. A man came over to the plane, dressed in dark trousers, a thick jumper and a beret.

'We will be ready in thirty minutes. Myself and one passenger. Will that be all right with you?'

Probably French, he thought. Taylor told him that it was all right and sure enough twenty-five minutes later a dark Humber with curtains drawn across the back pulled alongside the left-hand side of the plane. The man with the beret opened the rear passenger door and two women got out. One briefly shook hands with the other before getting straight back into the car, which quickly pulled away from the plane. The woman stood alongside the man in the beret, handed her bag to him and climbed into the Lysander, followed by the man. Once they were settled and strapped in the back, Taylor spoke to Tangmere, was cleared for take off straight away, and gunned the Bristol Mercury engine into life. The plane bounced down the field and was soon airborne, clearing the hedges (which had slightly bothered him) with ease.

They were still climbing when the blue moonlight picked out the Sussex coast disappearing beneath them and then glinted off the sea.

'I wouldn't get too settled,' Taylor shouted into the back of the plane. 'It's only a few minutes now until we land.'

Chapter 16

Pas de Calais, April 1944

She had survived as Nathalie Mercier when she came to England, because she became Nathalie Mercier. It was not who she pretended to be: it was who she was. That was the only way. She managed to lock her true identity away so successfully that she had to think carefully before she could find the key – so much so that if she ever heard her real first name, she no longer reacted instinctively to it. And being Magpie was easy enough. You treat that part of your identity as a job. When she became Nathalie Quinn, she realised it was just an extension of Nathalie Mercier. You had to believe who you are. If you don't believe it yourself, how can you expect someone else to do that? She had never had much trouble compromising her beliefs. In any case, she thought, it was not as if there was too much to miss in her previous identity.

So somewhere between the noisy and uncomfortable plane taking off from that field in southern England to it landing in a field in northern France, she knew that she had to discard Nathalie Mercier and Nathalie Quinn over the Channel and never let them enter her mind again. Any regrets or emotions that Nathalie may have had should go into the sea along with that identity. But she was unsettled. It may be easy enough to discard your identity and the details that go with it, but the emotions – they were an altogether different matter. On occasions she had surprised herself in England, and nothing had surprised her more than the fleeting glimpses over the past few months of the feelings that she had for Owen. Very fleeting at first, but recently they had been far more frequent. They had taken her aback at the time and she had attempted to dismiss them; maybe she had simply been reciprocating his very strong feelings for her, playing the part as always. It simply meant she had been doing her job well, but it would be wrong to pretend that they had not confused her and made her think. It would certainly account for why she felt so utterly sad tonight.

It was Geraldine Leclerc who climbed down the steps of the plane in a field near Boulogne. Magpie was her job, and now Rider was a second job. It was all clear in her mind. And her true identity was still neatly locked away in her mind, although it had come somewhat closer to home.

The landing had been unpleasant. The pilot had crossed the French coast south of Boulogne and then dropped altitude quite suddenly. They approached the landing zone very low and very fast. The summer storms meant the ground was wet and this caused the plane to slither as it hit the ground. The pilot struggled with the controls – 'No one told me it was on a sodding slope!' – the Lysander skidding from left to right and back again as it bounced on the greasy field. They soon came to a halt, with the engine still running. The man with her unstrapped her belt, opened the window and told her to climb down the ladder.

'Quick.' No 'goodbye'. No 'good luck'. No time.

A man helped her down at the bottom and passed her over to a woman who took her by the arm and led her quickly over to a copse, part running, part walking and part slipping over the greasy ground. She glanced round and saw that the canisters were being unloaded. Behind the copse was a narrow track, with bicycles propped against trees, and beyond that a field, with a mass of trees in the distance.

When all the equipment was out of the plane, the engine revved up and within a minute it was airborne again, its grey shape quickly merging into the black sky and soon becoming invisible. Three men were still carrying the canisters into the copse. The woman who had led her by the arm had run back into the field to extinguish the beacons. A hole had already been dug between the trees and the canisters were being lowered into it and then covered up.

A young man with dark hair covering his brow smiled at her as he spread leaves and twigs over the area. He pointed to the canisters. 'We will collect them tomorrow.'

He and another man were both carrying guns, which she recognised from her training as American Mark 3 sub-machine guns. The older man – the one who had helped her from the plane – held a Colt automatic pistol in one hand as with the other he checked the covering over the hole into which they had hidden the canisters, kicking an extra covering of leaves over the surface as he did so. When the woman rejoined them in the copse the older man motioned for them all to crouch down. The five of them sat in a small circle, surrounded by the trees. The ground around them was covered in bluebells, their colour just evident in spite of the darkness. Geraldine was fascinated by their presence. High above them, the wind was causing the leaves at the very top of the trees to rustle. There was a smell of wet earth and of France. She was conscious of her glasses and kept removing them. The bridge was hurting her nose. She was quite unused to wearing glasses.

The older man leaned over to her, offering his hand. 'Pierre.'

'Geraldine,' she replied.

The others introduced themselves. 'Françoise', the woman who had brought her over to the copse. 'Lucien', the older man, and 'Jean', the younger one with the dark hair flopping down his face and the smile.

'We wait here for a while. It is a very clear night. If the Germans head this way we will soon hear them.'

And so they sat in silence. There was a rustle in a field on the other side of the track, causing Geraldine to turn sharply.

'Germans?' she whispered.

'Don't worry,' said Pierre. 'Just cows.'

'Same thing,' said Jean. Nervous smiles and more silence.

'Do you have your pistol?' asked Pierre.

Geraldine got out her Webley, struggling to pull it out of her jacket pocket. Pierre nodded, with a quizzical look on his face. 'You prefer it? That's good.'

After what was probably only ten minutes but seemed much longer, Pierre sent Jean and Françoise out in different directions to check all was clear. When they came back, Pierre spoke in a dialect she didn't recognise.

'*Asteur.*'

He made an apologetic gesture towards her with his hand.

'Sorry. I was saying now. We use the local patois here a lot. The Germans don't understand it, so it is a useful habit to have. We leave here one by one, at five-minute intervals. Apart from you. You will go with Jean. You will be staying at his father's house. Lucien will come back with Jean tomorrow to collect the canisters. You stay in the house all day tomorrow. I will call by at some stage. I will have more papers for you then.'

They moved off into the night, like bats darting silently in different directions. She and Jean were the last to leave. When they moved out of the wood into the field, she could see him clearly in the moonlight. He was barely a man, probably not yet out of his teens, but he moved with the confidence and experience of one much older. He guided her with an arm round her waist to the side of the field and, under the cover of first the hedge and then trees, they walked for a good fifteen minutes. They crossed two roads, sat silently while dogs in an unseen farmyard reluctantly stopped barking and then climbed over a stile. Ahead of them she could just begin to make out the silhouette of the village. They edged down a gentle hill, hopped over a small river and landed on the springy grass on the other side. They were now just yards from the back of a row of a dozen cottages, with not a flicker of light in any of them. To their right the dark shape of a church was picked out against the sky. It was two in the morning. An owl hooted and she thought she heard the sound of a vehicle moving away on a distant road. A line of tall trees towered above the cottages, the tops of them gently swaying in a strange unison.

They waited while she caught her breath. Suddenly she heard a dramatic screech ahead of her, like a cat screaming out, four times in a row. A pause, then three more times. She jumped and Jean placed a reassuring hand on her thigh. He leaned close to her and whispered.

'Don't worry. It's the peacocks. They live at the château. You'll have to get used to them.' He pointed ahead of him. 'The second house on the left is my father's. I will go first. When I have been in for one minute, I will send a signal with my torch, one short flash, two long ones. That means it is clear. Come to the house then. The back door will be open. If you see no signal from me after three minutes you will have to go back the way we came as quickly as possible. When you come to the second road we crossed, follow it into Boulogne. Hide when you get to the town then go to the station when it is busy and ask for Lucien. You saw him tonight. But be careful, Boulogne is full of Germans. Everywhere.'

Within a couple of minutes, she had entered through the tiny kitchen of the little house. Jean was already in the small hall, pointing up the stairs. He took her into a tiny bedroom, checking that the curtains were shut. There appeared to be just one other bedroom.

'This will be your room. It used to be mine. I will get you a drink. Are you hungry?'

'No, I am fine. A drink would be good though. Where is your father?'

'Germany. Compulsory Work Service. Thousands of men from this region have gone, like slaves. My father is an electrician. They need people like him in their factories.'

'How long has he been gone?'

'Two years now, nearly. He writes every week. It is much harder for him.'

'And your mother?'

'She died when I was eleven.' Jean smiled, not wanting her to feel embarrassed. She realised she was probably asking too many questions, but she had one more.

'How old are you, Jean?'

'Eighteen, but I am nineteen on the sixth of June.'

As she lay down in bed she did not expect to sleep that night. Her body was exhausted, but her mind was everywhere. She had failed to completely dispose of Nathalie over the Channel; part of her last identity remained stuck inside her, which meant that Owen did too. She tried to stay awake, fearful that she would call out his name, but drifted into an uneasy sleep which only became a deep one after Owen told her not to worry, that he understood. She was woken just after seven as Jean tapped on her door and asked her to come down. Pierre had arrived. She dressed quickly and went into the small front room, which the front door opened straight into, shielded by a curtain. The room was sparse, more utilitarian than comfortable. The dark wooden floor was covered by two frayed rugs, which overlapped. An oak table with six chairs around it was the main feature of the room. There was a battered armchair in front of the fireplace. The mantelpiece held a few photographs: the young Jean; the young Jean and his parents, and a beautiful woman in her thirties. She presumed this was his mother. Like most of the surfaces in the room, they needed dusting. The other side wall of the room, opposite the mantelpiece, was dominated by a large gilded mirror. Some of the mirroring had faded away in patches, but the gold-coloured frame was ornate, sitting incongruously in the room.

There was a half empty bottle of Calvados on the table. She noticed it was the proper Calvados – farm produced. She remembered her father making a big fuss about buying some from a farmhouse when they had holidayed not far from here. It was his favourite drink. A sticky glass was beside the bottle, along with two unwashed cups that appeared to have once held coffee. A small sideboard contained a dusty

Bible, three unopened bottles of red wine, and another picture of the beautiful woman.

Pierre was at the table. She could hear Jean in the kitchen and water boiling.

'It is unusual that you stay here with another member of our group, but the situation has been helpful for us. Last month the Germans checked all the houses in the village and told people who had spare rooms that they must allow workers to stay in them. The bigger houses have Germans billeted with them. So, you are staying here with the approval of the Germans, I suppose.

'I teach at a school in Boulogne. Jean was a student of mine until a year ago. He is a bright boy, he could have continued his studies, but it was too risky for him to stay at school. He now works at a farm on the other side of the village – most of the men in the village work in agriculture, or at least they did before the war. It means that the Germans class Jean as essential labour and so he is less likely to be sent to Germany, for the time being. It also gives him good cover to move around the countryside.

'Lucien is a *cheminot*, a railway worker. He is based at Boulogne-Ville, which is the main station in Boulogne. The railway line passes just south of here. Lucien is married to Françoise, who you also met last night. Françoise is a supervisor at a factory in Boulogne. They assemble electrical equipment like light switches and plugs. Some of it is for the German Army. They are very short of staff, so it was very easy for her to find you work at the factory. You start there on Monday. Françoise was also born in the village. With all the Allied bombing of the town, she and Lucien were worried about the children when she was at work, so now they live with her parents in the village. They are on the other side of the church. This was a very small village before the war, but the bombing in Boulogne has been so bad that many people have moved out here. And then we have our guests: the Germans don't want their troops to be staying in the town either, so we have plenty of them staying here. We need to be careful, of course, but there has been very little resistance activity in this immediate area. We've only come together as a cell in the last few weeks. We assume that we were brought together as a cell to help you.

'You have a bicycle and that is how you will travel into the town. It is not safe in Boulogne. The Allies bomb it all the time. The port is important to the Germans and, of course, it is a big submarine base. You just have to be very careful there.

'Today you can cycle into the town. You will need to register with the authorities and also get your work documents from the factory. Here, I have drawn you a map of where you need to go. Memorise it, don't take it with you. If you get searched and they find something like this on you, they will find that very rewarding. Your cover is good, you should be all right when you register. It is good that you are from Arras, that was a clever touch by London; it has been so badly destroyed that it is almost impossible for the Germans to check out someone's details if they say they are from there. Try to affect a Picardy accent. It's not easy.'

Geraldine nodded. The accent was one of the most distinctive in France, so she had to concentrate on subtle differences, like pronouncing the final 's' in a word.

'The Germans will certainly believe your accent,' said Pierre. 'But it is not them you need to worry about. I am ashamed to say, it is other French people you need to worry about. Even in this area, too many people have been happy to have an easy life and go along with the occupation. And the collaborators, there are too many of them. The police, local officials. Trust no one, assume nothing. Anyone could be an informer. Say very little and just remember to keep what you say as simple as possible, otherwise you can get caught out by your own detail. Do you understand?'

She was lost in her thoughts, realising just how vulnerable she was.

'Do you understand?'

Geraldine nodded. 'Sorry. I must still be tired.'

Pierre spoke with a sense of urgency. Jean had come into the room and placed a large bowl of coffee in front of her and Pierre, along with some bread and jam. Pierre gestured – 'You must eat. Now, what can you tell us about your mission?'

She sipped at the scalding coffee, which was better than anything she had tasted in England. 'The Allies will invade through the Pas de Calais. We do not know when exactly, but it must be in the next two or three months. We will get warning of the invasion. Our main task is to take part in *Plan Vert*: sabotage of the railway lines. We will plan where to blow them up. The BBC will broadcast the coded messages that will tell us when to do it, but it will be essential if we are to stop German reinforcements coming in to the area once the Allies land. Until then, the orders are to do very little. They don't want to risk us being caught before D-Day. So we will continue to undertake reconnaissance of the area, plan the exact points where we are going to plant the explosives once we get the message, and concentrate on not getting caught.'

Pierre nodded. He understood. He stood up to leave, drinking the last of his coffee before he did so.

'Jean will leave soon. He will go to work at the farm and Lucien will join him later. They will take a truck from the farm and move the supplies you brought with you to safer locations. We have a house in the village where we can keep the transmitter. Remember this map. You will leave for Boulogne after Jean leaves for work. If you have any trouble when you register with the Germans, you must stick to your story. The paperwork you have is very good and the Germans are not always as efficient as people think they are. Just act normally.'

And then, as if as a casual afterthought: 'If they don't believe you, hold out for as long as possible. That will give us time to disappear. Good luck. I will see you later.'

After Pierre left, Jean came and joined her at the table. He had opened the curtains fully and the sun was now streaming into the room. As he pulled back the curtains he released a cloud of fine dust.

Jean smiled at her as he ate his breakfast. His eyes were jet-black, like hers, and when he smiled, he had a perfect set of white teeth. He looked uncannily like the woman in the photograph. 'You don't wear your glasses all the time?'

Geraldine realised that she had forgotten to put them on. She had also forgotten to tie back her hair. From the way Jean could not take his eyes off her, she clearly did not look as plain as she did when she left England. She realised that, in her haste to dress when Pierre had arrived, the top three buttons of her shirt were undone, and Jean was trying hard not to stare at her. His own shirt was open to halfway down his chest. Any Germans bursting in now would assume they were lovers enjoying a drink and that unspoken intimacy that comes after making love.

'I will return around six this evening. The curfew starts at eight o'clock. I will bring food from the farm for us to eat. Usually I eat with the Gironds next door, but I told them I now have a lodger. Don't worry, people know better than to ask too many questions around here these days. Enjoy your day in Boulogne.'

She was surprised at how badly damaged Boulogne was. She knew that there had been air raids and it made sense that the RAF would be attacking the area ahead of the invasion, but the scale of the damage still shocked her. Apart from what she had seen in Dunkirk, the France she had left behind four years previously had been the France she had grown up in. But this place was barely recognisable as a town, let alone one in France: buildings spilled onto the pavement and the road; road signs were in German as well as French; shops stood empty; the few civilians that were around looked dishevelled and beaten, and there were German troops everywhere.

The registration at the Hôtel de Ville in the fortified part of the old town had been easy, though it had, inevitably, taken time. All of her papers were in order. She went from one desk to another to get them stamped, then had to go to the factory to have another document cleared, before returning to the Hôtel de Ville for her final clearance. At no stage did anyone ask her difficult questions. She was treated with something approaching disdain. What she was unused to was the fact that none of the men who dealt with her gave her a second look. It made her realise that for as long as she could remember, she was accustomed to that lingering stare, the smile held a bit longer than was proper, the eyes following her around a room, the eagerness to help even when it was not required. That had been part of her life for the past ten years and it occurred to her now how much she relied on it. She only realised the extent of it now that it no longer happened. Not for Geraldine Leclerc, it didn't. The thick-framed glasses held together by tape and the uncombed hair pulled back tightly had turned her into one of the anonymous grey characters inhabiting the crowd scenes of life whom she had always despised. The British, she had to admit, had done a good job with her. No one cared about Geraldine Leclerc, the thirty-year-old factory worker from Arras billeted in a small village outside Boulogne. She was anonymous, someone who would easily fade into the background.

By now it was twelve noon. Since leaving the village she had worked on the assumption that the resistance would be following her. They had little reason to suspect her; after all, they had seen her climb out of an RAF plane with their own eyes. But at the same time, she knew just how cautious they were. Her communications with Paris had been very limited since she was first approached by the SOE, but one of the messages back from them had been that she should do everything that the resistance asked of her once she arrived in France. It was critical that they suspect nothing of her. The miserable little Belgian had given her a telephone number to memorise. Once she arrived in France and it was safe to call, she was to ring that number.

Outside the Hôtel de Ville she asked an old man how she could find the post office. He turned his whole body slowly to face her, allowing his rheumy eyes time to focus on her.

'Where are you from?'

'Arras.'

He looked around. 'Is Arras as bad as this?'

'Worse.'

He shook his head. 'Head down towards the port. The Grande Rue will take you there. Not that they call it that now.'

She looked at him quizzically. He edged closer to her and lowered his voice. His hand grasped her firmly by the wrist, pulling her nearer to him.

'They now call it Rue Maréchal Pétain.' He turned round very slowly, checking no one was watching and then very deliberately spat on the pavement.

His eyes blazed at her. She was finding this tedious, but did what was expected of her and shook her head in a mildly shocked manner.

The post office was on Quai de la Poste, facing the River Liane. She parked her bike and sat on a nearby bench eating the bread and jam she had brought with her from the house, observing what activity there was around her. She would have spotted any of the people in her cell, but what concerned her was anyone else who may have been following her. If only she could get into the post office without being observed. By the side of the post office was a narrow cobbled lane. A German sentry was posted at the entrance to the lane and only allowing a few people through. If she could get through there, it was unlikely that anyone following her would risk trying to get through too. She waited until a small queue had formed in front of the sentry. A man in a cheap suit approached the sentry.

'My office is just down there, it is easier for me—'

'*Nein.*'

'I have to collect a parcel from the back of the post office, here is my ticket...'

The cheap suit was gestured through.

'I need to go to the baker's—'

'*Nein.*'

And then Geraldine. She had already removed her glasses and untied her hair, shaking it as she did so. She flashed a smile at the young sentry.

'I have to collect a parcel but don't have a ticket. They told me that if I showed them my identity card, that would do and I...'

The sentry was not looking too closely at her identity card. He looked into her eyes and smiled, which she returned, at the same time allowing her hand to brush his.

'All right. But don't get me into trouble!'

She gave him another smile and wheeled her bike through, taking care to put her glasses back on and tie back her hair. At the rear of the post office was an open door, from where she could see a man emerging with a parcel. She propped the bicycle against the wall. There was no one to be seen. She removed a plain brown headscarf from her jacket pocket, wrapped it round her head and walked in.

An elderly woman behind a window asked her for her ticket.

'I am sorry. I have left it at my office. My boss will be so angry with me.'

'Do you remember the number of the ticket?'

'No, but if I could phone him then he could give me the number.'

'I cannot let you use this phone. You must use one through there. I will let you in.'

She unlocked a door into the main part of the post office. Along the wall to her left was a bank of eight telephone booths. Three were being used. She chose one that had vacant booths on either side and turned to ensure her back was to the room.

She dialled a Paris number.

'Yes?' The person answering was speaking French, but in a strong German accent.

'Is that the dentist?'

'It is. Which tooth do you have a problem with?'

'My molar.'

'And when did it start hurting?'

'Last night. Very late last night.'

'And is anyone with you?'

'No. I am phoning from a post office. No one is near me.'

A long pause.

'Welcome back to France, Magpie. So long since we have spoken! Welcome home.'

The conversation was urgent and to the point. Where are you? Where are you staying? Who are the people you are with? Where are you working? What is your identity card number? Her answers were quick and equally to the point. She turned round once, but no one was taking any notice of her. She affected a smile, as if in a conversation with a friend or family.

'Is everything as expected?'

'Yes. They are definitely coming in through the Pas de Calais. In this area. I am part of the advance guard.'

'Good. You carry on as normal. I will come up to Boulogne in the next day or so. I will make contact with you when we know it is safe. From now on, it will be easy for you to pass information on to us.'

The whole conversation had taken no more than five minutes. She returned to the parcel office, explained that her boss could not find the ticket so she would have to return and cycled back to the village alongside the river.

As she got back on her bike, a man in his early thirties casually stepped back into a dusty shop doorway. Just in case, he covered his face by cupping his hands to light a cigarette. Anyone standing very close would have seen his pale blue eyes and brown hair momentarily catch the glint of the match. Jolly good, he thought to himself. He was carrying the blue coat he had been wearing when he waited for her inside the post office. He had made sure to turn it inside out, so only the beige lining was exposed. She was doing exactly as expected. London would be pleased to hear that. Very pleased.

-

Georg Lange had lifted up the receiver of his other phone from its cradle even before he had finished talking to Magpie.

'Get me Major Schmidt in Tirpitz Ufer,' he ordered the telephonist. This development was so important that Berlin needed to know first. Who could you trust in Paris? He stood up, preparing to talk to his superior. He had once been told that you should always stand up when making an important phone call. It gave you an air of authority apparently. At his height, that was important. He called his secretary in as he waited to be connected to Berlin.

'Gertrude.' He had lowered his voice and was cupping the receiver with his hand. 'I need to travel to Boulogne this evening. I may be there some time. Please arrange for a car and for somewhere to stay. But please be discreet. The whole of Avenue Foch does not need to know.'

'Lange?'

'Major Schmidt, a very good afternoon. I have some very good news for you. Magpie has returned to her nest. The British flew her in last night as an SOE agent. They saved us the cost of travel.' He chuckled at his own little joke.

'And where is she?' The voice in Berlin was steady.

'In Boulogne, Major. She landed in a field outside the town last night. She linked up with a small resistance cell based in a village on the outskirts of the town. She is certain that she is here to help prepare for the main Allied landings in the Pas de Calais.'

'That is excellent, Lange. Excellent. And what do you propose to do now.'

'I will travel to Boulogne myself this evening. I will be able to handle her personally.'

'Well done, Lange. We have her just where we want her!'

'Indeed, Major.'

–

As Lange prepared to travel north, Major Schmidt went to pass the good news to his superiors.

Since Admiral Canaris had been forced out of office in February, the Abwehr had become part of the SD, so it was General Walter Schellenberg who was informed of this development just before he left for a briefing with Hitler. He liked to be the bearer of good news.

London, 12th May 1944

On 12 May 1944, Dr Clarence Leigh's office in Baker Street was so crowded that he had to bring in extra chairs himself from the room next door. If his secretary had been around she would have sorted it all out, but it was a Friday afternoon and for reasons that he had never quite fathomed, she had to go and do things in the country at the weekend, which meant she was allowed to leave at Friday lunchtime. Let's hope D-Day is not on a Friday, he thought as he struggled in with another chair. At Oxford there were porters to do this kind of thing.

Apart from himself, there were Newby and Nicole from F Section, along with that frightfully self-satisfied Major Edgar, who was still acting as if he was winning the war single-handed, and another chap from the London Controlling Section. Leigh had not met Captain Archibald before, but he seemed a very different kettle of fish altogether. Quite charming. Appeared to possess manners. Very distinguished Navy man in his time, apparently.

'Rider has been in France for three weeks now. Thought it would be a useful opportunity for us to have a catch-up. See how she has been getting on.' Leigh was flabbergasted. *He* had called the meeting because SOE had concerns about the whole operation. Now Edgar was trying to take it over. In *his* office. It was *most* irregular.

Leigh cleared his throat. He was determined to be very calm.

'Major Edgar, Captain Archibald. As you know we have had to put ourselves out *considerably* to accommodate this operation. We had to find a country house we had never used before, nor will be able to use again. We had to bring in a French officer to do the training and escort her over to France. Nicole here was the principal contact with Rider, which restricts her opportunities for working directly with agents again. And we could not even fly her out from our normal base, we had to use a special airstrip.'

'We are, as you are aware, Dr Leigh, most grateful—'

'But what most concerns myself and F Section now is the *extreme* danger posed to the resistance in Nord Pas de Calais. The occupation there has been especially brutal. I am unsure if you are aware, but that region is actually run from Brussels by General von Falkenhausen and they have suffered greatly. Notwithstanding that, the FTP have—'

'FTP?' Captain Archibald asked.

'I do beg your pardon. Stands for *Francs-Tireurs et Partisans*. Key resistance organisation, even if many of them are communists. As I say, they have been very active in that area. Very well organised and disciplined. Typically they work in detachments of around thirty-five men… and women. But within each detachment, they are organised in cells and the cells do not have contact with each other. That way, we cut down the risk of people betraying other cells if they are captured.

Usually, two cells of four come under a *chef de groupe*. The chief will command one group of four and his or her *adjoint*, or assistant, will command another cell of four.

'Clearly we did not want to risk the whole resistance structure in Nord Pas de Calais, as important as this Rider operation is. So what we have done is create a new cell, which was not too difficult, as the FTP is especially strong in the Boulogne area. The cell is four strong, so Rider makes it five. And that cell now has no contact with anyone else in that detachment. The *chef de groupe* has been told this is because Rider needs to be kept isolated for reasons of D-Day security. So we believe that we have managed to protect the rest of the detachment. But in doing that, we have effectively cut that cell of four loose. That means, gentlemen, that four gallant resistance fighters are at very great risk...'

Edgar shifted impatiently in his chair and interrupted. 'But as we keep telling you, Dr Leigh, they are perfectly safe as long the Germans need them. If they touch them, then they expose Rider, and if they do that then they will stop getting all of the information that she provides.'

'Oh, we do understand that, Major Edgar. But at what point will the Germans decide they don't need Rider? An hour after D-Day starts? What is going to happen then? Will they realise that they have been deceived and arrest her along with the four people in the cell?'

Captain Archibald noticed that Dr Leigh was getting red in the face and somewhat excited. He attempted to calm things down.

'That will not be the case. Rider has already been given information alerting the Germans to the possibility that the initial Allied attack on D-Day itself will, in fact, be a feint. As soon as D-Day happens, we will reinforce that message to her. The longer we can keep that going, the better. Anything to tie the Fifteenth Army and Panzer Group West down in the Pas de Calais for as long as possible. We know from Ultra that the Germans are anticipating a feint, so we believe that they will swallow this information. If we can keep them believing that for at least a week, then we will be buying valuable time, but frankly even if it buys us a day or two it could save thousands of Allied lives.'

'And are the Germans really still buying into Pas de Calais?' Leigh was trying hard not to sound too sceptical.

Edgar nodded.

'We think so. Had a bit of a scare in February when Canaris was arrested. He seemed to believe the Pas de Calais line, mainly we think because that's what his agents like Garbo and Magpie were telling him. So as long as he was running the Abwehr, then we knew that the Pas de Calais was a favourite inside German military intelligence. It's still a bit unclear about what happened in Berlin in February. Most likely thing is that Himmler finally had enough of Canaris and got Hitler to dismiss him. Canaris is now under house arrest, so he appears to be out of the picture. We'd be surprised if he re-emerges. A chap called Walter Schellenberg who runs the SD is also looking after the Abwehr. But we don't think that this is affecting the Pas de Calais intelligence we're sending them. The most important factor is that Hitler remains convinced that the invasion will be in the Pas de Calais, and so long as he thinks that, the Pas de Calais is odds-on favourite in the Berlin bookies, so to speak. Having said that, I'm not sure what the Nazi line is on gambling.'

'And how long can you – we – keep this pretence up?' The sceptical tone was still apparent in Leigh's voice.

'Well,' said Major Edgar, 'there will be a point after D-Day – probably a few days after, possibly a couple of weeks, a bit longer if the Gods are with us – when Ultra and everything else will tell us that the Germans no longer believe that Normandy is a feint. Then they will know that there is going to be no invasion in the Pas de Calais. At that point, we tell you, and you somehow get the message to the cell to go into hiding. With some luck, that should only be for a few days.'

'And what are they meant to do with Rider?'

'That,' said Edgar, 'is up to them. If she is still around.'

Silence in the room. Leigh knew what Newby from F Section was thinking and he saw the rationale of it himself. They had taken every precaution they could, but there was a very good chance that the cell of four *résistants* in Boulogne would have to be sacrificed. Greater good and all that.

'Very well. We shall proceed on that basis.'

'And how,' asked Captain Archibald, 'is she getting on over there?'

Leigh waved his open hand in the direction of Major Newby.

'Major Newby is handling the case personally. Major?'

'She has taken to it rather splendidly. The new cell was a bit of a hotchpotch, to be honest. We weren't going to risk anyone very experienced, but she seems to have knocked them into shape. We're getting all your messages through to her loud and clear but, of course, we don't know what she is doing with them once she gets them. We assume that it is fairly easy for her to make contact with the Abwehr over there. One of our chaps is watching them from a distance so to speak. She seems to have rather taken a shine to a young man in the cell. How is her husband, by the way?'

'Missing her. Poring over his charts and drinking rather too much whisky,' said Archibald. 'Convinced they'll be back together soon and strolling arm in arm down the Champs Élysées.'

Chapter 17

Pas de Calais, 5th June 1944

By nine o'clock on the evening of Monday, 5th June 1944, the unseasonal storms that had been whipping down the Channel from the Atlantic all week and battering northern France had begun to relent. It now felt a bit more like the typical seasonal bad weather common to all coastal areas.

It was not just to the sea that anxious residents of the Nord Pas de Calais region would glance. For the past few weeks, the Allied bombing of the region had intensified. '*Bientôt*' was the word with which locals now tended to greet each other when they were certain they were out of the earshot of any Germans. '*Ce sera très bientôt.*' 'It will be very soon.'

In the village of Hesdin-l'Abbé, five miles south of the port of Boulogne, a young man and woman were walking arm in arm by the side of the Rue du Mont de Thunes. Although the road was normally quiet, dozens of German troops were billeted in the village and their lorries and cars had a habit of speeding along with their lights too dim, so the couple chose to wheel their bicycles along the side of the road. To their right, the grey steeple of the seventeenth-century church of St Leger loomed in the distance. To their left was Château Cléry, where the villagers swore that Napoleon had once stayed – though it would be an unusual French village if there was no property to claim a visit, however brief, from the Emperor. Now, the château was the residence of German officers. The village began to merge into the countryside and opposite one of the rich ploughed fields that sustained the area was a row of five detached houses, more substantial than the others in the village. The couple paused and fell into each other's arms, holding the embrace just long enough to be able to observe over each other's shoulders that all was clear. Satisfied that it was, they turned sharply into the narrow driveway of the second house, which was shielded from the road and its neighbours by tall rows of conifers.

As the couple approached the side entrance of the house, the door opened. They were expected. They silently acknowledged the elderly lady behind the door, propped their bikes behind the curtained alcove in the hallway and climbed two flights of stairs. On the upper landing the man picked up a broom resting against a wall and gently tapped the trapdoor above his head. Two taps, a pause and two more taps.

The trapdoor opened and a ladder lowered to the ground. The couple climbed into the attic to join an older man in there. They nodded to each other.

'You are both all right? Certain you weren't followed?' said the older man.

'Pierre, trust us. You always ask.'

'And I will continue to do so, Jean. Geraldine, how are you?'

She said she was fine as she made sure the trapdoor was firmly closed. Pierre fiddled with the dial on the radio in front of him, Geraldine adjusted the aerial in the rafters of the roof and Jean slipped the safety catch off the American Colt automatic pistol that they had only had for two weeks and were yet to use.

Within a minute they were tuned into the BBC French programme. Listening to this programme in a nearby house the previous Thursday, Pierre had heard the message:

L'heure des combats viendra.

'The hour of battle will come.' The invasion was imminent. The message was telling the resistance that the invasion would take place in the next fifteen days. That night he had risked breaking the curfew to inform as many of the others as he safely could. From then on, at least three of them would listen to the broadcasts every night.

The following night, 2nd June, they had heard the next message:

Les sanglots lourds
Des violons
L'automne.

It was the first three lines of a poem by Verlaine. The schoolteacher had questioned why the poem was not being quoted accurately. There are two mistakes, he said. '*Don't worry,*' Geraldine had reassured him. '*You're not in the classroom now.*' They knew that when they heard the next lines of the poem, that would be the signal that the invasion would take place the following day.

Now, three nights later, they were crouched in the attic, the dusty history of a family's life stacked around them. Tennis racquets, children's toys, old clothes, a chair without a seat and, wrapped in brown paper, parcels of the resistance newspaper, *La Voix du Nord.*

The three of them gathered as close as they could to the radio, the volume so low that they could only just hear it. If the Germans were going to detect them, it would be because of the radio's signal rather than any noise, but old habits were hard to break.

The dial of the radio threw up just enough yellow light to catch their faces. Pierre's lined and tanned, someone who had spent a lifetime catching the sea breeze. Jean was tense, chewing his fingers, his dark hair dropping over his eyes as he listened to the broadcast. Geraldine still wore the scarf she had been wearing outside, her hair flowing from under it, her dark eyes managing to pierce through the gloom.

The broadcasts comprised of a series of coded messages to the French resistance. Each of the messages would be meaningless to anyone else listening, even to other resistance groups. But for the particular group that each message was aimed at, the meaning would be very clear. Tonight, the messages were preceded by an announcement:

> *Today the Supreme Commander directs me to say this: in due course, instructions of great importance will be given to you through this channel, but it will not be possible always to give these instructions at a previously announced time. Therefore, you must get into the habit of listening at all hours.*

The list of messages then followed. Normally, this would last five minutes, certainly never longer than ten. But tonight, the list of messages lasted for an unprecedented twenty minutes. The final message caused hairs to stand on the backs of necks and tears to well in eyes throughout occupied France:

It was the lines of the Verlaine poem: 'Wound my heart/With a monotonous languor.'

The two men clasped each other's right hand. Pierre bit his lower lip and inclined his head away from the other two. Jean put his left arm round Geraldine, gently caressing her shoulder and pulling her towards him. She looked at him with her piercing black eyes and with her long fingernails, carefully flicked a tear from his face. She nodded and spoke one word.

'*Demain*.' Tomorrow.

From the vineyards of Bordeaux to the arrondissements of Paris, from the coalfields of the north east to the châteaux of the Loire, from the Pyrenees to the restaurants of Lyon, and from the villas of Provence to the great cathedral cities of Chartres and Rouen, groups of *résistants* who had kept the flame of France flickering – some for as long as four years – knew the same as the small group crammed in the attic in the Pas de Calais.

The liberation of France would begin tomorrow.

Paris, 5th June 1944

The *résistants* were not the only people in France listening to the BBC broadcast that night and understanding its deep significance. One hundred and seventy miles south of where the little group in the Pas de Calais were gathered round the radio in their attic, a slight, bespectacled man was doing the same in a more comfortable room in the lee of the Arc de Triomphe.

Avenue Foch was one of the twelve avenues branching out from the Place de l'Étoile in the centre of Paris, and 72 Avenue Foch housed the substantial headquarters of two much-feared organisations: the secret police, known as the Gestapo, and the *Sicherheitsdienst* – the security service, known to its few friends and many enemies as the SD. As head of the SD's radio monitoring section, Karl-Heinz Gratz was certainly no admirer of the BBC, but for the past few weeks, even months, he had been doing little else but listen to its broadcasts. Fourteen hours a day, seven days a week. He was now starting to hear the broadcasts in his sleep. Even when he was awake, he found it difficult to get the annoying *di-di-di-dah* refrain from Beethoven's Fifth that the BBC used to announce the broadcasts out of his head.

Ironic, he thought, using the music of a good German like that!

The Gestapo and the SD had tortured just enough information out of captured resistance fighters in the dungeons below Avenue Foch for

Gratz to be aware of what to listen for. Tonight he had sat through the twenty minutes of coded messages, scribbling furiously on his notepad as he did so. The messages had never lasted so long. That morning he felt he had reached a point of exhaustion, now he knew that he would certainly be up all night and probably well into the next day. He could feel a sense of excitement which he did not really understand, tempered by a feeling of fear, which he did understand.

For one brief moment he pulled off his headphones and yelled 'Jürgen!', but his young assistant was probably asleep, again. No stamina, these young people. His heart was beating so fast that he had to turn up the volume on the radio. He could hear the sound of laughter in the corridor and there seemed to be some kind of party or gathering in a nearby office. That would all end very soon.

When the broadcast ended, Gratz pulled off his headphones, sat still for a moment and then banged the desk with his fist, shouting:

'*Ja. So ist es. Das es bevorstehend.*' So that is it. It is imminent.

Within minutes, 72 Avenue Foch had sprung into life. People ran from office to office, shouting at one another, desperate calls were made to try to raise senior German officers from the beds of their French mistresses. 'Most Urgent' messages were sent to Army headquarters in Berlin and to the different German Army groups in France. Gratz stood in the entrance to his office, watching the chaos take hold around him. He was like a schoolboy who had mischievously pressed a fire alarm, not imagining what the consequences would be. Two SS colonels pushed past him. Field Marshal Rommel, it seemed, was back home in Germany, celebrating his wife's fiftieth birthday. The invasion is imminent. Some birthday present.

At eleven o'clock that night Gratz stood at the large window in his office, looking down Avenue Foch towards the Arc de Triomphe in the centre of the Place de l'Étoile. The great symbol of French republicanism now had long been overshadowed by an enormous swastika hanging inside the arch. The flag was picked out by the spotlights trained on it, swaying awkwardly in the breeze as if it knew it was an imposter. Paris was the favourite posting for Germans. Gratz knew that it could soon be over.

He took a deep breath, and as he exhaled allowed an ironic '*Heil Hitler!*' to pass his lips, although not before carefully glancing over his shoulder to be certain that he was alone in the room.

Chapter 18

London, 6th June 1944

Owen Quinn woke with a start from a deep sleep on the morning of that first Tuesday in June. He would not sleep properly again for the next eight months.

Bright shafts of light pierced the blackout and the curtains. He had overslept, and the two-thirds-empty Talisker bottle on the floor by the bed was part of the reason why.

According to the bedside clock it was just after a quarter past nine. The alarm had not been set for its normal time of a quarter to seven. He should have been in work over an hour ago.

As his body reached that moment where it was more awake than asleep, he began to remember. Yesterday had seen a never-ending stream of charts and weather reports, a sense of growing urgency, whispered conversations in the corridor, 'all hands to the pump, chaps', even more photographs arriving by the hour.

Unfamiliar faces appearing in the office, little time to chat with those he knew. Security at the highest state of alert. On Monday, he had been stopped three times by security between entering the building and arriving in his office. A military policeman was outside all day. And the WRENS – with their smart uniforms and busy manner – they were a sure sign something was up. He and the others were told they weren't to waste precious time gathering files. Then the midnight finish. The office had filled with uniforms during the evening, and it was the familiar one of Captain John Archibald who took him aside as he was about to leave.

'Good work today, Quinn. Not long now. Looks like we may have cracked it. Top brass happy. Done our part. You've been splendid. Lieutenant Commander Quinn before you know it!'

Archibald always talked a bit louder than necessary and in short phrases rather than proper sentences. It was a result of years at sea, where it was hard for someone to hear you, so he had learned to be spare with words. Owen Quinn knew the feeling. Archibald had a noisy cough and had to pause to catch his breath.

'Take this, Quinn, and enjoy it. You deserve it. Late start tomorrow. Need to let security check the place out, so best keep out of their way until noon.' Archibald had pressed a bottle into his hands.

Quinn glanced down and saw it was whisky. He was grateful, but suspected he would drink far too much of it. He checked the label. Talisker. A malt meant it was serious.

As Quinn turned to leave, John Archibald did something which at the time struck him as unusual. It would be some hours before he began to realise the true significance of it.

The elder man gently held Quinn by the elbow and guided him towards the empty cloakroom, looking over his shoulder as he did so. When he spoke, it was in an unusually quiet voice.

'Good luck, Quinn.' He was shaking his hand now, placing his left hand over Quinn's wrist as he did so.

'I may not be around here for a few weeks, but all the very best, Quinn. Whatever happens, remember you've played your part.'

In the two and a half years that he had known him, Captain John Archibald had always behaved in a proper manner. He was spare in his emotions – not exactly cold, but not very far from it either. But tonight, as he released his grip, Quinn could have sworn that he detected a catch in Archibald's voice.

Realising now that he had not overslept, Quinn's panic subsided. He stretched out, his right arm swinging over to the empty side of the bed, a cold reminder of her absence. The pillow next to him was still plump. For a few weeks after she had gone, he could still smell her on it. Now, he could not be sure if the increasingly rare hints of her scent were just in his imagination. There had been times during the torment of a restless night when he had sunk his face into her pillow and would wake up in the morning to find it still damp.

He waited for the pain in his back and his leg to ease before slowly getting up. That is what the doctors had told him. Your first movements of the day will be critical. Stretch out when you wake up, wait and then get out of bed. Slowly. No sudden movements. When the bed wasn't empty there had been less chance of that in the mornings, when Nathalie had been at her most attentive. He had even fallen into the habit of setting his alarm twenty minutes early. Since she had gone, his back had felt much better and he always arrived at work on time.

He started to run the bath in what he expected was the forlorn hope that there would be hot water actually coinciding with the time when he wanted a bath. You took your chances when you could with the hot water, in the same way that you did with everything else that was in short supply. After nearly five years of war, that covered most things.

The water ran cold. Quinn pulled on his dressing gown, unaccustomed to this enforced relaxation on a weekday morning.

This was when he missed her most, the unplanned moments when there was little to do. He was fine when he was busy, which was most of the time, or exhausted, which often accounted for the rest of the time. As long as he had a schedule to work to, he could cope. But quiet moments like this, on his own in the flat, walking by the river or awake in bed – they were the hardest. Then, he could not avoid his thoughts; there was nothing to distract him, nothing to stop him reflecting on what he would have said had she been there and how she might have replied. She had only been away for a matter of weeks, but it was beginning to feel as if it was far longer than that. At times, he struggled to remember the tone of her voice, the way her eyes dazzled as she came into a room and her scent that lingered long after she had left. He was worried that his memories of her were fading away. He would then get angry at himself for being irrational and maudlin; it was uncharacteristic. Then he'd shrug it off and get on with life. *It won't be long now.*

The tiny kitchen was just a galley area off the lounge, so Quinn was able to sit in the elderly armchair that had come with the flat, and would remain long after he and Nathalie had left it. As he waited for the kettle to boil, Quinn turned the radio on. For a while, the noise of the kettle struggling to the boil blended with the crackle of the radio as it was tuned to the BBC Home Service. For a few seconds, it merged into one confusing sound.

The kettle whistled, the music on the BBC flooded into the room and Quinn began to feel relaxed. The pains in his leg and back were still there, but the stiffness after a night's sleep was easing off, and soon he would be able to take the first of his tablets. He made a large mug of tea, shovelled in two teaspoonfuls of sugar, hesitated, and then added a third. The toast could wait. He would listen to the radio, have his breakfast, shave, try the bath again, and stroll into work with plenty of time to spare. He began to feel relaxed. From what Archibald had hinted last night, from all the activity he had seen around him and from what he had heard, it felt that the war could be over soon. Not as soon as everyone hoped and some expected, but possibly by the end of the year and certainly within a year. By then Nathalie would be back and they could lead a normal life for the first time.

The hot, sweet tea was making him feel quite optimistic and even happy. On the radio, the music was fading and a familiar voice was taking over. Quinn placed his mug on the small table in front of him and turned up the volume on the radio.

> *This is the BBC Home Service – and here is a special bulletin read by John Snagge. D-Day has come. Early this morning the Allies began the assault on the north-western face of Hitler's European fortress. The first official news came just after half past nine, when Supreme Headquarters of the Allied Expeditionary Force issued Communiqué Number One. This said: 'Under the command of General Eisenhower, Allied naval forces, supported by strong air forces, began landing Allied armies this morning on the northern coast of France.'*

Quinn could not be sure how long he had sat there. Certainly, by the time he reached for his mug, the tea had turned stone-cold and an unpleasant film had appeared on the surface. '*D-Day has come.*' Those words were going round in his head. He should have been euphoric, but instead he found himself feeling uneasy at first and then confused. D-Day was what he had been working on for more than a year. He had devoted most of his waking hours to its preparation and for the last three months his wife had been even more deeply involved in it. But any sense of relief or excitement was dampened by a sense of unease. The Allied assault, the broadcast had said, was on the '*north-western face of Hitler's European fortress*'. What did this mean? Could they really have made a mistake in such an important broadcast? It could be a deliberate mistake. Maybe he was reading too much into it. After all, the statement had gone on to say that Allied forces had landed '*on the northern coast of France*', but the northern coast of France stretched from Dunkirk on the Belgian border across to where Brittany fell into the Atlantic. The north-western edge of Nazi-occupied Europe. Every word of the first official announcement of D-Day would have been carefully weighed and considered and referred to a sub-committee. Quinn had a good idea of how these matters were dealt with. Why would they say 'north west' when, as Quinn knew only too well, the real assault was taking place many hundreds of miles further up the coast, in the Pas de Calais?

There was no point in worrying, he decided. He worried too much. The important thing was that it would be over soon.

The boiler in the large house in Alderney Street was evidently aware that it was D-Day and Quinn found he had enough water for his first deep and truly hot bath for weeks. He shaved, made himself some toast on the grill that hadn't been properly cleaned since she left, had another mug of sweet tea, and put on his dark blue naval uniform.

Owen Quinn left his flat in Pimlico just before eleven and set off on the two-mile walk to Duke Street in St James's. When he first began this job, he had been told at his security briefing to vary his route to and from work. It was advice that Quinn happily adhered to. He preferred to walk, the exercise helping his back, though he would take the bus if it was raining. Depending on when he left the flat, he could take the more direct route through the heart of Victoria, across St James's Park and then over Pall Mall. Or he could take a more roundabout route, heading for the river, down Millbank, past the Houses of Parliament and then down Whitehall. This was the route he was most likely to be stopped on, especially if he tried to cross St James's Square. Sometimes it would be for a security check, or because the road was closed, but Quinn's pass usually saw him through. Or he could take a middle route. Or a combination, sometimes doubling back on himself just to be absolutely sure he was not being followed, and occasionally darting into a turning he had never used before just to vary the routine. He was, after all, a navigation expert.

By the time he set off, any doubts caused by the wording of the broadcast had dissipated and there was a spring in his step. Even though it was the same way he had gone the previous day, Quinn broke the habit of a year and took the same, direct route. That morning he arrived at the office in Lincoln House twenty minutes before midday.

There was no familiar face among the guards on the ground floor of Lincoln House that morning. That was unusual, but not unprecedented. Sometimes they would bring in a new unit, so Quinn thought nothing of it at first. There was none of the good cheer and bonhomie from familiar faces, no 'Good morning, Lieutenant. Not too much of a crosswind I hope, sir', which he would affect to be amused by as if it was the first time he had heard it. Instead the lance corporal who took his pass handed it straight to a corporal who asked him to 'Wait here a moment if you don't mind, sir' and who then disappeared in through the door of the guardroom.

After five minutes, Quinn became mildly irritated. Never before had he had to wait in the reception area of the building where he worked, and his enquiry of the lance corporal if there was any problem was met with a dismissive 'I wouldn't have thought so, sir.'

He sat down in the small reception area, the guards managing the feat of keeping an eye on him while avoiding any form of eye contact. They were trained to do that, he told himself. That and handling clipboards. The metal chair was uncomfortable. He had walked fast and now he was feeling the familiar twinges in his back and a dull ache in his leg.

By the time he had been kept waiting for twenty minutes, his irritation had turned to an ill-concealed exasperation, which was studiously ignored by the guards.

Five minutes later, the corporal returned, along with a sergeant wearing the distinctive uniform and red cap of the military police. 'If you care to come with me, Lieutenant Quinn, we'll have this sorted in no time. Just a small problem with your pass, sir.' He was being passed through the ranks.

Quinn followed the sergeant up the stairs, past the first floor, through whose heavy doors he had once heard people talking in German, beyond the second and third floors where he had never seen the doors anything but firmly shut, past the fourth floor which always had a sentry on the stairwell, and past the fifth floor where the door was sometimes ajar and through which he had seen a mass of electrical equipment. As they approached his office on the sixth floor, two guards carrying large boxes were coming down the stairs, forcing Quinn and the military policeman to go in single file, pressed against the wall. Quinn found himself ahead of the officer, who had had to step further back to allow the guards more space to descend.

Quinn pushed his way into the entrance to the sixth-floor offices, half hearing but ignoring the sergeant's cry of 'Not in there please, Lieutenant.' By the time the sergeant had caught up with him, he realised why. He was clearly not meant to see this. The large central room, from which three small offices led, was deserted. The walls, which twelve hours before had been covered in charts and maps and photographs, were bare. The large map table in the centre of the room had been disassembled and was propped against the heavily barred windows. The filing cabinets containing thousands of photographs were gone, as were the boxes of letters, postcards and other documents. There was a box in the centre of the room full of black phones and alongside it were the two large office clocks. One of the clocks had always been on Greenwich Mean Time, the other on Central European Time. One clock had stopped just after three, the other just after four.

'Please, sir, not in here.'

'But this is my office.'

'I'm afraid we need to go up another flight of stairs to get this sorted, sir.'

'But I don't understand!'

Quinn had moved into the centre of the large room now, puzzled and determined to see what had become of his own small office. He moved quickly across the scuffed green linoleum floor to escape the attentions of the sergeant who was now at his shoulder, but as he did so he found his way blocked by a familiar figure dressed in a black greatcoat, towering well above his own six-foot frame.

'Captain Edgar!'

The tall man nodded to the sergeant. 'Leave it to me.'

And then to Quinn. 'Not happy with you bounding ahead like that, Quinn. Having a bit of a clear-out in here as you can see. Sergeant had instructions to bring you to the top floor. And by the way, it's Major Edgar now.'

From his very first encounter with Edgar in the hospital two years previously, any dealings with him had had an edge of menace to them. Had he been asked to explain that in more detail, Quinn would have struggled. He would have talked about the major's coldness, about his quiet voice with no discernible accent that nonetheless appeared to dominate the room. He would have remarked on the fact that, despite having met the major a number of times, he found it almost impossible to recall in any significant detail any of his physical characteristics, other than his height. But most of all, he would have recalled the feeling of near-fear that he instilled in Quinn. No threats, certainly no violence, but an overwhelming sense that anything the major asked or required was beyond discussion. The effect was almost hypnotic.

By now the major had led Quinn out of the sixth-floor suite of offices which had been his life for the past two years and out into the stairwell. The major hesitated, looking up towards the seventh floor, where Quinn had never been.

'I'll tell you what, Quinn. Let's go for a walk.'

Outside in Duke Street, the major fixed his familiar trilby to his head in a precise manner, twisting it carefully so it sat just right. He wore it lower than Quinn had observed in other people and the brim of the hat appeared to be wider than usual. The effect was to cast much of the major's face in shadow.

They headed south, across Pall Mall and The Mall, entering St James's Park near the bandstand. The walk had been conducted in studied silence, but throughout it Quinn kept thinking of what Captain Archibald had said the previous evening, 'I may not be around here for a few weeks, but all the very best, Quinn. Whatever happens, remember you've played your part.' And now, the abandoned office, along with the BBC announcement of D-Day and the reference to the north west of France. The sense of unease that Quinn had felt when he first heard the BBC broadcast in the flat had returned.

They strolled down to the lake, still silent as they had been since leaving Lincoln House, apart from Major Edgar's occasional cough. And so they stood, their backs to The Mall, facing the lake, silent for a good two minutes.

When the major did start to speak it was in his usual quiet voice. The noise of the city around them obliged Quinn to shuffle closer to Edgar than he felt entirely comfortable with, but he did not want to miss a word.

'Quinn. I want you to listen very carefully to what I am about to say. I don't expect you will like one word of it, and I have no doubt that by the time I have finished speaking you will hate me. But it is important that you listen, take it all in, and then forget the last two years and get on with your life.'

Major Edgar paused as two men in bowler hats got up from a bench to their right. As they moved away, Edgar gestured towards the bench and that is where they sat for the next twenty minutes.

During that time, the major spoke in his quiet, commanding tone, leaning forward for most of the time, his elbows resting on his thighs as he looked around him, anywhere other than directly at Quinn. Quinn had to lean forward himself to catch every word. To a passer-by, it may have looked as if an impromptu confession was taking place, which was perhaps not too far from the truth.

'You have obviously heard the news, Quinn. The landings?'

Quinn nodded. *Of course.*

'I need to tell you something, and from your point of view, it's not going to be very pleasant.'

There was a pause while Edgar carefully straightened his shirt cuffs and adjusted his tie, while at the same time nervously prodding away some gravel with the tip of his highly polished shoe. He coughed and shifted on the bench.

'How long is it now since you've seen your wife, Owen?'

Quinn looked puzzled. This was not what he imagined they had come here to talk about.

'Six… seven weeks? Something like that.'

'And, of course, you only saw her intermittently in the months immediately before that?'

'While she was training, yes.'

'I expect you miss her.'

Quinn looked unsure. Edgar was not the kind of person he imagined having a conversation like this with.

'Well, of course. Naturally.'

'Have you… adapted to her not being around?'

'Well, I cope, if that's what you mean. But I do miss her an awful lot. Perhaps more than I expected. Look, I'm not sure why you're asking me these questions.'

'Owen, I have to tell you that Nathalie is not who you think she is. We do not know her real name, but it is certainly not Nathalie Mercier. What we do know is that she did enter this country in June 1940 with that identity. She is indeed a nurse. There is no easy way of saying this, but I have to tell you that she came here as a German spy…'

There was silence and no movement from Quinn's end of the bench. Edgar glanced over at him; he had been expecting more of a reaction than this. The younger man had a puzzled expression on his face, as if he had trouble hearing what Edgar had said. Edgar wondered whether he needed to repeat it. The silence was broken by a pair of ducks waddling noisily in front of them, arguing furiously.

Quinn's brow was starting to furrow now as first disbelief and then anger appeared to take hold. He was shaking his head.

'No, no – don't be so bloody ridiculous, Edgar!' Quinn stood up, then rapidly sat down again, but hesitantly, as if he were about to stand up again. 'If you think I've come here to listen to nonsense like this then—'

'Listen Quinn – Owen. I know this is hard, but as it is I am telling you more than I should. Just listen. It may be the only time you hear it.' Edgar had adopted a firm tone. He could not afford to leave Quinn in any doubt about what he was saying.

'We became aware that your wife is a German spy only very recently. Certainly after she was sent to France – goes without saying, of course, that we wouldn't have sent her over there if we'd known she was a German spy. I cannot tell you much, but I can tell you this: soon after she arrived in France we came across certain intelligence that made us suspect her. You have to trust me, Owen. We checked this intelligence out most carefully. We had to be sure and I am afraid that we are. We've been back over her movements since she arrived in this country and I can tell you that there is no doubt about it. We feel pretty bad about it, as I'm sure you do. But at least we've found out now, or rather a few weeks ago. If we hadn't done so then I think the consequences could have been quite dreadful.'

Owen laughed.

'Oh, I see! And they aren't "quite dreadful", as you put it, now?'

Edgar shifted uncomfortably at his end of the bench, holding his hands out in front of him in a conciliatory manner.

'Of course they are dreadful for you, Quinn. I am sorry. We're not fools. I don't want you to think that we are being insensitive to your predicament. We can see that you are going to be absolutely devastated. But it is better to know than not to know, eh?'

Quinn was not so sure. As far as he was concerned, ignorance was bliss – at least it had been up until a few minutes ago. He didn't know what to make of what Edgar was telling him. It sounded so far-fetched as far as he was concerned, but then why would Edgar concoct such a ridiculous story? He was not sure what Edgar meant and he could not even be sure that what he was being told was true.

'And who was she supposed to be spying on – me?'

'Quite possibly. Until – if – we get the chance to interrogate her, we simply won't know. We don't know if she was spying on you, or just trying to get into a position where we recruited her. As I say, we only discovered that she's a spy a few weeks ago.'

'And is all this connected to the Normandy business?'

'What do you mean, Quinn?'

'Well, the invasion started a few hours ago in Normandy, apparently. Everything I've been working on has been on the assumption that the invasion would be in the Pas de Calais. So what's going on, Edgar? And where is Nathalie? In Normandy or the Pas de Calais?'

Edgar made to speak and then hesitated, as if he had not been expecting this question.

'She could be anywhere in France, Owen. I can't tell you any more than that and nor would you expect me to. As to the Pas de Calais, well… all I can say is that the D-Day operation is barely twelve hours old. It is far too early to say what is going to happen when… and where.'

More silence from Quinn's end of the bench. Edgar shot him another glance and noticed that his eyes were moist and he was blinking rapidly. He appeared to be in shock and was tapping his feet on the ground. Quinn pulled a long white handkerchief from his uniform pocket and blew his nose.

'So why are you telling me all of this, Edgar? Why didn't you continue to keep me in the dark like you seemed happy enough to do since you apparently discovered she was a spy a few weeks ago?'

'We are telling you now because you need to be aware of it. If I am to be absolutely honest with you, Owen, then I would have to admit that we weren't going to tell you quite so soon. But something unexpected cropped up today that meant we needed to tell you much sooner than we had planned.'

'And what is that?'

'There is a German spy loose in London. Elusive chap, this one. We've prided ourselves on having a pretty outstanding success rate in capturing German spies in this country, but not him. We've been after him since 1940, never been able to get our hands on him. From a professional point of view, one has to admire him. He is quite an outstanding operator. Caused us no end of trouble. However, a few weeks ago, we spotted him tailing you, just after we discovered your wife was a spy. What we think happened is this: the Germans wanted to be sure that what your wife was telling them was true, so they got this chap to verify you really do exist – that you work where she was telling them you worked, in the Navy – that kind of thing.

'A week or so ago, this agent disappeared into the ether again, as he is prone to do. However, this morning we intercepted a transmission he made to Berlin. Couple of hours later he's spotted near your flat. Had to wait around, of course, but once you left at eleven he followed you all the way to Duke Street. It was important that you came into work.'

Quinn was looking round the park. He had stopped dabbing his eyes now, but they were still red and damp.

'And what about if he has followed us here?'

'Of course not, wouldn't have been so foolish as to bring you here if he had, would I? We watched him follow you to Duke Street then he hopped in a taxi and headed north. My bet is that even as we are speaking he will be making his final transmission from his place in north London, then he will head off to a new place. He probably has two or three on the go at any one time. He'll be back on to you, Quinn. Probably go and check you're around this evening and then be out there in the morning. Which brings me back to why we need you to play ball with us.'

The younger man huffed and pulled a face.

'I do understand, Quinn. I daresay that is the last thing you feel like doing. We need you to do this. I am afraid that you really have no alternative – regard it as orders. Please listen carefully.'

Edgar outlined the plan. It was quite detailed. Quinn was surprised that he was able to take it all in. Edgar looked across at Quinn, as if to check that he understood.

'I'll have to be heading off soon, Quinn – you know what you have to do then.'

Edgar was leaning forward, his forearms resting on his thighs, hands pressed together in his familiar prayer-like pose and head bowed towards the ground. Quinn was very still again, speaking in a quiet voice, with no trace of either the anger or the sarcasm that he had shown before.

'You are certain about this, Edgar – Nathalie and all that?'

'I am afraid so.'

The younger man stared ahead, the emotion appearing to rise up in him again. He was biting his lower lip and clasping his hands together very tight. Another long spell of silence followed as he sank deep into contemplation. The pair of ducks walked in front of them again, their argument unresolved. Edgar and Quinn watched them as they noisily climbed back into the lake before Quinn spoke again.

'If… and I say *if*… *if* it's true what you say, where do you think that leaves me? Do you think that any of her feelings for me could have been genuine?'

'I think that only she can answer that, Quinn. We have to assume that her relationship with you was part of her work as a German spy. That doesn't mean, of course… that…' Edgar stopped. He really did not know what to say.

'I presume you had… marital relations? I mean, did you have a healthy physical relationship?'

Quinn blushed and nodded.

'There we are then. Look, you are a good-looking chap. Good personality, charming. I am sure she had feelings for you.'

When he had finished talking, the major leaned back against the bench, his hands pressed together in his familiar prayer-like pose, looking up at the white clouds picked out against the blue sky. Quinn sat perfectly still. They stayed like that while nearby bells pealed two o'clock. As if on cue, Major Edgar got up and stood awkwardly in front of Quinn, patting him gently on the shoulder before silently walking away.

Quinn waited a moment before turning round to watch Edgar walk back to The Mall. A black car was waiting and as Edgar approached it, a uniformed figure emerged to open the rear door for the major. Within seconds the car had sped off in the direction of Whitehall.

Quinn turned round and started to get up, but his legs felt so heavy that he was unable to move. He was weighed down by his thoughts. Recollections of times he had spent with Nathalie, snippets of what Edgar had said and flashbacks to his childhood, but as these memories evaporated he was left with the stark reality of what Edgar had told him. Although it seemed unbelievable, he kept coming back to the conclusion that Edgar would not have made it up. There would simply be nothing to be gained from telling him something untrue.

He stayed on the bench in a state of shock until three o'clock, and when a policeman who had already passed him twice asked pointedly if everything was well, Owen said that it was and got up slowly to leave the park.

Quinn was far too wrapped up in his own thoughts to notice anything that was going on around him. He certainly never noticed the small man watching him from the bridge to the right of where he had been sitting. He might be described as 'round' rather than 'fat' by anyone who looked at him long enough, which few would bother to do. His red face was topped by a bowler hat perhaps one size too small. He effortlessly slipped in some fifty yards behind Quinn.

Quinn never turned round as he left the park and crossed Birdcage Walk, but even had he done so, it is highly unlikely that he would have noticed that same man following him from a careful distance.

Chapter 19

His initial thoughts in the first few seconds after he awoke were always about who he was. A few days previously, he had attended a lecture in London on existentialism. 'Who Are We?' it was called, and he sat, amused, at the back of the hall, smiling at the thought of the earnest audience worrying about their purpose in life and who they really were.

You want to try being me. You want to know what it is like to have to be a different person every few weeks, to be constantly changing your identity. And try keeping that up for years.

After all that time, the effort of remembering who he was each day was beginning to exhaust him.

He had never before heard the telephone ring in the main hall of the house at that time of the morning. From his bedsit on the first floor the sound reverberated across the hall with its chipped and noisy floor tiles, up the pretentiously ornate staircase with its cheaply varnished banisters and missing balustrades and along the threadbare carpet to his room, the acoustics making it sound as loud as if the phone was ringing outside his door, rather than some way below it. The first ring came at six in the morning. Two shrill blasts, then silence. He turned over to go back to sleep and realised he was not alone. Whoever it was, she was fast asleep and did not look nearly as attractive as she must have done the night before, which was usually the case. Through the prism of a glass, they all acquired a flattering sheen at some stage of the evening. Daresay they thought the same of him. He would not learn his lesson, but from what he could recall, and from the state of the bedclothes, it had probably been worth it.

Something beginning with 'S', he seemed to remember. Not Susie, not Sheila – though there had been a Sheila not that long ago. Sheila from Stockwell. Sandra? Could be Sandra. Sandra was in a deep sleep, lying on her back, head tilted back on the pillow at an odd angle, mouth slightly open, the make-up which she had not bothered to remove smeared across her face and the pillow case, and probably somewhere on him too. The sheets were gathered around the top of her thighs.

He lay there for a moment, contemplating her breasts and the nipples which were somehow still hard. Maybe, if he was very…

The phone rang again. Just the two shrill blasts. He looked at his watch. Five past six. He wondered. No. Not possible. Impossible, in fact. Only in a dire emergency.

He touched the small strip of flat bone between Sandra's breasts, though he was now not sure if it was Sandra after all. Maybe Stephanie. It didn't matter if you couldn't remember the right name, just so long as you did not use the *wrong* one. He walked his fingers slowly down her body, a light touch at first, then firmer. She started to respond in her sleep, writhing at first. His hand was just past her belly button when she began to wake up, trapping his hand between her legs. She opened her eyes and turned over to face him, her wide smile revealing teeth stained with a cheap lipstick. Some of her eyelashes were stuck together with blobs of mascara and she reeked of cigarettes. He had seen better in the hardest bars in Hamburg, but once they started to respond, it didn't matter. She pulled him towards her.

Three more blasts of the phone.

This time there could be no mistaking it. Two normal rings then the phone cutting off halfway between the next two. Three rings. And exactly five minutes after the last call. He could hear Mr Fraser come out of his downstairs flat and talk angrily as he answered the phone.

'Hello? Hello… anyone there?'

There wouldn't be.

She was working hard on him now. No subtlety but plenty of experience to compensate. She made him respond soon enough. He was already inside her and could be finished in a minute if he wanted. He always could in the morning. Two more minutes and he could even satisfy her, which was not necessary but always a bonus nonetheless. Helped ensure a return visit, was how he liked to put it. But the phone calls had signalled something more urgent. He did not even have one minute.

He pulled out of her quickly, roughly pushing her hands away as she tried to coax him back in.

'You have to leave now.'

'What! At this time of the morning? Who was it who was all over me a minute ago? You woke me up for it!'

'You have to leave. You must go now.'

He was out of bed now, naked.

'I can see you still want it…'

He walked round to her side of the bed and hauled her out of it, quite roughly. He picked up her clothes from the pile by her side of the bed and thrust them at her.

'I am sorry. I suddenly realised I was late for something. You must go. Here, take this.' He had picked up his wallet from the desk and handed her a one pound note.

'What kind of a girl do you take me for?'

'I take you for a very nice girl who I would like to see again and take out for dinner. This is for a taxi.'

'Crikey. I could buy a taxi with that. Where am I going to get a taxi at this time in the morning?'

'Please be quiet on your way out. Look…' He wondered whether to try using the name Stephanie, but in the circumstances it was too great a risk, getting her name wrong. '…I promise I will come and visit you at the bar tonight, and I promise I will take you to dinner at the restaurant of your choice.'

'You promise?'

'Of course.' The easiest thing in the world was making a promise that you had no intention of keeping. You just… promised. It was what he did.

He waited until she was out of the front door and watched her disappear down the street. Of course, Mr Fraser would not be happy about this. Even now he would be writing down what time she had left in his little notebook in his spidery handwriting ('I have the evidence here, Mr White, in my own fair *hand*'). He preferred landladies; he could always count on being able to charm his way around any woman. But Mr Fraser and charm lived in different worlds.

'You know it is quite against my rules for you to have visitors…' he would say.

So far, a pound or two pressed into Mr Fraser's bony hands had worked. Probably wouldn't again, but it didn't matter. He would have to be out of this place before noon anyway. That was the procedure: if you get the emergency signal, get out within six hours. The sooner the better.

He checked that the door was locked, then slid the extra bolt into place, used his overcoat to cover the gap at the bottom of the door and moved the dresser away from the window. The floorboards opened easily enough, as he had made sure they would. The radio was on the dresser now. He hooked the aerial high inside the window, just inside the net curtains and turned it on. He was connected surprisingly quickly. He scribbled the coded message on a pad on his right. The transmission only lasted a minute. He decoded it even before he stored the radio away, which was the wrong way round.

'Large scale invasion Normandy underway. Clarification urgently required on first sector. Urgent you check Nero to confirm movements.'

The best advice he had ever received in this business was not to panic. It was easy to say that, everyone did. It was an obvious thing to say. But the man who had taught him had been an intelligence officer in the Great War and had survived an interrogation by the British by convincing them he was a deaf mute. His advice was this – when you find yourself in a really difficult position: stop. Have a cigarette and think. Five minutes.

So he stopped for five minutes, had a cigarette and thought. He would have to leave the flat – too risky to stay. Of course, he already had somewhere to go – he would never be in the position of not having a fallback position. But the message was clear. Check on Nero. That meant being in Pimlico sometime around eight so he could follow him again. He was always having to do that. Nero was not bad, he always varied his route, but for someone in his mid-twenties he was slow, which must be because of his injuries. Not quite sure of the whole business, not that it was his business to be sure anyway. When he had first come here the work had been more varied. Travelling around the country. More excitement. Now it was just following this man and, until a few weeks ago, his wife. But it was what Berlin wanted, and what Berlin wanted…

He started to pack. Everything he needed in two large suitcases and a smaller one. He would leave the house at seven – before that would feel a bit too early. It would be pushing it a bit; he needed to get down to Clapham first, but if he then took a taxi from Clapham to Victoria

Station, that would help. It was an old trick, if you have to resort to using a taxi, take it to a train station. No one ever thought there was anything unusual about that. He could take one large suitcase with him now, drop it off at the place in Clapham and then be in Pimlico by eight to pick Quinn up on his way to work. Back here, pick up the other cases, send one last message to Germany before he left this place, pay off Mr Fraser ('No, no – please keep the deposit, for your troubles. You have been very accommodating. Thank you.') He had learned that the word 'accommodating' worked wonders with the English lower-middle class, which is what Mr Fraser clearly aspired to. It was what they spent their lives doing. Then he would take the other cases over to Clapham. Tonight he would have to start finding a fallback for Clapham. It was going to be a long day.

Funny thing was, he had never expected them to use the emergency code to get him to contact Berlin. Two rings on the phone. Gap of five minutes, two more rings. Another gap of five minutes, then three rings. That means contact Berlin. Urgent. Very urgent. The most intriguing part of it was that there was someone else in England who would have made the call and somehow Berlin would have been able to contact them. The British had picked up so many Abwehr agents that he had come to assume he was the only one left in the country. It was a little comfort that he wasn't.

'Large-scale invasion Normandy underway.' Well, there's a surprise. It was, actually. Not a surprise that the invasion was underway, although they'd taken their time about that. But Normandy was a surprise.

'Urgent you check Nero to confirm movements,' the message had said. What else have I been doing the past few months? Pimlico to St James's. And back. Two or three times a week. How often did Berlin want reassurance that yes – that's where he works, yes – he's there every day, all day.

'Clarification urgently required on first sector.' How on earth was he to find that out? Walk up to Quinn and tap him on the shoulder 'Excuse me… How come you chaps aren't on the beaches of the Pas de Calais this morning?' Follow him into the office and ask 'What's all this about Normandy then?' He'd have to work on that one.

He finished his second cup of tea, decided it was going to be a busy day and poured a generous measure from the brandy bottle before packing it in a case. He had already denied himself one pleasure that morning, so he was entitled to a small drink.

Edgar had been up since four in the morning. The initial reports were quite good, though the Americans seemed to be taking a bit of a hammering on the western beaches.

At six thirty he took a call from one of the MI5 duty officers.

'Cognac had an early morning alarm call, sir. Three calls to the house phone between six o'clock and ten past six this morning. Caller hung up after just a couple of rings.'

Cognac. The man who had caused them more trouble than entire German divisions. They knew he had entered the country early in 1940 and assumed it would be a matter of time before they picked him up, like they had with all the others. He was a well-known Abwehr agent. One of their best. He'd been spotted in the West End in May 1940 by MI5 and there were other confirmed sightings in Manchester, Liverpool and Glasgow. But they were never able to lay a hand on him. He had an ability to vanish – thin air and all that.

He had assumed almost mystical qualities in MI5 circles, but along with luck on Cognac's part and sheer incompetence from some of those following him, Edgar put Cognac's ability to evade them down to two factors: one was his sheer ability, and the second was his way with women. Edgar had sat in on one interview with one of them. A woman in her late forties whose husband was a prisoner of war in the far east. Cognac had stayed with her for a couple of months in 1941, originally moving in as a lodger. She was totally besotted with him. 'I have never been satisfied with a man before, sir. I would have done anything he asked,' she admitted, staring intently at a lace handkerchief she was twisting in her hands as she spoke. She had made a good stab at appearing ashamed, but it was not difficult to see the passion in her eyes as she spoke about Cognac.

Then a stroke of luck. In September 1943 they had been following Quinn to work, which was routine. They did it once or twice a week, as part of their monitoring of him and his wife. The man following Quinn that morning, who was especially good at his job and had the ability to follow someone from a very long way back, spotted Cognac in between him and Quinn. Instead of panicking like the rest of them had – and allowing Cognac to get away – he followed Cognac. Back to a house in Hendon, where he had a small flat. After that, it was a matter of keeping an eye on Cognac, who in turn was keeping an eye on Mr and Mrs Quinn.

Edgar assumed that the Abwehr were so pleased with what they were getting from Magpie that they had put Cognac on to them to be absolutely sure that she was where she said she was, and Quinn was doing what she said he was doing. So in turn, MI5 kept an eye on Cognac, but let him get on with it. He kept them busy enough, checking out Quinn and Magpie, and then hanging around the second- and third-division bars in the West End. He was usually lucky, Edgar noticed. He preferred to go back to their place or book a cheap hotel room where the manager was prepared to ignore the form filling for an hour in return for double the rate. It was rare for him to take one of them back to his place.

'Yes, sir,' said the MI5 man. 'Those phone calls to the house were obviously a signal for Cognac to contact Berlin. Post Office have traced the calls as coming from a series of telephone boxes in and around Waverley Station in Edinburgh. Cognac contacted Berlin around six twenty. Radio boys triangulated the transmission to his road in Hendon, but Bletchley traced the transmission anyway. Still working on the final version, but they reckon it's to do with D-Day. Seems Cognac has been asked to keep a close eye on your man today. Reference to the first sector too. Bletchley working on that.'

Edgar called Archibald.

'John. I think that you had better come over for a chat. I know that we weren't planning to do so, but I think we are going to need to tell Quinn today.'

Chapter 20

London, 6th June 1944

Quinn remembered little of the walk back to Pimlico. He was vaguely aware of a lighter mood in the air, people slapping each other on the back, strangers exchanging smiles.

'Good afternoon.'

'It most certainly is, isn't it?'

'Not long now.'

As he walked past Westminster Abbey he noticed a steady stream of people going in. The relief that people felt as they anticipated the end of the war could not be exaggerated, although the euphoria was a long way off.

Owen Quinn could not imagine feeling more depressed. The shock that had numbed him since Edgar began talking to him in the park was beginning to wear off. It was being replaced by a boiling rage against the injustice in the way his life had been ruined. The physical effort of walking was difficult. As often happened in times of stress, his back was beginning to ache.

Once he was in Alderney Street his pace quickened. He would get out of his uniform, have a bath and, most importantly, a drink. He thought about Edgar's plan. He would have to go along with it, there was no alternative. He would need to pack a case. At least it would get him away from the flat for a few days.

He climbed the steps into the house, holding the door open for the odd-looking civil servant who always wore a bowler hat and who lived in the flat next to him. *So he's come home early today too.*

Quinn checked the table in the hall for any post. The tall aspidistra, covered in a sheen of dust, stood sentry over a few bills and some handwritten correspondence. Just one letter for him, the envelope bearing his mother's distinctive script. Its theme would be familiar

– '…looks absolutely splendid, as does the front garden… so please, Owen, do make an effort to come and visit your father and I, neither of whom are getting any…'

Roger. That was what the neighbour was called. He had been useful enough when they first moved in, even offering the services of his own cleaner.

There had been a forgettable evening just before their first Christmas here when Roger had invited Nathalie and himself in for drinks. Roger, it turned out, didn't drink. Not alcohol, anyway. An evening of tea and barley water and some hard biscuits apparently baked by Roger's mother. They nodded at each other as they stood in the hall. Two men and a woman were following Roger, who held the door open for them. Quinn hadn't seen them before but he did not give it a second thought, it was a transient sort of a house anyway.

He ran up the stairs as fast as his back and legs would allow him. He decided he would have that drink before the bath as well as after it. Roger was behind him too, which was odd – he hadn't stopped outside his own flat.

'Owen – are you all right?' Roger was standing immediately behind him now. He could hear more people climbing their staircase. Owen nodded.

'Mind if I come in, Owen?' Before Owen had time to say that actually, yes – he did mind, Roger had pushed past him in his tiny entrance hall and walked into the lounge. Owen stood in the hall. The two men and one woman who had followed them into the house were now standing in the entrance to Owen's flat, waiting for the hall to clear so that they could enter too.

'Come through, Owen. Let me explain.'

Roger had sat himself down in one of the large armchairs. It was the one Owen usually sat in. It was the one he had been sitting in less than seven hours previously when he had listened to the news. Owen sat in the other armchair. No one had sat in it since Nathalie had left. He heard his front door shut and voices in the hall.

Roger was a small, rotund man, florid of complexion and given to perspiring extensively. He had obviously been walking faster than normal because he was struggling to catch his breath. His neck bulged against his tight collar, the knot of his tie concealed by the excesses of his neck. He wiped his damp face with a large handkerchief.

'Can I ask what on earth is going on with you barging into here?'

Eventually, Roger caught his breath enough to attempt conversation, though it was punctuated by frequent pauses.

'Owen. It is not simply a happy coincidence that I am your next-door neighbour. I am a colleague of your friend Major Edgar, as are my three colleagues currently squashed together in your hall. I moved in just before you did. My brief was to keep an eye on you and your lady wife. Make sure nothing odd happened. I think that Major Edgar has explained your plans for the next few days?'

'Yes.'

'Good. I have two tasks now. The first is to ensure that when you set off tomorrow, our new friend goes with you. It is vital that he sees where you are going. His code name, by the way, is Cognac. He has a taste for it, so I am told. Can't see the attraction of it myself, foul stuff actually, but then most foreign drinks are. Where were we? Ah yes. Tomorrow. The streets around here will be well covered. We anticipate that Cognac will come by here tonight just to check that you are in. Our guess is that in the morning he will also be watching out for you too. We're rather counting on that, actually. As soon as we are sure he is there, you will leave. You don't need to worry, I will be here to tell you when and where to go. Is that clear?'

'So far.'

'Splendid.'

'But—'

'Hang on, Quinn. My next task is altogether less pleasant. We need to thoroughly search the flat, and I am afraid that my orders are to ensure that any trace of your wife is removed. For reasons of security, I am told. I think that Major Edgar has explained her new… security status? Well, it rather follows that he needs to go through all of her possessions, don't you agree? Everything, I'm afraid. Apparently even the tiniest or most inconsequential-looking item could be crucial, so there we are. Not my field as it happens, but I'm told they can find almost anything these days, eh! I know this is not nice, but I am told that after a time some of it could be returned to you. If you want it, that is. My colleagues in the hall will take care of this. Did your wife have any valuables here?'

'Some jewellery – not much. Earrings, necklaces, that kind of thing. Trinkets, really, but I wouldn't—'

'Very well. I am sure that eventually anything of value will be returned. Now, if you don't mind.'

Owen spent the next hour slumped in the armchair as all trace of his wife was carefully removed from around him. A large whisky had been pressed into his hand and refilled as the two men and the woman methodically worked their way through the flat. He was never introduced to any of them. Roger fussed around the flat, annoying the other three who seemed to know what they were doing, and being unctuously attentive of Owen – 'Another whisky? Tea? Biscuit? Put your feet up old chap…'

Drawers were emptied and every item gone through. Anything to do with Nathalie or his work was put straight into a case. Other items were checked with Owen. All paperwork went into the case too. Even the bills.

As his world was efficiently dismantled around him, Owen sat slumped in the armchair, creased in defeat and resignation. The glass of whisky was refilled yet again and he was beginning to feel very tired.

By the time they were done, Owen was fighting an urge to curl up and sleep. He heard Roger telling the other three to put the cases in his flat next door. 'We can remove them tomorrow when the coast is clear.'

Roger explained the plan for the evening. The two men would stay with him – 'Don't worry, Owen, they will be fine in the armchairs!' – to make sure everything was in order. To guard me, you mean, thought Owen. Roger would stay next door with the woman 'She will have my bed! I'm on the settee.'

A supper magically appeared from the kitchen and Owen picked at it while his two protectors ate theirs with gusto. Barely a word passed between them. Conversation was restricted to the occasional solicitous remark – 'Pepper?… Salt?… More water?' After supper they brought him a mug of tea that was too strong and tasted almost bitter, but which he drank nonetheless before he ran a bath. He did not enjoy sounding like his mother, but there was no doubt that milk did go off much quicker these days. Looking round the bedroom, it was clear that there was now no evidence remaining that Nathalie had ever existed, let alone lived here. The photos of their wedding had gone along with all of her clothes, her make-up, jewellery, hairbrush, the silk stockings which hung on the inside of their wardrobe door and which he allowed to brush his face when he opened it, her few books and even the tiny, imperceptible scent of her which he would pick up from time to time and would take his breath away.

If anyone came to the flat now and he explained that his wife had once lived here, they would surely question his sanity. She had vanished in more ways than one.

He undressed for the bath, packing as he did so. 'Two weeks you'll be away,' Edgar had said. 'Maximum three. You'll be in uniform.' Not too difficult to pack then. The last item he threw into the case was a travelling toiletries bag that Nathalie had bought him in November for his birthday. He had not used it yet and she had been annoyed. He unzipped the bag. Handy little thing. Neat compartments for his razor and shaving brush, a travelling toothbrush, a soap holder, hairbrush, comb. As he picked it up he felt a rattle, coming from inside the soap holder.

He closed the bedroom door – 'Just getting undressed' – and opened the soap holder. It was empty, apart from something weighty wrapped in tissue paper. A strip of gum-paper had held the little packet in place, but one end had come loose which was why the packet had rattled.

He opened it. Carefully wrapped inside the tissue paper was a beautiful cameo brooch, the cream head of a woman with long ringlets of hair carved out of black shell, mounted on a gold base. He turned it over. Just under the pin was inscribed one word.

Toujours.

Always.

–

After his bath he had sat by the open window in his bedroom, the curtains and blackout pulled aside. The merest hint of a breeze drifted into the room, but its impact on the stifling heat was marginal. It stayed light until just before ten o'clock, but as darkness fell he began to feel angry again. He was surprised that since returning to the flat he had felt exhausted rather than upset or even angry. Perhaps he was still in shock. He remembered how he felt after being rescued from the sea. The exhaustion overwhelmed every other emotion. A packet of Senior Service lay open on the windowsill. Just two cigarettes remained. He had smoked eight since getting back to the flat. The road outside was quiet, the occasional couple returning home, one always slightly more drunk than the other. A cyclist. An elderly lady being pulled along by two dogs. An air raid warden with a limp and a dipped torch that threw out a yellowy light just a foot or so in front of him.

Which one of you is Cognac, then?

One of his two guards knocked gently on the door, opening it before Owen had the chance to tell him to come in. He was carrying a tiny tray with a large glass of whisky, another mug of tea and a plate of biscuits.

The tea was a bit weaker than before, more to Owen's liking, but it still had the bitter taste of the previous drink. It was odd. He looked again at the cameo brooch, turning it in the half-light, feeling its every contour, studying it for clues.

Was it possible that anyone other than Nathalie had put the brooch in the case? He could not imagine who. He racked his brain to see if he could picture her at any time wearing the brooch. Had she written '*toujours*' herself or had she had it specially inscribed? Had that word already been on the brooch? As far as he could tell, the brooch was not new but the word '*toujours*' looked fresh. The cream head of the woman looked as if it had once been whiter in colour and the gold reverse had tiny scratches. From somewhere at the back of his mind he recalled his mother and grandmother discussing a cameo brooch and remarking that tiny imperfections in the shell were a sign of authenticity. He imagined the brooch was a family heirloom that Nathalie – or whatever her real name was – had brought with her from France. For some reason, she had hidden it, wanting only him to find it. He brought it closer to his eye. At the very top of the reverse, in the centre, were two tiny capital letters. 'CT'? He pivoted the brooch in his hand. The C could be a G, part of it having faded. He went and held it directly under his bedside light. It was a G. GT. Who was GT? Were those Nathalie's real initials? Or those of her mother? And if so, was it her maiden name or married name? Or a grandmother? Or an aunt? In truth, it told him little, but it took him a bit closer to her.

On one level, the brooch gave him some hope. Would a German spy really leave a keepsake behind? Maybe she was trying to reassure him. But then he thought that perhaps it was her way of leaving him with one memento and hoping he would be satisfied with that.

He lay back on the bed, pulling an extra pillow across from Nathalie's side of the bed, and had another sip of the tea, but decided to give up on it. Whisky was always a preferable option anyway. He held up the tumbler with its generous measure of whisky. Like the cameo brooch a few minutes before, it caught the fading light. He noticed something strange. Tiny white crystals floating at the bottom of the glass. A dozen of them and only visible if he held the glass at eye level and directly against the light.

He wondered and then he realised. The tiredness and even calmness that he had felt since returning to the flat were no coincidence. He must have been drugged. The endless glasses of whisky and the bitter tasting tea. They were to make him compliant. It would ensure he was easy to handle for what they had in mind the next day.

He placed the whisky glass back on the bedside table and lay there, becoming increasingly unsettled as the effect of whatever they had been sedating him with wore off. The breeze had picked up now as the darkness took hold, and as it did so a most terrible thought came to his mind, which he dismissed as ridiculous.

He got up to close the curtains. He climbed into bed. He needed a good night's sleep.

But sleep turned out to be a hopeless prospect. The terrible thought that he had had before gnawed away, crushing him. He sat bolt upright in bed, totally awake.

What was it that Roger had said earlier when he came into the flat? *I moved in just before you did. My brief was to keep an eye on you and your lady wife. Make sure nothing odd happened.*

They had moved into this flat in June 1942. Two years previously. But according to Edgar, they had only discovered that Nathalie was a spy after she went to France. It didn't make sense. If they really had no idea that his wife was a spy, why had Roger been keeping 'eye on you and your lady wife' for almost two years?

And then there were other things that had played on his mind when they had happened, and which he had dismissed. Maybe they now had a plausible explanation.

The happy coincidence of her arrival at Calcotte Grange; his being told so unexpectedly that he wasn't going back to sea despite the assurances he had received from the doctors until then; the way in which the Royal Navy had been so understanding over their relationship and so accommodating about their getting married – even helping to find them this flat.

He had thought it odd, and these thoughts never really strayed too far from the back of his mind. It was equally odd that she was allowed out on her own from the safe house in Holland Park. And then the fact that he had earlier been allowed to take secret papers home, and even use his wife as an unofficial translator. Even at the time he had been surprised that Archibald had allowed that, especially as it coincided with his starting work on the Pas de Calais landings.

He wrenched open the door to the darkened lounge where the two guards were both slumped in the armchairs.

'Get Roger for me.'

'It is rather late, sir. Perhaps in the morning?'

The shorter of the two had stood up; he had clearly not been asleep. He was adjusting his jacket, discreetly moving his hand inside it.

'I don't give damn how late it is, I want to see him now.'

The other guard got up.

'Very well, sir. Just keep your voice down though, if you would. We don't want to disturb the neighbours.'

A minute later Roger bustled in wearing a large check-patterned dressing gown over striped pyjamas. He wondered what the matter was.

'I'm not doing it.'

'Doing what?'

'Doing what you want me to do tomorrow. I've decided not to do it.'

'I'm afraid that is not an option that you have, Owen. I know you're upset, but you are also tired. Get a decent night's sleep and you'll feel fine in the morning. Be a good chap. Another whisky, perhaps?'

Quinn moved to stand right in front of Roger, towering above him. One of the guards moved towards him but Roger gestured him to hold back.

'What is it, Owen. What is the matter? Shall we talk in your bedroom?'

So he and Owen talked. Not for long. Five minutes was enough to convince Roger that this was above his rank. He opened the bedroom door and spoke to the guards.

'I need you to go and get Major Edgar and ask him to come here. It is rather urgent. Thank you.'

—

Edgar arrived within the hour, clearly none too pleased at his summons. He told Roger and the two guards to go and wait in Roger's flat.

'I gather that there seems to be some kind of a problem, Quinn?' he said with calculated understatement. His meaning was clear: '*This had better not be a waste of my time.*'

'How long have you known?'

'Known what, Quinn?'

'How long have you known that my wife is a German spy?'

'I told you in the park. We found out not long after she went over to France. A matter of weeks ago.'

'And you didn't know before that?'

'No.'

'I don't think I believe you, Major Edgar.'

'Quinn,' said Edgar, his earlier irritation now having turned to anger, 'it is not your place to disbelieve what I say. Your attitude is bordering on insolence and—'

Quinn carried on, ignoring Edgar, his voice shaking with fury. 'I'll tell you what I think, Edgar. I think that you knew long ago, before she went to France, that Nathalie was a spy. I am not sure when you found out, but I'm beginning to think that you may have known all along, certainly before I met her.'

'Don't be ridiculous, I told—'

'I think that I've been set up, Edgar. I think I've been used as part of some complicated, clever plan of yours. Your chap Roger out there, he let slip earlier that he'd moved into the flat next door just before we moved in. "To keep an eye on you and your lady wife" were his words. Why would he do that, Edgar, if you had no idea then that Nathalie was a spy? Tell me.'

Edgar said nothing. He sat still, eyeing Quinn like a boxer trying to find his way through an opponent's tight defence.

'You see, Edgar, I think that you were counting on me being in shock at first, which, of course, I was. And then when I got back here – well, Roger and his friends were busier than the waiters at the Savoy, plying me with tea and whisky. Plan was to keep me nice and sedated and calm and not causing any trouble, eh? So as soon as I realised that, I stopped taking your liquid refreshment. And then I began to think more clearly, helped along by poor old Roger's little slip. And do you know what I think? I think that you knew all along that Nathalie was a German agent. I even think that you knew that long before I met her.

'And I'll tell you why I think that. When your sedatives started to wear off, I asked myself why I believed what you told me in the park. Why didn't I just get up there and then and tell you to get lost? How, despite the fact that you gave me no evidence, did I know deep down that what you said may well be true? I'll tell you why. Because at the back of my mind, there were things that I ought to have been more suspicious about. Small things. Like the fact that I knew so little about Nathalie. Why did such an important project like the one I've been working on have such a small office with such a frankly second-rate group of people to work with? And why was I allowed to take work home with me? It was terribly convenient, of course, for me to do so, but it didn't really make sense, did it?'

Edgar started to speak, but Quinn raised his hand. *Wait*.

'So, I'll do a deal with you, Edgar. You tell me the truth. Everything. Then I'll go along with your plan. Otherwise, I'm not playing. You can arrest me, beat me up, put me in the bloody Tower of London, I don't care. But I know that you need me to co-operate with you, so I think that you are going to have to tell me everything.'

'For Christ's sake, Quinn. Stop behaving like a schoolboy who's had his bat and ball taken from him. This is war, not some silly game which you decide whether you want to play or not. I think you'll find that you have to—'

'Oh, really? And what are you going to do? Drag me along there in handcuffs? That will look good, won't it? That will convince whoever's watching. Tell me the whole truth, Edgar.'

Quinn was breathing heavily through his nose, arms folded tightly across his chest.

Edgar leaned back and removed his trilby, which he had been wearing since he came in. He looked carefully at Quinn. Maybe he had underestimated him. There was more steel there than he could ever have imagined. He slowly turned the trilby round in his hand, carefully studying the brim and flicking a piece of fluff from it. They had not expected Quinn to cotton-on quite so quickly. Roger would be made to pay for this. He would have to tell him. If he did not co-operate tomorrow – later today, actually, he thought glancing at his watch – then this carefully crafted operation was buggered, not to put too fine a point on it.

He placed his hat on the small table in front of them and turned to face Owen.

'The landings on the beaches of Normandy are our main route into Europe – our only route into Europe. There will be no landings in the Pas de Calais.'

Silence from Quinn, who looked stunned. His head had jerked towards Edgar and stayed in that position, his brow furrowed in confusion.

'What I am saying, Quinn, is that Normandy is and always has been our main choice for the landings. The Pas de Calais was an attempt to deceive the Germans. It still is. We need them to believe for as long as possible that Normandy is not our primary target and that the main landings will be in the Pas de Calais.'

'So then everything that I have been working on...'

'Everything that you have been working on is a vital part of the deception. I hope that as time goes on you will come to realise that you too have played your part. But, certainly – all the planning that you have been doing has not been for an actual invasion.'

'But what has it been for then?'

'I cannot pretend that this is not the difficult part, Quinn. Through you, we have been able to directly mislead the Germans. You have, if you like, been an unwitting but very necessary conduit for passing on incorrect information to them.

'Your wife was recruited in France before the war as a German spy. We did not pick her up when she came here. We only became aware of her after we arrested another German spy – a Belgian as it happens – in 1941. As you know, at the time, Nathalie was working at St Thomas's Hospital. By the time we became aware of her, she had already applied for a transfer to a military hospital. We had a choice at that stage. We could arrest her, but there would be little to be gained from that. We had no evidence against her for a start – just the word of our Belgian friend. Or, we could see what she got up to, and to do that we needed a helping hand. So we facilitated her transfer to a military hospital. She ended up at Calcotte Grange, where she met you.

'We knew that she had asked to go to a military hospital so she could have direct access to the kind of intelligence that you will pick up in that kind of place. It occurred to us that this gave us a perfect opportunity to enable her to meet someone who had access to top grade intelligence. She was allowed to see your file, which told her that you were going to be working on a top secret Naval Intelligence project. Even you were not aware of that, at that stage. It was not hard for us to arrange for you and her to get together. She was keen to get to know you, so to speak, and we knew that you would be keen too, though for altogether different reasons.

'We arranged for you to work in Naval Intelligence. At first the work was reasonably low-level and we knew that Nathalie would not be in a position to find out much about what you were doing. But the idea was to be very careful and very gradual about it. We did not want the Germans to get wind that this all may be too good to be true. That has always been one of the risks of this operation. But by the middle of 1943 we were well into planning the invasion of Europe, and a crucial part of this was a deception operation that would convince the Germans that the invasion would be somewhere other than where it was going to be, if you get my drift. Quite early on it was decided that Normandy was the preferred location. German defences are just too good in the Pas de Calais. They were expecting us there; everything we were intercepting from them was telling us that. So we simply told them what they thought anyway. If you like, we reinforced it for them.'

Quinn was staring down at the floor as he had been throughout the time that Edgar was talking. He appeared to be shielding his face. He was biting his nails.

'As you know, we allowed you to take some material home with you. Quite irregular, of course, but it was the best way to ensure that Nathalie was getting the information. Sure enough, she was passing it on back to her Abwehr control in Paris.

'Naturally I cannot go into any detail, but I can assure you that this was just one part of the deception. There are many other aspects of it. But what was critical was that the Germans were getting – are getting, indeed – a consistent story, whereby the different sources corroborate each other. If they know that Agent A has no connection whatsoever with Agent C, for instance, yet both are saying the same thing – then what they are both saying has added credibility.'

'If… if this is true, then why was she sent to France?'

'The icing on the cake, if you like. To help further convince the Germans. We've sent hundreds of agents over. They liaise with the resistance. In her case, she is there to prepare for the invasion in the Pas de Calais. Up until this morning, that is what we have been telling her. What she is being told now is that the main invasion will still be in the Pas de Calais, that what is going on in Normandy is actually a feint. If they believe it, even for a short while, then they'll keep their forces in the Pas de Calais and delay reinforcing Normandy. Absolutely crucial then that the Germans got that message, hence our sending her over there.'

'And what happens when it's all over?'

'If we get our hands on her then she will face the due process of law.'

Silence for a few minutes as Quinn took it all in, as far as he was able to. As much as he wanted to argue with Edgar, there was something about what he said that made sense, reluctant as he was to admit it. Despite having been with Nathalie for a year and a half, deep down, he felt that he had never really known her. The questions that he constantly asked about her life in France, the answers that told him nothing. The times when she appeared briefly distracted to the extent that she seemed to be a different person, only to snap out of it and return to him with a smile. On the other hand, her affection for him did not feel forced. When he came home, she appeared genuinely pleased to see him. She was an enthusiastic lover, he could not recall many occasions when she had rejected his advances and often she had instigated lovemaking.

'But you deceived me!'

'Unfortunately we did. We had to. It was the only way. Your wife has been such an important source for the Germans that we had no alternative.'

'Why are you telling me all this, Edgar? What if I do something about it?'

Edgar laughed. 'I'm telling you, Owen, because you insisted, rather had me over a barrel before, didn't you? Not sure that you're better off knowing what you do, ignorance being bliss and all that. But what are you going to do, Owen? Go to the police? Tell the newspapers. Come on, old chap. There's a war on. No one will believe you. We won't let anyone believe you. They'll assume you are mad. Anything you say will be denied. It never happened. Not true. Wife working for us, went to France and not heard of again. Happens in war.'

'But you just said that if you catch her she will go on trial.'

'I think that what I said was that if we find her, she will face due process. *If* we find her.'

'And if not?'

'Then that may be better all round. Look, Quinn. I've taken a calculated risk telling you now; you didn't really leave me with an alternative. But we need you to play ball with us. We are sure that they are still keeping an eye on you and, if that is the case, we need you to be doing what they'd be expecting you to do. May have been better for you to carry on drawing your maps, which was the original plan. But you would have found out in a matter of days anyway that there was to be no invasion in the Pas de Calais. Better this way: we can tell you in a controlled manner. We owe it to you. You have every reason for feeling that you have not been treated well.'

'But she deceived me – you deceived me! What am I to do now?'

The anger was coming now, Edgar thought. Long overdue.

'You get on with your life. Look, Quinn. No one is pretending that this is nice for you. But look at it from our point of view. We get one shot at D-Day. If it fails, it could be years before we can try again. We have to use every trick at our disposal to ensure that it does not fail. You, I am afraid, are one of the tricks. You'll get over it. The Navy will look after you, do the decent thing. Just play ball with us for a few more weeks. Come on. Busy day tomorrow. Try to get some sleep.'

–

After Edgar left, Quinn demanded a new bottle of whisky, so he could be sure of having a drink that had not been tampered with. A strange calm came over him. Maybe it was the whisky, maybe it was the quiet of the night, maybe he was still in shock. Quite possibly, it was a combination of all three. But most of all, the calm came from a determination to find his wife. Whatever happened and however long it took, he would find her – and the brooch was the first step.

One of the men in the lounge was snoring loudly and he could hear the other one shuffling around.

He climbed back into bed naked. For the first time since she went away, he rolled over to her side of the bed. Once again, he imagined he could smell her on the pillow case and feel her indentations on the mattress. He woke up frequently during the night and each time he stared at the cameo brooch on the bedside table before drifting back to sleep.

He awoke at four o'clock on her side of the bed and lay there thinking until the first hint of dawn, when he drifted back to sleep again. He thought of his grandfather, the only other person whom he had loved and lost. He remembered that last conversation with him, when his grandfather asked what he wanted to do when he was older and he had replied that he would like to play cricket for England, at which his grandfather laughed. And then he said he would like to marry a beautiful Frenchwoman. That really was what he had wished for then. 'Be careful what you wish for,' had been his grandfather's reply.

Those words had come back to haunt him now.

Chapter 21

London, 7th June 1944

Owen Quinn was woken by the sound of voices coming from his lounge. He had not slept for more than an hour at a time that night. It was seven o'clock.

He stayed in bed until there was a knock on the door. It was seven thirty. One of his guards, for want of a better word, came in with a mug of tea.

'Roger suggests we may need to think about moving in around an hour, sir. No sign of anyone outside, but just in case, before you open the curtains we'd better wait in the hall. Take your time, sir.'

He did take his time. Checking to see if anything else had been overlooked, drinking his tea, repacking his case and listening to the news. As far as he could make out, it was good news. More than one hundred and fifty thousand Allied troops had landed in Normandy the previous day, plus something like twelve thousand vehicles. It was the latter figure that impressed him. You could do all the planning in the world, but until you put a tank on a beach, you would not know what was going to happen.

At eight thirty Roger came into the lounge. Quinn was dressed in his uniform, in his armchair and drinking a third mug of tea. By the side of his bed was the bottle of Talisker that Archibald had given him, less than a quarter of the bottle still to be drunk.

'Good news, Owen. Cognac popped by last night on his bike. Had a quick look up, and back to Clapham. And the even-better news this morning is that he is back in the area, so he's behaving exactly as we were expecting – now we just need to give him the bait: you. Shall I just run through the plans one more time?'

Quinn left the house at a quarter to nine, after Roger had run through the plans. The exodus was carefully choreographed. Roger left at his normal time of ten to nine, though he would make his way via a circuitous route to Owen's destination. One of Owen's two guards, whose name he now discovered was Andrew, left the house immediately before him, the other man and the woman just after him. As he locked the door of his flat, the couple were waiting on the landing. 'We'll look after the key for you,' the man said, his hand held out towards Owen. He hesitated before handing over the key.

He paused at the bottom of the steps, looking back once at the house, not certain when he would enter it again and not sure that he wanted to. It was a pleasant day. Just the perfect weather for his trip. Carrying his case and so walking a bit slower than usual, he set off. A few minutes later he entered Victoria Station from Bridge Place.

'Take your time when you get there, Owen,' Roger had told him. 'Give Cognac a chance to catch up with you and get his bearings. Go and buy a paper, look at the departure board – that kind of thing – and then go and buy a ticket. First class. Whatever you do, make sure you get on a train that is not just about to leave. Can't risk him losing you.'

There was little chance of that. The station was a heaving mass of people, far busier than he would have expected. A crowd was gathered under the departures board and small but noisy groups formed around any member of the station staff who made the mistake of standing still. As he passed one group he overheard the plea from a harassed ticket inspector.

'If we all shout and push at the same time, we won't get anywhere today, will we? For the one hundredth time: there are severe delays on most of our services to the south coast. Some of you may have heard the news. It means that we are running far fewer trains. Now madam, if you care to...'

Quinn walked over to the departures board. It was now five past nine. It was clear that there were delays on all routes, especially those to the south coast. Some services seem to be cancelled altogether. The next train to Dover was scheduled for nine thirty, which would have been ideal, but that was showing as 'delayed'. Another harassed-looking ticket inspector walked by, doing his best to avoid any questions. Owen stepped in front of him and asked about trains to Dover. A small crowd joined him round the ticket inspector; people were anxious to find out what was going on. He just hoped that whoever was meant to be following him would catch what was happening.

'No trains to Dover so far and I doubt if there will be any through trains all day, sir. If you want to try your chances, I would go to Maidstone East and then see what they can do there. If you're lucky, you'll then get a connection via either Faversham or Ashford. Good luck, sir.'

A train was about to depart from platform three: a cloud of pure white steam travelled more or less horizontally into the station concourse. The guard's shrill whistle, a cry of '*Come on now!*' and a sudden rush to the gate as it swung shut. A Canadian soldier put down his bag and tenderly stroked the face of the girl he had been hugging next to Quinn, before picking up his bag and vaulting over the gate. Three sailors hurried past, saluting him as they did so. On a small bench a woman was bent double, her face covered. A young boy, no more than ten, stood next to her. He looked confused; his hand uncertainly placed on her heaving shoulder.

It was going to be hard for Cognac to keep tabs on him in this chaos, Quinn realised. He walked slowly over to the newspaper kiosk, to join a long and disorderly queue. People were keen to read whatever they could of D-Day, and that had led to a run on the papers.

'As I have just told the gentleman in front of you, sir, we have no copies remaining of either the *Daily Herald* or the *Daily Mail*. *Daily Telegraph?* Very good, sir. Yes, sir?'

Quinn bought one of the last copies of *The Times*. He was careful not to look around. 'Avoid the temptation. You won't spot Cognac, of course, but he may well spot you looking around. Just act normally.'

As instructed, he waited until a small queue had formed by the first class window in the ticket office and went to join it.

'First class single to Dover, please.' Again following instructions, he spoke softly.

'Where to?' the ticket clerk asked.

'Dover, please. I understand I may need to go via Maidstone East. Is that correct?' Quinn repeated, a bit louder this time for the benefit of the clerk.

'It will have to be Dover Priory, sir. No trains to Dover Marine today or the rest of this week. Security. You'll understand. Head for Maidstone East. Next train due to depart ten o'clock. Probably another delay on top of that. Platform four, sir.'

An hour later he was wedged into his first class compartment as the elderly locomotive pulled the eight-coach train out of the station.

He had boarded the train as soon as it was announced as the one for Maidstone East, but even so he was lucky to have found a seat in the rush. There were even three people standing in his six-seat compartment. He had noticed a man bearing a distinct similarity to Roger, but wearing a trilby hat that was far too big. The man pushed his way through the crowded corridor, briefly glancing into his compartment. Owen opened his newspaper. He noticed that it was just eight pages today. It was rare these days for it to be more than that. By the time the train pulled out of Victoria Station he had already answered six of the clues in *The Times* crossword.

'He'll be following you,' Edgar had told him in the park the day before. 'What the Germans will want to know now is whether Normandy is a feint. Will there still be a main invasion through the Pas de Calais? That's what preoccupying them. So we've decided to send you to the seaside'.

Edgar and Roger had both explained his role in some detail. The Germans believed that Quinn was involved in planning the Pas de Calais invasion, so they would now be looking at his behaviour after D-Day to see if it was consistent with that. The Germans had also been relying on intelligence that a massive Allied army was gathering in the south east of England. This would be the army that would invade through the Pas de Calais.

'FUSAG,' Edgar had told him. 'Stands for First US Army Group. It's the US Fourteenth Army and the British Fourth Army, at least that is what the Germans think it is. Commanded by General Patton. Totally fictional, of course, apart from Patton. Although, as I understand it, quite a few of the top brass wish he was fictional. Tricky chap, apparently. We have every reason to believe that the Germans have bought it. Some of their agents – now working for us, of course – have spent quite a while in the south east, spotting the formations, tanks, landing craft. The whole place has been buzzing with radio traffic. Based around the Kent ports, short hop over to the Pas de Calais.

'So it makes perfect sense for you to get down there today. They'll think that the main invasion is imminent, so your moving down to Dover will fit in with what they expect. Cognac will be able to follow you to the Castle and watch you go in. Won't be able to go any further, but that doesn't matter. Our guess is that he'll then head back to London and let Berlin know that one of the Pas de Calais planners has moved down to FUSAG.'

Twenty-four hours ago, all had appeared to be well in his world. Then it collapsed. Now, like this train being led along on the tracks, he was being led along, with little control over his destination.

–

Cognac prided himself on his composure. He had always considered that to be a secret agent's most important asset – staying calm, making careful judgements, avoiding silly mistakes. His composure had been fully tested this morning.

The previous day had been hard enough. After the early morning excitement, he had taken the tube down to the bedsit in Clapham where he had deposited his large suitcase and then taken a taxi to Victoria. A short walk so as to be near Quinn's place for eight o'clock – and, of course, it was a full three before he emerged. He followed him to Duke Street, watched him go in, waited five minutes – which was as long as he could risk – and then took a taxi back to the house in Hendon for the last time. He made his final transmission to Berlin, letting them know that Quinn was at work as normal, then he packed up his remaining bags.

He settled the rent with Mr Fraser. The stooped figure of his landlord had opened his door before Cognac had finished knocking on it, no doubt he had been peering through the spy-hole as was his habit whenever the front door of the house opened. Mr Fraser's slightly hunched back made him appear shorter than he was. His accent had the very slightest trace of Scotland from where he had moved many years ago. As ever, he had a cold and was constantly dabbing at his nose with a crumpled handkerchief that may once have been white. Whatever his landlord's intentions had been, they soon changed. Not only did Cognac tell him to keep the deposit – 'I am sure there will be the odd scratch and chipped saucer' – but he also pressed a five pound note into his grateful hands – 'Just in case any of my lady friends or their fathers come looking for me! If you could tell them as little as possible. I am a married man myself, you'll understand.' A knowing nod from Mr Fraser, who would very much have liked to be a married man himself, but was flattered that the gentleman thought he would understand. He left Mr Fraser a fictitious forwarding address and then embarked on a series of criss-crossing bus journeys to Clapham. They confused him and hopefully would have the same effect on anyone following him. As the day wore on he had the occasional pang of regret: Stephanie, which he was now sure was her name, had been an enthusiastic lover – far more responsive than most women he'd come across in this country. It was a shame, he could have had a few more days' fun.

Later that night he cycled up to Pimlico, a journey vindicated by seeing Quinn's distinctive profile by the window.

Back there at eight o'clock the next morning. Good job that the warren of roads afforded plenty of discreet places to wait. Street corners were always good, a couple of small blocks that he could walk round, sure in the knowledge that if Quinn left his flat he would not have gone very far by the time he came back round the block.

The round little civil servant with the red face and the funny hat had come out as usual. Quinn left at a quarter to nine, but today he was carrying a suitcase – and not a small one either. This was interesting. He turned left rather than going right or straight on as he normally did. Cognac was not altogether surprised to find himself following him in the direction of Victoria Station.

The crowds in the station were helpful. Plenty of cover. Of course, he had to work that much harder to keep an eye on Quinn, but that was not too difficult – his quarry was tall and his Royal Navy peaked cap distinctive enough to be very helpful.

He stood in the queue alongside Quinn. The best way of following someone, he had been taught all those years ago, was by not being behind them all the time. People take too much notice of what's behind them. You would never be expected to be followed by someone in front of you. Bit of a risk, if he reaches the ticket window before Quinn, but he is a Dutch refugee today and his English is poor, so his failure to understand the clerk could delay matters long enough until he hears Quinn's destination.

Dover. He had never been there, though in the past few months he had had to make a few trips to Kent to see what he could find about all the Allied forces gathering there for the invasion. 'Lots of them' had been the essence of his subsequent reports. 'All over the bloody place,' as the English would say. Lots of security though. You needed to be careful down there. He was pleased he had chosen his Dutchman today, it was his most robust identity.

The journey ought to have taken just under two and a half hours, but by the time they changed at Maidstone East and then Faversham, it had taken them the best part of four hours. He had nearly lost his man at Maidstone East, the platforms were so crowded. On the final train, from Faversham to Dover, he had ended up sitting in the compartment next to another young navy officer. He chose a seat right by the door so he could keep a check on his movements.

But the journey itself had been most useful. Tanks parked in fields in the distance, hundreds of them, literally. Around five miles outside of Dover he noticed heavy guns mounted on rail wagons parked in some sidings. They were covered in camouflage and would have been hard to spot from the air. He counted five of them in total. He memorised all the details. Large troop camps were just outside the town. When the train pulled in to Dover Priory, the station master's announcement:

'This train terminates here. All change please. There are no services to Dover Marine.'

Even if he lost Quinn now – and there was a chance he would have a car waiting for him – he would still have plenty to report back tonight.

He made sure he went through the ticket barrier ahead of Quinn and then paused to light a cigarette. The station appeared to have been bombed quite heavily. The end of one platform was fenced off and one of the buildings had been reduced to a pile of rubble. Quinn waited outside the station, looked around, glanced at his watch, looked up at the skies and then set off.

The station was at the top of a hill. Quinn walked down the hill into the town centre, stopped to ask directions of a policeman and then carried on, this time up another hill. Around half an hour after leaving the station he arrived in front of Dover Castle. The security was very high. Cognac knew he had reached the end of his own journey. In the reflection of a tea shop window, he saw Quinn pass through the security barrier in the road outside the castle, and then through the heavily guarded main entrance, being saluted as he did so. Cognac would have to go into the tea shop and have a cup of disgusting English tea, in case anyone wanted to know the purpose of his walk up the hill. Then it would be back to London.

Cognac was weary by the time he arrived back at Dover Priory Station. It was four o'clock and the station was quiet. Three policemen were on duty outside the station, taking care to check everyone as they entered it. This was going to be too risky. Cognac had taken care to remove his coat and hat, but he still needed to be careful. It would be difficult to have to explain to a policeman why he had come to Dover for less than two hours to purchase a cup of tea. 'Don't they sell tea in London then, sir?'

He decided to go cross country. They taught you to do that, of course, but it was notable how tempting it was to disregard it. If you are in Manchester and need to get to London, it is very easy to take the direct route. But if you are being followed – and you must always assume that you are – then you are making it so easy for whoever is following you that you may as well have a sign on your back saying that you work for the Abwehr. Cognac had once left Manchester at seven in the morning and not arrived in London until nine o'clock that night. Four trains and six buses. Three department stores visited in between buses and trains. Hard to beat a good department store for losing someone in, with their lifts, back-stairs and gloomy corridors.

There was a small bus station across the road and he headed there. One of the three buses that displayed any sign of going anywhere that day showed Deal on its destination board and the driver had just started the engine. That would have to do. It was the opposite direction from where he was heading, but that was not a bad thing in itself. He knew the map of Britain better than his own country now.

He paid the fare and slumped in a seat at the back. A mother and two noisy girls were occupying most of the back row and Cognac chose to sit in front of them.

They arrived in Deal just after five. There was another bus waiting as they pulled in showing Ramsgate as its destination. That would still be heading away from London, but he could catch a train from there. Ideally he'd have tried to spend an hour or so in Deal, just in case he was being followed, but it was beginning to get late so he got on the bus.

The journey was another long hour. The bus stopped in Sandwich for a while, where it filled up with people, and then wound its way to Ramsgate. He went straight to the train station. The restricted service on the south coast routes that had been so evident this morning had not improved. His best chance, the man at the ticket office told him, was to go to Chatham. From there he ought to get a direct train back to Victoria.

The journey back was punctuated by a series of delays. Not long after the train left Chatham it pulled into a siding to allow three trains laden with troops and equipment to pass. He carefully counted the number of carriages on each train and even managed to spot some serial numbers on tanks. He closed his eyes as he tried to memorise the numbers, fighting sleep as he did so.

It was about nine thirty by the time he walked out of a now-quiet Victoria Station, buying a copy of the *Evening News* on the way. It was still light, although night was not too far away. He noticed four taxis waiting at the rank, but knew he must resist the temptation. He'd pushed his luck with taxis the previous day. Two bus journeys would be four times longer, but safer.

It was a quarter past ten by the time he arrived at the bedsit in Clapham. He would encode his message and keep it as brief as possible, though there was plenty to tell Berlin tonight.

He sank onto the narrow bed, with its greasy candlewick bedspread and a gentle tilt towards the wall. Not the kind of place he could bring anyone back to. He would have to find another place soon anyway. He fought sleep.

He knew he was good, quite possibly the best, which was why he had survived so long. From the little that he could gather, he was one of the few German agents still active in Britain. Maybe now that the woman was in France, he was the only one still around, though he did suspect that she possibly had a radio-man somewhere out there, and of course whoever had made the phone calls the day before. He had been careful today, he always was. But in his heart, he knew that they would catch him sooner or later. A policeman would be lucky, or he would make a mistake. He had been so exhausted on the journey back that he did not like to think what would have happened if he had been stopped by the police in Deal or Ramsgate, or if some officious train guard had decided to be difficult.

And all for what? Germany was going to lose the war. Even allowing for the Allied propaganda, the evening paper made it clear that the invasion of Normandy seemed to be a success so far.

What would happen then?

Where would he go?

Would someone in the Abwehr turn him in during an interrogation?

And had it been worth it?

For the first few years, of course it had been. He'd been a believer then. But now it was just a matter of survival. Maybe it was now time to put himself first. To contemplate retirement. He hauled the transmitter from under the bed. *Ask me if it has been worth it when they lead me from the cell, condemned. Ask me if it has been worth it when they slip the noose round my neck. Ask me then.*

Chapter 22

Pas de Calais, 5-7th June 1944

Just before ten thirty on the night of 5th June, Geraldine and Jean left the house on the edge of the village where they had been listening to the BBC broadcast. The curfew was well underway, so they left their bikes in the house and returned to Jean's cottage via the covered bridle path at the rear of the house. It brought them out into a country lane which they had to cross before entering the churchyard through the back gate. The graveyard was wrapped protectively around the church, the moonlight picking out some of the inscriptions on the gravestones. They crossed the graveyard, past the bleak memorial – a large cross on top of it and the names of the twenty-five villagers who had fallen in the Great War picked out in metal characters. In her less composed moments, she had imagined them pointing accusingly at her. The memorial had even started to appear in her dreams. The stone angels that adorned the gravestones had developed a habit of flying into her dreams, quick to arrive, reluctant to leave, like the worst type of guest. She could barely sleep at night for the noise they made on the windowpane. When she entered the churchyard these days she looked down all the time, doing her best to avoid the accusing looks. When she was very young, her father would take her to the cemetery where his parents were buried. 'The people here,' he would say, pointing at the statues and the graves, 'they are the only ones who know *everything* that is going on.' It had taken her nearly twenty-five years to come to believe it.

The peacocks in the château grounds could be heard in the distance as they entered the Impasse de l'Église and Jean's cottage.

The curtains in the front room were drawn tight and they sat around the table in darkness, apart from a band of pale light coming in through the half-open door that led to the kitchen. Jean poured two glasses of wine.

'What do we do now, Geraldine?'

When she had first met Jean, she had seen him as little more than a boy, deferring to her, seeking her approval and enjoying having a woman in the house. At other times, he was a man, strong and fast, and when they were out in the fields or woods at night, there was no one she would rather have with her. He never panicked and displayed a rare courage. She could never anticipate whether the Jean she was speaking to would be Jean the boy or Jean the man. The previous week she had got up in the middle of the night to fetch a glass of water and caught sight of Jean in his room, towelling himself down. What had unnerved her that night was not the sight of Jean, but the memories seeing him like that evoked of Owen. She lay in bed that night, not knowing what she would not give up for the chance to have him there with her for just one unsettled night. By the time dawn pricked through the thin curtains, she wished she had spent the night with the stone angels.

Now he was Jean the boy, relying on her to know what to do.

'You heard the message tonight. Plan Green, the railways. Tomorrow we will need to contact London, so we will have to use the transmitter. Then we will know when we are to begin the sabotage. They will also give us more information. We need to sleep, Jean, the invasion could be starting very soon. It could even be underway now.'

Neither of them slept well that night. Few people in the Pas de Calais did either. The Allied planes overhead were incessant. The sounds of bombs exploding in the direction of Boulogne and further to the north was deafening. At one stage Jean knocked on her door and asked whether they should be doing anything.

'Like what, Jean?'

'Maybe we should take to the hills, if the Allies are coming in tonight, they will need help.'

'We stay here. Try to sleep.'

He hesitated in the doorway. For one tense moment she wondered whether he was going to come in. She could not possibly risk that happening.

Pierre stopped by the house early the next morning. There were rumours that the Allied invasion had started, but much further west, perhaps in Normandy. The priest had told him that some villagers had reported seeing British paratroopers. No doubt there were other reports that General de Gaulle was already marching down the

Champs Élysees. Was the tricolour flying over the Hôtel de Ville in Boulogne?

'We will meet again this evening. By then we will know if anything has happened. Until then, we go about our lives normally. I go to school, Jean, to the farm. Geraldine, you go to the factory.'

There were more roadblocks than usual on the road into Boulogne and in the town itself. Each roadblock had at least one extra soldier on duty. One soldier who examined her card in the last roadblock before the factory looked no more than eighteen. His helmet was a size too big, but what was most noticeable was that his hands were shaking as he examined the identity card, holding it upside down at first. Geraldine gave him a smile when he returned it and he looked as if he was about to burst into tears of gratitude.

She could see plumes of smoke rising from the port area in the distance and she cycled past one block that had been reduced to rubble overnight. But if the invasion had begun, it was not in this area. Apart from the normal sounds of the town, there was none of the noise and activity she would have expected with an invasion. But the coded messages on the BBC had been very clear. The invasion should have begun by now.

The cacophony of noise in the factory made it difficult to talk. It also made it difficult to be overheard, which was always an advantage in her passing conversations with Françoise.

'Have you heard anything?'

'Just the same rumours that everyone has heard. Philippe says there has been a broadcast on the BBC that the invasion has begun, but no one has heard anything or seen anything.'

An hour later Françoise brushed past, pushing her slightly against the bench. Geraldine did not look up but carried on assembling a plug. When she had finished, she went to the toilet. Françoise was washing her hands, they huddled closer together. Françoise turned up the tap to help muffle her voice.

'One of the drivers has just returned from Calais. He says that German radio has announced a big Allied invasion in Normandy – on the beaches. They say that their forces are defending successfully.'

'They would do.'

'Surely they wouldn't report something if it hadn't happened. I thought that the invasion was supposed to be in this region?'

'I thought so too. It still could be. This could be an attempt to trick the Germans – to get them to move their forces away from this region.'

'We will see tonight.'

At lunchtime Geraldine went out, telling Françoise she was going to ride into town to buy some bread and to see if she could find out any information. A block past the factory she stopped, dismounted, and knelt down by the side of the road to tie her shoelaces. An open-top lorry full of troops drove past. She was used to them calling out to her, but this lorry drove by in silence, the troops all looking sternly ahead. Assured that no one was watching, she felt under the saddle and sure enough, a note had been secreted there. Lange had been in touch, she was not surprised. She glanced at it and hurried off to his meeting point.

She passed a bakery and noticed a smaller-than-usual queue and stopped to buy the bread, thankful that she had remembered her coupon.

The church of St Nicholas was halfway between the Hôtel de Ville and the post office. Barely one building around the church remained intact. Women were hunched in the rubble, picking through it as if it was harvest time, not knowing quite what they were looking for. There would have been a time when you could have seen the church from far off, but the top half of the steeple had disappeared during an RAF raid in May. Miraculously, all the stained-glass windows had somehow remained intact and the church still functioned, shrugging off the damage as an expected inconvenience.

Although he varied his meeting places like the experienced Abwehr man he was, this was Georg Lange's preferred rendezvous. He liked the mixture of noise and silence and the contrast between the damage, which shocked people, and the magnificence of the architecture, which left them in awe. People came to the church to pray, or to seek shelter, or just to sit for a few minutes. Some came to meet friends. Many, no doubt, liked to believe that its sanctity gave them a temporary immunity from the war, even if they knew that was fanciful.

Being lunchtime, the church was busy, but not packed – more people would be at the Notre Dame in the centre of the town. Lange was on a pew at the front of the church, to the side. He had taken care that no one was sitting around him and was on the seat closest to the aisle, apparently deep in prayer. Few people would feel able to disturb him and ask to be let through. Geraldine positioned herself in the row behind him, just to his left.

She crossed herself and was seemingly lost in prayer too. Lange leaned back in his seat, taking care to look around. There was no one anywhere near them.

'You have heard the news? The Allies have landed in Normandy. They are on the beaches, many of them have broken through. Tens of thousands of them. This is not Dieppe.'

'Is this the main invasion then?'

Lange turned round, looking directly into her eyes with the faintest hint of a very brief smile.

'That is what I was hoping you would tell us.' He turned back to face the altar, where an elderly and overweight priest with a dirty cassock was hobbling with the aid of a stick that threatened to snap at any moment. He picked up a candle holder and disappeared behind a curtain, releasing a shower of dust as he did so.

'The information you have been giving us was very clear – that the main invasion will be in this region. It is probable that this is still the case and that the invasion of Normandy is just a diversion, but we need more hard information. I cannot tell you what it is like today. Some generals want to move troops from here to Normandy now, others think it is a trap. The Führer is convinced that the main Allied forces will still land in the Pas de Calais. One minute they want me back in Paris, the next I am to remain here. You are very important to our intelligence, I hope you realise that. What are your instructions?'

'One of the coded messages last night was for our group. We are Plan Green, which means we have to sabotage the railway system. Heaven knows, we checked out the likely spots often enough. But we have to contact London tonight, we should get more detailed instructions then. We are going to the woodman's hut in the forest. Can you arrange for the patrols to keep away from there?'

'That is so difficult. I have not been able to tell anyone the real reason why I am here. The Gestapo just think that I am here for general intelligence duties, but they suspect something. They know that I am running an agent, they aren't complete fools. You know what those boys are like. They have no subtlety. They would just arrest the whole cell. They would ruin the operation. Lieutenant General Heim is the garrison commander here. I know him well enough, we've dined together a couple of times, we have mutual friends in Frankfurt. He has some idea as to why I am here. I will talk to him this afternoon and suggest he put extra patrols on the shoreline tonight. That ought to draw people away from inland patrols, but it would be too risky to ask for much more than that. You're just going to need to be very careful. And Magpie…?'

'Yes?'

'I don't want you blowing up railway lines, you understand?'

'I understand, but our orders are to attack the railway lines. How is it going to look if we don't do it? I am the one who has had the training. If we don't carry out the attacks, the group will get suspicious.'

'I know. You will have to be clever. But if the Gestapo finds out that one of my agents is blowing up a railway line, that will give them all the excuse they need. As it is, they would love to meet you. In any case, we can't risk damaging the railways. We need them to transport troops and equipment. It is the best way to move tanks. We must not shoot ourselves in the foot. I will see you the same time tomorrow. Notre Dame.' Lange had stood up now. As he walked past her he tapped her baguette and smiled.

–

The Forest of Boulogne lay to the north east of the village, across a range of upwardly sloping fields. The first line of birch and ash could be seen from the village itself and at night the forest gave the impression that an enormous black cloud had floated down to earth. There were some small roads and tracks through the forest, but its sheer size did afford them some safety. It was very rare for German patrols to venture beyond the roads and tracks. You needed the lifetime experience of the woods, such as Jean and Pierre had, to be able to find your way around it in the dark. Within just a matter of yards from a track, the trees stood improbably close together and the undergrowth was heavily carpeted with bramble and ferns.

Four of them went into the forest that night, the 6th of June. The plan was to travel in pairs, taking different routes to their destination. Geraldine would travel with Jean, Pierre with Lucien. Once they met up, Jean and Lucien would rig up the aerial then fan out to stand guard, while Geraldine and Pierre looked after the transmission. It was always perilous. There was the ever-present danger of German patrols, added to the risk of their transmission being intercepted. They would take the right precautions: keep the transmission short, change frequency if it went on for more than five minutes and then dismantle the equipment quickly as soon as it was over.

The Germans would almost certainly intercept the broadcast and then triangulate its location, but if all went according to plan, by the time the Germans arrived in the forest the group would be safely back in the village. The danger was either a passing patrol stumbling across them by chance, or if a mobile detection unit was in the area that night.

They met at a disused woodman's hut in what had once been a small clearing in the centre of the forest, well away from any track. The hut had not been used for years, but it was a good place to meet. The clearing was now overgrown and the forest had begun the process of reclaiming the small parcel of land.

The little moonlight there was that night struggled to penetrate the canopy of the forest as a steady stream of cloud streaked across the sky. It was as dark in the forest as Geraldine could remember. She and Jean were waiting in the lee of the hut for the other two. She shivered. Instinctively he put an arm round her. She moved closer to him, placing her palm on his chest. He was about to speak when silently the other two came upon them. A brief conversation. Pierre knew every inch of the forest. They would walk five minutes to the east. The trees were very thick there, but there were a few that were easier to climb.

When they found the spot, Pierre and Geraldine prepared the radio. Jean removed his jacket, strapped the aerial to his back and, with Lucien's help, climbed the tree – lowering down the cable so they could attach it to the transmitter. They were all carrying Sten submachine guns. Pierre and Geraldine lay theirs on the ground next to them. Jean and Lucien fanned out on either side. Within seconds they were out of sight.

Pierre hated this business. He much preferred to rely on receiving messages via the BBC, but recognised that there were times when they needed to contact London. As soon as they established contact he shone his torch on his watch. It was eleven thirty-three. If they were still transmitting at eleven thirty-eight then they would need to change frequency. The Germans would be able to pinpoint a position with an accuracy of around ten miles. That ought to be safe enough. It was the vans with the mobile receivers that bothered him.

Geraldine was tapping away hard at the Morse code key and scribbling down the response on a pad which Pierre was illuminating with his torch. At eleven thirty-eight he signalled to her – 'Need to change frequency'. She held up one finger: one more minute. Three minutes later she pulled off the headphones and turned off the transmitter. Pierre made a soft owl hoot and within a minute they had been rejoined by Jean and Lucien.

Pierre nodded at Geraldine.

'What do they say?'

'The main invasion will still be in this area. Soon. We are to be patient. They want us to begin the sabotage.'

Five minutes later the aerial had been dismantled and the transmitter packed away. They would bury it nearer to a track and Lucien would collect it in the morning in his father-in-law's car.

Pierre and Lucien left first, taking the most direct route back to the village. Geraldine and Jean stood silently against the trees. They would wait for three minutes and then leave in a different direction, which would take them to the north of the forest, further away from the village, at first. They would then skirt back round the outside of the forest, making sure to stay inside the tree line. They ought to be back by half past midnight. Geraldine stumbled once in the undergrowth and fell over. She allowed Jean to pick her up and he had continued to hold on to her.

It may have been because of this, or possibly because the cloud cover had grown thicker, that they did not see the Germans until it was too late. They were approaching one of the tracks that threaded across the forest. The normal procedure would be to halt well short of the track, and Jean would creep forward until he could see it properly. If all was clear, he would signal Geraldine forward, she would cross the track while Jean covered her and he would follow, with her providing cover for him.

For some reason, they stumbled across the track before they noticed it. They only came to a stop when Geraldine was on the track itself with Jean right behind her. It was too late. A German motorbike and sidecar was parked on the other side of the track, no more than five yards from them. Standing with his back to them, lighting a cigarette was a soldier. Jean and Geraldine froze. Jean made a reversing gesture with his hands. They would move back into the cover of the trees and hide. At that moment the soldier stepped out into the centre of the track and turned casually towards them. They had the advantage of having had their shock a crucial two or three seconds before his. In the second that he stood there, stunned and transfixed to the spot, momentarily unable to react, they both rushed him. Jean threw himself at the soldier, diving at his hips and using his speed and momentum to bring him down in a rugby tackle. The soldier's rifle fell as he went over. On the ground, the soldier and Jean struggled. The soldier was a large and strong man. Once he had got over the initial shock he seemed to regain his strength and worked his way on top of Jean, pinning him to the dusty ground. He was reaching for his holster.

'Help me,' Jean called out.

From her side belt Geraldine pulled out the knife that was standard SOE issue. The only time she had used it before was on a straw dummy in a barn in Lincolnshire. Now she plunged it into the soldier's back. There were two things that struck her in that moment. The first was that nothing had prepared her for the amount of bone that the knife would hit. She thought it would just go straight in. The other was the blood. She must have hit an artery, because a fountain of blood spurted up.

As this happened, Jean threw the soldier over and pinned him down with his hands round his neck. He held them there, tightening his grip. The soldier's eyes seemed to double in size and a look of utter terror was etched into every line on his face. Even in the dark, she could tell that he was turning bluc.

'Watch out, there will be another one,' Jean panted.

She turned round. Of course. A motorbike and sidecar. There would be two of them. The other one was coming towards her. He must have gone into the woods to go to the toilet because he was now running out with his trousers flapping loose around his thighs. He was using one hand to try to hold them up. Geraldine lunged at him with the knife, but he parried her blow, sending the knife skidding across the track. She remembered she must have put her Sten gun down when she got out the knife. The soldier was raising his rifle to her, his trousers now round his ankles and his finger on the trigger.

The bullet that she thought would kill her came from behind and sent the second soldier crumpling to the track. She turned round. Jean had one knee firmly on the throat of the now-still soldier. In his hands was his sub-machine gun with which he had shot the second soldier just before he was able to fire at her.

He checked the pulse of the first soldier, nodded and walked over to her. She was now kneeling on the track, drained of all her energy. He picked her up, holding her close to him as he did so. At that moment he shrieked. The second soldier had lunged at Jean. He must have found Geraldine's knife and, despite his wounds, was able to attack. Geraldine grabbed Jean's sub-machine gun. The soldier and Jean were in a frantic struggle. She took aim, but in the dark it was hard to see who she was aiming at. She stepped over to the two of them, held the gun at the soldier's back and pulled the trigger. His body muffled the noise and he slumped onto the track, a dark pool emerging from under his body.

For one moment she feared that she had also hit Jean as well. His shoulder was covered in blood, but he climbed out from under the second dead German. It was a knife wound.

'Quick,' he said. 'We have to move them. Now.'

They dragged each soldier as far as they could into the undergrowth. They would be difficult to find at night and that would give them enough time to get back to the village. But the track was covered in blood and in any case the dogs would find them soon enough. Then there was the motorbike and sidecar. They wheeled it into the undergrowth on the other side of the track, but could not move it more than five yards in before the undergrowth made it impossible to go any further. They spent a minute or two pulling branches and shrub on top of it. That might just about cover it during the hours of darkness, but at first light the search parties would spot it easily enough.

Geraldine checked Jean's wound. The knife had penetrated the front of his shoulder, but it did not appear to be too serious. She gave him her scarf. 'Keep this pressed against it.'

It was nearly one o'clock when they crept into the house on the morning of 7th June. Within hours the whole area near the forest would be teeming with search parties. Fortunately for them, they had killed the soldiers on a track on the eastern edge of the forest, which was in the direction of Boulogne. Other villages were nearer. There would be nothing to link the attack with this village. They went upstairs. Both of them were covered in dirt and blood. She needed to deal with Jean first. He sat on his bed. The curtain in his room was very thick, so they could risk lighting a lamp. Even in the dim light she could tell that he was pale.

'Remove your shirt.'

He peeled off his shirt. The wound had stopped bleeding, but it would need cleaning up before she could tell if it would need stitching. She was worried that he might need medical attention. A couple of years before a doctor from nearby Isques had been shot for helping a wounded *résistant*. From the bathroom she fetched a bowl of cold water and a sponge. They would need to burn their clothes. She cleaned the wound and then put ointment on it from the small first aid box that she had found in the bathroom. She placed a pad over the wound and told him to hold it while she found something to keep it in place. The wound did not seem too bad. The real concern now would be to make sure that it did not become infected.

The priority was to remove all trace of the dirty clothing. If the Germans did a house-to-house search they would find them both filthy and covered in bloody clothing. She was trying to remain calm. When Lange realised what had happened he would be furious, but she had no alternative. The most important thing was to maintain her cover. She knelt down, untied Jean's shoes, and removed them and his socks. 'You need to remove your trousers, Jean.' He couldn't do that while still holding the pad over his wound, so she undid his belt and unbuttoned his trousers before pulling them down. She sponged the filth and blood from a now-naked body.

A small pile of filthy clothes was now on the floor by the side of his bed. When she turned round, Jean had pulled over the bedspread to cover himself.

Pas de Calais, 7th June 1944

She was woken that night by the muffled noise of more bombing raids. They did not sound as close as Boulogne this time, but it had made for a strange and urgent background. She remembered she had to do something with the clothes. She tied them into a bundle and hid them in the loft. They would survive a random house-to-house search, but nothing more thorough. Jean would have to take them with him to work and destroy them. She was aware of vehicles speeding through the village, which was unusual at this time of the morning. The search was on for the missing soldiers.

In the morning she checked Jean's shoulder. It couldn't have been more than a glancing blow. She cleaned it once more and dressed it. He would be fine.

They went downstairs for breakfast. Jean prepared the coffee and they sat together in silence at the table. Neither of them felt like eating bread and jam. Yesterday had been Jean's nineteenth birthday, which they had celebrated by killing two Germans.

Pierre stopped by on his way to work. He commented on the amount of Germans on the road and they told him what had happened. Pierre paced up and down the small front room, trying hard to arrange his thoughts.

'And there is nothing that could link the deaths with you… with us?'

'Only the clothes and Jean will destroy those at work today.'

'No, too dangerous. There will be roadblocks everywhere. They will search everyone. Keep the clothes where they are for the time being. You didn't take their weapons?'

'No, we didn't think,' said Jean.

'Don't worry. Maybe it is safer anyway. There will be reprisals when they find the bodies. Just stick to your routine. We had better delay the sabotage until later in the week.'

So they stuck to their routine. Jean left as normal for the farm. He wore one of his father's jackets; the extra bulk would help conceal his shoulder dressing and any awkward movements.

Geraldine cycled into Boulogne. There were fewer troops at the roadblocks, so she assumed they had not found the missing soldiers yet and were still out searching for them. She did not say anything to Françoise at work. It would be too risky.

At lunchtime she left for her appointment with Lange at the Notre Dame inside the fortified old town. There were roadblocks everywhere and they were stopping and searching everyone. Maybe they had now found the bodies.

She was a few minutes late when she got to the church and there was no sign of Lange. She found an empty side chapel and went in, lighting a candle before sitting down. What if the Germans turned on her for this? Maybe they thought she was now an Allied agent who had misled them over the invasion and was killing German troops. Why had she told Lange yesterday that they would be transmitting from the forest? He was bound to know she was in some way involved in the deaths.

Lange shuffled into the chapel and sat down in front of her before turning round.

'You had better explain.'

She did her best. If she had done nothing then she and Jean would have been arrested. Her cover would have been blown. She would have been useless after that. 'You would get no more intelligence from the Allies. No clues about the invasion. Nothing.' What was she meant to do? And wasn't he meant to make sure that there were fewer patrols inland last night? It was not her fault. It was bad luck.

Lange calmed down. He was not so much worried about the deaths of two worthless conscripts, but if the Gestapo or the SD found that there was a connection with the Abwehr, well that was a different matter altogether. '*But they needn't find that out, eh?*'

What mattered to Lange was the information that she had received when she spoke with London. So there *would* be an invasion through the Pas de Calais after all. It would be soon. They were to be patient. The sabotage was to start.

An old woman dressed in black came into the chapel. Lange left as she did so, Geraldine following behind.

They walked down the steep flight of steps from the Notre Dame, turned left and then down a narrow alley, with tall buildings flanking either side. Lange was walking a few paces ahead of her. As they emerged, they could hear a commotion in front of them, from the direction of the Hôtel de Ville. She hesitated, unsure of what was going on. Lange stopped and waited for her to catch up with him.

'You ought to watch this,' he said as she came alongside. 'It may teach you to be more careful in future.' With that he doffed his cap, smiled and wheeled away.

She was in the Place Godefroy de Bouillon now, immediately in front of the Hôtel de Ville. It was teeming with German troops, who had ringed off the perimeter of the square. Crowds of civilians were being forced to assemble around the outside of the square. In the centre there were a dozen SS, dressed in their black uniforms, laughing and joking with each other. Standing separate to them was a detachment of around ten Wehrmacht soldiers, guarding a small group of civilians.

She was pushed to the front of the cordon. The sun was quite glorious now, streaming down into the square and bouncing off the neat rows of cobblestones.

An SS officer moved up to a large lorry, took a megaphone from the dashboard, tested it, and then addressed what was now a large and tense crowd in fluent French.

'Last night, two German soldiers were murdered in the Boulogne area.'

Murmurs in the crowd.

'These murders could only have been carried out by French criminals. Therefore, in accordance with the military orders governing the Nord Pas de Calais region, two French citizens will now be executed. If there are any further criminal acts, *two* civilians will be executed for the death of every *one* German soldier.'

She could hear sobs and gasps from within the crowd. Geraldine noticed some people surreptitiously crossing themselves. A woman behind her tried to walk away. A soldier shoved her back.

From the group of civilians held at gunpoint in the centre of the square, a young man was dragged out. As he was pulled nearer to where Geraldine was standing she could see that he was probably not much older than Jean, quite possibly younger. His shirt had been torn and his face was bruised. Two SS men went over to where he had been pushed to the ground. One of them said something to him and he shook his head and screamed '*Non*.' The other SS man lashed him across the face and kicked him hard in the stomach. The boy crumpled to the ground. The first SS man was now behind him, his Luger revolver drawn. He drew it slowly round, leaned down, held it against the back of the boy's head, and fired. The body lurched forward, the head contorting at a strange angle so that it was turned to the sky. Small streams of blood began darting through the cobblestones with surprising speed.

Shocked silence in the crowd. Geraldine could hear the man next to her mumbling a 'Hail Mary'.

There was more screaming from the group of hostages. A woman was pulled out, her shrieks reverberating around the square, bouncing off the walls and through everyone standing there. She was dragged towards the still-laughing SS men and pushed to the ground in front of them, no more than a yard from the body of the dead boy.

She rose up to a kneeling position, begging the soldiers, her hands clasped in prayer in front of her. The SS men were circling her, laughing and smoking. One of them grabbed hold of her dress and tore it. She held her head in her hands as two soldiers drew their revolvers. They both shot her at the same time, but they were body shots and her body was still moving after it hit the ground. Soft groans floated across the silent square. Even some of the soldiers guarding the cordon seemed shocked. After a minute, a Wehrmacht officer walked over and said something to the laughing SS men. They shrugged and the officer walked over and finished her off.

The crowd was ordered to disperse. Geraldine went to collect her bike. It would be easy to justify where she had been and why she was late. She had better remember to buy some bread.

Berlin, 8th June 1944

General Walter Schellenberg did not know what to make of these Abwehr types. Ever since Hitler had sacked Admiral Canaris in February, Schellenberg's *Sicherheitsdienst* – the SD – had taken over the intelligence functions of the Abwehr.

They certainly knew plenty about intelligence, with impressive networks of spies everywhere. But Schellenberg could see how Hitler had come to mistrust them. It almost seemed to be a badge of honour among the top brass of the Abwehr that you were not a Nazi. Indeed, Schellenberg was aware of a fair amount of evidence now emerging that some of them were actually *anti*-Nazis. He did not understand it.

One of the few Abwehr officers still in place was Major Reinhard Schmidt from Abwehr 1. This was the department that looked after foreign intelligence, not without some success. They were responsible for some very useful intelligence, not least in the immediate aftermath of the Allied invasion of Normandy.

Major Schmidt had now asked to see him in connection with that. His timing was good. He would have trouble naming one of the French-based generals or one member of the General Staff here in Berlin who had not contacted him in the past forty-eight hours.

They all wanted to know the same thing: is this the real invasion? I thought you told us it was going to be in the Pas de Calais.

Schellenberg did his best to reassure them. Normandy is a diversionary tactic and the main invasion will still be through the Pas de Calais. That is our assessment. '*We stand by it. Do not panic and, certainly, do not abandon the Pas de Calais. We must remain at full strength there.*'

But it's not easy, thought Schellenberg. They want *me* to tell them what to do with the Fifteenth Army and where to send their wretched Panzer divisions.

All he could think was that, for a feint, the Allies had landed an awful lot of troops in Normandy. It was not looking good. This damned Abwehr intelligence had better be good. Schellenberg did not fancy having to explain it away to Hitler.

There was a knock at the door and Major Schmidt entered.

'It had better be good news, Schmidt.'

'I think it is, sir. You remember I briefed you on our agent in London – Magpie? She is the one who ended up marrying the Royal Navy intelligence officer, and from whom we have been getting such good information about the Allied plans to have their main invasion in the Pas de Calais. It strongly corroborates the information we have been getting from our other agents in Britain.'

'I remember. Continue, Schmidt.'

'As you know she was then recruited to the SOE and landed in France in April, on the Führer's birthday as it happens. My man, Lange, has been up in the area since then to liaise with her. Magpie was in contact with London last night. She was told still to expect the main invasion through her area. We have also been following her husband. He went to Dover yesterday. He was seen entering Dover Castle, which we believe is General Patton's main base for the First US Army Group, FUSAG. So he is behaving exactly as we would expect him to behave.'

Chapter 23

When Jean heard the news of the executions in the centre of Boulogne he was inconsolable. There was no doubt whatsoever in his mind that he was responsible for them. Try as she might, it was impossible for Geraldine to persuade him otherwise. The boy who was murdered was just seventeen and Jean had been at school with his brother. The woman was a mother of two young children; her husband had been sent to work in Germany. If he had been in the square at the time, Jean insisted, he would have given himself up to save the lives of the hostages. He could not understand why she had not done that herself. He wanted to give himself up now to stop any more hostages being killed. They were responsible for this.

Their arguments had to be conducted in whispers in case the neighbours heard. That night, she could hear him pacing up and down and the sound of gentle sobs.

It was only when Pierre came round the next morning that they managed to convince Jean that there was nothing they could do. They had not set out to kill the German soldiers, so they had not been deliberately reckless with the lives of civilians. And they were far more use by remaining an active resistance unit.

By the Friday, Jean had calmed down. The prospect of beginning the sabotage at the weekend concentrated his mind.

The tension in the area had heightened since D-Day. Before then, the Germans who were billeted in the village had mainly used it as a place to sleep, restricting themselves to the occasional patrol, but now the Germans were constantly asking people for their passes. On the Friday evening they even saw a German radio detector van driving through the village. Pierre decided they must do everything to reduce the risk to the group.

'Our job is simple: sabotage the railway lines. If we are caught before then – doing something like breaking the curfew for example – that would be irresponsible.' He would listen to the BBC broadcasts on his own in the old lady's attic. Her house was just a few doors down from his and he could slip in and out without being spotted.

On the Saturday afternoon they all met in the house where Françoise and Lucien were staying. Her parents had taken the children to Samer, where Françoise's sister lived and was expecting a baby any day now. Her husband had also been sent to Germany.

They gathered round the table in the large kitchen. The cooker and oven were laden with food in different stages of preparation. If the Germans turned up when they were all there then they would say they had all come round for a meal. It would not be much of a defence, but even after four years of occupation, the Germans were still bemused at the French obsession with food. They might just believe it.

The kitchen was suffused with the aroma of roasts and baking and the noise of bubbling soup as Pierre opened up a large map of the area. It had been drawn on the reverse of a picture of cows and ducks painted by Françoise and Lucien's young son. If the Germans came in, the map could be flipped over. It would give them a small chance of persuading the Germans that they had happened upon an innocent gathering of friends.

From Boulogne, the railway headed in three directions. There was one route to the north, to and from Calais. That route then headed south out of the town. Just to the south of where they were sitting now was the village of Hesdigneul-lès-Boulogne, on the other side of the main Calais to Paris road. At Hesdigneul-lès-Boulogne, the line split: one track continued east towards Lille and then Paris. The other track headed due south, to Abbeville and into Normandy.

'The railways are the quickest way for the Germans to move large numbers of troops and vehicles. If the invasion is going to take place in this area, then they will want to send reinforcements, especially from here…' Pierre pointed to the east and the centre of France, '…and here.' Normandy. 'At the moment, they must be uncertain – as we are. They are not sure if Normandy is the main invasion area. If they decide it is, then they will want to move the Fifteenth Army from this area down to Normandy, along with the Panzers. If there is an invasion here, then they will come in the opposite direction. Either way, the railways are vital to the Germans. Without them, their options for moving around are much more limited. They will be restricted to the roads and remember that other resistance groups will be carrying out Plan Turquoise, which means they will have the task of sabotaging roads.

'So, our job is to stop the Germans being able to use the railways to either get in or out of the area. Lucien?'

Lucien was a man of few words. He had a large moustache and was built, Geraldine thought, like a locomotive. A typical *cheminot*.

'The RAF have been bombing the area, as we know. They have obviously been aiming at the railway lines, but with very limited success. It is difficult, they are flying at night and from their altitude it is hard to be accurate. Any damage they do cause tends to be fairly superficial – maybe a siding will collapse – but it is all repaired fairly easily, no matter how inefficient we try to be!'

The others laughed. They knew that the railway workers, the *cheminots*, were at the heart of the resistance movements throughout France. Thousands of workers risked their lives every day by doing their best to compromise the system. It was not always the acts of sabotage that counted. As Lucien liked to point out to them, if five workers were sent to repair some track and they took two days over a job that they could have done in one, then the Germans had lost five days' labour. Multiply that by what was going on across France and the effect was significant.

'You see, what would really cause major disruption would be a direct hit on a track, and that has not yet happened in this region. The only way to be sure, is by planting explosives in exactly the right position.'

'And,' added Pierre, 'doing that just before a train passes over.'

'Indeed,' said Lucien. 'That way it takes many more days to remove the train before you can even begin repairing the track.'

'Not forgetting, of course, that if it is a military train then you will kill troops and damage vehicles,' said Pierre.

'Our instructions are to concentrate on this area.' Pierre was using a fork to trace a small circle around Hesdigneul-lès-Boulogne. 'Where the line splits. That way, we disrupt the routes to and from Lille and the centre, and to and from Normandy. Other groups will look after the Calais line.'

'Will there be reprisals against civilians?' asked Jean.

Françoise placed a hand on Jean's arm. 'Jean. Everything we do will help to end the occupation. How much longer can people be allowed to suffer? If we stop and consider all the consequences of our actions, then there will be no resistance and without the resistance, the occupation will continue.'

'Tomorrow night,' said Pierre 'we will hit the track through Mourlinghen – where the Lille line goes through the woods. Geraldine, how much explosive do we have?'

Geraldine asked Pierre to repeat the question. She had been thinking. She had no way of contacting Lange today or tomorrow to warn him of the attack. They had agreed that when she knew the location of an attack, he would arrange for a German patrol to be on the line, which the group would spot and therefore abort their mission.

'Is Sunday really such a good day to do it, Pierre?' she asked.

'Why?'

'Maybe it will be… too quiet?'

'But the attack will be late at night. It will not matter what day it is. In any case, Lucien is working tomorrow and finishes at six in the evening. By then he will have a good idea of what movements there will be on the line that night. How much explosive do we have?'

'Enough for three major explosions. Maybe we could split some up and go for two major attacks and two or three smaller ones – like junction boxes or signalling equipment.'

'Very well,' Pierre was folding the map now and placing it back into the lining of his jacket. 'We go for a major attack tomorrow night at Mourlinghen. We will meet at Jean's house at eight. Be careful.'

–

They left Jean's house between nine and ten o'clock the next night.

Lucien's information was that a supply train would be leaving Boulogne just before eleven, heading towards Lille. He was unsure what was on the train – it didn't do to ask too many questions – but the important thing was that they had an opportunity to blow up the track with a train on it. As Lucien pointed out, if they could blow up the track where it went through the woods, it would be even harder to remove the train. With any luck, it would put that line out of action for three or four days at least, quite possibly a week.

The night before, Jean and Geraldine had retrieved the explosives and the detonation equipment from where it was hidden in the forest and concealed it in a culvert under the Calais–Paris road. They left the house one by one, at ten-minute intervals. Jean went first, heading due north and then working his way round anti-clockwise to Mourlinghen. It was a long route, potentially hazardous, but Jean knew the countryside so well that he could take the risk. Pierre also headed north from the back of the house, taking a clockwise route to the woods. The other three fanned out in a southerly direction.

By ten thirty they had all crossed the River Liane as it flowed across the gently sloping countryside and were at their meeting point in the Bois du Quesnoy. They crouched close together as Pierre carefully went through the instructions one more time. The railway line cut through the top of the woods, most of which was on the southern side of the railway track. Pierre and Françoise would guard the north east and north west corners, Jean would look after the south. Lucien would go down with Geraldine to the track. If all went well, four of them would be north of the track at the moment of detonation. From the position they had chosen, it was a relatively short distance across the fields back to their village, although it was uphill. Hopefully they would be back in the village before the Germans appeared on the scene. The real danger would be if the Germans billeted in the village heard the explosion and came out to investigate. There was no discernible wind that night and Pierre was concerned that the sound of the explosion would carry to Hesdin. They would just have to be very careful when they returned.

As Geraldine scrambled down the steep bank to the track, she remembered her training in Lincolnshire. It had been much colder then but, strangely, she felt calmer now. Back then she had been concerned that the training was a trap, that maybe they would discover her true identity.

If tonight's explosion worked, the SOE and the resistance would be pleased; if it failed, the Germans would be pleased. She still had no idea what to do; she would have to wait and see what opportunities were presented to her. In a strange way, it seemed to sum up her predicament; increasingly she felt that she had slid into a state of limbo. She knew which side she was meant to be on, but she was no longer convinced how distanced she was from the other side.

There was little cloud in the sky, but the tall trees made it difficult to see. She and Lucien waited by the side of the track, scanning up and down the line with their binoculars to see if there was any movement. They waited five minutes, listening carefully for any warning signals from the other three. *All clear.* Lucien crossed the track, crouching down by the southern side of the line. Geraldine got to work from the north side. Scooping the gravel away with her hands, she pushed the explosives in and then attached the wire. Until that moment, she was not sure which course of action to take. She thought of what Lange had said. She imagined what the reaction of the group would be. Lucien seemed more concerned with scanning up and down the track than with what she was doing. Once she had made her decision she finished her preparations, smoothed the gravel back over the wire and then ran it back towards the siding, taking care to scatter some stones on top to keep it in place. Lucien joined her and together they climbed up the bank and back into the woods. Geraldine had taken care to bring plenty of wire to enable them to reach the far edge of the woods. They had chosen a position that gave them a view of the line, so she could see the train as it was about to enter the woods. Two seconds after that, she would detonate the charge.

They had only just settled into position when they heard the first distant rumble. It was hard to work out where it was coming from at first, but within a minute it was the unmistakable sound of a train coming down the line from the direction of Boulogne. They heard the clatter as it slowed down and crossed the points at Hesdigneul-lès-Boulogne and seconds after that the dark mass loomed into sight. As the train entered the woods, they counted, '*One, two...*' together, and Geraldine pressed hard on the detonator. Instinctively, they all covered their heads – not so much because of the noise they were anticipating, but more because of the danger of any flying metal or exploding ammunition.

But there was nothing. Just the rush of wind as the train sped through the woods and the noise of the birds disturbed by it. In front of them, a small creature scurried through the undergrowth.

Pierre looked at Geraldine. '*What happened?*'

'I don't understand. It makes no sense. What do we do now?' she asked.

Pierre looked shocked. 'It's too risky to stay. We can't even risk getting the explosives back. We must try to pull in as much of the wire as possible and then go. There must have been a faulty connection. I don't understand. Did you check it, Geraldine?'

'Of course I checked it! What do you think I was doing down there, Pierre? We checked it, didn't we, Lucien?'

The railwayman nodded.

Pierre shook his head. This was close to a disaster.

'Lucien. You go down and recover as much of the wire as you can. I'll cover you. You two, back to the village. Jean will guess something has gone wrong, he'll make his own way back.' He was clearly angry and was muttering to Françoise in the local patois, something which he had avoided doing in her presence since her first night back in France. He shaking his head and saying '*dinon*'.

Jean arrived back just after midnight. Geraldine was already in her bed when he silently entered the house. He came into her room, leaning exhausted against the doorframe.

'What happened? Why was there no explosion?' He was angry, his tone almost accusing.

'I cannot explain, Jean. How do you think I feel? When I was training in England, sometimes it happened, the explosives didn't work. Maybe a rat got to the wire, maybe Lucien or I pulled it by mistake with our feet – I just don't know. It's possible the explosive got damp when it was stored. I did my best, I checked the connection carefully. I don't understand either.'

'Such a wasted opportunity. We cannot risk getting those explosives back.' He stood there shaking his head.

–

The 13th of June was a Tuesday, exactly one week after D-Day. Lange had left instructions in the usual place under her saddle telling her when and where she was to meet him. She had wheeled her bike up a narrow alley just beyond the old town and came across a shop with a dusty façade, improbably squeezed between two larger shops. She paused there, exhausted. She was getting tired these days and after the exertions the other night, her back was hurting. The shop sign said '*Levy – Chapellerie*'. There had been a clumsy attempt to scrub out the word '*Levy*', but the outline of the name remained visible, like a ghost haunting the new owner. Geraldine was looking at the tired display of just a few men's hats when a man materialised on her right. When he was sure no one was around, Lange spoke quietly in the direction of the window.

'Do they believe you?'

'Pardon?'

'Your comrades, who do you think I mean?' Lange said sarcastically. 'Do they believe you? About Sunday night?'

'What do you know about Sunday night? I was going to tell you about it.'

'Do not forget that I am an *intelligence* officer. I am trained to deduce matters. Yesterday morning a patrol found some loose wire by the track in Mourlinghen. They are aware of my interest in any matters relating to railway sabotage so I was called in. We found the explosive. You had not connected the wire to the explosive. It was not even subtle, was it? If one of them had gone back to check the connection that would have been obvious to them too.'

'Of course, I didn't connect it. Did you want me to blow up the train?'

'Absolutely not! All I'm saying is that you need to be careful. You did the right thing, but what I want to know is this: do they suspect you?'

'I don't think so. Pierre is angry, but I think he just believes I was either incompetent or unlucky. Lucien was near me but he never saw the actual connection being made, he was too busy watching the track.'

'Just so long as they don't suspect you. They'll kill you, you know. We infiltrated a man into a cell near the Belgian border. He was useful for a time, very useful. But he must have made a mistake. At the end of May he was found hanging from a tree. His ears and nose were not the only parts of the body they had cut off. Before they hanged him.'

'I am sure they don't suspect me.'

'The minute you think they do, you come to me and we'll get you out of the area. The Gestapo will be very keen to get their hands on your "friends".'

Geraldine looked shocked.

'Don't worry. You will be well out of the way. It won't matter to you, will it? It won't be long now. Soon we ought to know for sure whether there is going to be an invasion in this area. Once we know that, your job is done.'

The shopkeeper opened the door and gave them an unctuous smile, hopeful that their lengthy spell at his window might result in some much-needed business. No one was interested in hats these days. All they were interested in buying was food. He thought it had been too good to be true when he was offered the chance to take the shop over when the owner was sent away. His wife told him it was a mistake. 'It can only bring bad luck,' she had said. He regretted it now, of course, but it was too late. Even his own brother wouldn't talk to him. The neighbours crossed the road when they saw him. All these rumours he was hearing. He had nightmares about what would happen to him when the war ended. What about if the old owner returned? He shook his head sadly as the couple walked down the alley in the direction of the cathedral. It was a pity. They would have been his first customers that week.

Boulogne and the whole of the Nord Pas de Calais region continued to be battered by the RAF. One night just over a week after D-Day, three hundred RAF aircraft took part in a raid on the Boulogne area. Geraldine and Jean watched the sky turn black with swarms of Lancaster and Halifax bombers. By 20th June Boulogne was barely recognisable as a town, its identifiable infrastructure of roads, traffic signs, shops, houses and places of work all but destroyed. Its landscape now took on a strange dimension, the rubble resembling mountains formed over thousands of years.

Even hours after a bombing raid, the air would still be heavy with dust, and the streets running with water where the drains or sewers had burst. Geraldine was no longer going into work; the factory had been blown up in the big overnight raid. Half the remaining population of the town now seemed to be homeless. Many were living in cellars or the ruins of their houses. Food was in short supply. Any illusion of normality, which the Germans had been so desperate to encourage during the occupation, was now gone. Children were seen begging in the streets for food. Lucien told them that when he was leaving work one day he had seen a young Wehrmacht soldier slip a piece of bread to a young boy who could barely stand. A few minutes later, he saw a passing SS officer kick the same boy into the gutter.

There was a sense that law and order was breaking down. There were reports of looting in some areas and some German soldiers no longer appeared to be quite as rigorous as before, though no less brutal. The Germans weren't stupid. They would have an idea of what was going on, they would gossip in their barracks, rumours would be rife. They would know that the invasion of Normandy had not been repelled. They would suspect that defeat might not be long coming.

And it was not just the Germans that knew that. Françoise met a woman from the factory in a bread queue who told her about a young woman in her street who had done very nicely out of her relationships with a succession of German soldiers. People had been frightened of her, but recently they had started to laugh at her. Two nights ago she had thrown herself from the roof of an abandoned ruin.

One of the teachers at the school where Pierre taught had bumped into an official at the Hôtel de Ville. Before the war he had been a minor official, but his eagerness to co-operate with the occupiers had seen him promoted to a senior position. '*Rising like scum,*' they had said. He had been particularly efficient in carrying out their orders. In the autumn of 1942 the Germans decided to round up all the Jews in Nord Pas de Calais. He had been especially assiduous in tracking down the few Jewish families in Boulogne, a role he repeated in January 1944 when the Germans rounded up the Gypsies.

Now, according to Pierre's colleague, he was acting like a man condemned: pleading to be understood, desperate to assure anyone he met that he had acted in the best interests of France, that he was only doing what he was told.

Françoise did find the factory manager. He was telling any workers he could find that they should stay put. He did not know if the factory was going to reopen. So the people who still had homes stayed in them.

And that was the pattern for the remainder of June and into July. People trying to survive, the air raids, the anarchy of the occupiers, and the rising fear of the collaborators.

They were still getting messages from London that they were to prepare for the landing: very soon now. It was always 'very soon'. Lange continued to be encouraged by this and told her that in order to maintain her credibility she needed to carry out some limited but successful acts of sabotage. They successfully blew up some points and a branch line. The damage did not seem to be enormous to the group at the time and Pierre was disappointed, but Lucien reported that, according to the Germans at the station, the damage was far worse than at first appeared to be the case.

By the end of June, the BBC was reporting that half a million Allied troops had landed in Normandy. The coded messages were still telling them that the Pas de Calais was the main target. *Soon. Very soon.*

But a month after D-Day and with such a bitter battle still raging in Normandy, even from where they were, it seemed hard to conceive that the Allies could be holding even more men in reserve to invade the Pas de Calais.

One night in the second week of July, Geraldine and Jean were eating at the table in the front room. Food was in short supply in the whole area, and although Jean usually brought a bit extra back from the farm, he insisted on giving most of it to the family next door, where the children were noticeably hungry. Geraldine was toying with a watery stew that mostly consisted of thin carrots and turnips, with only a gristly hint of the rabbit that Jean had caught the previous night.

It was an unusually quiet night. The group had not been out for a night or two, they were very low on explosives and Pierre had decided that they should keep what they had until the invasion. For a few days now, it had not been a matter of 'when' the invasion comes, but 'if'. She wondered if it was her they disbelieved or the British. She was no longer sure who to believe herself.

'Pierre does not think that there will be an invasion here, you know,' Jean told her. He was staring at the plate, moving a piece of carrot around in the watery gravy with his fork.

Geraldine shrugged. 'None of us know, do we? We only know what the British tell us. The Germans must still think that there will be something going on. Otherwise, they wouldn't still have so many troops in the region, would they?'

Jean's turn to shrug now. 'I just know that Pierre is suspicious. About everything.'

He was trying to avoid eye contact with her, instead glancing uncomfortably around the room.

Silence.

'What will we do after the war?'

Geraldine was shocked at the question. 'Who?'

'Us. You and me. After the war. Will you go back to Arras?'

'I will have to. My family. They... what will you do?'

'I would like to go to college. Pierre always said I had the ability. I would like to be an engineer. I will wait until my father returns from Germany. I don't know...'

'You are assuming the Germans will be defeated, Jean!'

'Don't you think they will?'

'I don't know.'

They went to bed after that. Geraldine could not sleep. It was not the heat, nor the silence. Jean had said something that she could not get out of her mind: 'I just know that Pierre is suspicious. About everything.' She knew that he was. She had seen the glint of suspicion in Pierre's eyes. He now openly used the local patois in front of her and she suspected that he was often talking *about* her. She had seen his lack of trust in her on the night the explosives had failed and she had seen it since, when she kept reassuring them that the invasion would come. She knew that the moment they realised who she was, she would be finished. The best she could hope for would be enough time to make her escape. She thought of the man hanging from the tree near the Belgian border with most of his extremities hacked off. Maybe one of them had seen her with Lange? Could she have been followed from the factory one lunchtime?

That night she made up her mind.

For some reason she decided that a Monday would be best, though she was not sure why. The others would be at work and not back in the village until the evening. Lange had started worrying about how to contact her and had taken to leaving messages under some bricks by a farm gate between the village and the town. The last time she had seen him he was tense and blaming her. He was talking about having to go back to Paris. He was no longer even sure whether he was supposed to be working for the Abwehr or the SD. She was almost as afraid of him now as she was of Pierre. She was unsure of whom she was really escaping from, the Germans or the resistance. The very fact that she was so uncertain only made her more confused.

A message had been waiting for her on Sunday. Lange wanted to see her on the Tuesday morning near the post office. If she left on Monday, she reckoned, she would have a day to get away from all of them.

She waited until Jean had left before going to the farm that Monday morning and then packed a few belongings. She had some extra money from Lange and an identity card in the name of Hélène Blanc that she had found in the rubble of a house near the factory when she had been helping to dig for survivors a few days ago. The identity card came from the purse of a corpse she had helped carry from the building. Nathalie had made a great play of placing the body carefully by the side of the road, removing its coat to cover her and using that opportunity to remove the purse from the coat. The woman was older than her, thirty-seven, but she could just about pass. The glasses were similar. It would have to do. She would just take a knapsack to carry some food, a jumper, some underwear, and a spare pair of shoes. And the Webley. She would not be able to take the revolver very far, but she might need it for the first part of her journey.

She paused in the front room and looked at the photograph of Jean with his parents. They were all smiling. He was still a boy. She hesitated and then opened the drawer where Jean kept writing paper. She paused for a while, then closed the drawer. She must not allow sentiment or emotion to get in her way. She was being foolish. She half opened the drawer again and pulled out a yellowy sheet of paper and started writing. She left him a note on the table, under the bottle of wine. He was sure to see it when he got in that evening.

And then she left, not looking back once. She was well used to this, leaving one life behind, plunging uncertainly into another one. Now she realised that it was never without a cost, there was always a small part of her that remained. And the more a part of her remained, the more diminished she was as she moved on. She cycled out of the village, heading south east for Samer on the N1, the main Paris road. This was the most dangerous part of the journey. If one of the others had seen her then, she would have probably needed the Webley. The ride took longer than she had expected; her cycling was definitely slower now. After about three miles, with Samer in view, she pulled into a small wood and buried the pistol along with her old identity card, after ripping it up into small pieces. A few weeks ago she had abandoned Nathalie Mercier along with Nathalie Quinn, somewhere over the Channel. Now, the remains of Geraldine Leclerc were buried under a tree. The wood was quite dense and showed little sign of being used, so she shoved the bicycle deep into the undergrowth and did her best to cover it.

It was Hélène Blanc who walked the last mile into the market town of Samer.

In Grand Place Foch a contingent of grey-uniformed Wehrmacht troops were climbing into lorries. She waited in the shadow of the *Mairie* until the lorries sped off. It was silent in the large square, even though it was still the middle of the day. Outside the church she spotted a woman of her age, struggling to push a pram across the cobbles. 'If there are any buses today,' she said in answer to her question, 'they'll go from just over there.'

She was worried now. She had not thought what would happen if she couldn't catch a bus from Samer. Not wanting to draw attention to herself, she walked slowly round the square. After about forty minutes, a bus pulled noisily into the square.

She approached the bus as the driver was changing the destination sign from Samer to St Omer. She asked for a ticket to St Omer.

'We'll see,' said the driver without looking at her. 'First, we go to Desvres then we'll see if they let us continue.' An exhausted-looking *gendarme* checked her identity card and allowed her onto the bus.

She was lucky. After a short stop in Desvres the bus continued on to St Omer, arriving there in the middle of the afternoon. She had planned to move on as quickly as she could, but the town was teeming with Germans and one of them looked at her and the identity card two or three times before nodding her through a checkpoint. Maybe the card was not good enough. She was concerned that it might attract attention if she caught another bus straight away, so she walked around the town for a short while and sat quietly on a bench in the Square St Bertin. On a bench directly behind her were two women of a similar age to her. One of them not only looked a bit more like her than Hélène Blanc, but even seemed to have a hint of the accent from her own region. No one noticed as she leaned quickly under the bench and swiftly got up, heading back to the bus station, where she was relieved to see that the sentries had been changed.

She was already on the bus to Lille before the woman on the bench in Square St Bertin realised that her handbag had been removed from under her seat.

When the bus pulled into Lille just after six that evening, she had two identity cards on her: Hélène Blanc and Nicole Rougier. She had been having serious doubts on the journey to Lille. Nicole Rougier would almost certainly have reported her handbag missing by now. The French police would have reported the fact that it contained a missing identity card to the Germans. It would be too risky to use. She had become careless. She would have to stick with Hélène Blanc.

She glanced at her watch: Jean would be arriving home around now and would see the note. 'Go to the forest as soon as you get this. Stay there,' she had written. 'Do not tell the others. It is not safe. I

251

will find you.' The last part was not true, but it ought to keep him away from the village for long enough for her to escape. She owed him that much, but she still found it hard to believe that she had allowed sentiment to get the better of her. So out of character.

She went into the toilet of a small café and looked through the handbag. She took money, a clean lace handkerchief and some perfume from the handbag, tore up the Nicole Rougier card into tiny pieces and flushed it down the lavatory, then stuffed the empty handbag behind the cistern, where it couldn't be seen.

She only thought briefly about what she had left behind her. There was too much that she had left behind too many times to give much thought to it.

–

It all would have worked out if Georg Lange had not been so impatient, and Lange was only so impatient because Berlin was so impatient. Now that the show was being run by the SD there seemed to be a sense of panic about everything. They had been on the phone that Monday morning. He knew it was urgent as they were communicating in the clear, no attempt at code.

'We must know what is going on… situation in Normandy is desperate… What is she being told?… Can we still trust her?… What do you mean you were waiting until Tuesday?'

So he agreed he couldn't wait until the Tuesday as they had arranged. He would go and see her now, in the village. He would pretend to be an official from the factory. They had reopened, he would say, in another location, and needed her. That would be his cover if he saw anyone else. But she was not in. A woman in a cottage at the end of the row said she had seen her heading east on her bike earlier in the morning. He began to get concerned, so let himself into the house. 'Don't worry,' he told the neighbour, 'I'm from the factory.' She did not look reassured. Inside the house there was no sign of anything. Maybe she had just gone out.

He was about to leave when he noticed the bottle of wine on the table and under it a sheet of paper. His hands shook when he read her note. Apart from any other consideration, this could mean the end of him. He realised that somewhere very deep down inside him he had never completely trusted that woman.

Long before Hélène Blanc arrived in Lille, the Gestapo had got to work.

Jean was arrested as he walked home from the farm: a Traction-Avant Citroen slewed across his path and he was bundled into the back before he could react. Lucien was arrested at the station: in the noise of the engine shed, he didn't hear when they came up on him from behind. They never arrested Pierre. He was in an upstairs room when he saw the Traction-Avant pull up in front of his house. He knew this was the favoured car of the Gestapo. He reached for his pistol as five men rushed into the house. He heard his wife scream. If he had been able to get to his Sten sub-machine gun, he may have stood a chance, but he must have known that this was hopeless. He put the barrel of the pistol into his mouth and pulled the trigger as the first Gestapo man reached the top of the stairs. He was not quite dead when they found him, but he was by the time they had carried him downstairs.

Françoise and her father had been visiting her sister, who had just given birth in Samer. When the Gestapo raided her parents' house in the village, she was not there, so they took her mother and her two boys. When it became apparent what had happened, a neighbour went to tell the priest. Father Raymonde cycled all the way to Samer, where he told Father Pierre, who was able to warn Françoise just in time. Father Raymonde was back at church in Hesdin to say Mass that evening to a larger than normal congregation.

Chapter 24

Berlin, August 1944

Admiral Wilhelm Canaris had seen it coming. It was inevitable, which did not make it any easier. The irony of his situation now was that he had always found visits to 8 Prinz-Albrecht-Strasse distasteful enough, even when he was head of German military intelligence and had to deal with the SD on a regular basis. However unpleasant, it had been part of his job. After his meetings, he had been free to leave, even if it was with an unpleasant taste in his mouth.

And now he was back here. This time, it was not for meetings on the ornate top floor. Now it was as a prisoner of the SS in the cellars.

The truth was that he had been playing a dangerous game since the beginning of the war. If there was one event that set him off on the path that led to this cell then it had been in Będzin in Poland in 1939. He had been in Poland just after the start of the war to visit the front line. And it was in the small town of Będzin that he had witnessed SS troops push two hundred of the town's Jewish population into the synagogue and burn it down, killing everyone inside.

After that, he made sure to appoint non-Nazi Party members to the senior positions in the Abwehr. He did not stop there. There was discreet support for non-Nazi Wehrmacht officers who had got into trouble. He had helped some Jews to flee Germany. Earlier in the war, his intelligence reports overstated Britain's defences, which some in Berlin believed helped delay and eventually stop any German invasion of the British Isles. There were discreet contacts with the British. Some of these had been through trusted intermediaries, others direct. He used his frequent visits to Spain to meet with British Intelligence. He passed on information. And then in 1943, he started to co-operate with other senior non-Nazi officers who knew that the only way to save Germany from utter humiliation and ruin was to get rid of Hitler and his cohorts.

And that had been his motivation. He wanted to save Germany. He could see what would happen. Germany would career madly towards total defeat and then the communists would take over. The sooner the war ended, the better.

The SS and the SD had had their eyes on him, of course. The beginning of the end was in February 1944. Hitler sacked him, and most of the work of the Abwehr then came under the SD and General Schellenberg. He had ended up with a desk in some anonymous ministry, but it was only a matter of time. He could have escaped, but he stayed. The plots against Hitler were thickening now. The big one was Operation Valkyrie on 20th July, but somehow Hitler had survived the bomb planted under a table in the Wolf's Lair. Canaris was arrested three days later, along with dozens of others, and taken to the Border Police Academy at Fürstenberg. To add to the irony, he was not even directly involved in the 20th July plot. Maybe if he had been, he thought, it would not have failed.

He had been roughed up a bit in Fürstenberg, nothing too bad. Maybe he would be able to cope with it; there might even be a chance to escape. But once they brought him here to Prinz-Albrecht-Strasse, he knew there was no chance.

He had been here a couple of weeks. Every day and sometimes at night, he was tortured. It was never clear what they wanted him to tell them. Perhaps everything, but the secret of surviving interrogation was to work out what the interrogators did not know. Once you knew that, you knew what not to tell them. And when you knew what they did know, there was no harm to be done by telling them that. That is what they had taught the Abwehr agents. But what made sense in theory was difficult in practice.

It did not take into account what the lack of sleep did to your mind. They kept the sharp lights blazing day and night and if he ever fell into a deep sleep, he would be woken up with slaps or by cold water being chucked over him. Then there was the hunger. They must have put him on reduced rations, because there was hardly anything to eat. If you had any chance of getting through an interrogation you had to concentrate and it was difficult to concentrate when all you could think about was food.

Nothing, of course, that the SS did came as a shock. Since that day in Poland when he had seen them herding men, women and children into the synagogue without a flicker of emotion on their faces, he knew that these people were capable of anything.

They kept him in chains and on occasions, to amuse themselves, the SS guards would take him into the corridor, force him onto all fours and walk him around like a dog.

For most of the time, he was in solitary confinement. Some of the 20th July plotters were being interrogated there too, and Generalmajor Oster, his former deputy in the Abwehr, was also a prisoner.

But from time to time there was contact with other prisoners. Such contact as there was tended to be fleeting, but two mumbled sentences could sustain you for days. You had to be careful, of course – make sure they weren't SS stooges, planted there to get you to reveal something.

This man hunched on the floor next to him was no SS stooge, he was certain of that. He had known Franz Hermann before the war. A very clever lawyer, an expert in banking law as far as Canaris could recall. Canaris was aware that Hermann had been a social democrat in the early thirties, but not very active. He had continued to practise during the war and had kept a low profile, but Canaris knew that he had been involved with the resistance in Berlin. The last time he had come across him was when he had been sent a report suggesting that Hermann had arranged for a Jewish family in hiding in Berlin to escape to Switzerland. Luckily the report had come to the Abwehr rather than the Gestapo, which is really where it should have gone. It was conveniently filed in the wrong place and forgotten.

Now Hermann was slumped next to him, his face badly bruised and blood crusted around his nose and mouth. He was trembling.

'When did you get here, Hermann?'

The lawyer turned and looked at Canaris through swollen eyes.

'Canaris? I didn't recognise you. They brought me here two days ago, maybe three. I don't know. I have no idea anymore.'

'What for?'

'Better to ask what *not* for.'

'What is happening outside?'

An ironic laugh from Hermann.

'Haven't you heard? We've won the war and Hitler is calling free elections. The Social Democrats are favourites to win.'

Canaris pulled a wry smile. Hermann dropped his voice and through broken teeth and a badly split lip he spoke urgently.

'The last I heard was that the Allies have broken out of Normandy. They're racing through France now. Our defences aren't holding. All this talk about the main Allied invasion being further east along the French coast, apparently it was not true. It was never going to happen.'

Canaris nodded his head. A guard had spotted them talking and was marching over, twirling a long truncheon in his hand.

'Of course not,' said Canaris. 'It was a clever deception all along. It is a good job we persuaded Hitler to believe it as long as we did, eh?'

Chapter 25

There was no single moment when Owen Quinn knew for sure that it was over. There was no single moment when he knew that there would be no Allied landings in the Pas de Calais, even though he had been told as much on D-Day. There was no single moment when he finally realised that Edgar had not made a dreadful mistake. There was no single moment when he knew that his wife had indeed deceived him, as had the Allies. In short, there was no single moment when he gave up hoping he was having a nightmare and realised he was living through one instead.

He remained in Dover until the end of July, which was far longer than he had anticipated. Edgar came down to see him once a week, visits which were certainly not occasioned by concern for his welfare. Quinn got the impression that Edgar came to check that he was neither being too difficult nor going mad. He felt quite close to the latter. He had precious little to do in Dover Castle. The Royal Navy were perfectly happy to have him there, and he was able to help with the weather reports, but it was obvious that work was being created for him.

He had far too much time to contemplate his pitiful predicament. After a while, he realised he must have been in shock for the first few days. If he had that time again, he would have attacked Edgar or tried to do something about it. Quite what, he didn't know, but he resented himself for the way he had sleepwalked home from the park, and allowed Roger and his friends to remove all traces of Nathalie from the flat, and then be led like a compliant beast to Dover.

His visits to the edge of insanity were driven in part by the sheer injustice of his situation. He was a loyal Royal Navy officer who had come within minutes of losing his life on active service, and who was then denied the opportunity to return to sea so that he could be used as part of some secret scheme, the efficacy of which was uncertain. He had been deceived by the people whose side he was meant to be on. But far worse than this injustice was the grief that he felt. Had Nathalie been killed, that would have been bad enough. But now, not only had he lost her, he knew that she too had deceived him. He doubted that she had ever loved him; she probably never even cared for him, and her only interest in him was for the information she could supply to the enemy.

When he reached the very edge of madness one thing stopped him inexorably tipping over. The cameo brooch. It was hard to conceive of any circumstances in which it could have been secreted in the soap dish by mistake. It must have been a sign from Nathalie of something. Possibly it was a way of saying sorry, or she could have thought that leaving him one little memento like that might be a way of filling some emotional void. He did not know. He doubted it was meant to offer any clues as to either her identity or her whereabouts. The brooch was not especially distinctive and the initials 'GT' not particularly helpful. He could hardly walk round France asking strangers if this brooch meant anything to them.

But what the brooch did do was allow him the slenderest of reasons to believe that maybe there was some point in his searching for her. At the very least he might get an explanation. Beyond that, he had no idea.

Edgar seemed satisfied that Quinn was not going to do something stupid. Quinn was tempted sometimes to stand on the ramparts of Dover Castle and shout out what had happened. But he could not be sure what they would do to him. The first night he arrived at the castle, a Navy doctor came and had a chat with him. It was an 'understand you've had a difficult time, old chap' kind of chat. The end result of this chat was a large pill being pressed into his palm. 'One of these each night, you'll soon be as right as rain.' He slept twelve hours that night and when his lethargy began to wear off the next afternoon, he found himself craving the next pill. He took it, slept just as well, felt just as lethargic the next day, and the craving for the next pill was even stronger than the day before. After that, he took no more pills. He accepted them all, of course, very gratefully, even eagerly. But they all ended up down the sink, every single one of them. He did not sleep well and there were many times during the day when he would have happily traded his rages, the insomnia, his anxiety, and his grief for a spell of lethargy, but at least he felt he was in some kind of control of his own feelings. He was not going to end up in some military nursing home shouting at passing clouds, and telling anyone who would listen that the sheep were Nazi spies and, by the way, my wife was one too.

Just play along with them.

On his first visit Edgar told him that the trip to Dover on 7th June had worked out well. The German spy had obligingly followed him up to the point of his entering the castle. They did not know whether anyone was still watching him, so a routine was agreed just in case they were. Quinn would leave the castle between nine and nine thirty every morning to walk down the hill to buy a newspaper. At around five in the afternoon he would emerge from the castle to stroll around its perimeter. Anyone watching him could be sure he was still there.

By the end of July, Quinn knew that the deception game must be over. From what he could gather from the BBC and what he overheard in the castle, more than half a million troops had landed in Normandy and now they were breaking out of the region into other parts of France. After a bitter battle, Caen had fallen, and that convinced the divided German military that there would be no invasion in the Pas de Calais after all. By the end of July, the powerful German Fifteenth Army and its Panzer divisions were moved from the Pas de Calais, but it was too late. The generals – on both sides – could only ponder at what would have happened had these forces moved into Normandy straight after the invasion. The Germans had been well and truly deceived. It was no consolation to Quinn.

On Tuesday, 1st August, he left Dover Castle. Major Edgar came to collect him in a black car very similar to the one in which he had been driven away from St James's Park on D-Day.

'Look on this as the first day of the rest of your life, Owen. You seem to have put what happened behind you. Well done for that. There is almost no family in this country that has not suffered during the war. You have lost your wife. Imagine she was killed in a bombing raid. But how old are you now… twenty-six, twenty-seven?'

'Twenty-six.'

'Well, that's no age, Quinn. You have years ahead of you. Plenty of time to start a career, find a new wife, have a family, nice house somewhere. Mark my words, you will just look back on this whole business as something unpleasant that happened in war. You'll be in the same boat as thousands of other people.'

'I doubt it.'

Edgar was gazing out of the window of the car as it sped through the Kent countryside, but was slapping Quinn's knee in a jolly manner.

'I know it is of no consolation to you now, Quinn, but you have played your part in a hugely successful deception operation. Can't go into too many details of course, Quinn, but all in all we must have saved tens of thousands of Allied lives. Germans have been giving us a hard enough time as it is in Normandy. We've picked up over two hundred thousand casualties in the Battle of Normandy. Something like 35,000 of those killed. If we had not helped persuade them to tie up forces round the Pas de Calais, the casualty rate would have been much, much higher – and it is possible that Normandy may even have failed. If that had happened, we would not have been able to invade again for years, and with all this talk of the Germans getting new weapons… who knows? It doesn't bear thinking about.'

'So the end has justified the means?'

'If you put it like that, then yes, I am afraid that in your case, it has.'

'And what happens after the war?'

'What do you mean?'

'With Nathalie, or whatever her real name is. Will she be arrested? I mean, where is she now?'

Edgar furrowed his brow. The thought of her being arrested had not occurred to him and he hesitated while he contemplated it.

'She disappeared a couple of weeks ago, Quinn. No contact, nothing. Hard to make out what is going on in the Pas de Calais, as it is still in German hands, but we do know that the resistance cell that she was with was pulled in by the Gestapo. There has been no contact at all. My guess is that once the Germans realised that there was going to be no invasion through the Pas de Calais, she had outlived her use to them. They may have arrested her, who knows? She's a smart young lady, as you know. Maybe she just left the area. We just don't know. Whatever happens, I cannot see her hanging around for when our chaps roll in, coming running up to one of our tanks waving the Union Jack and shouting, "Oh, by the way, I was a German spy", can you?'

Be careful, you are talking about my wife. 'But what about if she is arrested elsewhere in France, Edgar?'

'For that to happen, we would have to be very lucky and she would have to be very unlucky. We do not know her real identity, never could crack that. We don't know where she is from. Owen, we are talking about a country twice the size of this one, with a population of forty million. Once the whole country is liberated, it will be chaos over there. We would not know where to start.'

'But just say she is caught. Then what?'

A long pause from Edgar.

'Then we shall cross that bridge when we come to it, eh?'

'And if she turns herself in?'

Edgar laughed. 'Nazi spies tend not to do that, Quinn.'

'Sounds to me that it would be rather inconvenient to you if she was caught. Am I right, Edgar?'

Edgar stared out of the window. They were now entering the southern London suburbs.

'Possibly. But have you thought how you would feel if your wife were to go on trial as a Nazi spy? Anyway, I thought you'd pretty much got over it. No signs of you being too bothered while you were down in Dover, I'm told.'

'Indeed,' said Owen.

The rest of the journey back to London was taken up with the plans that had been put in place for Owen's life.

'The Royal Navy are going to look after you.' They had rented a very nice flat for him behind Marylebone High Street – 'Assumed you wouldn't want to return to the old flat, all the memories and that.' He could live there until the end of the war, and then for a few months after until he sorted himself out. He was to be promoted to lieutenant commander, with a desk job at the Admiralty that he would keep at least until the war ended, and longer if he wanted. A generous stipend was to be paid when he did decide to leave. His new flat was a bit further away from work, but it had been chosen carefully: he would have no need to return to Alderney Street or even go anywhere near it. They clearly did not want to risk him getting any more upset than was inevitable. And everyone would agree on an official line regarding his wife: missing in action while on operational duties in France. Not allowed to discuss any details.

'Try and stop feeling so sorry for yourself Quinn,' were Edgar's parting words, delivered with a thin smile.

–

Cognac gave up at the end of July. He could not see the point of carrying on. He had performed miracles by keeping going as long as he had, but the trip to and from Dover had a valedictory air to it. 'Living on borrowed time' was the English phrase. He had delayed sending his final message to Berlin on the night of 7th June because he had no back up, nowhere else to go in case they managed to trace the transmission to that miserable bedsit in Clapham. So he found a room in a house in Kew and moved in there, making the final transmission to Berlin just before he left Clapham for the last time. Immediately after that last transmission he burned everything incriminating in the hearth. He took the transmitter to Kew, but only briefly. It disappeared into the Thames at high tide one night from a footpath under Kew Bridge. He took a risk throwing it in, but it was a calculated risk of the kind he had been taking every day for the past few years. Once the transmitter sank silently he knew that there was nothing to incriminate him. He had some money left and a decent identity that he had been keeping for this eventuality, which even the Germans were unaware of. But his prize possession was his ability to outwit and outthink the British, an ability which had served him so well up to now.

He would stay in Kew for a few weeks and then he had a plan. But most important of all, he had retired.

–

Owen Quinn behaved in the compliant way that he realised was expected of him that summer. He moved into his very pleasant flat in a neat street between Marylebone High Street and Portland Place. He turned up at work every day at the Admiralty, where he found himself in an office full of charts and maps, and was fastidious in ensuring he caused no trouble. He was suspicious of everyone, of course. He had no idea whether the charming neighbour in the flat next to his really did work at the Colonial Office or whether he was there to keep an eye on him. The three or four people who worked with him at the Admiralty were all pleasant enough, but whether they were really who they said they were, he had no idea. He always checked whether he was being followed, but was never sure. The truth was that what he did and where he went probably did not matter to anyone now.

He had a plan. *Keep your head down, do not cause any trouble, and when it's all over, go to France and try to find her.*

Sitting on his own in his flat in the evening he would go through the plan, fuelled by his first glass of whisky. He would go to the Pas de Calais. He would find people who knew her there. He had the brooch. Somehow, he would trace her. But by the second or third glass, he worried that it might be a fanciful plan. Edgar was right. He would not find her. *'Needle in a haystack and all that. It would be impossible.'* She had disappeared.

By the fourth glass of whisky he would start thinking about what he would do in the unlikely event of him ever finding her. That varied according to whether he ever got onto the fifth glass, but in truth it was never really a question he could begin to answer.

On Saturday, 26th August, Owen went to visit his parents in Surrey for the first time since May. His contact with them had been minimal: he had told them he was leaving London for a while, and that Nathalie was away too. That was all that they needed to know, and his father at least knew better than to ask.

It was a glorious weekend. The day before, Paris had been liberated, and that was another significant milestone towards the end of the war. He took the train down in the morning and was planning to stay overnight. After lunch they sat in the garden, bathed in the warm sunlight and the still of the afternoon. Conversation during lunch had been easy enough; he just let his mother talk about life in Surrey and the lives of their friends and relations. But there was obviously an unspoken presence that could not be avoided.

'So, Owen,' said his father, trying to be as matter of fact as possible, 'what have you been up to?' The question was framed in very much the same way as when his father came home from work and enquired of Owen's day at school.

'Been away for work, told you that in the letters.'

'And you cannot tell us where?' his mother asked.

'You know he can't, Marjorie.'

'We are your parents, Owen, and we have been worried sick that you may have been in France. We had no idea of what you were doing and what was going on,' said his mother, close to tears.

'Well, wherever I've been, I'm here and I am safe, so there's no need to worry now, is there?'

His parents shot worried glances at each other. This attitude was so uncharacteristic of their son. *That woman*, thought his mother. *She has a lot to answer for.*

'You must have done something right if they have promoted you. We are so proud of that. If only you had let us invite some people round today, we could have had a small celebration.' A son who was a lieutenant commander would clearly do his mother's advancement in her social circle no harm whatsoever, if only he would play ball.

'And this new job, Owen, at the Admiralty. Good prospects?' said his father.

'Possibly. Let us see what happens at the end of the war.'

'Both your mother and I do feel that the Navy has treated you in a splendid way.'

'Absolutely, father. I could not have been treated better.'

Time now for the other unspoken beast to emerge.

'And... er... Nathalie? What news there? Is she still away?'

Thank you so much for asking. Everything is fine! Turns out that she is a Nazi spy and the Royal Navy who have treated me so splendidly, as you put it, arranged for her to get together with me so that they could use me as a conduit for her to pass false information on to the Germans. Then she was sent as a British spy – please keep up – to France to work with the resistance, but has now disappeared and I doubt that I will ever see her again. But don't worry, it's fine. At least I have a brooch, and many people are far worse off than me, or so I am told.

'No – I mean yes. No, there is no news and yes, she is still away. I think... I think I have to... to tell...'

'Yes, Owen?' His mother was leaning forward anxiously.

'I think I am going to have to ask you not to raise the question of Nathalie again, if you don't mind. It is very difficult, you see. She was sent back to France on operational work and has... well, she has disappeared.'

A long silence.

'Owen, how dreadful. I am sorry.' His father got up and somewhat awkwardly placed his hand on his son's shoulder. His mother said nothing, unclear how she was meant to react.

'I mean we just don't know what has happened, and I can really say very little, I hope you appreciate that. I just have to accept the fact that she has gone. Maybe... who knows...?'

He struggled to hold in the tears now. Somehow, crying in your childhood home was much easier, having done it there before.

His father plied him with whisky, which was not something he tended to do in the afternoon and, after a long and awkward silence, his mother was as tactless as ever.

'What do we tell everyone?'

'As little as possible please, mother. Just say she had to go back to France. Just say you cannot discuss matters, which I would rather you didn't anyway.'

'I always thought that a foreign marriage would not last.'

'Marjorie!' His father's tone towards his mother was reproachful.

'Well, I did,' Owen responded. 'Wouldn't have got into it if I hadn't thought it would last.'

His mother stood up, smoothing out the front of her dress and adjusting her hair after catching sight of herself in the mirror. 'At least there are no children. I suppose, Owen, that is one small blessing for which one ought to be grateful.'

And so on. For the first time since Nathalie had gone to France, Owen felt that there was a danger he was losing control in front of other people, even if these other people were his parents. It was out of character. He shouldn't behave like that. He realised he needed to get a grip. If he carried on like this – the drink, the open displays of emotion – then the only thing that was certain was that he wasn't going to find Nathalie.

By dinner that evening his parents were taking heed of his request for them not to raise the subject. His mother was back to her inconsequential tales of local life and his father talked about cricket. He suspected that his mother's overriding emotion was one of relief. She had never really liked Nathalie and would now no doubt consider that dislike vindicated, not that she would say so in as many words.

He left after lunch on the Sunday. Before he did, he found his father standing by the mantelpiece in the lounge, looking at Owen's wedding photographs.

'Not sure whether you want us to take these down?'

Owen realised that he did not have his wedding photographs anymore. After Roger and his friends had so thoughtfully cleared out the flat in Alderney Street and helpfully moved his possessions into the new flat, the wedding photographs were not included with all of his other photographs. He had repeatedly asked for their return, and had been assured that that was imminent, but he doubted it. He had no photographs of Nathalie, apart from an increasingly creased one that he kept in his wallet.

'Don't worry. Maybe best if I take them.'

Towards the end of September, he recognised that he quite possibly might be heading towards depression. He had seen people behave oddly at Calcotte Grange, especially when they thought no one else was watching, and he was concerned that when he wasn't with other people and having to act normally, his behaviour was not natural. When he returned home from work it was the whisky that helped him through the evening and into the night. If he thought about it, he realised that he was drinking too much, but he didn't bother to think about it often. Too often he would wake up in the early hours of the morning slumped in his armchair, still dressed, the lights blazing and the cameo brooch lying on the floor from where it had slipped from his grasp. Most times he would haul himself up, have a wash and brush his teeth and climb into bed, but there were nights when he would curl himself into a ball and wait for a restless sleep to return.

He was functioning well enough during the day. A couple of strong cups of tea, a bath and a shave and brisk walk to the Admiralty helped with that, and his work was not too demanding either.

At the end of September, he realised he needed to sort himself out. The emotions that had surfaced at his parents' were still there and, if he was to find Nathalie, then he needed to get back in control. Most of the Pas de Calais was now in Allied hands: the Canadians liberated Boulogne on the 22nd and Calais on the 25th. Quinn realised that if he was to be of any use when he did manage to get over there, he needed to pull himself together.

He could not remember the last time he had visited the doctor. They had registered at a surgery in Pimlico when they moved into the area, and he been there a couple of times for prescriptions for painkillers when his back or leg had been playing up. Nathalie had been there more often, but in his case it must have been a good year since he had visited.

They would sort him out. Something to help him sleep, nothing like the heavy-duty stuff they had tried to get him addicted to in Dover. Then he would just be able to get away with one drink after his evening meal and have a decent night's sleep.

He left work early one afternoon and walked all the way to the surgery. It was a pleasant day and he was feeling buoyant. Not quite optimistic, but he had a feeling that he could soon be in France, and until he did that, he would not be able to move on.

The surgery was crowded. An elderly receptionist with tiny glasses perched improbably at the end of a very long nose asked him twice whether he had made an appointment. '*No, I didn't realise I was going to be unwell.*' She tilted her head so as to be able to shoot him a disapproving glance through her glasses. '*Very well, you'll have to wait your turn.*' It had not occurred to him that he would have to do anything other than that.

He waited the best part of an hour, leafing his way through *Punch* and *Country Life* and being forced into conversation with a ten-year-old boy who wanted to know what ships he had sailed on and what battles he had taken part in.

'Quinn. Owen Quinn?'

He followed the GP into his surgery. He recalled having seen him before when he needed some painkillers. Dr Peacock had spent much of the time then explaining how his retirement golfing plans had been disrupted by this 'wretched war'. They also serve, thought Quinn. Delaying the doctor's retirement would have to be listed as another Nazi war crime.

His surgery was a fug of cigarette smoke. The small window was locked and the ashtray was full of spent cigarettes, some of the ash spilling onto the desk. A lit cigarette was stuck in the side of Dr Peacock's mouth, and every so often he paused to move it to the centre of his mouth, inhale deeply and then return it to its resting place. Dr Peacock was a tall man, with bright red braces, a matching tie and frayed cuffs. Owen noticed damp patches spreading under his shirt armpits.

'Now then, Quinn. How are you? Having a decent war?'

'Based in London now, Dr Peacock. Haven't been back to sea. Promoted though.'

That would appeal to Dr Peacock, who had now perched his glasses on his forehead and was studying Owen's file.

'Splendid. Very good, well done. And how's the back? Is that why you're here?'

'Back's not too bad, thank you. I have come about something else.'

'As long as it is not in-growing toenails. That is all I seem to have this week. Why people can't go straight to a chiropodist, I don't know.'

Owen explained he was having trouble sleeping, '…nothing serious you understand, but you know, Doctor… probably to do with the back…'

Dr Peacock understood. No problem. Quick listen to the heart and look at the blood pressure, no problems there. Hard for everyone to sleep these days. The German rockets didn't help. Had to send Mrs Peacock up to her sister's. Here's a prescription. Should help. Good long walk in the evening helps too. Go easy on the booze, not that I'm much of a one to be telling you that. Come back and see me in a month.

And that was that. Owen slipped his jacket back on and Dr Peacock stubbed out his cigarette, but not before removing a new one from the pack.

'And how is Mrs Quinn getting on these days?'

Owen was momentarily taken aback. Nathalie.

'Oh… she's, you know… the war and that…' He had not really expected Dr Peacock to ask about his wife, but his response was the standard anodyne one he had ready for whenever he was asked about her. He relied on people's reluctance to pry.

'As long as she is keeping well.' Dr Peacock was glancing down at his file. 'Beginning of April I last saw her. Told her I only needed to see her if there was a problem, so I'm assuming no news is good news, eh? She must be what… seven months pregnant now? Anyway, not long to go. Make the most of the peace and quiet while you can!'

Chapter 26

Lille, August 1944

The bus ride from St Omer to Lille in the middle of July had been more hazardous than she had anticipated. The elderly man sitting next to her on the bus held her arm as he spoke and looked at her carefully through moist eyes. 'Lille and the countryside around it have been moved into Belgium by the Germans,' he told her. He looked around, making sure no one could overhear them and moved closer to her, his whisper even louder than his hushed voice.

'This all comes under Brussels now,' he said, gesturing outside the window. 'All of it.'

He shook his head and coughed violently. 'To think…'

He remained lost in his thoughts, but still clutching her arm, until they reached a checkpoint on the outskirts of Lille. Her confusion gave her an air of genuine innocence which seemed to help with the exhausted-looking German sentry, who appeared to be having problems with his feet and was probably the wrong side of fifty.

Hélène Blanc, the identity she was now travelling under, had a blank against 'Profession' on her identity card, but she was able to persuade the sentry that she was a nurse. 'For some reason it has been omitted from the identity card,' she told him. She was going to visit an elderly aunt in Lille, and maybe find work there as a nurse.

'You look like you could do with a rest,' she told him, managing her sweetest smile and allowing her forefinger to brush very slightly against his hand as she handed him her identity card. She had switched to German now and he returned the smile.

Behind him an officer was laughing inside the guardroom, a phone pressed to his ear. He was leaning back in his chair with his jackbooted legs on the table.

'You can say that again,' said the elderly sentry. 'We're on double shifts now, you know. Shouldn't be telling you that. Half our lot have been sent to either Normandy or the east. I just sleep and then stand here. That's my life. "If you don't like it," they tell us, "then you can go out east."'

He continued to scrutinise her identity card. She could tell from his eyes that he was not inclined to believe her, but he seemed too tired to probe.

'I'll tell you what. Because you're a pretty nurse I'll believe you. You really should have had the papers sorted before you set out, but the curfew starts soon and I just want to go to bed. How long were you planning to stay in Lille for?'

A day, a week... a year? She had no idea.

'I'm not sure. A few weeks, certainly.'

'The longest I can do myself is one month.' He had pulled a sheet of paper out of a folder and was organising some rubber stamps. 'More than that and he'll have to get involved and we don't want that, do we?' He gestured to the guard on the phone behind him.

She shook her head. Behind her the bus driver hooted. All the other passengers had been cleared and he was waiting to continue the journey.

'Hey!' The officer had sprung out of the guardroom and was shouting at the bus driver. '*You* don't hoot *us*. Do you understand? Otherwise you'll find yourself driving buses in some very unpleasant places.' He turned to the sentry. 'Get a move on, Schmidt.'

The sentry was busy stamping a permit.

'If he finds out, I'm off to the east – but he won't find out, will he?'

She shook her head. *He wouldn't find out. She was very grateful.* She turned to climb back on the bus.

'And you take care, won't you? How long now?'

She was confused, until she noticed he was glancing at her stomach. She looked down and realised how much she was showing now. It was the first time that anyone had noticed, or at least commented upon it. She was surprised no one had said anything at the village, though in the past few weeks she had made an effort to wear looser-fitting clothes.

–

From that very first night, Lille was close to a disaster. All of her ingenuity and luck, her ability to anticipate trouble, seemed to desert

271

her in this strange city which seemed to be French one minute and Flemish the next. Possibly, it was because it was like her: not sure of what it really was. First one thing and then the other.

She had found a small guest house a few roads from the enormous Grand Place. The sign in the dirty window said there were rooms vacant, but she had to keep knocking until the door was opened by an enormous landlady whose body seemed to fill the hall.

'Yes, we have a room. You wait here while I finish my dinner.'

She had to sit in the narrow front hall while the landlady and her husband, who seemed to be half her size and twice her age, finished their meal.

She could see them through the open door into their small kitchen, peering out at her.

'How long are you here for?' The landlady was speaking with her mouth full.

'Perhaps a month.'

'You have papers?'

She nodded, taking the permit out of her handbag.

'Because I don't do anything I shouldn't do, you understand? The authorities keep an eye on these places, and I don't intend getting into trouble for anyone.'

She nodded. She understood.

'Got money?'

She nodded.

'Let me see it then.' A long piece of dark green cabbage was dangling from the landlady's mouth.

She opened her purse and waved a wad of notes towards the open door. Behind the landlady she could see the husband helping himself to another potato while his wife was distracted.

When the landlady had finally finished her meal, she followed her up the narrow stairs to the top floor. The landlady was so wide that once or twice it looked as if she might get wedged between the walls. The room was tiny, with a bed against one wall and precious little else. A grey net curtain hung in front of the small window and there was a smell of dust and mice. The floor was just bare floorboards with an old rug next to the bed.

'What do you think?' The landlady was leaning against the door, struggling to catch her breath.

She couldn't begin to say what she thought.

'It will do me fine. Thank you.'

'I want a week's rent in advance.'

'But what if I only stay for a few days?'

The landlady remained impassive, shrugging her broad shoulders. Beads of sweat dotted her forehead. 'A week's rent.'

She handed the money over. The landlady noisily licked her thumb before carefully counting it.

'No visitors, you understand?'

'Of course.'

'Your husband?' She had removed her coat and the landlady was staring at her stomach.

'Taken away… a couple of months ago.'

The landlady nodded. She would have liked to know more about her new tenant, but there was plenty of time.

That night, she lay on the bed fully clothed, unwilling to crawl between the greasy sheets which had evidently not been changed since the last occupant. She removed her shoes and covered the pillow with the one jumper she had in her bag. The bed itself was not uncomfortable, though it felt as if it would not be able to withstand too much movement. Despite the narrowness of the window and the state of the curtains, the moonlight filled the room. She could hear scratching under the floorboards. In a room somewhere below a couple were having noisy sex that lasted an improbably long time. She tried hard to avoid imagining that it was the landlady and her husband.

For the first time since leaving the village she was able to stop and think. She lay on her back, her hands crossed over her stomach and she could clearly feel the kicking inside her. She thought of the couple below her and of the trail behind her. And to her surprise, she thought of Owen. Part of him was moving inside her and perhaps for that reason she realised that her thoughts about him were now so different from before.

She imagined that he had entered the room, as pleased to see her as always: the broad smile showing his white teeth and hardly creasing his smooth face, the blue eyes sparkling and the fair hair flopping down over his forehead. She'd shift over slightly to allow him to sit at the end of the bed and he would perch there, taking care not to disturb her and taking her foot in his hands and gently massaging it.

Previously, she had always had to think of Owen in strictly practical terms. How to inveigle him, how to be sure of where he was at any given time, how to convince him of who she was and that she cared, how to find out what he was doing and trying to remember where she had told him she was going to be.

His presence in the room was very real now.

'I've never thought about you like this before, Owen,' she found herself saying. She had started to sob gently now and the kicking in her stomach was growing stronger.

'Everything I had to do, I was forced to. Do you understand?'

And he would have nodded. In an innocent way, as if he didn't fully understand, but couldn't see what all the fuss was about.

'I couldn't tell you how I really felt about you because I could not even allow myself to contemplate such thoughts. But you were always so happy, so grateful for everything, so keen to show how much you cared about me. And I couldn't give anything back to you. At first, because I didn't really want to. You were just my work. But then I couldn't because the one thing I could not do was give in to my emotions.'

Her crying was so strong now that she turned her face to the pillow. She thought of the first time she had been waiting for him to come back from work and had realised that she was looking forward to his arrival. That had shocked her and worried her. That evening they had made love three times before either of them properly spoke to the other, and she had lain in bed afterwards wanting to tell him that she loved him. That was when she knew she had to get a grip on herself. Carry on that way and she would make mistakes. She had convinced herself that she was deluded.

'I'm not sure now, Owen. Maybe I wasn't deluded.'

The crying had subsided and her stomach was still. She hauled herself up into a sitting position against the bedstead. At this point, Owen would finish massaging her feet and slide his hands up her legs.

'I must have cared about you. And what will become of us now?'

She had no idea. She was beginning to feel the chill of the night now and crawled under the dusty bedspread which smelled of tobacco and human bodies. She was still fully clothed.

She was utterly confused. She was shocked at her expression of feelings about Owen. At that moment, she would have given anything for the opportunity to return to him, with all the consequences that that entailed.

The hospital in Lille had enough nurses, the matron told her. Hang around, she told her, when the fighting starts we'll need more. She was desperate, she said, following the matron down the corridor. She had spent most of her money on a week's rent and some food. She had been to the cobblers that morning to get her shoes repaired. Before the war, she could have bought a decent pair for the amount she'd just paid for these to be repaired. She would do anything. The matron paused and looked her up and down.

'How many months are you?'

'Five or six.'

'Fit and healthy?'

She nodded.

'Husband?'

'At war,' she answered without hesitating.

'Aren't they all,' said the matron, who was staring at her left hand. She realised she was not wearing a wedding ring and that that was going to be a problem. She felt the need to explain and held out her left hand.

'A German soldier took my ring from me at a checkpoint.'

The matron wiped her hand on her apron, her eyes showing that she was not entirely convinced by that explanation.

'You can start on Friday night. We always need more help then. I'll give you a trial for a few days to see if you're really up to it. I'll put you on the wards. You clean and help the nurses out. When we get busier there may be more for you to do, if you are still able to.'

For three weeks, the best that could be said of the work was that it allowed her to eat and paid the rent. For that privilege she was able to grab the few hours' sleep that the daylight and the noise would allow her in that rank-smelling room, where the landlady seemed to resent her coming in or going out.

Whenever she could, she would take refuge in one of the small cafés behind the Grand Place. She avoided those in the Grand Place itself; they were more expensive, even if the coffee tasted very slightly more like coffee. The main problem, though, was the number of Germans in them. Previously, their presence would not have bothered her. She would have been wary not to draw attention to herself, but would have done her best to ignore them.

But the atmosphere was very different now. Maybe it was Lille, but she doubted it. The news from Normandy that people discussed in corners and behind their hands was not good for the Germans. The Allies would be moving through France soon. She sensed that the German troops knew it and their presence had an added air of menace to it.

In a café one morning she watched a young SS officer deliberately barge into two local women who were negotiating their way towards a table, causing them to spill their drinks and plates over a group of young Wehrmacht soldiers.

'You animals!' the SS officer shouted. He was in his early twenties and his face was flushed and sweating as if he had been drinking. With the back of his hand he lashed out at the women, connecting with the one nearest to him, causing her to stumble and then crumple to the ground. One of the Wehrmacht soldiers put his arm out, to stop her falling further.

The SS officer was incandescent.

'You,' he said to the women, both of whom were white with shock, 'will pay for this damage. Give me your purses.' They handed them over and he emptied the contents of both straight into his jacket pocket. 'Now go away. And you…' he was pointing to the soldier who had helped the woman up '…come with me. Now!'

On the Thursday evening of her third week in Lille she had given up on sleep early. The house was hot and the top floor unbearable. The landlady was shouting at her husband and a band seemed to be rehearsing nearby. The aroma of dinner rose up through her window, which was by far the most disconcerting sensation of all.

She was not due at the hospital until nine, and by the time she reached the small café on the corner it was only just seven thirty. She had more than an hour to kill, but she found solace in these small cafés, where she could always find a seat alone and an obliging *patron* who would allow her to move the food around on her plate for an hour and sometimes refill her drink with a wink and a smile. And then she would talk to Owen. His imagined presence would comfort her. She had decided on the first night in Lille that Owen would forgive her. He would be angry, perhaps even furious, but in time he would understand. So on those evenings in the cafés of Lille she would revisit their relationship; the little things he had said, the questions he had asked but she had not answered, the nuances that would have made another man uncertain or jealous, and the episodes of affection.

Alone with these thoughts, on this night she was startled by the *patron*, a large man with an enormous moustache who had decided that the price of an occasional free drink was that he could confide in her.

'Not long now. They'll be running with their tails between their legs before the autumn, mark my words,' he would mutter at German soldiers on the other side of the glass. 'Another drink?'

Shocked, she glanced at her watch. Ten to nine. The hospital was a fifteen-minute walk away. She paid and left in a hurry, running across the cobbled streets, straight across the Grand Place and towards the hospital. She was no more than five minutes' walk away when she passed an abandoned industrial building. There was not a soul in sight.

'Hey. Pretty girl. Come here.'

She looked round. In the doorway of the building was a young soldier wearing the black uniform of the SS. She looked around; maybe he meant someone else, maybe there would be other people around.

'Yes, you. Come here.'

If she took her shoes off and ran fast, she might make it to the main road before him. But the ground was scattered with debris and she remembered her condition. Any thoughts of escape ended with the distinctive metallic click of a catch of a gun being drawn.

'Where are you going?'

'Home.'

'And where have you been?'

'At work. I'm a waitress at a café in the Grand Place.'

She realised she was panicking. Maybe she should have told him the truth about where she worked. She was so used to avoiding the truth that to lie was now her natural response.

'And where is home?'

She panicked. She did not know Lille well enough to know what to say. She pointed in the opposite direction that she had come from.

'Change of plan. Follow me.' He pointed his long-barrelled Luger revolver straight at her and then, using it as a finger, waved her towards him and into the building.

He waited until she was inside the building before opening a door off a dark corridor and pushing her into a dim room. It must have been an office at one time. The only windows looked out onto what would have been a factory floor. A desk had been pushed against the wall, a half-full bottle of brandy on it and an empty one next to it. A torn leather office chair was in the centre of the room, circled by a collection of empty beer bottles. A calendar had stopped at January 1943 and there were the remains of a dead pigeon in the fireplace. In one corner was a large pile of sacks with two or three torn blankets on top.

'Over there.' He was pointing to the sacks with his revolver. 'Get over there and get undressed.'

'I can't.'

'Really?' he asked sarcastically. 'And why is that?'

She opened her jacket to show him her swollen stomach.

'Oh, don't worry. That really doesn't bother me. If anything, it adds to the pleasure. It would be my first time with a woman in your condition!' He was leering at her, slightly unsteady on his feet.

'Look…' She was breathing heavily and could feel herself panicking. She was not thinking rationally. Should she tell him that she was on his side really, that he was making a terrible mistake? *I have the name and telephone number of someone important in Paris who would vouch for me.* But she knew it was hopeless. He would not believe her, and anyway, she was no longer sure whose side she was on now. And if he did believe and act on what she said, she would be in even worse trouble than she was now.

Having been in the unusual position of having been trained by both the Germans and the British, she felt she was prepared for this. Not prepared for being raped in an abandoned building, or for the extreme fear that she felt now, but prepared for a confrontation of this nature. Treat it like an interrogation, she thought. She tried to remember her training.

You are an attractive young woman. There may be occasions when men may try to take advantage of you. If so, appear to go along with them. Do not encourage them, but do not antagonise them either. Do anything to take the edge off a situation. If a man tries to rape you then he will not be thinking about his own security during the act. This will be when he is at his weakest. That is when you must act.

So she calmly removed her jacket, taking care to fold it and remove a handkerchief from the pocket, which she used to dab her face, and she sat down on the coarse sacks. Her tactic seemed to be working. The young SS man smiled and removed his own jacket, placing it with his cap and revolver on the chair. He took off his boots, undid his belt and lowering his trousers, crawled on top of her. He was breathing deeply now, his hand inside her skirt and beginning to hurt her. She could smell the alcohol on his breath as he became rougher. *If he carries on like this I am going to miscarry.* With his other hand he had been holding her down, but now he paused while he removed his trousers altogether and started to pull down his pants. Her head was pushed back against the rough skirting board, its dull green paint peeling, revealing damp wood underneath.

'Don't be so rough,' she whispered, 'there's no need.'

And with that she pulled him closer to her, feeling the skin of his back, hot and clammy, through his shirt. She kept one hand, with the handkerchief inside it, on his back, stroking him with it. With the other hand she started to caress him. He reacted straight away, breathed in sharply and started to moan, his body relaxing and tensing at the same time.

With her fingers expertly working at him, she carefully moved the handkerchief to her other hand. Now was her chance.

At first he didn't realise what was happening and for a very brief moment carried on moaning as before. She pushed the nail file in far as it would go and then twisted it. As his moan turned into a childlike high-pitched wail she rolled him over and crawled away from him as fast as she could. He was already doubled up into a foetal position, his face white and his body shaking. She had seconds to act before the immediate shock wore off.

She gathered up her shoes and jacket. He was starting to react now. Blood was pouring through the hand that was clutching his groin and he was trying to get up. She grabbed the revolver from the chair and thought about using it, but feared that the noise would attract attention. *As long as he doesn't have it.*

She fled the room, taking time to jam a plank of wood against the outside of the door. It would buy her a few seconds. The Luger disappeared through a hole in the floorboards. Before she left the building, she put on her shoes and jacket and straightened her skirt. There was some blood on the hand that had plunged the nail file into him, but not enough to attract attention.

She was almost twenty minutes late at the hospital, but the ward sister believed her story about being given a hard time at a checkpoint. Much later that night she was sitting alone in the canteen, as she always did. Two nurses moved to the table behind her, discussing their shift in casualty.

'No more than twenty-five, I'd say.'

'Really?'

'Yes. They had to bring him in here, he was so bad. Didn't have time to get him to the military hospital.'

'You don't say!'

'Surgeon operated on him straight away. They've had to remove both of them.'

'He won't be prolonging the master race then!'

'We shouldn't laugh really. There'll be hell to pay when they find out who did it. Probably one of the prostitutes who hang around there.'

The other nurse lowered her voice. 'Or the resistance.'

It was a monumental effort of will for her to remain at work for the rest of her shift. When she finished at six she returned to the guest house on a long route that kept her well away from the abandoned building.

She lay still and wide awake on the bed until she heard the landlady stir at eight o'clock. Already packed, she went down and explained that she had received some bad news. Her aunt in Amiens was gravely ill and she had to go to see her immediately.

Grateful that she had so many aunts around France, she pressed a week's rent into the landlady's outstretched palm.

The Germans were checking everyone's papers at the bus station, but hers passed a quick inspection.

When you have to escape from somewhere, get on the first bus or train out. Don't wait for a preferred destination. Do not look around a station as if you are unsure of where to go. They look out for people behaving like that. You can plan where to go next on the journey. When you are queuing for a bus, try to get behind a family or an elderly person. The guards will be relieved to deal with someone straightforward. It is a good idea to act slightly annoyed at the delay, but blame other passengers, not the guards. If the situation allows, pretend you recognise someone on the bus or in a queue as your pass is inspected. It will make you appear more credible.

She couldn't remember which side had told her that, probably a bit of both.

A bus was about to leave for Lens and her priority now was to get out of Lille.

Chapter 27

'It just does not feel right to me, Edgar. I am afraid that I don't see how we can help you. I'm sorry, but you have to understand that it's a mess out there and I cannot see how this is going to help anyone.'

A silence ticked away the seconds in Major Newby's office in the mews house off Portman Square. Major Edgar had listened to what he had said and had yet to respond. He was sitting in a low chair in the corner of the room, still wearing his coat and trilby and staring intently at Newby through his hands, which were held together as if in prayer, his fingertips touching.

Newby was unnerved by the silence and felt obliged to break it.

'Look, Edgar. You have to agree that we did all that we could to help. We sent her out there, we linked her up with the resistance – we did all that you asked. We—'

'I simply feel,' interrupted Edgar, 'that if we allow him to go over in a supervised and, above all, controlled manner, then hopefully he'll get it out of his system. He can meet the people she knew, see where she lived, ask a few questions and then realise that he is never going to find her. If he goes over on a semi-official visit, so to speak, then we can control what happens. What we don't want is him rampaging around the French countryside, shouting her name from every hilltop. We want him to realise that it is a hopeless task. Of course, we can stop him doing that while the war is still on and he's in the Navy. But once it's all over, then there's nothing to stop him going over there and causing all manner of problems.'

Major Newby walked over to the window and had to bend down to be able to look out of it. An unlit pipe was in his mouth, bouncing up and down as he spoke.

'As I said, it is a bit of a mess over there, Edgar. You chaps had promised us that when she was no longer needed we would be able to get a warning to the resistance group. That never happened, did it, Edgar?'

'No it didn't, but then we didn't know that she was just going to disappear – and from what we gather from the boys at Bletchley, neither did the Germans. Something probably spooked her and off she went. Wherever she is, my guess is that it is an awfully long way from the Pas de Calais, so he's not going to find her.'

'As I say, Edgar – it is a bloody mess out there. Gestapo moved in on her little group as she moved out. There are only two of them left now and I don't think that they are going to welcome Quinn with open arms.'

'Do they suspect that she was a German spy?'

'No. They have enough on their minds as you will find out. They are just suspicious, but I think that they are suspicious of everything, to be frank.'

Newby turned round to face Edgar.

'And you say that he's being a bit difficult?'

'That's a recent development. Up until a week or so ago he was as good as gold, in the circumstances. Remarkably so, actually. Took it much better than we could have hoped, to be honest. We have looked after him, of course; nice desk job at the Admiralty, promotion, comfortable flat. But something happened at the end of September. Don't know what, maybe the enormity of it all just dawned on him. But something made him snap, in rather dramatic circumstances, as it happens. Read this.'

From a thin briefcase Edgar had produced a sheet of paper, covered in dense type. He handed it to Newby.

Belgravia Police Station
202-206 Buckingham Palace Road

Crime Report

My name is Neville Priest and I am a police constable with eighteen years' service in the Metropolitan Police. I am currently based at Belgravia Police Station in Buckingham Palace Road.

On Wednesday, 27 September 1944, I was on a routine patrol in Pimlico Road. I was on the south side of the street, heading in a westerly direction towards Chelsea

Bridge Road. The weather conditions were unremarkable: there had been some light drizzle around lunchtime, but visibility was clear.

At around 4pm I was alerted by a passer-by to a commotion that was coming from a street on the other side of Pimlico Road. I made good haste to the scene of the disturbance, which I discovered to be halfway along Passmore Street.

Upon arriving at the scene I saw that a small crowd numbering approximately seven persons had gathered outside number 25 Passmore Street, which is a residential building. I observed that a long ladder was on the pavement along with two empty buckets and a pool of water. A gentleman approached me to explain that he was a window cleaner who had been retained by the owner of number 25 to clean the windows of the house. He had placed his ladder against the small first floor balcony and gone to collect water. When he returned, he found that a man had used the ladder to climb onto the balcony and had then thrown the ladder down to the pavement.

I then observed that a man in his mid-twenties wearing a Royal Navy uniform was on the balcony. His uniform was in a dishevelled state and he appeared to be distressed. I noticed that his Royal Navy cap was on the pavement. He was holding on to the wrought iron railings to the side of the balcony and appeared to be trying to climb onto the ledge.

I asked him what he was doing and he shouted that he wanted everyone to get out of the way as he was planning to jump from the balcony and did not want people to get hurt when he did so. I urged him not to jump. The window cleaner, who I now know to be a Mr David Osbourne, thereupon shouted abuse at the man and said he would sue him for damage to his ladder. Mr Osbourne also told the man that he should go ahead and jump, but from that height he was unlikely to do much damage to himself.

I told Mr Osbourne that were he not to desist he would find himself under arrest. A lady in the crowd asked the man on the balcony why he was up there. The man started shouting in an incoherent manner. He did, however, keep repeating the phrase 'Why didn't she tell me?' At this point I asked a young man in the crowd to go and find other police officers. I asked the man on the balcony to come down and he replied in an abusive and offensive manner which I do not intend to repeat verbatim in this statement. He then shouted 'It's not Normandy – they are all lying. Edgar is the biggest liar.' He repeated this a number of times and I was able to write it in my notebook.

The balcony railings must have still been wet from the earlier rain because the man slipped as he moved along them.

I noticed that he was crying now and after a while he climbed down from the railings and sat on the floor of the balcony, holding his head in his hands. At this point three Canadian army officers passed by, and with their assistance I was able to place the ladder against the balcony and climb up. The man did not acknowledge my presence; he was just staring ahead and not responding to anything that I said. I was able to escort him through the doors of the balcony into the house. At no time did I form the impression that the man was acting under the influence of alcohol. By this time assistance had arrived and I was able to arrest him for breach of the peace and take him to Belgravia Police Station.

Upon searching him at the police station we discovered that he was a Lieutenant Commander Owen Quinn of the Royal Navy, based at the Admiralty. The matter was then referred to Inspector Page, who I understand liaised with the Admiralty. I am told that the man was released without charge that evening.

Neville Priest (Police Constable)

Addendum to above report

With reference to the very thorough report by PC Priest: I was informed that a Royal Navy officer was in custody at the station and I rang the Admiralty. Within twenty minutes two gentlemen presented themselves at the station and said that they had come to take Quinn away. I told them that this was a police matter. At this point one of the men used my telephone to call Scotland Yard. Within five minutes I received a call from a senior officer at Scotland Yard telling me to do as the men asked and release Quinn without charge. I was informed by the men that Quinn had recently lost his wife in an air raid and was under some pressure. I was asked to instruct PC Priest not to discuss this incident further and was told that I myself should regard the matter as closed. Quinn was released into the gentlemen's custody at a quarter to six that evening.

Frank Page (Inspector)

Newby finished reading the statement and handed it back to Edgar, knowingly nodding his head as he did so.

'Poor chap. I rather see what you mean, Edgar. And you say that you have no idea what may have triggered this off?'

'None whatsoever. As I say, he'd seemed to have taken the whole business terribly well, once he found out what was going on. We gave him some pills at the time to calm him down and I can only surmise that they must have been working. Whether he was relying on them and then stopped taking them, I just don't know.'

'And I presume you were one of the two gentlemen who turned up at the police station?'

'Indeed. Carted him off to a safe house in Surrey. He didn't say a word. Stared out of the window the whole way there. Doc then pumped him full of something that sent him to sleep for the next twenty-four hours. Calmed down a good deal when he woke up, quite apologetic, actually. Desperate to find her, though. Has to go to France – that kind of thing. "Before it is too late" he kept saying; not sure what he meant by that. If I told him once, I told him a dozen times, "You are not going to find her, Quinn". But he wants to go. So, as I say, let him go out there, get it out of his system.'

Newby walked back to his desk and toyed with a pouch of tobacco and a box of matches.

'And any idea as to what caused this behaviour?'

'Told us he had run out of his tablets and thought he could cope. Doctor gave him another batch and he promised to take them. Seems to be more or less back to normal, apart from this obsession with going to France to find her. One of our psychiatrist chaps came to have a look at him and said we need to let him get it out of his system. Quite bonkers.'

'Who? Quinn?'

'No, Newby. The psychiatrist. So that's where we are. Apparently if we send Quinn on a trip to France then he'll be as right as rain.

'I am prepared to sanction him going out there, but it does have to be controlled. Nicole is in France pretty much most of the time now, looking after the SOE agents we sent out there, finding out what has happened to those who disappeared – the genuine ones that is, Edgar – so I would remind you that this is a sensitive situation. I ought to tell you that the FTP leadership are hopping mad about all this. They suspect that we may have put a German spy in their midst, so they may want their pound of flesh.'

'Meaning what, precisely?'

'Ideally, they would like to get their hands on Nathalie, or whatever her real name is. Failing that, you may want to consider giving them… someone else? Would certainly help us if we could get them off our backs for a while. If you could offer up some other sacrificial lamb, that would help. The atmosphere is pretty vengeful out there, I can tell you. Can't say that I blame them. Have a think about it.'

A thought occurred to Major Edgar. 'I think I may have just the right person for them. In time.'

'Very well then. Quinn can go out there, for what it is worth. I will tell Nicole to meet up with him and she can take him to meet the surviving two members of the group. Let him wander around and realise he is not going to find her. With some luck, he'll appreciate that it is a hopeless situation. As you say, let us hope that he gets it out of his system. One thing occurs to me though, Edgar.'

'What is that?'

'It is not exactly in your interests for him to find her, is it?'

'Meaning?'

'What is going to happen if he does find her, Edgar? Are you going to put her on trial? Let the whole world know what happened? I doubt it.'

It was Edgar's turn now to walk over to the small window. He had to go down on his haunches to be able to peer through it. Sacks of coal were being hauled off the back of a lorry in the courtyard below and two dogs were fighting over an empty sack.

'I really do not think that is going to happen. Certainly not if I have anything to do with it.'

Pas de Calais, October 1944

Edgar managed to find Owen Quinn a seat on an RAF flight to Le Touquet in the last week of October. He fixed it up on the Monday afternoon, but did not want Quinn to have too much notice; he certainly did not want him going round broadcasting his trip to anyone who would listen. So he let his man at the Admiralty know on the Tuesday that Quinn would be away for a few days on official business, perhaps a week, certainly no more than that.

He waited until Quinn returned home from the pub at around eight o'clock. He was staying longer there each day now and Edgar was getting concerned. *Sooner we get him out there and back here, the better.* And then he called. 'Good news – going to France in the morning. I'll pick you up. Be waiting outside at seven thirty. Only room for a small case. Get a decent night's sleep.'

Edgar duly picked him at the appointed time. Quinn cut a forlorn figure, standing alone at the bottom of the steps leading up to the main entrance of the house where his flat was, anxiously studying his watch, a small Navy kitbag resting against his leg.

Within a couple of minutes they were on the main road to Oxford and by nine o'clock they were at RAF Benson in Oxfordshire. Two hundred and seventy-one Squadron were flying de Havilland Dragon Rapides into France and Edgar had called in one or two favours to get him aboard, along with a lot of documents, a crate of whisky which he was concerned that Quinn might think was for him, an army padre and a couple of Canadian Army officers. Edgar looked after such formalities as there were, which seemed to comprise having a chat with a group captain in a Nissen hut.

At quarter to ten they were led out across the tarmac to the plane. Edgar came with him as far as the steps and shook his hand – 'Good luck and bon voyage!' – and by ten o'clock he was airborne.

Owen Quinn left England for his first ever visit to France with the last vestiges of summer hanging uncertainly in the air. When he landed in France an hour later, the winds had a colder edge to them and the sky was more grey than blue. The plane landed and taxied back to the small cluster of buildings.

'Don't worry, Quinn, you'll be met at the other end,' Edgar had told him.

'By whom?'

'Don't worry. They will know who you are. You will be well looked after. It has all been taken care of.'

A light brown Renault was parked between the De Havilland and the buildings. As he climbed down the steps a woman climbed out of the car, struggling to tie a scarf around her head as the wind took hold. As he came past the car she asked him whether he was Owen Quinn and he told her he was. 'How did you recognise me?'

'The Navy uniform. My name is Nicole. Glad to meet you.'

Nicole was immaculately dressed and extremely proper. Quinn realised after just a few minutes that she was one of those people who would say as much as she needed to and then no more. Her silences were not to be interpreted as rudeness, it would just be that she had said what she needed to. He suspected that it was a natural trait, reinforced by years of secret work.

'We will head straight for Boulogne sur Mer. It should take an hour, but it is difficult to judge,' she said as the car headed north from the airport. 'The roads are a bit of a mess. There are some good stretches though and apparently this machine can do seventy miles an hour, although I've not yet managed to get up there yet.'

'What car is it?'

'A Renault Primaquatre. Courtesy of a German official in Calais. Apparently, he purloined it at the beginning of the war in Paris, so as long as I don't drive it down there I should be all right.'

Owen was shocked when the car entered Boulogne just after one o'clock. He had not been expecting the extent of the damage that he saw all around him. Groups of German prisoners of war in their grey uniforms were clearing rubble away without much enthusiasm.

Nicole glanced over at him in the passenger seat and smiled. 'We're responsible for most of this you know. RAF. Hit the town very hard. Big submarine base in the port. Lots of bombs went astray, as you can see. Canadians had a bit of a battle coming in, but luckily we are being treated as liberators so there is not too much ill feeling.'

The Renault pulled up in front of a small hotel in the town centre, which appeared to be the only undamaged building in its block.

'You're booked in here. I'll give you an hour to check in and get unpacked and then I will meet you in reception.'

By two o'clock they were the only customers in a café near the Notre Dame in the main square, apart from a young Canadian officer talking intently in French to the waitress. When they were finally able to attract her attention they ordered one of the two dishes remaining on the menu and ate their omelettes in silence. When Nicole had finished, which was some time after Owen, she neatly arranged her cutlery on the plate. She could now start talking.

'Very well. I do understand that this is a very difficult situation for you. I hope that you will appreciate that it is also a very difficult situation for the people out here, especially those that I will be taking you to meet this afternoon. People here do not know the truth about your wife, and it ought to remain that way. As far as they are concerned, she was an SOE agent who came out here and who then disappeared. It is best that they do not know she is your wife. I have told them that you are a British officer who has come to find her. They are suspicious, but then suspicion is endemic at the moment. It is everywhere. Do you speak French?'

'Some.'

'Are you familiar with the word *épuration*? No? It means purge, or purification. There is plenty of it going on at the moment. This country was occupied for four years, parts of it still are. The Germans could not have managed such an orderly occupation without a good deal of co-operation from the French population. Most people just got on with their lives, did not want to cause trouble. A few collaborated with the Germans, far more than the French would have you believe. And then a few joined the resistance – but this time far fewer than the French would have you believe. Do you realise that it was almost a year into the occupation before the first German soldier was killed by the resistance? A bit of a myth has grown up around the resistance, I ought to tell you. For most of the occupation, *résistants* were seen as a nuisance by the general population. They just wanted to get on with their lives. Then as the tide of war changed, suddenly everyone is in the resistance. The *résistants* even call them the *Septembrists*, the people who only emerged once the invasion of Normandy began.'

Nicole stood up and left some money on the table and put on her coat. She did not continue talking until they were back in the car. They had to drive slowly. Enough rubble had been cleared to make the roads passable, but in most cases the road was not yet wide enough for two vehicles to pass. As most of the other vehicles were military, the Renault was constantly having to pull in.

On the outskirts of the town she halted in front of a badly damaged building.

'This is the factory where your wife worked, or at least the remains of it. She assembled electrical parts.' They paused for a few moments and then drove on. The road became easier outside the town. Quinn noticed that they had entered a village called Hesdin-l'Abbé, where they appeared to be the only car on the road. Just by the church they pulled up outside a row of cottages.

'And this is where your wife stayed while she was in the area. This house here.' It was the only one in the row where all the curtains were drawn. 'She lodged here with another member of the resistance group. They were all based in this village. We are going to meet two of them now. You need to know that while she was here, your wife was known as Geraldine.'

'Was that her real name?'

'No, of course not. No one knows her real name. Geraldine was the name we gave her. Geraldine Leclerc. And remember. They do not know the truth about her, whatever they suspect. They wanted to be able to tell you what happened themselves and I agreed to that. We owe it to them.'

The house was larger than some of the others that Quinn had noticed in the village and it was set back from the road, behind a low stone wall and a pretty though slightly unkempt front garden. It was on the outskirts of the village and Owen could see a forest rising in the distance. Nicole signalled for Owen to pause halfway down the path while she went in. A minute later she signalled for him to enter.

A man and a woman in their late thirties, or perhaps early forties, were sitting around the table in a large kitchen. Neither of them smiled when he entered the room, though the man did point to an empty chair where he should sit. Through the kitchen window, Owen could see an older man in the garden.

'Françoise, Lucien – this is Lieutenant Commander Quinn from the Royal Navy.' They both nodded. Owen noticed that the man was sitting in a wheelchair and winced whenever he moved. 'He has come to France to try to find Geraldine. He may have a few questions for you, but first, please could you tell him what happened?'

Lucien made a hand movement towards his wife. She would speak. Owen noticed that her eyes were red and she was tightly clutching a large white handkerchief, twisting it as she spoke.

'We were not really an active resistance cell until March or April this year. Pierre had joined the FTP earlier in the war but was not very active. In March they asked him to put together a group in this village. The FTP operates in cells of four people, a leader and three others. So he asked Jean to join him. He was one of his pupils and was a bright boy, very strong and knew the countryside very well. And then he asked us. In fact, he did not want a husband and wife to be in the same group, but he needed us both. Lucien is... was... a *cheminot*, he worked on the railways. I was a supervisor at a factory in Boulogne. Because it was supplying equipment for the German Army I had good security clearance, it was easy for me to get in and out of Boulogne. In any case, this village is not exactly full of people queuing up to join the resistance. Geraldine joined us towards the end of April, I think it was. Lucien?'

Her husband nodded.

'At the end of April then. She landed not far from here and brought a transmitter with her, and explosives. I got her a job at the factory and she lodged with Jean in his father's house. It was only Jean there as his father had been sent to Germany and his mother is dead. It was fine, there were no problems. We would make transmissions to London and Geraldine would get the information that we were to prepare for a landing in this area. We carried out some sabotage on the railways.'

Lucien muttered something. His wife continued.

'Geraldine had been trained in explosives in England, so she was our expert. Lucien wonders how much of an expert she really was. What would have been our biggest act of sabotage did not happen. It was near here actually. Lucien had information that a German supply train was going to be passing through a wood late at night. If we could have blown it up it would have caused major damage. Because of the position, it would have taken days for them to recover the train, and then they would have had to repair the track. Lucien went down with Geraldine to lay the explosives while the rest of us stood guard.'

'I never saw her make the connection, so I do not know the truth,' said Lucien. 'All I know is that afterwards, Pierre was very suspicious.

He just could not understand why the charge had failed. But I never checked the connection, that was her job. I was keeping an eye on the track.' He shifted himself uncomfortably in his wheelchair and continued.

'But we did carry out some successful sabotage after that. Not very big jobs, we had lost too much of our explosives already on that first attempt, but it was enough to cause a bit of trouble.

'We carried on through June and July. Transmissions, sabotage. Our main job was to wait until the invasion here and then do what we could to help. But then in the middle of July, Geraldine disappeared.'

'Do you remember the date?' asked Owen. He was looking up from the small notebook he had in front of him.

Both Françoise and Lucien laughed bitterly. Françoise's eyes filled with tears as she carried on speaking.

'Oh yes, we remember the date. The 17th of July. It was a Monday. Monday, the 17th of July.' There was a long and complete silence, apart from the thud of wood being chopped in the garden.

'I had gone to Samer to see my sister who had just had a baby. My father came with me.' She nodded towards the older man in the garden. 'We were about to return when Father Pierre turned up. He is the priest in Samer. The priest from this village, Father Raymonde, had come to see him. The Gestapo were raiding our house and looking for me.' She broke down into a sob. Lucien continued.

'I was at the station in Boulogne when they arrested me. The Gestapo. I was taken to their headquarters in the town and thrown into a cell. Jean was already in the cell next to me. He had been badly beaten. I think he must have fought with them. There was blood everywhere. They took it in turns that day and through the night to torture us. Who else was in the group, where was Geraldine, what did we know about her, where is the transmitter, our weapons. They wanted to know everything.

'Pierre told us that if we ever got caught, to hold out for as long as possible – even a few hours will give the others time to get away. Of course I did not know that Pierre was already dead.'

Quinn looked up, raising his eyebrows.

'Yes, he shot himself when they came to arrest him. And, of course, I had no idea whether Françoise was safe. But I said nothing. Jean, he argued with them the whole time, he fought them. At about six in the morning – that would be the Tuesday – they must have been doing the most terrible things to him. I heard him cry for his mother. He let out this terrible howl and then there was silence and soon after that I saw them carry his body from the cell. I don't know what they did to him in the end, but it was terrible. I have heard animals caught in traps and this was far worse.

'Of course, they could concentrate on me after that. They broke every toe. They pulled out my fingernails. They broke my knees. They put electricity in places I can't tell you about but the pain was so bad that I passed out. When I was coming round on one occasion I heard them talking – they must have thought I was still unconscious. They said something like "We just need to find his wife now". So I reckoned that meant Françoise was the only one who had escaped, which meant I could tell them about Pierre. So I took a risk and when they tortured me next, I told them about Pierre. I also told them that I had no idea where Françoise was. There had been an argument I said and she had left home. I don't think they believed me but they weren't sure. I had told them about Pierre and they were not to know that I had overheard them talking. Then I just collapsed. It was like a coma. They could not wake me up. I was taken to the prison near Calais. I was freed by the resistance there just as the Canadians came in.'

'And you, Françoise. What happened?'

'My father and I went into hiding. There is a lot of forest and marsh in that area and my father knows it very well, it is where he was brought up. We survived. It would have been better if I had not survived.'

Owen started to ask a question, but Nicole put her hand on his arm to stop him. Françoise continued.

'When they came to this house to find me, my mother was here with my children.' She gestured to a photograph on a shelf of two boys. 'They took my mother and the boys. They took them to a barn, where no one could hear anything. They must have tried to make them to say where I was, we do not know exactly what happened. But we do know what happened next, one of the workers on a nearby farm was hiding in the trees and he saw it. They locked the three of them in the barn and set fire to it. He heard their screams. Apparently, they lasted for ten minutes.'

For a full five minutes Françoise wept into her handkerchief before she could continue.

'Georges was ten, Charles was seven. My mother was in her sixties. So you see, Lucien and I survived, but for what? We have each other and we have my father, but we now have no life. We have entered the winter of our lives and it will only get darker, it will never be warm again. People do not know what to say to us. They are very nice, they bring us food,' she pointed at a kitchen top with bread and baskets of vegetables on it, 'but we have little appetite. They say things like, maybe you can have more children.'

Lucien shook his head.

'After what the Gestapo did to Lucien, that is impossible. Ten and seven they were. Georges and Charles. A life without children, it is unimaginable.'

Another long pause. He was shocked beyond belief at the grief and the dignity in this room. His own problems now seemed so irrelevant that he felt embarrassed. Françoise's father came in from the garden; he walked over to his daughter and placed a hand on her shoulder, and she reached back to place her hand on his. When he spoke again, Owen tried to sound as sympathetic as possible.

'And what do you think alerted the Gestapo? Was it Geraldine? Did she inform on you?'

Françoise spoke now.

'We don't think so, because they were so desperate to find out where she was. From what we have found out since, a man went to Jean's cottage to look for her. He said he was from the factory but, of course, he was not. One of the collaborators who was working for the police was arrested after the liberation and he gave some information before he was… dealt with. He said that this man was from German Intelligence. The Abwehr I think it is. We do not know what he was doing there, there must have been some information that she was a British agent. But apparently, he found a note Geraldine had left for Jean. We do not know exactly what it said, but it was a warning of a type, telling him to escape. Jean thought a lot of her and he protected her. Maybe it was her way of thanking him.'

–

Nicole waited until they had left the village before she pulled off the main road and parked on a verge. To either side of them were rolling fields and trees. A flock of sheep was grazing in the field closest to them.

'It is Wednesday today. I can assist you until the weekend and then I have to continue my work.'

'What do you do?'

'You don't know what I do?'

'I have an idea.'

'My section of the SOE trained agents to work in occupied France and then sent them out here. Nearly five hundred of them. Over a hundred of them have not returned. Some of them, we know, were killed, but others are missing, some are still in occupied areas like Alsace. My job is to try to find out what happened to them.'

A shepherd had now joined the flock in the field to their right and his dogs were herding it up the hill. The shepherd bent down to pick up one of the lambs. Nicole continued.

'You know, I often accompanied these agents to their plane before they were flown out to France. Many of them were parachuted into France, some landed in Lysanders, like your wife. But it was always a difficult journey. I often felt that I was sending people to their deaths. But they were all so brave. They all thanked me, you know.

'With your wife, it was different. Did you know that I was with her during her training too? We had to make special arrangements, we couldn't let her be trained with other agents or at the places we normally used. I tried not to get close to her, but that was not difficult. She never gave anything of herself. She was as cold as steel. I always thought that if she had been one of ours, she would have made a very good agent. Did you love her?'

Owen was surprised by the question.

'Yes… I did. More than anything else in the world. I know that I shouldn't, that it's wrong, but I…'

'Don't worry. It is not a crime to love the wrong person. Most people manage it at least once in their lives. I can see you need some answers.'

'Do you think that we will find her?'

'Honestly? No. The Abwehr were good, very professional. Probably only one or two people in it were aware of her true identity, no more than that. She has shown how resourceful she is and how she copes under pressure. Can you imagine living the lies she has led – here and in England? I mean, did you think you had a normal relationship?'

'Of course.'

'Exactly my point. You are an intelligent young man. You believed that it was a normal relationship, and maybe in some respects it was.

She was clever. Come on now. We go back to the hotel and tomorrow we resume our search.'

Owen Quinn felt humbled by the grief and the dignity he had encountered at Françoise and Lucien's house, although it had done nothing to diminish his determination to find his wife. But he was equally determined to do what he could to help Françoise and Lucien.

—

Quinn came down for breakfast at eight the next morning. Nicole was waiting in the tiny reception area. 'We are going to Samer,' she said. 'We will talk in the car. There is no time for breakfast.'

'Françoise contacted me last night,' she said as they headed out of Boulogne. 'She felt guilty, I don't know why. Maybe she picked up that there was a connection between you and her. She has one clue that she didn't bother to tell us about, but she has now. She hasn't told anyone about it, which is lucky for you. Apparently, Geraldine was seen in Samer the morning she disappeared. She was seen getting on a bus to St Omer.'

'By whom?'

'By one of the villagers from Hesdin who happened to be in Samer that morning. She knew that Geraldine was staying with Jean, but she only mentioned it to Françoise last week. This villager did say that a local *gendarme* was checking people's identity cards as they boarded the bus. So now we are going to the police station in Samer.'

The small police station was inside the *Mairie* and it did not take them long to find the policeman who had been checking the passes that day. There were not many policemen in Samer.

'Yes, I think I remember,' he said.

'Please look at this photograph.'

'Yes, probably.'

'Where was the bus going?'

'Desvres first, then St Omer.'

'You sure? Yes? And what was her name?'

'Hélène something or other.'

'Not Geraldine?'

'No! I told you, Hélène.'

'You sure?'

296

'Yes, of course I am sure. My mother is called Hélène. And my wife. I don't forget a Hélène, as much as I might try!'

So they drove to St Omer, the roads crowded and progress slow. They tried all the hotels in the town. No one recognised the photograph. They had split up by now to try to cover more places. Owen slipped into a couple of jewellers on Rue Carnot.

'Does this brooch mean anything?'

'It's cameo.'

'Thank you – other than that?'

'No, nice example, good quality, nothing exceptional.'

'And the 'GT' on the back?'

'Maybe someone's initials, sir.'

'Thank you. Thank you very much.'

It was getting dark now and they booked into one of the hotels. It would give them the evening to ask in the restaurants and bars. When they emerged from the hotel to do that, Nicole had an idea. 'We know the date, don't we? Let's check at the police station.'

The sergeant was having a quiet evening and was very happy to help, especially an officer from the British Army and such a beautiful lady. 'Thank you very much sir, even our darkest hour, you never forgot France.' He was puffed up with his own self-importance. As long as they didn't ask any awkward questions about what he was up to during the war. He was only doing his duty. He had a family to consider...

Quinn bit his tongue. He thought better of explaining the difference between the Army and the Navy. At least we have one of each, he thought. And he decided not to ask the *gendarme* what he did in the war.

'The seventeenth of July, you say?'

'Yes, it was a Monday.'

'It was. That's what it says in my book too.' A loud, toothy laugh. Both Owen and Nicole briefly joined in

'And you say an identity card was stolen that day?'

'No. We are just wondering whether one was reported as stolen that day. We are not sure whether one was.'

The sergeant looked puzzled, but carefully studied the book.

'Ah yes. Two reported missing that day.'

'Can we have the details?' asked Nicole.

'Were they your cards? Because if not, this would be most improper.'

Nicole smiled very sweetly as she palmed a couple of folded bank-notes across the desk.

'Of course, for the British Army, this is not a problem. Henri Laporte from St Omer reported his card missing that day.'

'Age.'

'Sixty.'

'And the other?'

'Nicole Rougier. Aged twenty-seven.'

Nicole Rougier. 'And where is she from?'

'Place of residence, Béthune. That is near here. Place of birth, let me see… Mulhouse. In Alsace.'

It was a breakthrough. Of sorts. They had done well to trace Geraldine from the village to St Omer and now, acting on Nicole's instinct, they had established that the identity card of a women of a similar age to Geraldine had been lost, presumed stolen, in St Omer on the same day. It didn't prove anything, of course. It was probably complete coincidence. But Nicole had a growing regard for Geraldine's prowess as an agent. It was possible that she had stolen the identity of Nicole Rougier.

She was quite probably going to continue her journey home in stages and at each stage would try to assume a new identity. She would presumably target women of a similar age and, where possible, from a similar part of the country. It was a risky strategy in the short term, but once you had stolen a new card, it would help keep the scent cold.

They returned to the hotel. Had they bothered to turn round after they had left the police station that evening, which, of course, they had no reason to do, they would have seen a tall figure wearing a long dark coat and matching trilby enter it.

–

Friday was the last day that Nicole could help Owen. They decided to stay in St Omer to see if they could trace where she had gone from there, possibly as Nicole Rougier. But they drew a blank. No one at the train station or the bus station could recall seeing her. They asked in shops and cafés, they revisited the places they had tried the day before.

The truth was, she could have gone anywhere. Nicole had to continue with her own work. They sat in a small bar by the train station. She was heading back towards Normandy. Where would he go?

'Paris. I will try there. I am not sure why. She said she came from there, but I suppose that was a lie like everything else. But it seems like the best place to go next.'

Nicole had torn a scrap of paper from her notebook and was writing on it. Truly professional, thought Owen. Avoiding leaving an impression of the writing on the blank sheets underneath. Impressive.

'Here. I didn't give this to you, understand? If you are going to Paris, visit this man. That is his address. I met him when I was there last month. He will be very helpful. Tell him that I sent you. See how you get on with him and then judge for yourself how much you want to tell him, but if I were you, I would trust him. You don't have many other options.'

'Why are you helping me like this?'

Nicole thought long and hard.

'I was wondering that myself. I am certainly doing more than I was told to do. I was meant to keep you with me all the time, not let you out of my sight and deliver you home in one piece with no harm done. If I am honest, Owen, I don't think they want you to find her. I was asked to report any leads we found. So why am I helping you? I'm not sure. Maybe I am helping you because you aren't after revenge. I think it is because when I asked you whether you loved her, you admitted you did. "More than anything else in the world," I think was what you said. I admire honesty. You deserve to find her. But you had better think carefully about what you'll do if you do find her.'

Chapter 28

Like a river, she meandered without any obviously logical route down the eastern edges of a France steeling itself for liberation. She knew where she was heading but was seemingly reluctant to arrive there. Like a naughty child afraid of facing up to punishment, she procrastinated throughout her journey, looking for excuses to avoid moving on.

To a great extent her journey was dictated by the circumstance of war. She had arrived in Lens to find the town in a state of panic in the aftermath of an Allied bombing raid. The bus was stopped by a German tank pulled across a road just before the town centre. A soldier came onboard and shouted at everyone to get off, although few passengers needed to be told.

The German garrison was in the process of evacuation. An army truck had pulled up on the other side of the road and soldiers were loading it with food and other provisions from a large shop with broken windows. The owner was pleading with an officer not to take everything.

The officer walked over to the entrance and told his men to stop. The owner, a thickset man in his late thirties with a large, clean, white apron, smiled and put his arms round a couple of children who were standing with him on the pavement. The officer adjusted his gloves, briskly walked over to the owner, removed his pistol from its holster and shot him through the temple. He nodded at his men for them to carry on.

Hélène Blanc was shocked – not so much at what she had just seen, but rather that she was no longer so shocked by it. She had been considering staying in Lens but, from what she could see, she would soon be on her own. On the journey from Lille she had realised that she had to regard her Hélène Blanc identity as compromised. It was likely that when the Gestapo started to investigate the castration of the soldier in Lille they would be looking at reports of anyone matching the description of the attacker who had recently left town. They could identify her through the hospital and certainly through her landlady, who would have registered her with the authorities while she was staying at the guest house. She doubted the landlady's capacity or inclination not to co-operate with the Germans. Her priority in Lens, she decided, was to find a new identity but, judging by the speed at which the town was being deserted, that appeared to be futile.

The army truck had pulled away and a small group of people had detached themselves from the stream of civilians wending their way out of the town. The two children were howling and a woman was bending down asking them where their mother was. Another woman and two men carried the shot owner into the shop. Hélène followed them in and, feeling she at least ought to do something, knelt down by the body and felt for a pulse.

'I wouldn't bother. He was dead before he hit the ground.' The man who was speaking was about her age and height. The collar of his jacket was turned up and he was not wearing a tie. As he lit a cigarette the match briefly illuminated a thin and unshaven face. His green eyes appeared translucent. He looked as if he could do with a good meal and a few days in the sun.

'I'm a nurse.'

'Congratulations,' he said, bowing slowly and grinning. 'You ought to have known he was dead then. Not many people survive a German bullet through the head. I'm a teacher and even I knew that. My name is Laurent, by the way.' He stretched over the corpse to shake her hand, as if they had been introduced by friends while strolling. Ash from his cigarette floated onto the body.

'And do you have a name?'

'Pardon?' She was lost in her thoughts, unsure of whether to stay or to leave, to take some food from the shop or not.

'My name is Laurent,' he said slowly, as if she were hard of hearing. 'What are you called?'

'Hélène. I arrived here just before from Lille. I really don't know where I'm heading. What is the latest news?'

The shop was quiet now. The other people who had helped carry the body in had left and the hysterical children must have been taken away. Flies had begun to buzz around the dead body and the food that had been strewn across the floor by the Germans in their haste to take as much as they could. A smashed jar of jam was getting particular attention.

'The Allies are pushing in from the west, mostly Americans and Canadians. In most places the Germans are staying and fighting. I wouldn't stay around anywhere like here where there is going to be fighting. People seem to be heading into the country to hide until they can then go to somewhere liberated by the Allies. Hard to think it will all be over soon. That is when life will get interesting. Why don't you join me? We can go for a long walk in the country together.'

They headed south and stayed together as travelling companions for a month. Laurent had made the most of his asthma, he told her, to avoid being sent away as forced labour and he was able to remain in Lens throughout the war as a teacher. He made a passing reference or two to helping out the resistance. Nothing much, he emphasised, just passing messages and things like that. He wasn't brave enough to do much else, he assured her.

'You watch though,' he told her. 'Soon everyone will have been in the resistance. It will turn out that France was a country of heroes while the Germans were here. It wasn't at the time, that's all!'

On their third day together, as they looked over Cambrai from a nearby hill, she confided that she had been involved in the resistance too, in Lille. Like him, nothing too important, but there had been 'an incident' with a German soldier and she had decided to leave town.

Laurent nodded, not probing any further. He didn't ask too many questions, preferring to have her as an audience to whom he could give the names of the trees and plants they saw, and for whom he could recite poems, tell her about medieval French history and the books he'd read and reread during the war.

They headed south, following the Reims road, and by the second week in September they were deep into the Champagne region.

'If the Germans had any sense they would have taken it all with them,' he said. 'The true taste of France.' But they hadn't. Just to the north of Reims they came across an abandoned château by the banks of the River Aisne where the liberation of the city was being celebrated by anyone who was passing by.

An elderly gardener, wearing his Great War medals for the first time in four years, told them that the château had been requisitioned by the Germans in 1940. Before that it had belonged to a family with German connections, so none of the dozens of people who had converged on the château seemed to have any qualms about partaking of its hospitality.

'They never treated me well,' the gardener confided in them as he led them through the cellar.

On their second night in the château, Laurent and Hélène were sat by the banks of the river, halfway through their second bottle of Mumm Grand Cru. Their shoulders were touching, though during their time together, Laurent had made no attempt to go further than a friendly arm around her shoulder.

'You are married, Hélène?'

She was slightly startled. He asked so few questions and when he did, nothing intrusive. She was about to say no, but realised that she was playing with the cheap wedding ring she had bought in a second-hand shop in Lille. It was something she had felt obliged to do after being questioned by the matron in the hospital.

'My husband was killed. A few months ago, by the Germans in the Pas de Calais. It was in a forest near Boulogne. I had no idea I was pregnant at the time.' She held out a hand in front of her, palm down. Enough.

Laurent was silenced by the amount of detail along with the lack of it. Hélène was drawing jagged patterns in the grass with a twig. He pulled her close to him as the tears began to streak down her face, their lines illuminated by the moonlight bouncing off the river.

'I suppose that at a time other than this, it would be a consolation. When is the baby due?'

'Late October, maybe early November.'

Her head was bowed down, her hair covering all of her face and the tears flowing quite freely.

'At least your baby will be born in a free France. You must have loved your husband very much.'

For the next few minutes she was so inconsolable that even Laurent, never lost for the right thing to say or to do, was helpless. All he could do was apologise, rub her back and pour her another drink.

When she regained her composure she assured him that she was fine. He was not to worry. It did her good to cry. She felt better. In any case, it was more of a wartime romance than anything else. Probably wouldn't have lasted.

What had disconcerted her so greatly was her reaction to Laurent's statement that she must have loved her husband very much. She had not hesitated to think about his question, because there was no doubt in her mind that she did love her husband very much. Not the fictional French husband apparently killed in a French forest, but the real one in England, who she could only wish was here with her now.

They remained at the château for two more days. By then it had been drained of champagne and American troops had arrived to take the estate over.

They took a circuitous route into Reims: not long after leaving the château they came across a platoon of American soldiers who told them that there was still some danger in the area. Small pockets of Germans remained and it was especially hazardous around the airport. That was their most direct route into the city, but the Americans advised them to head east. That side of the city was safe. 'Once you've crossed the River Vesle you know you can enter the city.'

Which was how they arrived at the small village on the banks of the Vesle. On the outskirts of the village a group of around thirty German prisoners of war were being led away in a column. An American Army jeep pulled up alongside them and a sergeant leaned over, shouting above the noise of the engine.

'Speak English?'

'A little,' said Nathalie.

'You planning on going into the village?'

'We're passing that way.'

The sergeant stood up in the jeep and looked back at the village.

'Just be careful. They're in a vengeful mood. We had to do a deal with them. They've let us take these prisoners in return for leaving the officers behind.'

The village opened out slowly in front of them: the houses were large with small plots of land between them. The road leading through the village and the two or three that they passed leading off the main road were all wide, with well-kept verges. They could not see any people, and so headed in the direction of the church steeple. Ahead of them was a commotion that grew louder as they approached.

Next to the church was a large house, set back from the road and linked to the church by a high wall, which appeared to have been recently whitewashed. A row of trees peered out from behind the wall, some of the leaves beginning to turn brown. A large crowd was facing the wall. Standing with their backs to it were two men in steel-grey German uniforms.

'What's going on?' Laurent asked a man at the back of the crowd.

The man took a step back so as to talk to them away from the others.

'The Germans carried out a reprisal shooting here two months ago. The resistance blew up a German truck just outside the village and the Germans shot four local men against that wall. The Americans captured the German unit that carried out the shooting and brought them back here so they could be identified. There was almost a riot: people want revenge. Eventually it was agreed that the two officers who were in charge of the unit would be left behind.'

'What's going to happen to them?' she asked.

'What do you think?'

An elderly man wearing medals and holding a rifle was shouting at the two officers.

'You have to answer our charges!' he kept repeating.

'No comprehends,' the older of the two officers replied, shaking his head. He was around fifty and plump, his face a deep red and his eyes imploring. His hands were tied behind his back and his nose bloody. He was trembling violently. His companion was much younger, perhaps in his twenties. He stood very still, his face impassive and with possibly the faintest trace of a smile, as if he was a man resigned to his fate. His trousers were bloodstained and he was jacketless, the front of his white shirt ripped.

A woman came and joined the old man who had been shouting at them.

'You cannot pretend that you don't understand. We know that you speak French well enough, you bastards. You certainly spoke it when you shot those men against this wall.'

Between the two Germans and the crowd an elderly priest stood to the side. He was holding a tall cross in his hands. The priest appeared to be terrified and he was leaning on the cross for support.

The man turned to Laurent.

'The Germans have been pretending that they don't understand us. Some of the villagers are insisting that we cannot do anything to them until we know that they understand what we're saying. Others just want to shoot them straight away. It's crazy.' He lowered his voice.

'It is anarchy, to be honest. We would have been better letting the Americans take care of them. You don't speak German by any chance?'

Laurent shook his head and looked at Hélène. Purposefully she strode to the front of the crowd.

'I speak German. I can translate for you.'

There was a murmur of approval.

'Tell them,' said the old man, 'that they are accused of shooting the four hostages here. We want to know if there is anything they have to say.'

She stepped forward and translated what the man had said into German.

The older officer leaned forward.

'Please, *madame*, you must understand. We were acting under orders. I actually managed to persuade my superiors that we should only shoot four people: they wanted us to kill one hostage for every German soldier killed on that lorry – twelve! We should be treated as prisoners of war. This is not a proper way to deal with us.'

She translated back into French.

The woman and the man with medals conferred. The man then spoke.

'Tell them that is as good as an admission. They are going to be shot.' Behind him two men emerged from the crowd carrying what appeared to be German machine guns.

'No!' said the older officer. 'This is a terrible mistake. *Madame*, please… I have a wife and children… you must tell them to save me. I would have been shot if I had not taken the hostages. Please…'

He was weeping and had sunk to his knees. The younger officer next to him spoke for the first time.

'Get up, sir, and shut up. You know what they are going to do to us. Let them get on with it. We're finished.'

'Do not speak to me like that! I am your commanding officer!'

'Then act like it, sir. Where is your dignity?'

The two men with machine guns had stepped forward now.

'Ask them,' said the woman, 'if they have any last words.'

She translated.

The younger officer shook his head and looked slowly around him. The older one spoke quickly, looking at the priest as he did so.

'I am a practising Catholic, even during the war. Please allow me to confess. Please.'

She glanced over to the priest who appeared to have caught the gist of what the German had said. He looked quizzically at her, the cross quivering in his hands as he did so.

She allowed the silence that had descended to linger. In that time a small flock of ravens descended on the trees behind the white wall.

She stepped towards the two officers. As she got nearer, she could smell the fear.

'You've lost, haven't you? Accept that.'

With that, she turned round and walked back towards the crowd.

'What did he have to say?' the woman asked her.

She shook her head. 'Nothing. He just said to get on with it.'

One of the two men had trouble releasing the catch on his machine gun. When they fired, it was clear not much had been planned. Both fired at the older officer, leaving the younger one still standing – unscathed and shocked. There was no smile or defiance on his face now, just a wide-open mouth, unseeing eyes and a look of utter fear. The two gunmen stepped towards him. One man's gun jammed and the other only let out a short burst before stopping.

Above them, the sky had blackened as the ravens flew off en masse, their panicked shrieking merging with the ring of the machine gun fire.

The younger officer had slumped to the ground, where he was groaning loudly and writhing on the bright green strip of grass. The old man with the medals stepped forward. He was holding a pistol and stood no more than two feet from the officer. He was taking careful aim at his head, but he was shaking violently. His first shot missed completely, ricocheting off the white wall. One of the gunmen put his machine gun down and went over to grab the pistol from the old man. The officer had lifted his head off the grass and was trying to say something, blood seeping out of his mouth. The gunman knelt down next to him, placed the pistol against his temple and fired.

No one in the small crowd moved for a good minute, shocked at what they had seen and shocked at what they had done.

Hélène and Laurent were offered a bed for the night but decided to move on.

'Victor's justice,' said Laurent as the village began to fade behind them.

'What other kind is there?' she asked.

They moved on to Reims, where they stayed until the end of September. Laurent had decided that he wanted to return to Lens. By now, he was beginning to be open about his desires towards her. The occasional friendly arm around the shoulder became more frequent, pulling her closer to him and trying to hold her there. The kiss on the cheek moved closer to her mouth and there were references to 'we'. She realised that he was beginning to assume that 'we' had a future. She allowed herself to contemplate the prospect for a while. It was not without its attractions. Laurent was a decent man; intelligent, witty, and resourceful. She could disappear into the anonymity offered by being a schoolteacher's wife in Lens. Life there would be dull but safe, something that she could not contemplate.

She also realised that she needed to head on. He had no idea where she came from and she needed to escape his attention and his affection before it became a problem. One morning when he was helping to clear roads she fell into conversation with an American officer who couldn't believe she spoke such good English. The officer was about to head down to Lorraine and if she wanted a lift, he would be happy to oblige.

–

Nancy had been liberated by the US Third Army on the 15 September after a ten-day battle, but in other parts of Lorraine the war continued.

She had intended to stay in Nancy until it was safe for her to move eastwards on the last leg of her long journey. Lieutenant Larry Jones had spent much of the first half of the journey from Reims to Nancy with his hand on her knee, and most of the second half of the journey with it on her thigh. She wondered if she had made the right decision to abandon Laurent. But she needed Lieutenant Jones, even more than he apparently needed her.

'Civilian control, ma'am. My mom is French-Canadian and I speak it as well as all of you, so I'm running the office in Nancy making sure everyone has the right documents.'

His French was not as good as he thought it was, but it was passable.

'I'll let you practise on me later,' she promised, which was all the encouragement he needed to book her into the one hotel that was still standing and pay for the room.

But more importantly, she needed new documents. He bought her story that her papers had been lost in Reims without too much difficulty and so the first thing he did when they arrived in Nancy was fix her up with an impressive new set. She was exhausted now; tired of moving, tired of not being sure of who she was meant to be, and in no real physical state to do much other than rest.

She thought hard about the new identity Lieutenant Jones was fixing her up with. She could be anyone, apart from the one person she wanted to be, and be with. Instead, she decided to revert to her real identity, which was something she had never given much thought to. It seemed to make sense. She had come full circle.

The hotel ought to have been the perfect place for her to stay: the sheets were clean and the small bathroom always had water. Downstairs there was a bistro attached to the hotel which had some food, if you liked potatoes, and Lieutenant Jones had assured her that her bills would be taken care of. He had even arranged for her to have a check up with an army doctor. All was well, she was assured. If only it was, she thought.

But there was an air about Nancy that made her uncomfortable. She had imagined that liberated France would be euphoric, that people whose dreams had come true and whose suffering had come to end would be happy. Yet all she could sense was an edge to the city. A tension that she found hard to describe flowed in on the River Meurthe and attached itself to the elegant but war-scarred buildings on the Grande Rue.

On her second night in Nancy she was in the bar adjoining the bistro. It was ten o'clock and Lieutenant Jones had just left. He had joined her for dinner and, realising that he was going to get no further than the ground floor of the hotel, reluctantly but politely bade her goodnight.

The barman was polishing a beer glass in an extravagant manner.

'Not your boyfriend then?'

'No. He'd like to be. I'm married.' She held up her left hand and wriggled her fingers

The barman smiled. 'What brings you here?'

'The war. I got a lift here. I'm moving on soon.'

Outside there was a crashing noise, the sound of glass breaking and people shouting. The barman went into the street and returned, still polishing the same glass.

'They've found another *collabo* then. It's not a nice sight. Go and have a look if you want to see what a free France looks like.'

She got outside just in time to see a crowd of people disappearing down the small road outside the hotel. She followed them into the Place Stanislas, where a larger crowd had gathered.

A young woman, perhaps in her early twenties, had been pushed to the ground and was being made to kneel. A man was tying her hands behind her back while another had yanked up her long hair in his hands.

The crowd was quiet, muttering disapproval of the girl.

'What is going on?' she asked the woman next to her.

'You don't know? Sleeping with Germans. And she's one of the lucky ones. They shot six men two days ago for helping the Germans.'

She was fixed to the spot, appalled at the spectacle in front of her, yet fascinated by it too. It was carried out in silence, the girl bowed and compliant, accepting of her fate. The older man finished tying her hands and then produced a pair of large tailor's scissors and proceeded to hack away at her hair. The younger man had his hand under the girl's chin, keeping the head upright. When most of the hair had been removed the younger man took out a cut-throat razor and scraped away at her scalp, nicking it and causing it to bleed. All along, the girl kept quiet and still, with not a tear in her eye.

She backed away from the crowd as it nodded its approval. A fear was gripping her now. She had been deluding herself over the past few weeks. She was worse than a collaborator, she was a traitor. If the truth were known about her, a far worse fate awaited her.

She ran back to the hotel, her worn shoes sliding against the cobbles. Outside the hotel she held herself against the wall while she vomited. She knew she must move on.

Inside the barman was holding the same beer glass, the bar still empty.

'Not pleasant, is it?' he said.

She nodded. A large cognac was on the bar in front of her.

'I imagine you'll want this. On the house.'

The next morning she told Lieutenant Jones that she was leaving Nancy. He understood. He had already realised that his interest in her was not going to be reciprocated. Frenchwomen looked like a lot of trouble anyway.

—

By the time she realised she had made a mistake it was, of course, far too late. If only Lieutenant Jones had tried to persuade her to stay in Nancy. He wouldn't have had to try too hard. She would have been comfortable there, there were hospitals, and it was away from the fighting.

The lorry that Lieutenant Jones had arranged to give her a lift had left Nancy early that morning, hugging the line of the Meurthe towards the Vosges Mountains. She was only about sixty miles from home. The front line was nearby and the lorry was delivering supplies to it. The driver apologised in the way that she had discovered Americans were good at. 'I can't take you any further. Sorry ma'am.' He sounded genuinely sorry.

The late summer sun was streaming down into the square of the village where she had been dropped. There was no shade in sight. Some of the trees were beginning to lose their leaves and a pyramid-shaped pile of them had been swept into a corner of the square. She deeply regretted leaving Nancy: she had been impetuous again, driven on by some kind of nesting instinct. She was feeling exhausted – weighed down by her pregnancy. She had underestimated how tired she would feel. Her back was hurting as it had been on and off for the past few weeks and her ankles were swollen. If only Lieutenant Jones had not been so obliging in helping her leave Nancy.

The *Mairie* next to the church was decorated with a row of bullet holes. Stacked up on one side of the square was a collection of dismantled German road signs. At first she assumed that the village was deserted, given its proximity to the fighting, but then an old lady dressed in black left a building ahead of her, slowly walking round the square, never taking her eyes off her. A family left the church, followed by a young priest with a wide-brimmed hat and a long black cassock, who carefully locked the door with a key on a long chain tied around his waist. A *boulangerie* looked as if it had closed for the war and was yet to be informed it was over.

She sat on a bench at the edge of the square for a while. Her eyes filled with tears. Until a few weeks ago she could not remember the last time she had cried. Now, she seemed to do so most days.

She couldn't stay in this village, she must keep moving. *I can't draw attention to myself.* A large black cat had circled her bench and was now sitting in front of her, its head cocked as if it was expecting to be fed, the yellow eyes burning into her. A gentle breeze rolled across the square. If she was going to move, she'd need to do so now while there was still plenty of daylight.

She carried on walking. Heading east, always heading east. It did not take long for the village to fade behind her as if it had never existed, like a strange dream, and for the countryside to open up. Ahead of her, far in the distance, was the crump and smoke of artillery fire. Her urge to go home was instinctive, but she had no idea where she was going to spend the night. She wondered whether there was any way she could get back to Nancy.

She was climbing uphill and her pace had slowed to a near-crawl. As the incline became steeper, she stopped every few paces. There was no breeze now and she felt lightheaded. Although the sun had dropped, she felt unaccountably hot and nauseous. She paused, leaning against a narrow tree. She peered up through the branches; the sun appeared enormous, its yellow edges bleeding into the sky. As she looked down she was sweating profusely and felt unsteady. She had to hold the tree trunk tightly as she was violently sick. Strange, she thought: she had, mercifully, avoided morning sickness in the early part of her pregnancy. She carried on walking painfully slowly. The birds were silent and the land swayed gently around her. She was concentrating so hard on reaching the top of the hill that she never heard the car until it stopped alongside her.

The last thing she remembered seeing was a tiny black car alongside her, with a man dressed in black in the driving seat. The words 'Where are you going?' were the last ones she remembered hearing.

Chapter 29

Lorraine-Alsace border, October 1944

That night she was back home, being dragged through the Place St Étienne, stripped naked by an angry crowd hacking at her with razors.

That night she was curled up in bed with Owen in a large London house, their children sleeping peacefully in adjoining rooms.

That night she had her hands round the neck of the German soldier in Lille, her well-practised smile fixed on him as she squeezed the life out of him as slowly as possible.

That night was the fourth in a row in which she had endured an interrogation by the British in a dank basement, insisting that she regretted what she had done and had been looking for an opportunity to tell them, but please let me rest now.

That night she was chased down the Avenue Foch; she knew that when she reached the Place d'Étoile she would be safe, but the faster she ran the further the enormous arch slipped into the distance.

That night she told Owen that she loved him and begged for his forgiveness, over and over again, but his face faded away as he began to speak and she never heard his reply.

That night stretched over three days and two nights.

She woke bathed in sweat, with an elderly man and a middle-aged woman at each shoulder, both looking anxiously at her. As far as she could tell, she was in large dark room, with a high, beamed ceiling and no windows but the sun leaking in through a part-open door. There was an earthy smell about, and outside the noise of a farm. She tried to get up, but the man held her down. His touch was firm, but not harsh.

'Lay still. A moment, please.'

He spoke French, with a heavy accent she couldn't place. He had a kindly face, with deep wrinkles, silver eyebrows that gave him an

313

owl-like appearance, and just a few wisps of white hair. Her head was spinning. The woman wiped her brow while the man placed a stethoscope on her chest and told her to relax. He moved the stethoscope around her chest, placing it in different positions, listening carefully.

'Good. You're strong,' he said after a while. He was holding the pulse on her wrist as he spoke to her.

'My baby?'

He patted her stomach. 'Strong too. But you must rest. You were found just in time. Drink.'

The woman held a flask of water to her lips. The water was cold and she drank the whole flask quickly before slumping back on the pillow.

'What happened to me?'

'The priest found you collapsed by the road – *collapsing* to be more precise. He brought you here. We are about five miles east of the village you stopped in. The priest saw you in the square there. He is a good man and has been keeping an eye on us. You have a fever and exhaustion. I gave you a dose of sodium barbiturate and you've been asleep for two days, nearly three, in fact.'

He spoke to the woman in what sounded like a strange dialect of German. She nodded and went away.

'We'll get you something to eat, but you must be careful. Not too much for now.'

'What about the baby?'

'Don't worry. The baby is getting all the nutrition it needs from you. It's you we need to worry about. For now, you must rest. You will stay here with us. When are you due?'

'Maybe a month? I'm not sure. Soon.'

He moved his hands from her wrist and held them around her stomach.

'It could be sooner. Have you been healthy throughout the pregnancy?'

She nodded.

'And active?'

She laughed. 'I think that you could say that I've been active.'

'Well, now it is time to rest. I'm a doctor, by the way, in case you were wondering.' He lifted up his stethoscope and dangled it. He was smiling, his eyebrows dancing as he spoke.

'What kind?'

'Before the war, I was a cardiologist in Kraków. In Poland. I studied in Paris for a while.'

'And during the war?'

The smile dropped and his long fingers drummed on the side of her bed. 'You don't want to know. Not now. Here, some soup and bread. Thank you, Rachel. Sit up and drink it, then we'll talk.'

The woman helped her drink the soup and spoke to the doctor in the German dialect.

'*Ask her about...*' the woman seemed to be saying.

'Ah yes,' he said. 'I meant to ask you. Who is Owen?'

'What?'

'You kept shouting it out in your sleep. You were delirious. It sounded like you were calling the name of someone.'

She shook her head, doing her best to look puzzled. 'It's not a name I know,' she reassured them.

–

It was four days before she was well enough to get up and only then did the doctor tell her how ill she had been.

'Another hour and I think you would have lost the baby. You were very sick. The fever was strong, but the priest found you in time. He was pleased. It helps confirm his beliefs. They were quite challenged after he met us.'

They were sitting around a large table in the dining room of the farmhouse. The top floor of the house had been destroyed by either a bomb or a shell, but the ground floor was functioning, despite the lack of glass in the windows and long cracks down the walls. The atmosphere was heavy with dust. The barn and another out-building alongside the main farmhouse had been made habitable, and now she was learning who else was in the odd community she had ended up in.

The doctor was sitting across the table from her.

'Do you want to tell me about yourself?'

She hesitated. 'I'm French – a refugee. I was working in the north. Now I'm heading home... south.' She felt the tears welling again.

'Don't worry. In time. Everyone here has a story too big to tell. That's the story of Europe now. Let me tell you who we are.'

315

Before he started talking he walked into the kitchen and came back with two apples, handing one to her. 'Eat. It's from the orchard. You need to eat more.'

There was a pause while he ate his apple, including the core and the stem.

'Imagine, four years I went without fruit,' said the doctor, shaking his head. Another pause.

'Let me tell you about your new companions. The girl who looks after the animals. Elisabette. This is her farm, or her family's. Her parents and brothers were killed when it got caught in tank fire. A shell took out the top floor when they were all asleep. She was the only one who survived.

'The rest of us, we had been inmates at a German camp near the village of Natzweiler, which is further into Alsace. The camp is about fifty kilometres south west of Strasbourg. Until 1943 they kept mainly political prisoners and resistance fighters there. You see Hans and Ludwig over there?' He was pointing at the two Germans, both sitting on a low wall, surveying the surrounding countryside. 'Both socialists who refused to help with the war effort in Germany. They were sent to the camp in 1940. It shows. They're both insane now. It's probably how they survived this long.'

The doctor got up and stood at the glassless window, his back to her.

'The rest of us – well, we were taken to the camp from Poland over the past few months. You know about me. The woman who was nursing you, she's called Rachel. From a city called Łódź. The four boys, they were all in the Warsaw ghetto. The Jewish ghetto. Last year there was an uprising in the ghetto, which the Germans crushed. These boys were found in a sewer weeks later. All six of us were at a camp in the south of Poland called Auschwitz. It's near Kraków. If you imagine hell on earth, you won't even come close to what happened there. Not even close to it. We're all Jewish, you probably gathered that.'

She nodded, though she was not sure that she had gathered that.

'The two women, the mother and daughter. They're Roma – Gypsies. The Nazis hate them as much as they hate us. They were also in this camp in Poland.'

'So how come you're now in France?'

'The Germans did not bring us to France for a holiday; I can assure you of that. It was not for the mountain air. When I arrived and they found out that I was a doctor, I was sent to work in the camp hospital at Natzweiler. From working there, I discovered why people had been sent to Alsace from Auschwitz. A German doctor was – still is, as far as I know – running an Institute of Anatomy at the University of Strasbourg. He's a proper Nazi, this doctor. His work is to help prove that people like the Jews and the Gypsies are a subhuman race: inferior to the Aryans. You have heard that theory, of course.'

Her eyes were wide open and she nodded just once. Of course, she had heard those theories. It was not that long ago that…

'What this so-called doctor was doing, I am told, was conducting experiments on the bodies of Jews and others to try to provide medical evidence for the Nazis. But he needed his bodies to be fresh, if you understand what I mean. So the Nazis arranged for people to be brought alive from Auschwitz in small groups, thirty or forty at a time. They were then kept at the camp and when their bodies were required, they were killed and taken to Strasbourg to be experimented upon.'

'How were they killed?'

'One day, maybe everyone in Europe will know. Maybe not. The Germans do not like to waste bullets, so they have devised this method of killing a lot of people at the same time. It's called a gas chamber. They force a group of people into a large, sealed room and then pour lethal gas in. The people suffocate within minutes. They didn't have a gas chamber at this camp, so they converted a nearby building. I don't know how many people died there altogether. What I do know is that we were next. Then one day, a few weeks ago, the Germans evacuated the camp. With no warning. Some of us just wandered out. Prisoners were heading in every direction. The French ones wanted to head for their homes, the Germans were heading for anywhere but home. And us… we somehow randomly came together as a group and just walked. I didn't think we would survive; the Germans still controlled the area, but near a small town called Raon-l'Etape a farmer hid us in his cart and put some distance between us and the Germans. We then carried on walking and came across this place. We should really head towards the Americans, I suppose. We'll be treated as refugees. If it was just me, I would. Rachel too, I imagine, and the Roma women. But the boys, they are terrified. I think if they saw another person with a gun, it would finish them. At the moment, they would not be able to distinguish between Germans and Americans. They would only see men in uniform. They trust me, so I'm trying to make them understand what is happening. They may be ready to move on in a few weeks. That is my hope. Maybe they are young enough to recover. They are the main reason we are staying here, for the time being.'

'And the Germans?'

'Look at them.' Hans and Ludwig had climbed onto the roof of the barn now and were scouting the sky with their hands turned into the shape of binoculars.

'I don't know what their countrymen have done to them, but it has had an effect on their minds, you understand? The taller one, Ludwig, he was an architect before the war, apparently. A very intelligent man. In his sane moments, he will talk passionately about Bauhaus. Now he tells me that the owls have been sent to spy on us. He passes onto me confidential messages from the chickens.'

She did not know what to say, and was not certain she was able to speak. Her throat felt tight. She was staring down at the table, drawing patterns on it with her fingers. Between them, she noticed through blurred vision that the light surface of the table was darkening with her tears.

She felt guilty. If she told the doctor the truth now, would he believe her? And if he did, would he then forgive her? It was not as if she had no idea. As much as she would like to believe that she had made one mistake, that there had been a misunderstanding, that she was not aware of what the Nazis were really like, she knew that was not true.

The doctor was sitting opposite her again, his soft hands gently placed on top of hers.

'Don't be upset. The people of France are not to blame. You look so guilty! It's not your fault. You look like a good person to me.'

Later that night she was sitting in the barn with the doctor and Rachel. The Roma women were in the house, the sound of the folk tune they were humming floating across the farmyard. The Germans were asleep and the four boys were cautiously walking around the farm, their heads looking in every direction.

'What happened to your families?' she asked them.

There was a long silence. Eventually, the doctor translated her question for Rachel. His translation lasted a long time and then a conversation between the two of them followed.

'We don't know.'

More silence.

'No idea at all?'

Another long pause as the doctor carefully straightened his shirtsleeves.

'When a transport arrived at Auschwitz, people were separated. The old, the very young, and the sick – they were sent to these gas chambers straight away. People who looked fit and who had a skill – they would be spared, for a time. I was with my wife and my son. When we came off the train, it was chaos. I have no idea what happened. I just don't think about it. Rachel, she had five children. She has decided in her mind that at least one of them must have survived, but she can hardly bring herself to think about it. Your question was a difficult one for us to answer.'

'How old was your son?'

'Twelve.'

'I'm sorry.'

'I keep telling you, you don't need to be. You're not to blame. And what about you? Do you have family?'

So far, he had not asked where she came from, or where she was going or what she did and she had told them as little as possible. They knew her as Hélène and had no idea that she was a nurse or that she spoke English and some German.

'My mother…' She could not say much more. Rachel spoke to the doctor, who replied at length.

'She asks about your husband, your baby's father. Where is he, is he alive?'

She gazed through the open door of the barn where the moon had lit up the farmyard, casting a silvery glow on the four boys as they silently walked round in a circle, one behind the other.

'I hope so.'

The night before she gave birth, she was woken by a commotion in the farmyard. Autumn was in full grip and, outside the warmth of the barn, a frost had already taken hold. She gathered a blanket around her and went out. Rachel beckoned her to stay back but she pushed past her.

At the end of the yard was a gate; beyond that was the farm track which, in turn, lead up to the road. Some twenty yards beyond the other side of the gate, standing on the uneven track were three men. They were all tall, standing stock-still in the shadow of the night, so it was not possible to make out any features. The two Germans were at the gate, pointing excitedly at them. The four boys were petrified, cowering in the middle of the farmyard. The doctor walked towards the gate.

'What do you want?' he called out in French.

The three men remained perfectly still. There was no breeze that night, but the noise had started to disturb the farm. The dark shape of a cow could be seen moving in the field behind the men. One of the chickens clucked its disapproval.

'Who are you?' The doctor's voice was firm, but his French was not convincing.

The three men moved forward by one step, staying within the shadow.

She walked up behind the doctor. 'Please go away,' she called out loudly, making sure they would be in no doubt that she was French. 'We are a French family. This is our farm. We have nothing of value here.'

The three men remained motionless.

To her left, she could see Elisabette in the broken doorway of the farmhouse, out of sight of the men. She had a rifle in her hands and was carefully releasing the safety catch.

'I don't think they are French,' the doctor said very quietly to her. The air was steamy with his breath.

'What are you after? We are French,' she called out in English. The doctor glanced quizzically at her.

Still no response. Had she been on her own, she would have wondered whether it was an illusion. But there was no doubt that the three men were there.

'Who are you?' the doctor cried out again, this time in German, his voice trembling.

The men stirred and appeared to be muttering to each other.

'God help us,' the doctor whispered, taking two or three steps back, fear etched onto his face.

She walked right up to the gate and called out in German.

'We are French. Leave us alone. There are Americans nearby. In one of the fields next to our farm. They will come if they hear anything. They promised us that.'

More muttering from the three men. Two turned and started to walk away from the farm. The third waited a moment and took one step forward. The moonlight caught his body and the lower part of his face. He was dressed all in black, in uniform. She leaned forward to get a better view of him.

'*Dreckige Juden,*' he said. Filthy Jews. It was said softly enough for just her to hear; his voice did not carry as far as the doctor. She had no doubt as to what she had heard. He paused a moment and then turned sharply and joined the other two walking away from the farm.

Shaken, she walked back to the doctor. SS renegades, she thought, evading capture, just realising that their dream was over. There was the sound of whimpering from inside the outhouse where the four boys had shut themselves in. Elisabette had put the safety catch back on the rifle.

'What did he say? I thought I heard him say something?' asked the doctor.

She looked at the doctor, at Rachel, at the two Roma women, at Hans and Ludwig who were both smiling, and beyond them at the outhouse door, where the four boys were now peering anxiously from behind a half-open door.

What could she say to them?

'Nothing,' she said, her hand reassuringly stroking the doctor's forearm. 'He didn't say anything.'

Chapter 30

Paris, October 1944

Owen Quinn had the first of a number of lucky breaks on that Friday afternoon in St Omer, not that he realised it at the time.

After Nicole had left, he had planned to take a train to Paris, but when he went into the station there were long queues and very few trains. He stood very little chance, they told him in the ticket office, of making it to Paris by train that day.

Then he remembered that, at the café where he had been with Nicole just before she left, there had been a couple of US Marine officers who were talking loudly about driving down to Paris that day. He returned to the café and they were just about to leave.

'Sure kid, as long as you don't mind a jeep ride.'

Had he taken the train, it would have been possible for the very tall man in the trilby watching him from the back of the station to have followed him. When he saw him leave and then hitch a ride in a jeep, he realised he was beaten, for the time being.

Half an hour later, and Quinn wished he was back on the platform at St Omer, going nowhere. The two Marine officers had a driver called Bob. Owen thought that Bob drove very nicely, if a bit too fast. The officer who was called Bill thought that Bob was driving too slowly, but was not complaining. The other officer, Earl, thought that Bob was driving far too slowly. As Earl outranked Bill, Bob had to drive very fast. Owen hung on to a side-rail with one hand and an overhead bar with the other as their death-defying journey gathered pace. On a number of occasions they came across groups of refugees heading in one direction or the other, clogging up the road with handcarts. Bob would drive round them by cutting into a field and then back onto the road. It was, without doubt, the longest one hundred and fifty miles of Owen's life.

They entered a city apparently unscathed by war. The French had General Dietrich von Choltitz to thank for that, Bill shouted at him. Hitler had appointed von Choltitz as commandant of Paris just a matter of days before its liberation with orders to destroy the city. Von Choltitz instead negotiated an orderly surrender and thus saved it.

'Where do you want be dropped, kid?' The jeep had slowed down to a speed one degree below suicidal and Earl had turned round from the front passenger seat to shout at him. 'Want some girls? With that uniform, kid, and your accent, you'll get a very good discount. I know a good place. Here's a card. Mention my name. Earl from Chicago.'

'The centre will be fine thanks.' Owen was now able to breathe normally and remove one numbed hand from the rail. He was not sure if his wrist was broken; he would need to wait until some feeling returned to it.

Five minutes later and they were picking up speed again down a very broad avenue, before screeching to a halt under the Arc d'Triomphe. He had said that he wanted to be dropped in the centre of Paris, and they had taken him at his word. Some passers-by were shaking their heads disapprovingly. They did not want to appear ungrateful, but...

'OK, kid. Guess this is as near as you're going to get to the centre of Paris. Good luck.'

It was six o'clock now and he decided to find somewhere to stay. Twelve avenues emerged like spokes from the Arc de Triomphe. Avenue de la Grande Armée was the nearest and felt appropriate, somehow. He passed a number of hotels and eventually found one that was much the same as the others he had walked past, and checked in.

That evening, he walked up and down the Champs Élysées, with the infatuation common to all first-time visitors to the city, and an aching sense of regret that this was where he had planned to come with Nathalie. This was where they were going to walk; this was where they would have eaten. Lovers, some recently reunited, others quite probably newly acquainted, sat quietly in the bars, not needing to speak. He could only be a spectator.

What was most noticeable was the number of men in uniform. Americans, British, French, Canadian, Polish. Not many Royal Navy, he had to admit. The River Seine had not been too much of a military problem. He was saluted by a couple of Royal Navy ratings, who looked as surprised to see an officer in the Champs Élysées as he was to see their salutes.

The photographs of Nathalie he now carried in his pocket were not to prop by his bedside, but to help trace her. But what was he meant to do in this city? Show them to every shopkeeper, every bar owner? Would the police help? He had heard all about the Paris concierges who knew everything that went on in their block and even their street. Should he try some of them? There would be tens of thousands in this city. It would be hopeless. The one clue he had to go on was from when they had had dinner at Archibald's club and Mrs Hardisty had asked Nathalie where she came from in Paris. And what had been Nathalie's reply? 'Oh, we moved around. Usually south of the 14th.'

He had picked up a map of Paris in the hotel and settled into a bar to study it. He bought a *Pastis* because he imagined that was the thing to do, a decision he quickly regretted. The 14th arrondissement was a large area in the south of the city, criss-crossed by large avenues and boulevards like St Jacques, du Maine, and Raspail, with the Montparnasse cemetery at its heart. If he knew for sure that she had a connection with the 14th then he could base himself there for a week, or even a month, and work his way through it systematically. He would need a lot of luck, but it was not impossible. Some shopkeeper, concierge, or schoolteacher might recognise the photo. No one can live in a city and not leave a single trace, he thought, though he was beginning to realise that if anyone was capable of doing it, Nathalie would be.

But Nathalie had not actually said she lived in the 14th arrondissement. She had told Mrs Hardisty that they lived *south* of it. *Usually*. Quinn shook his head and downed the *Pastis* in one go without thinking. It was hopeless. *The Pastis* – and the situation. Two thirds of France was south of the 14th – for heaven's sake.

–

He woke up early the next morning to the rank smell of drains that he had noticed throughout the city the previous day, and more sun streaming into the room than he imagined possible. That was because he had forgotten to draw the curtains, and he had forgotten to do so because of what had happened in the bar after he had downed his *Pastis* in one go.

He must have pulled a face because a couple of corporals from the Royal Northumberland Fusiliers came over to join him. Reg and Ron, or it could have been Ron and Reg. They were from the Fourth Battalion and had fought in the Battle of Normandy, and wanted him to know it. They had fought hard and now they were drinking hard. 'You don't want to be drinking that muck, pal.' For one dreadful moment he thought they might have found a supply of Newcastle Brown Ale in Paris and he would have to make his excuses and leave. But no, Reg and Ron had found a wonderful drink. Made with herbs. Absinthe they called it. 'Good for you.' And that was pretty much all he could remember. Maybe if it made you forget, it *was* good for you. Something about it not being legal, but they had befriended a bar owner. He remembered little more than that.

He did remember a taxi back and promises of lifelong friendship, and now he was on the bed, fully clothed.

He bathed, shaved, and went out in search of coffee and his wife. His first inclination was not to wear uniform, but as a non-Frenchman he would have stuck out like a sore thumb in civilian clothes, and in any case, the uniform of an Allied officer counted for something in this city, and that wouldn't last long.

It was a glorious autumn morning and in a noisy café on the Avenue Hoche where everyone was smoking strong cigarettes, he had a coffee and the first croissant of his life. He was surprised to see a couple on the table next to him already sharing a bottle of wine.

From his wallet he took out the piece of paper Nicole had given him with the name and address of her contact. It was in Rue Taitbout in the 9th arrondissement. He found it on the map. There were some Metro stations nearby, but he decided to walk. He didn't have a schedule, and by walking he might get a feel for the city. At the end of Avenue Hoche he turned right onto Rue Faubourg St Honoré and then left into Boulevard Haussmann. It was a long walk, much further than he had imagined – and he was supposed to be a maps expert. He imagined his map was not drawn to a proper scale. Despite having been occupied for so long, Paris felt more at ease than London. Maybe, he thought, it was *because* it had been occupied. It had not suffered air raids, and the city itself had remained intact. The buildings are the heart of a city. The people come and go, and give it its soul, but the fabric of the buildings, the style and atmosphere that they evoke – these are what gives a city its character. He admired the sweeping boulevards and the height of the buildings, which made it feel as if he was walking through an elegant ravine. He had been in the city for less than twenty-four hours and could already see why people were besotted by it, even though it smelled entirely different to anywhere he had been before. The smell of drains and the ever-present aroma of strong cigarettes. If only his first visit here had been for a different reason.

Just after the Opera he came to the junction with Rue La Fayette, and then turned on to Rue Taitbout. He noticed small groups of people, in twos and threes, dressed smartly in dark clothing, moving hurriedly to his right. They all seemed to be going in the same direction, and appeared to be glancing anxiously at him. There was an atmosphere that he could not put his finger on. It felt like a classroom which all the children had suddenly left, although the sense of noise remained. The area felt abandoned.

The building he was looking for was four blocks to the north, just before Rue de Châteaudun. The front door was open and the ground floor comprised the mailboxes for the flats. He checked the note and studied the names on the mailboxes.

'Can I help you?'

The old lady was peering at him from inside her concierge's room. 'Who do you want. Are you police?'

After all these years of occupation even a Royal Navy uniform obviously had these connotations.

'No, I am looking for… André… Koln?' She turned away, speaking as she did so. 'Top floor. Number nine. The lift is broken, so don't bother with it.'

He walked the eight flights of stairs. These days, his back and leg were fine, but a climb like this could trigger stiffness. He paused on a landing halfway up, before continuing, eventually ringing the bell for number nine. There was no reply. He rang again, still no reply. He had walked a long way to find no one in. He would leave a note and return in the afternoon.

He was not sure whether '*I am a British officer, and a friend recommended I come to see you*' would be of any use, but that is what he wrote, and slid it under the door. He would return in the early afternoon.

He had descended one flight of stairs when a door above him opened and a voice called out, 'Wait! Come up!'

The figure, leaning against the door of apartment nine and eyeing him coming up the stairs, was tall and thin with a dark complexion, but an unhealthy pallor, and a couple of days' growth of beard. His hair was long and he had a bohemian air about him that Quinn felt was in keeping with the surroundings. He held out his hand, taking care to do up his shirtsleeve as he did so.

'André Koln. Hello.'

'Owen Quinn, I am glad to meet you.'

'Come in.'

The main room of the flat was chaotic, books and papers piled everywhere. On the sofa was a stack of framed pictures and photographs. The floor around the sofa was dotted with used cups and wine glasses. The table by the window was piled high with papers and a typewriter. Those surfaces that were still surfaces were covered with a veneer of dust. One wall of the room was dominated by a large glass-fronted cabinet, part-covered by a dust sheet. Where that sheet had slipped down, ornaments were visible. On the walls he spotted a series of square and rectangular dark patches, outlining where pictures or mirrors had once been.

Yet despite the chaos and the untidiness, there was a quality to the room. A woman must have lived here, Quinn thought. The curtains were clearly good quality and they matched the carpets and the wallpaper.

André sat at the table, next to a large ashtray which contained the remains of a number of packets of cigarettes. His hand slightly shook as he took one out of a packet, and he had to use two hands to light it, closing his eyes briefly as he inhaled deeply.

'What's the uniform?' He pointed at Quinn with the now-lit cigarette.

'The Royal Navy. The British Royal Navy.'

'Really?' He laughed. 'The Royal Navy. Have you jumped ship?'

'Not exactly. Nicole gave me your name. She said you could help me.'

'The reason I didn't answer the door when you kept ringing is that I have a problem with uniforms – I could see you through the spy hole, you see. When you have been through what I have been through, you'll understand.'

'Can I ask what have you been through?'

A long stare at Owen through the white smoke.

'When I know you a bit better. You obviously need help. I can help. It is what I do. It is all I can do, now. Nicole would not have sent you along if I was not the right person. So you tell me what you need. But I warn you. Tell me everything. If you miss something out, then it is your problem.'

'Can I ask first what it is you do? What is your job?' Owen risked.

'I have had many jobs – you can choose which one you want. I'm a lawyer. And a journalist. Now I put all these skills together and I find people. Go on, tell me your story.'

It took Owen Quinn an hour to tell his story to André Koln. The whole story. He left nothing out. He had no idea why he was able to open up so freely to a stranger. And not just a stranger: André Koln was a *strange* man. Sitting in his peculiar flat, in a foreign city, with his distrusting eyes, which darted around as if there were things that only he could sense. Possibly it was because Owen was in such a different environment that he felt able to let down his defences, for the first time since June. At one stage, he found himself weeping and not feeling the need to apologise for it. Only once in that hour did Koln react, and that was when he told him that Nathalie – which was the name he was using for the want of anything else – was pregnant.

When he finished, Koln disappeared into the kitchen and came back a few minutes later with a strong pot of coffee and poured them each a cup.

'So your child will be born very soon?'

'Yes. She was two months' pregnant at the beginning of April, so nine months is the end of October. So, yes. Any day now. It may have been born already.'

'So, you are going to be a father. Congratulations. It is good. It's the best thing in the world.'

It was an unusual reaction. Not the one he had been expecting. In return for being so frank over the past hour, he was expecting a bit more than this. '*How can I help?*' was what he had in mind. Or better still, '*I can help, I know how to find her*'.

Koln walked over to the window, which looked onto the Rue Taitbout, and flung it open. It was now noon. It had turned grey outside and a cold blast swept into the room.

'I'll tell you my story, Owen. Then you can decide whether you want me to help you.'

He pulled his chair directly in front of Owen's, so the two men were sitting virtually knee-to-knee.

'You are in the 9th arrondissement. A lot of Jews lived here before the war. Some still do – you may have seen them going to synagogue as you walked here. But not as many live here now as did before the war. It's not a ghetto like you have in other parts of Europe, or used to have. We don't have these in France. No need for it. Not everyone is religious. My family is not religious. I'm certainly not. My family have lived here for over a hundred years, they came from Germany originally. My wife, her family came here more recently, from Poland. Sophie.' André paused, taking a sip of coffee before concentrating on his cigarette for a moment or two.

'But before the war, it was fine. I was a lawyer, and I was also a journalist. I was active in politics too, with the socialists. My wife taught literature at the Sorbonne. We had a good life. Our son was born in 1940. Daniel.'

He leaned over to the sofa and selected a picture from the pile stacked there, and showed it to Owen. André Koln looked ten years younger, with a beaming smile, standing next to a beautiful woman with long, dark, wavy hair and amazing eyes. She looked not unlike Nathalie, and was holding a tiny baby.

'A happy family, eh? That's what I thought. You should know that something is going to go wrong when everything is going right. We were very happy, but not for long. The Germans entered Paris in June 1940. It all happened so fast, we couldn't believe it. Half the population left the city, but where could we go? To Germany? In any case, we had a young child. Look Owen, I am an intelligent man. I am resourceful. I know what to do. I know people. I'm not religious, I didn't think everything would be fine, that God would sort it out. But in this case, we had no idea what to do. We were like rabbits caught in lights. We just stood still. And by the time the shock had worn off, there was nothing we could do. We were trapped in the city. There was nowhere to go.

'Life became difficult – but then it was for everyone in this city, apart from those who collaborated with the Germans. And let me tell you something, Owen, there were plenty of those. Everyone you meet in France now will tell you they were in the resistance, and for most of them that is a lie. Most people did nothing, perhaps you can't blame them for that. But those who helped the Germans, they deserve everything they're getting.

'Sophie lost her job at the Sorbonne, so she stayed at home to look after Daniel. I was not allowed to work as a lawyer, and funnily enough there was not much demand for a socialist journalist, so I worked for my uncle. He had an electrical repair workshop in the Marais, and I used to help him in the holidays when I was a student. I had my one stroke of luck, if you can call it that. I had to get a new identity card to show that I was a Jew, and on it I made sure that my occupation was shown as "electrician". So, I was no longer a troublesome lawyer or journalist, but I was an electrician.

'Then, in 1942, things got worse. In May we were told that we had to wear yellow stars to show that we were Jewish. Everyone over the age of six. We had to buy them from the police station, three each. Let me show you.' He opened a drawer in the cabinet and took out an envelope and put two pieces of cloth on the table.

'Here we are. This was one of mine – "*Juif*", and this was one of Sophie's – "*Juive*".'

Owen noticed again that André's hands were trembling slightly.

'But worse was to come. In July that year they started the deportation of the Jews. They called it the *grande rafle*. It was terrible. That first day, they rounded up more than ten thousand people. After that, hundreds more every day. Old men who had fought at Verdun, babies, everyone. Some people did not go. In the next block, a woman threw herself and her baby out of a top floor window as the police hammered at the door.

'I made plans for us to escape to the country. A lawyer friend of mine had moved his family to his family's farm in the Loire and he said we could stay there too. It was complicated, it was in a different zone, but I managed to sort papers, and as long as we could get there, we would stand a chance.

'We were going to go on the 19th of August. They came for us on the 17th. I don't know why. Maybe someone informed, maybe it was our turn. I will find out one day. I had made plans for when they came. I thought we would hear them coming, and I would hide Sophie and Daniel in the apartment next door; they were away and we had the key. I would be able to get out across the roof. But they hammered on the door at four in the morning, and by five o'clock we were in Drancy.'

'Drancy?'

'It was a housing estate they were building near Le Bourget airport. It was only half-built, so there was no sanitation, no electricity. It was very primitive, the conditions were terrible. Everyone was sick. People died. One morning they put us on trains. Not ordinary trains, these were like cattle trucks. Thousands of people stuffed together. We were on them for days. When we got out, we were in a place called Auschwitz. Have you heard of it?'

Owen shook his head.

'You will. It is in Poland. It is a death camp, where Germans murdered the Jews and other prisoners. I will tell you something now, Owen. It was only when we fell out of the train at this terrible place that I saw German soldiers. Until then, from the moment we were arrested here, to when we were taken to Drancy, and to when we were put on the train to Poland, it was all French policemen.

'There was a selection process once you came off the train. Old people, children, anyone who looked less than fit and healthy, they were sent to the gas chambers and murdered. You look shocked, Owen? I know. You don't understand? You will. I never saw Sophie and Daniel again, I did not even get a chance for a last look. It was so chaotic as they sorted everyone out, but I know they were murdered that day.'

Owen was aware that he was rigid, as if any movement might appear inappropriate. There was a pause as André flicked the long piece of the ash off his cigarette, checked whether it was still alight, and then lit another one. Owen noticed that André had to hold the lighter with both hands to steady it.

'I was fine, which sounds odd to say. I was fit and I was an electrician, so I was able to work. At first, I didn't care, actually. I knew that my wife and my child had been murdered, so what was the point of struggling to stay alive? But there was a man from Lyon in the bunk next to me; he was about ten years older. He had lost his wife and all four of his children, and he looked after me. He said that I had a simple choice to make: whether to give up or to carry on. And he said that we owed it to our families to carry on. So, I made that choice and I decided I had to carry on. I worked in a quarry like everyone else, and then I was sent to work as a slave labourer for a company called Siemens – they were using a lot of the prisoners at Auschwitz. I survived that first winter and then, in late summer of 1943, myself and some other prisoners who were electricians – or so they thought – were moved. We were taken to a place called Nordhausen, which is in the centre of Germany. And there they were building another concentration camp, which they called Dora. This was also a factory to make rockets. So I became a rocket engineer – can you imagine!

'I had the advantage of speaking very good German; remember my family were originally from Germany. My friends and I were clever; we had to be to have survived so long. We did our best to ensure that they were not very good rockets. But then, at the beginning of this year, a few of us were moved again, this time back to France. The Germans were building a new rocket factory, underground at a place called Helfaut-Wizernes. It is in northern France, very near to where you were yesterday in St Omer. So, the Germans brought me back to France. They abandoned the site in July, and we managed to escape. I returned to Paris.

'The concierge, she had moved her nephew into this apartment. She assumed we weren't coming back. They looked like they had seen a ghost when I returned. He said he was looking after it for me. So I threw him out, literally. Down the stairs. He broke his shoulder and both his legs. The concierge does not like me, and I do not like her. I suspect she may have tipped off the police that we were leaving the apartment. If I find that out, I will deal with her too.

'So, let me finish my story. I remembered the policeman who came to arrest us. He was a sergeant. I remembered his number, I memorised it. When I got back here, I decided to look for him. It seems that I was not the only person who was looking for him – the SOE were too. He had arrested one of their agents who had then disappeared. This is how I came to meet Nicole. When I found him, I handed him over to her. By the time she had finished with him, they found out what had happened to their agent. He was murdered by the Gestapo, apparently. I am not sure what happened then, but this policeman is not around anymore. I now use my skills as a lawyer and a journalist to find people. I have good contacts, but the truth is that people feel obliged to help me. I seem to have acquired a certain moral authority; I don't know how long that will last. Perhaps one day, I will find myself. I can't live here properly, there are too many memories. That is why everything is piled up. I don't want the apartment to look or feel like it did before. One day, I will move out, but at the moment I can't do that either. So you see, Owen, our stories are similar!'

'Not at all, André. I cannot begin to compare what I have been through with what you have.'

'Maybe not, but we have both lost a woman we loved, and a child...' He shook his head then looked up. 'That is why I will help you. You need to find your child. Come, let's get to work.'

André soon realised that there was precious little to go on. Owen gave André a photograph of Nathalie and the cameo brooch, and they went through all the details again. It was agreed that Owen would return to England and see what he could dig out, and then return to Paris, perhaps in December. 'You need to find one small fact to help me, Owen. Anything, just one decent clue to help me.'

Owen started to write down his address in London, then decided better of it and gave him his parents' address in Surrey. He had no special reason to, but it did no harm to be cautious.

They walked up into Clichy for lunch, which did not finish until after four in the afternoon.

Walking back to his hotel Owen came across an RAF crew who were flying back to RAF Northolt that night and said he could hitch a lift if he bought them all one more drink.

By six that evening, and three drinks later, he had checked out of his hotel on the Avenue de la Grande Armée and was on his way to Orly Airport. His timing was impeccable. Just half an hour after he left, a harassed and very tall Englishman wearing a long dark coat and a trilby entered the hotel to enquire of an Owen Quinn, only to find out that he had just left.

It was most annoying. The man had been checking the hotel registration cards that recorded the names of all guests in the city's hotels since early morning and had only come across Quinn's at five o'clock. He was proving to be an unexpectedly elusive quarry.

–

Owen Quinn had returned to London buoyed by a sense of his own resourcefulness and his meeting André Koln. At last, he now felt in control or at the very least, no longer *not* in control. He felt that if anyone could help find his wife, it would be André. Over lunch in Clichy that Saturday it had become clear that André had, if anything, played down his influence. It transpired that he was well connected in resistance circles and would be able to tap into that enormous body of people who were now effectively in control of much of French society.

333

'Don't keep asking me why I'm helping you, Owen,' André said. 'It's a challenge for me. It's good to help someone. I need to be doing things all the time. If not, then I have too much time to think.'

And Owen knew what he had to do. So far, he had given André precious little to go on: a couple of photographs and the cameo brooch along with the names Nathalie Mercier, Geraldine Leclerc and Nicole Rougier, though all of these identities would have been discarded long ago. Without something more substantial, it was going to be a hopeless task.

There were all of Nathalie's possessions that Roger and his team had removed from the flat on D-Day, but he had little hope that there would be any clues there, and in any case, they were hardly likely to return them to him. He could imagine Roger and Edgar and the lot of them sifting through everything to try to find some clues themselves.

He reflected on something that Nicole had said to him: putting aside whatever personal feelings he had for Nathalie, and whatever one thought of her as a Nazi, her skill as a spy and at leading a double- and then triple life had to be admired. She had managed to enter England undetected, had remained that way for a year, and then conducted herself as an active German spy with poise and bravery for the best part of three years before going to France. She had then managed to disappear. The idea, thought Owen, that this careful and clever person would have made the mistake of leaving some meaningful clue as to her real identity among her possessions was fanciful. The cameo brooch was, if anything, he now thought, probably designed to put him off the trail.

He had flown back to London on the Saturday night and, leaving the Admiralty after work on the Monday evening, found himself walking down Whitehall with Edgar, whose distinctive figure had materialised alongside him out of the early evening fog.

'Welcome back, Quinn. Any souvenirs from Paris?'

Quinn ignored him and carried on walking, attempting to quicken his pace.

'Not very happy, Quinn, have to tell you. I organised that little trip to France for you to answer one or two questions for yourself. I had to pull a number of strings with the SOE to get you over there. The idea was that you would play ball, not go gallivanting all over France. And did you get any answers?'

'No. Which is probably why I went gallivanting all over France, as you put it.'

'I see. Part of me is quite impressed, Quinn, actually. You obviously have some skills that you had previously kept well concealed, that at a different time we could do well to tap into. Avoiding the train in St Omer, palling up with those Americans, managing to fall off our radar in Paris for the best part of twenty-four hours. Very impressive, I have to say.'

'How did you know about all that – I mean the Americans, Paris and that?'

'It's my job to know, Quinn. And out of interest, what did you get up to in your lost twenty-four hours in Paris?'

'You know, the usual sightseeing, like half of the British and American armies – that kind of thing. I seem to remember having a drink or two. Anyway, why are you asking me – I thought it was your job to know?'

'Now look, Quinn.' Edgar was angry. 'Let me get something clear. We have all acknowledged that this situation with your wife is unfortunate, to say the least. We are sorry. But we really cannot have you going off on some freelance operation to find her. And in the highly unlikely event of you actually finding her, what are you going to do?'

'As you say, Edgar, that is highly unlikely, so...'

'But you may just be lucky. Very lucky. If that happens, we don't want anything embarrassing happening. We would rather matters were dealt with in a quiet manner. Diplomatic. We can help you. I am not sure what happened in Paris that Saturday, but mark my words, we will find out. So the minute you get a whiff of where your wife is, I am the first person you call. I can help you. Do I make myself clear?'

'Perfectly.'

And with that, Edgar peeled away into the fog filled night. For the first time, Owen Quinn had a sense of perhaps holding the upper hand over Edgar.

Chapter 31

London–Lincolnshire, December 1944

It was now December and London was just a few days away from what everyone hoped would be the last Christmas of the war. Owen had only a vague memory of what it was like before the war. Before the war, there had been plenty of cheer on the streets, of course, and you could sense a jollier atmosphere. Nowadays, it was altogether more restrained, but inside the pub around the corner from work there were some decorations and some attempt at cheer.

Owen had stopped in for a quick drink after work. Another week at work, and as short a time as he could get away with down at his parents' over Christmas. It would be dreadful, of course, and the New Year would be awful. André Koln had written to him at his parents' address. 'I really don't know why you didn't give these people your own address, dear,' his mother had said, eager to know who the letter was from and what it was about. Although there was no news, Koln suggested a longer visit in January. Thousands of collaborators had now been arrested, and Koln had some thoughts about how they might be able to find out something. It was all a long shot, but that was all he had, and he needed that to get him through the festive season.

He pushed his way towards the bar.

'Quinn, isn't it?'

Owen's face was clearly a picture of confusion. He could only just about hear the man he was shoulder to shoulder with in the pub.

'Hardisty? Don't you remember me? Air Ministry? Met up for dinner at Archibald's club? Both our wives are French.'

'Yes, yes, of course! I remember. Sorry, not quite with it today. How are you?'

'Can't complain, and wouldn't do much good if I did, would it!'

They both laughed. They agreed it wouldn't.

'I see you got promoted. Well done. Back at sea?'

'Not quite. At the Admiralty, round the corner. And you?'

'Still at the Air Ministry. Was hoping for a posting back to Paris, but there is some talk of sending us out east when that show is over. And how is your wife?'

He still didn't know how to deal with these questions. They always took him aback. Mumbling tended to help.

'Oh, you know – the war and that. She's over in France at the moment. Can't say a lot, you understand.'

'Of course, of course. My wife did enjoy meeting her though, that evening. Nice for her to be able to have a good old chinwag in French. Good for her. She hates London, actually. She was a bit confused though.'

'About what?'

'Where exactly your wife is from. She told my wife she is from Paris, but Amée noticed that once your wife had drunk a couple of glasses of that rather decent Côtes du Rhone her accent had a definite ring of Alsace to it, rather than Paris. She's a bit like that, Amée. Prides herself on being able to spot where people are from. Difficult in France, because they have less regional accents than we do, apparently. She can spot an Alsatian accent though: her grandfather was from that part of the world. It's got a slightly Germanic ring to it and sometimes they'll use German phrases, but in French, if you get what I mean. It was draughty in that room and Amée noticed that your wife said "*ça tire*". Apparently her grandfather used to say that too. Means "it pulls" and stands for nothing in French, but the German does. Maybe she had an Alsatian boyfriend, eh! Before you, of course, old chap.'

'Quite possibly.' He felt his breathing tighten. The first chink of a possible clue.

'Must push off, Quinn. We'll have a proper drink in the New Year, shall we? I say, it's bad news about old Archibald, isn't it?'

He had not seen or heard from Archibald since the night before D-Day, but didn't want to let Hardisty know that. He furrowed his brow and leaned towards him, adopting a confidential tone.

'What have you heard, Hardisty?'

'That he's taken a turn for the worse. Thought you'd know more than me. Apparently, he has been poorly on and off for a year or two, but since the autumn there's not been much they can do.' He lowered his voice. 'Lung cancer, I believe. Lost his son on D-Day. Must have

337

been a blow, can't have helped. Bad show all round really. He's at home in Lincolnshire apparently. Anyway, you're more likely to see him than me, so when you do, please do give him my very best.'

'Of course, I will, Hardisty.'

-

He had to wait until the gap between Christmas and the New Year before he had an opportunity to head up to Lincolnshire in search of Archibald.

He had already booked a couple of days' leave and did not want to arouse any more suspicion than necessary. He decided that it was inconceivable now that Edgar did not have someone at the Admiralty keeping an eye on him. A few days' leave at his parents after Christmas would seem innocent enough.

He would also be able to use his uncle's car. He had hinted to his parents that there might be a lady in Lincolnshire whom he wanted to visit. He did not tell them as much, but when he was reluctant to disclose his reason for wanting to drive up there – other than an unconvincing 'I fancy seeing the countryside' – his mother optimist-ically jumped to a conclusion that he did nothing to discourage.

'We're so pleased for you, Owen. A chance to put everything behind you.'

On Christmas Day itself, he pored over maps of Lincolnshire. His only clue was his first meeting with Archibald, at Calcotte Grange. Archibald was telling him about how he had tried to retire to Lincolnshire. 'Between Boston and the sea,' he had said. He studied the map. It was a start, but not much more than that. There was quite a lot between Boston and the sea, but much of it was fields. Due east of Boston, there were around a dozen villages. He could certainly work with that, but then there was the possibility that 'between Boston and the sea' could also be north of Boston and south of it.

On his many solitary walks that Christmas, he racked his brain to try to remember what else Archibald had said in describing his idyllic life in Lincolnshire. They didn't live in a village, but near it. He remembered that much. There was something about a telephone box next to a war memorial on a village green. That would narrow it down. A bit.

He drove up to Lincolnshire the day after Boxing Day in a Ford Anglia borrowed from his somewhat reluctant uncle. Uncle Jimmy had bought the little black car when it first came out, just before the war started in 1939, and it was his pride and joy. But given that he managed to run it on the proceeds of his black market activities, he was not in a strong position to resist his nephew's increasingly firm requests over Christmas.

Boxing Day was a Tuesday and he was not due back at work until the following Monday, which was New Year's Day. He would need to head back to Surrey on the Saturday at the latest, so that he could return to London on the Sunday.

He set off at six in the morning. His parents had both decided to get up and wave him farewell from the front porch, his father already wearing his tie and his mother wrapped anxiously in her dressing gown.

By eight o'clock he was on the Great North Road, driving through grey sleet and slush, struggling to coax every bit of the 900 cc horsepower out of the Anglia. By eleven o'clock he was in Peterborough. He stopped to fill up the car with petrol and then had a cup of tea in a café, eating his mother's sandwiches and feeling thoroughly miserable. He headed towards Spalding and into Lincolnshire, wondering whether he was on a pointless journey. The chances of Archibald having any idea as to his wife's real identity were remote, but given that he had been involved in the case from the outset, he had to at least ask him.

The countryside had turned grey, the weather was showing no sign of improvement and, even before he reached Spalding, it was beginning to get dark. It was noticeable that all around him the land was flat, completely unbroken by hills or any interesting geographical features. As he got nearer to Boston he could sense that the Wash was just to his east. In reality, he knew that it was some miles away, but with little to keep his attention other than the long road and empty space all around him, it felt as if he was driving on the edge of the world.

It's possible, thought Owen, that Archibald may be too ill to help, even if he did know anything, and even if he did want to help.

He arrived in Boston at four o'clock and decided he would go no further. It all felt so bleak that it almost seemed as if there was nowhere to go. The town appeared to be deserted. It may be the largest town in the area, he thought, but that was about as much as you could say for it. He could see why the Pilgrim Fathers were so keen to leave.

If anything, the sleet was heavier now and he drove round what he took to be the town centre in an attempt to find somewhere to stay. He stopped at a small police station, where the desk sergeant insisted on seeing some form of identification. 'Satisfied' was not the quite word to describe his reaction, implying as it would some evidence of a positive attitude. But he did, at least, scrawl down the name of a hotel with the most basic of directions.

The hotel was approached down a narrow side street which was only just wide enough for the car to pass. At the end, the road widened into a small square, which had probably been a coaching stop. Any thoughts of a comfortable room and a roaring fire were soon disabused.

The owner wanted to know why Owen was up here. 'Having a few days break' sounded unconvincing enough to him when he said it, so he had no idea what it sounded like to someone else. The owner was a tall man who had to constantly stoop to avoid hitting his head on the broad beams in the low ceilings. He also seemed to be oblivious of the fact that he needed to wipe his nose. There was no evidence of a roaring fire, just a faint smell of gas and boiled vegetables. It was a good two minutes before the owner informed him that they were full. All twelve rooms. He helpfully informed Owen that it was the time of year. Quite why he could not have told him as soon as he came in, Owen was not sure. Or even have invested in a 'No Vacancies' sign. But Owen was partially relieved. He was feeling miserable enough without risking either his dinner or breakfast being served by a man who needed to wipe his nose.

The owner did at least give him details of a nearby pub, which ominously 'always' had vacant rooms. It was only 'round the corner. You can leave your car here. Please tell them Clifford sent you. Remember – Clifford.'

He never bothered to tell them Clifford sent him. If the hotel was strange, the pub was downright peculiar. Owen was wearing civilian clothes but, had he walked into the pub wearing a Waffen SS uniform, the reaction could not have been any less friendly. He had barely stepped inside the door, clutching his small overnight bag, when the whole pub fell silent. In itself, that was not too difficult; there were no more than twelve locals in there. But all of them stopped talking and drinking and stared at him.

With the whole of the pub intently listening in, he asked whether there was a spare room, was informed that there was, and gave his details. He had to spell 'Owen' twice and 'Quinn' three times and eventually offered to fill in the registration details himself. Otherwise, he risked checking out before he had checked in.

The room itself was basic, but not as dirty as he feared. It was lit by a single, low wattage light bulb with no shade, had a single bed that seemed to rise in the middle, and a wardrobe that only had three legs but somehow stayed upright, the back balanced optimistically on the skirting board. Most of the floor was covered with a large rug, but around the sides were just bare floorboards. The curtains closed with some difficulty, but even when they did, there was little to prevent a vicious draught.

He lay down on the bed, and was just thinking how tired he was after all the driving when he must have drifted off to sleep. He was woken by a gentle knocking on the door. When he opened it, a girl who could have been no more than sixteen carried in a tray, which she placed on the small dressing table by the window. He had paid for dinner, bed and breakfast, but was nonetheless surprised to find a plate of stew and some grey bread being deposited in his room at six in the evening.

He needed little incentive to be up early in the morning to start his search for Archibald. He had two full days, maybe part of Saturday if he really needed it. He spent the whole day driving around the villages between Boston and the sea. Not just the villages: if he passed through hamlets or even went past isolated farmhouses, they too were scrutinised.

By mid-morning, the foul weather of the previous day had been replaced by some quite pleasant sunshine, and he began to revise his opinion that this was the bleakest place he had ever visited. True, there was an ever-present biting wind, but the isolation of the countryside did have a certain attraction to it. The sky seemed to go on forever, and you did not need actually to see the sea, or even hear it or smell it, to be ever aware of its enormous and constant presence.

Not quite the end of the world, he thought – *but you can certainly see it from here.*

He subjected every village to a mental checklist. Was there a village green? A telephone box? A war memorial? Most of them had village greens of sorts, and telephone boxes. Only three that whole day had war memorials, and none of those had a telephone box near it. From what he could recollect, he was certain of two things: that the location was between Boston and the sea, and there was a war memorial with a telephone box next to it. On the village green.

In one village, he did make further enquiries. The village had a green and war memorial. The war memorial was near the village green, but across the road from it. Further down the road was a telephone box.

He had prepared a line of enquiry during the long journey up. 'My father served in the Navy in the Great War, under a Captain John Archibald. Told me he's retired to these parts. Married, possibly living just outside the village.' Much shaking of heads in the village shop, where the combined age of the shopkeeper and her two customers must have been well in excess of two hundred years.

By late afternoon he realised he had driven in pitch darkness for the past hour and his chances of spotting a village, let alone a telephone box, had diminished. He headed back to Boston, and this time when he entered the pub, one or two of the regulars even carried on speaking.

The next morning he decided to head up the coast road in the direction of Skegness. He had looked carefully at the map the night before: he had visited all the villages in a corridor directly between Boston and the sea. South of The Haven, it was more The Wash than the sea, so north seemed a better bet.

The weather was somewhere between the sleet of the first day and the previous day's sun. It was grey, but the wind was not as biting as the day before, and for the best part it was dry. He had not been driving long when he came to a road that he knew from the map that led to a cluster of three villages, so he came off the main Skegness road and headed in that direction. The complete absence of road signs had probably added hours to his search: he was constantly having to refer to his map, checking the tell-tale stumps by the road that indicated a road sign had once been there.

The first thing he saw in the first village he came to was a village green, with a war memorial very definitely on it. *Next to a telephone box*.

He pulled the car up outside the church, just as the priest was unlocking the large wooden doors. He followed him in.

'My father served in the Navy in the Great War, under a Captain John Archibald. Told me he's retired to these parts. Married, possibly living just outside the village.'

The priest shook his head.

'Is your father close to him?'

'Not terribly, they were in the Battle of Jutland together and he has always talked fondly... I just happened to be in the area you see, thought I'd look him up.'

'He's not in a good way, I'm afraid. Very ill. He is at home and I visit most days. Iris takes good care of him. They are a bit isolated. You would have passed their lane as you drove into the village without spotting it. I'm sure he would be happy to have a visitor. Here,' he guided Owen out of the church, 'let me show you how to get there.'

The sound of the car coming down the lane must have alerted Mrs Archibald, because when he parked up in the drive of their very pretty cottage, she had come out to see who it was. The location was certainly isolated; the lane petered out just past the cottage, and there were no other houses or buildings in sight.

She was wiping her hands on her apron, looking at him quizzically, as if she was not sure whether she could remember him.

'Good morning, Mrs Archibald. I am not sure if you remember me. I am Owen Quinn. Lieutenant commander Quinn. I am – was – a colleague of your husband's.'

'Yes, I remember. What a surprise – you ought to have let us know you were coming up. Do come in. You know he is ill, don't you? He is actually quite comfortable today, so you are lucky. The doctor was here earlier. Let me see if he's awake now and I'll see if he wants any visitors. Please do sit down.'

He was in a large lounge that opened from the hall. The room was replete with sofas and armchairs and a large piano, on top of which was a display of framed photographs.

He was about to walk over to the window to admire the view from the large picture window when Mrs Archibald returned.

'John was surprised you'd come, but he will see you. I cannot let you stay long. It doesn't take much to get him tired, and in any case the district nurse is due here at twelve.'

She led him into a large downstairs bedroom. Captain John Archibald was propped up on a number of pillows in a large bed, next to which an array of tablet bottles and other medicines lay on a small table, along with a jug of water and a half-full glass. His appearance was transformed. He looked gaunt, he had clearly lost a lot of weight and his skin was drawn tightly over quite visible bones. He appeared to move with some difficulty, but did hold out his arm when Owen came in to shake his hand.

'Owen Quinn. Owen Quinn.' There was a long pause after Captain Archibald repeated his name. 'Good chap. I always wondered whether you would find me. Rather glad you did. Thought you'd come looking. We underestimated you, I think. How are you?'

'I am all right, sir. I am sorry that you aren't.'

'So am I. Damned thing started a couple of years ago. Doctors thought they had it under control, but it turned out to be something nastier than they suspected. Thank you, Iris, I'll be all right, dear.' Mrs Archibald left the room.

'I've not got terribly long, Owen. I'm glad I've had Christmas here, and if I can hack it through to the spring, I may get a bit longer than the doctors said I would, but I know it is not too long. Tell me, why did you come here?'

'I heard you were unwell, sir, and I thought—'

'Now come on, Owen. You and I know each other well enough. If you are honest with me, I can be honest with you. Tell me the truth. You're not going to be allowed to stay terribly long, you know. Iris will have you out in half an hour. She seems to have this rule, thirty minutes per visitor. Go on.'

'You obviously know the full story about my wife, sir. I have not come here to discuss the whys and wherefores of what happened. I have come to ask for your help. I need to find her, and I need to know if you can help me in any way.'

'I've thought about this. Why do you want to find her, Owen? What good can it do?'

'Because I need to know why she did it, sir. I loved her with all my heart, and I need to know whether she ever had any feelings for me. Edgar keeps saying that I should just get on with the rest of my life, move forward. Maybe I should but, until I've seen her, I am not sure that I am going to be able to do that.'

'Owen, I am sorry about what happened. I did have reservations about the whole operation. In the end, the deception was so successful that perhaps anything we did to bring it about was justified, but from a personal point of view, the way we treated you, I'm not so sure. But I cannot see what useful purpose can be gained from finding her. Edgar and his lot are ruthless. He's always been determined that the truth about her should never get out. They won't want her put on trial, either here or in France. On the other hand, if you actually find her then they're not going to let her go. There will have to be some kind of justice. She is a Nazi spy, after all. But you have to think carefully about this. Do you want to see her strung up from a tree in some isolated wood?'

'But do you have any clue who she really is?'

Archibald shook his head. He started to cough and pointed to his water for Quinn to pass it to him. Mrs Archibald half opened the door.

'I am all right, Iris. Don't worry.'

'There is another reason, sir. Why I want to find her.'

'And what is that?'

Owen hesitated. He had decided earlier not to utter a word about this to anyone in England, but he was prepared to risk doing so now.

'She went to our GP in April, sir, not too long before she left for France. She was two months pregnant. She would have had the baby by now. My child. I have a right to know. I must see my child.'

Archibald sank back into his pillows, his eyes filling with tears and his head moving slowly from side to side.

'I can see why you're so keen to find her.'

'No one else knew, sir, apart from her GP, and he has no idea what Nathalie has been up to. And now you, of course.'

'We lost our only son in Normandy, you know. William. He was a second lieutenant in the Royal Scots Greys. Fourth Armoured Brigade. Killed on the 10th of June somewhere near Bayeux. Iris wept the night we heard, and has not mentioned his name since. Lord knows how she will cope when I'm gone. God Almighty, this war… what has it done to all of us?'

Archibald slumped back in his pillows and closed his eyes, silent for a few moments while Owen wondered whether he'd fallen asleep. The door opened and again Mrs Archibald's head popped through.

'John?'

'I'm all right, dear, just a few minutes. Pass me that notebook, Owen.'

There was a small notebook on the bedside table. Archibald leafed through it and eventually found what he was looking for.

'Here we are. Come here.'

Owen moved closer to the bed as Archibald dropped his voice and gripped his visitor's arm.

'Edgar came to see me in November. Never really liked the man. He warned me that you may try to find me, to see if I could help you find your wife. He wanted to know if I had any idea about who she really is. He insisted that if you came here I was to call him. I told Edgar that I had no clue about who your wife really was or where she was from. That was more his side of things. Annoyed him a bit. Told him he should have found out more himself. Every week or so one of his chums pops by. Just happens to be in the area, they say. Checking to see how I am. But they always ask me two things: have I heard from you, and have I thought of anything that could help them identify who Nathalie really is.

'Edgar does not know what I am about to tell you. And I hadn't planned to tell you this. I felt that it would not serve any purpose for you to find your wife. But when you told me about your child... and then, having lost William... I think you have a right to know, and I have no right to withhold it from you.

'The SOE are a funny lot. Your wife came under F Section, which looked after France. But there is actually another section in the SOE which looks after France too: RF Section. They worked with de Gaulle's lot over here. Never the twain could meet, I am told. Lord knows how that country is going to get sorted out once the war's over, but that's their business. A friend of mine works for RF Section, and they got wind of the operation with your wife. Of course, they would not do anything to jeopardise it, things were not *that* bad.

'Because of the connection I had with them, I was sent over to RF Section to try to patch things up, warn them off this case. They trusted me. Less confrontational than Edgar, so they said. Turns out that they had a woman in Paris who had very successfully infiltrated the Abwehr – that's German military intelligence, the people your wife was working for. They came across a reference to Magpie, the code name that the Germans use for your wife.'

'So do they have her real name?'

'No. They had very little, and because they weren't aware of the operation, they weren't able to put two and two together. But they did have something that I think could be most helpful to you. It's something that until now I had decided to keep to myself.'

Owen's eyes widened as Archibald painfully leafed through the pages of the notebook.

'Here we are. It is the name of the officer who recruited your wife and seems to have been her liaison. I wrote it down here. Take it.'

He ripped out a page from the notebook and handed it to Owen.

'I never thought I would do anything with this information, but there we are. If you find this chap, he will most likely know Nathalie's true identity. Whether he cares to tell you is quite another matter.'

Owen looked at the sheet of paper, which contained the name of the Abwehr officer written in large block capitals.

'I wouldn't bandy that piece of paper around, if I was you. Be careful with it. Destroy it once you have memorised the name. Never let on to Edgar that you got this name from me. Not that there is much he can do about it now, but still. He never really trusted me. I think he suspected that I might be disposed to helping you one day. Be careful though, Owen. Edgar will do everything he can to stop you finding your wife. He doesn't know about the child, does he?'

'No, sir.'

'Maybe that's as well…' Archibald's eyes were slowly closing as tiredness visibly crept over him.

'Thank you, sir. I do hope you…'

'What? Get better?' He laughed and coughed at the same time. Iris opened the door.

'Owen is just leaving, dear.' He beckoned him to come closer and grasped him by the wrist. The older man's touch was cold and bony.

'I felt bad about what we did to you. You were deceived. I know that we saved thousands of lives, no doubt about that. But you suffered. This,' he tapped at the piece of paper in Owen's hand 'clears my conscience. This is my absolution.'

—

Owen was away from the isolated cottage by noon. He drove straight back to Boston, checked out of the pub and headed west along the Holland Road towards the Great North Road.

He felt quite elated as he drove along, the expansive countryside to either side glistening under a cloudless sky. He had got the breakthrough he needed. Coming up to Lincolnshire had been a long shot: he'd had no idea whether he would find Archibald, or then whether Archibald would have either the information or the inclination to help him. He would pass this name onto André, and then see what happened. He kept repeating the name '*Georg Lange, Georg Lange, Georg Lange*' out loud. Back in the pub in Boston he had decided that this was a name that he would never forget, so he had burned the piece of paper and flushed the ashes down the toilet.

Georg Lange, Georg Lange, Georg Lange.

He had slowed down now behind a tractor caked in mud, its wide plough taking up the width of the road and allowing him no space to overtake. After a mile or so, a small convoy of cars had built up behind him as the tractor slowed them all down. A mile later and the tractor turned right onto a farm track. He tried to get as much out of the little Anglia as possible. It would start getting dark soon and he needed to be on the Great North Road soon if he was going to find a petrol station open.

He was struggling with the Anglia on the greasy surface and slowed down to allow a car and a van to overtake him. One car remained behind him, seemingly in no hurry. He wound down his window and waved to indicate that it could pass. But the car stayed with him, dropping a bit further behind.

I know that it's the mood I'm in, he thought, *but it's unsettling me.* As far as he could tell, it was a large black car, certainly one that could overtake him with ease on the empty country road. Ahead was a lay-by. *Pull in there, get out to check a tyre or something, let him carry on, and stop being so silly.*

The black car stopped too, some way short of the lay-by. He could see at least two people in the car, apart from the driver. The front seat passenger appeared to be wearing a black coat.

His heart was beating fast and his breathing heavy. *This car has been following me for miles, it won't overtake me and now it's pulled into the lay-by behind me. Either I get out now or drive on, or...*

He could feel the sweat under his shirt and his face was burning. This was no coincidence. He sat still for a moment, tapping his hands on the steering wheel as if in time to music. *Maybe it's all in my imagination, Archibald going on like that and getting me worried. Let's give it one last try.*

He pulled out without signalling and hit the accelerator as hard as possible. The little Anglia swayed a bit on the surface, but he was travelling much faster than he had done before. The black car pulled out and within seconds was close on his tail. Ahead he could see a turning to the left. He slowed down without braking and turned left without indicating. In his rear-view mirror he saw the black car shoot past.

He pulled in to the verge and breathed a heavy sigh of relief, allowing his head to rest for a moment on the steering wheel. *I need a break, this is all getting to me. It's beginning to affect my judgement. Maybe a couple of drinks and a decent night's sleep.* He found himself actively looking forward to seeing his parents again. *Let them look after me for a day or two. Slow down. Relax.*

The interior of the car was very slightly darker when he lifted up his head. He looked to his left where a car had pulled up alongside him, so close that it was virtually touching his passenger side. The brown gloved finger of the driver was beckoning him to get out.

He scrambled out of his door and across the muddy verge. Two men were already waiting for him on the road. The long black Jaguar quietly pulled up in front of his car.

Two of the men were wearing police uniforms, the other was a civilian. One of the police officers came over and showed him his warrant card. *Police Constable Peter Sutton, Lincolnshire Constabulary.*

'Good afternoon, sir. Do you have any identification upon you?'

He found his Royal Navy identification card in his wallet.

'Lieutenant Owen Quinn, Royal Navy,' muttered PC Sutton, sounding both impressed and sarcastic as he handed the card to the other uniformed officer. He passed it behind him to the civilian in the black coat with an upturned collar, who had been standing a bit further away, impatient.

'Not at sea then, sir?' asked the man in the black coat, looking carefully at the ID card.

Quinn looked around him at the fields and the occasional tree swaying in what was now a fading light. It was going to be dark before he was on the Great North Road.

No, he wasn't at sea – at least not in the way that they meant it.

'Routine stop, sir,' said PC Sutton. 'We have had reports that a Ford Anglia with a single male passenger may be carrying black market goods. We would like to search you and the car, please, sir.'

'What kind of black market goods might they be?' Owen asked.

The two police officers turned round to the man in the black coat.

'Meat and other produce,' he said in a well-spoken and irritated-sounding voice.

'Well, you're welcome to search the car, but I can assure you I have nothing in it that shouldn't be there.'

The man in the black coat walked over.

'What have you been up to in this part of the world, sir?'

'Few days' leave. Thought I'd have some time in the country before going back to work in the city.' Quinn smiled.

'Very nice, sir. You're lucky to be able to get hold of enough petrol coupons to get you here and back.'

'I've been saving them up.'

'Very prudent, sir. Now if you don't mind, I just need to search you, so if you could start by removing your coat and your jacket.'

'You're welcome to, but I can assure you that you are not going to find any meat or other produce about my person!' Owen removed his coat and handed it them.

The man in the black coat did not respond. He was carefully going through all the pockets and even checking the lining of the coat and the jacket. Behind him, Owen could see the two policemen thoroughly searching the car, looking under the seats, lifting the floor mats, even running their fingers along the inside of the car roof.

'I'm sorry; I didn't catch your name.' Owen asked the man in the black overcoat.

'I'm with these two officers, sir. If you don't mind, I'm going to empty the contents of your wallet, just need to check.'

'What, for rashers of bacon between the pound notes?'

He said nothing, spilling the wallet onto the bonnet of the Jaguar. One of the policemen had a torch and was looking under the Anglia. When they had finished with the boot they even had a look at the engine. The black overcoat was now subjecting Owen to a very thorough body search.

By the time they had finished it was nearly dark.

'No meat or other produce then?' said Owen.

'No, sir,' said PC Sutton.

'So I can be on my way then?'

The black overcoat stepped forward.

'Can you tell me where you have been today?'

'I've told you, seeing the country. I have been staying in Boston and driving around the area.'

'Have you visited anyone?'

'Today?' asked Owen, trying to buy himself a bit of time as he attempted to judge what was behind this question.

'Yes. Today.'

'No.'

'Sure?'

'Yes. I am sure.'

The man in the black overcoat looked exasperated, as if finally beaten at a long game of chess. He put his gloves back on.

'So I can go then?'

The man in the black overcoat looked past him, well into the distance.

'Yes. You can go now, Lieutenant Commander Quinn.'

One of the policemen had walked back to the main road and was directing Owen as he reversed onto it. They waved at each other and he was on his way.

Probably a coincidence after all. They do stop people they think are handling black market goods. Odd how they had been following him, but he was worrying too much.

He didn't feel quite right about the whole business, nonetheless. For the time being, he was more concerned with getting on the Great North Road and finding enough petrol to get him back to Surrey.

The feeling of elation he'd had before had evaporated. He had worked out his plan. Tomorrow he'd write to André. 'Coming over to Paris early in the New Year,' the letter would say. 'And maybe in the meantime, André, you would like to see if you could trace the whereabouts of a Georg Lange, formerly of the Abwehr in Paris?' He'd wait until he was back in London before posting the letter, in a postbox that was near neither where he lived nor worked. *Best to be safe.*

But it was hard to concentrate. Something was niggling at him about the way he had been stopped, and he could not put his finger on it. Maybe it was nothing to do with being stopped, but everything that was going on, and going back to work next week. It was only much later – as he was driving through Bedfordshire and the pitch-black night enveloped the road and everything around it – that it hit him so hard it was as if the little car had been rammed from behind. He braked hard, the car skidding to the verge of the road just as a roundabout loomed into view.

He sat still, gripping the steering wheel, his heart pounding. He could feel the familiar symptoms of fear. The cold feeling sweeping through the body, the prickling of sweat all over, the sick feeling in the stomach, the tightening of the chest, the suddenly dry mouth and the need to look nervously around. He wound down the windows, breathing in the earthy taste of the country night. The man in the black overcoat. The smug, well-spoken man in the black overcoat who never said who he was and clearly thought he was so clever.

Well, thought Owen, he was so bloody clever that he had made a bloody stupid mistake, hadn't he!

Owen's emotions were all over the place: he was pleased with himself for spotting the mistake, but fearful now that he realised what it meant. Of course, they had not been looking for 'meat and other produce'. Stopping him had been no coincidence. They were onto him. There was no question about it.

It was thinking about going back to work that had done it, and more specifically his Royal Navy identity card, which he had shown to the policeman. The name on the card was Lieutenant Owen Quinn. *But that was the thing.* He had not yet got round to getting a new card, to reflect his promotion a few months ago to lieutenant commander. They had been nagging him at work to get it changed.

But what was it the man in the black coat said a few hours ago in that desolate lane in Lincolnshire?

'You can go now, Lieutenant Commander Quinn.'

If they weren't looking for him, how on earth would they have known that he was really a lieutenant commander rather than a lieutenant, as stated on his ID card?

The shivers were still running down Lieutenant Commander Owen Quinn's spine when he arrived back in Surrey just before midnight.

Chapter 32

Paris, January 1945

Georg Lange.
*   Georg Lange.*
*   Georg Lange.*

As soon as he had the name of his wife's Abwehr controller, Owen had felt the urge to go straight to Paris to find him. But the realisation that he had been followed in Lincolnshire had a sobering effect. He now knew for certain that Edgar was not far behind him. He needed to be cautious.

André had replied to Owen's letter by return of post. He would need time to trace Lange, he wrote. When Owen did come to France, he should allow at least a week for his visit, said André. Possibly longer.

Owen devised a plan based on the assumption that Edgar would find out soon enough that he had gone to France, and would follow him. He realised that he needed to steal at least a day on Edgar, ideally two.

He was certain that Edgar knew nothing about André Koln. He realised now just how lucky he had been to get the lift with the Americans from St Omer to Paris, gaining precious hours on Edgar. If he could get to Paris this time without Edgar realising straight away, he stood a chance. So he booked a week's leave at the end of January, telling colleagues that he was going to play golf in Scotland. On a visit to his parents, he borrowed the passport of a cousin with a different surname, but a decent enough resemblance. He explained that the Admiralty needed to see it to get him to the next level of security clearance. It seemed an implausible story to him, but it appeared to play well enough in Surrey.

He knew that word would soon get back to Edgar that he was going away, so he avoided telling colleagues at work that he was going on leave until Friday the twenty-sixth. He had no idea who at work was Edgar's source, but he was determined to make it as difficult as possible for them. He had actually booked the whole of that Friday as holiday, but came into work as normal in the morning. He was thus able to disappear at lunchtime, take the train to Folkestone, and was in Boulogne before half the office had retired to the pub at the end of the day and realised they had missed Owen leaving.

He had thought of calling in on Françoise and Lucien in Boulogne. Their loss had haunted him and made him ashamed of his own self-pity. But he knew he needed to keep moving, so caught the train straight to Paris instead.

André greeted him like an old friend when he met him at the Gare du Nord that evening. To Owen's slight embarrassment, he found himself being embraced by André on the platform.

'How are you, Owen?' Despite wearing a woollen hat, a heavy overcoat, and what looked like at least two scarves, André appeared to have lost weight. 'Excited?'

'Yes – and nervous.'

The station was busy and as they walked to the Metro he had to lean close to André to catch his words.

'The war has not improved this city, Owen. We're having a terrible winter. There's a shortage of everything: food, fuel – and even women! Food and fuel are one thing, but the women! For Paris, that is a problem.

'The worse thing though, Owen, is the atmosphere. You would have thought people would have learned something from the occupation, that they would have realised how fortunate they are. But no. The atmosphere here is terrible; it's like anarchy but without the revolution. So many people are denouncing so many other people, the accusations of collaboration… it makes the air… poisonous.

'You know me. If I think someone is a collaborator, then they should be dealt with. I have dealt with some myself. But Noisy-le-Sec, Santé, Fresnes – all the prisons, they are full of people who have been denounced as collaborators. And the officials – the people who allowed the Germans to carry on as normal – they are still around. You understand?

'I saw my friend Pierre the other day. He said that Paris has become a city of denunciations. Before the liberation people were being denounced, and there was hardly a pause after it for those denunciations to continue. The only difference is who they are being denounced to.'

They took the Metro to Notre Dame de Lorette and were walking to André's apartment in Rue Taitbout. Owen could see what André meant. He sensed that with the New Year, the city appeared to have lost some of its charm and replaced it with an unpleasant edge. When he had last visited in October, the city was still drunk with the euphoria of the liberation two months previously. Now it appeared to be suffering from the hangover. The short day hurriedly merged into a dark night, giving the city an ethereal quality that was not altogether peaceful. The vents set into the side of buildings and the drains and Metro outlets sent up small plumes of steam. Walking along the cobbled streets and boulevards, slippery with ice and slush, it felt as if tiny clouds had descended to the ground and were gently bouncing up again.

The apartment was much less chaotic than he remembered it. The table was clear and possessions were now neatly stacked into large boxes. There were still no photographs on display, but the apartment looked as if an attempt had been made to tidy it. André showed Owen into a small room.

'You can sleep in here. It was Daniel's room. We had a spare mattress. It is safer than staying in a hotel. I won't ask you to register.' He smiled. He put his arm round Owen's shoulder and led him back into the lounge. He sat Owen down on the sofa and he turned an armchair round to face him. As he lit a cigarette he poured red wine into two large glasses which appeared to have been rinsed rather than washed. He handed a very full one to his guest. Owen tasted the wine and noticed the bottle.

'Pétrus. Isn't that meant to be rather decent?'

'You could say that.' André paused while he held the wine glass back to admire it, then sniffed it appreciatively. 'I think it is probably the best Bordeaux. The collabo we removed it from was not so decent, I can tell you. Some friends of my parents had been hiding in the Dordogne. When they returned to Paris they found that their former bookkeeper was now living in their apartment and was refusing to move. He told them that he had bought the apartment legitimately. He had a document. It turned out that he had developed a very lucrative business redistributing the possessions of Jewish families. Of course, he never imagined them returning. So I visited the apartment with some colleagues from the FFI—'

'What is the FFI?'

'Sorry. *Forces Françaises de l'Intérieur*. It was the main resistance body. It is still very active. As you can perhaps imagine, it still has a lot of influence. Anyway, we visited the apartment. It was a very successful visit. My parents' friends got back their home, the FFI got their hands on another *collabo*, and I got a case of very good wine. The apartment was a treasure trove of things he had stolen. Maybe this was from a good restaurant. Your health. *Santé.*'

'And what would have happened to the *collabo*?'

'Who knows? Who cares? The jails are full of them at the moment, all pleading their innocence and telling anyone who'll listen that they love France and how it was a terrible misunderstanding. The big *collabos*? Some of them are being put on trial, but not many of them. The ones just below them, like the one who had taken the apartment, some of them are being dealt with. People say that many have been killed, perhaps hundreds maybe even thousands, but who knows what to believe? I daresay that in a few months most of them will have crept back into society. It may be a bit uncomfortable for some of them for a while, but it will soon be forgotten. You'll understand if I sound cynical, Owen, but I saw what happened when the Germans arrived. Life for most people here carried on as normal. Unless they were directly affected, the majority of people did not really care. The collaborators, yes, of course, they were a problem – but the real problem was the silent majority who quietly went along with the occupation, and suddenly appeared on the side of the resistance on the sixth of June.'

André shook his head and was lost in thought, finally lighting another cigarette and finishing his glass of wine. Owen had never tasted anything quite like it. He felt good. He had reached the magic moment which always came to him just after halfway through the first glass of wine, when things begin to feel better.

'I want to know, André. Why are you doing this to help me?'

André leaned back in his chair, balancing himself on his heels.

'Because I like you. Because you have had your child taken away from you, and I had mine taken away from me. Sure, the circumstances are very different, but I know how it feels, and if there was ever anything that anyone could do to get my son back for me, I would expect them to do it. And because it gives me something to do. Look,' he gestured around the apartment. 'I'm on my own here. My only company is my memories, and I can promise you that they are not good company. So I keep busy. I go for long walks. I have projects that interest me. Yours is one of those.'

André looked around the apartment, which showed all the signs of a life interrupted. For a while, he was lost in his thoughts, looking down at the ground, his forearms resting on his thighs, his feet bouncing restlessly up and down. He glanced at his watch, coughed and composed himself. 'We'll go and get something to eat soon, Owen, but first, let me tell you what has happened since I got your letter.

'It was a good job you got that new information. Before that, I realised that it was going to be impossible to find your wife if we had no proper information. The cameo brooch – I have shown it to jewellers and they cannot help. The strange thing is that it is gold, but there is no hallmark. But it is not going to help us find her. The possibility that her accent may have been from Alsace... that would narrow it down a bit, but only a bit. Alsace is a big region, and it was only liberated from the Germans in November. It makes some sense; many people in that area regard themselves as more German than French, but do you think she would have gone back to Alsace in July, when it was still under German control? I don't know. I could have gone to Alsace, but it would have been very difficult. The fighting there has only just stopped. I'd have needed some more information to help me there anyway.

'But Georg Lange – that is different. Very different!' He leaned forward and slapped Owen on the knee. The wine swayed violently in his glass.

'Getting that name made all the difference. I have made a lot of progress. We know that Lange was an Abwehr case officer, his job was to recruit and then look after various agents. We know that he was based at the German Embassy here since 1937, so was probably recruiting agents as far back as then - certainly before the war started. At some stage during the war, he moved from being based at the German Embassy in the Rue de Lille to the headquarters of the SD and the Gestapo in Avenue Foch. That would certainly have happened last year when the SD took over the Abwehr, but he may have gone before. Anyway, it is absolutely feasible for him to have been the person who recruited your wife and would then carry on as her case officer. It all fits very nicely. Have some more wine.'

André leaned back in his armchair and lit another cigarette.

'And how do we find out for sure, André, whether there is a connection between Lange and my wife?'

'It is simple, Owen. We go and ask him.'

André was now smiling. It took Owen a few moments to realise that he was being serious.

'And when do we do that?'

'Tomorrow!'

Early the next morning they were waiting in the street outside André's apartment for a contact of his from the resistance who had helped him track Lange down and had made the arrangements for going to see him. Gaston, André told Owen, had been a leading member of the resistance in Paris and was now involved in the FFI.

'He escaped from the Gestapo twice, he is a very brave man. It is important that we have him with us,' André said as they waited outside the apartment building at seven o'clock, the early morning chill eating into them with a surprising speed.

'As I told you last night, the FFI carry a lot of authority here. Lange is now being held by the French authorities. They look into the background of all German prisoners. If they are not senior officers, or are not suspected of any war crimes, or are not members of the Nazi Party, they will be the first to be released when the war ends. Otherwise, we would have to hold too many German prisoners for too long.'

A silvery-grey Renault with a long bonnet and wide running boards pulled up. A large man wearing a dark coat and scarf got out, embraced André, and shook Owen warmly by the hand. Before they got in the car, Gaston spoke to them on the pavement.

'Look, Émile is our driver today. Don't think he's rude or anything, but he doesn't talk these days. Not a word. He had a terrible time in August and was in a clinic until a few days ago. He checked himself out and we need to keep him busy. Don't worry, he's reliable and very trustworthy. Just don't expect him to be sociable.'

'What happened to him?' asked Owen.

Gaston looked down at the pavement, his hands deep in his coat pockets.

'One of tens of thousands of stories. He was in the resistance here in Paris. Émile was captured at the end of July and tortured in the

Avenue Foch. Émile knew some of the details about one of our key cells in Paris liaising with the Allies, so they really needed him to sing, but he didn't say a word. He had sent his family to the country, near Clermont-Ferrand. Someone told the Nazis where his family were, we have no idea who. So, one evening, Émile was taken to a cell and had to watch his wife being raped by four German officers. The last one, when he had finished, put his revolver inside her and shot her. Still, he said nothing. The next morning they took him to another cell. His two children were in there. His young son was hanging by the neck from a rope. He was dead. There was another rope next to him. They told Émile that unless he told them everything, his little girl would be next.'

Gaston made towards the car. Owen started to speak, but André put his arm across to stop him.

'Don't… don't even think of asking.'

Émile turned briefly as they got in, a dark beret pulled down just above his hooded eyes, which surveyed them through the rear-view mirror. As they headed south through the quiet streets of early morning Paris, Gaston briefed them.

'We are going to a prison for German prisoners of war. Those that are cleared – that is, the non-Nazis – will be sent to a holding camp. They will be released when it is safe, when the war is over. The others, those suspected of war crimes, they will face further justice.

'We managed to track Lange down to this prison. He is being processed at the moment. I have to tell you though, it looks like he is in the clear. There is no evidence that he is a Nazi Party member or has committed any war crimes. He was probably a typical Abwehr officer – not a Nazi. He's clever, apparently. Smart is the word they used to describe him. He was wearing a Wehrmacht uniform when he was caught, and there is no evidence against him. It is not going to be easy.

'We used to have free access to these prisoners. Straight after the liberation, we could even take them away and do what we wanted with them. If it was up to us, we could get the information you want out of him in an hour, probably far less. It would be no problem. But with the authorities, it is not so easy now. We can no longer have open access to the prisoners. That is why we are going early on a Saturday morning. The governor of the prison is away. The senior officer on duty today is very sympathetic to us. He will give us access to Lange, but on one very strict condition – we are not to harm him. Understand?'

Owen had expected the prison to be on the outskirts of the city, but they had driven for some time and Paris was long behind them. They passed Fontainebleau and soon after turned off the main road. The land was flat and covered in a layer of rolling mist, the open landscape broken only by islands of trees and isolated farm buildings. The road had narrowed and was now well above the level of the land on either side of it, which had taken on the appearance of soggy marshland. After about twenty minutes, a large grey building appeared out of the mist ahead of them. They slowed down for a police checkpoint and there were two more before they drove through the main prison gates.

They were ushered into the office of a tall man whom Owen took to be Gaston's contact. From the way they embraced, Owen imagined that they had been *résistants* together at some stage.

He looked at André's pass and nodded, and then spoke in a fast Parisian accent to André, who translated.

'He wants to remind you that there is to be no physical violence against this man. Lange is not expecting us, by the way.'

The senior officer led them through the warren of corridors. It appeared that the building may originally have been a castle, with various prison buildings being added at different stages. The overall effect was of a confusing collection of blocks and rooms, linked by gloomy corridors and courtyards. After walking down a corridor they came to a door which the senior officer unlocked. They were now in a courtyard, surrounded by high, grey walls. The air was damp and oppressive, the stone walls glistened. A group of German prisoners were milling around the courtyard, hunched against the rain, staying close to the walls and what little shelter they offered. They were guarded by three French soldiers.

Owen was shocked. Apart from the German prisoners he had seen clearing rubble while driving through Boulogne, this was the first time he had come face to face with any Germans, despite being at war with them for over five years. Gaston spat on the ground, in the direction of the prisoners. André shot them a mocking smile. But it was not Owen they were looking at, nor Gaston, nor the officer. This group of men with their grey prison uniform and hollow eyes, huddled together in the drizzle against the grey brick, could not take their eyes off André. It was unsettling, as if they recognised him.

The senior officer unlocked a door at the end of the courtyard and they were now climbing down a series of steep steps.

'Why were they all staring at you, André?'

'Don't you realise, Owen? They know my type, they've had years of training. I was supposed to have been eliminated, remember?'

They waited in a narrow corridor while the senior officer went into a small office. The steps had taken them down into what now felt like a dungeon. The only light came from a series of yellow light bulbs, all protected by steel mesh, and the atmosphere was distinctly damp. They were now joined by a guard who led them down another corridor, through further locked doors and into a small corridor with four more locked doors. They paused in the corridor.

'I will carry out the interrogation,' said Gaston. 'Leave it to me. André will translate for you. We do not want him to know at this stage that André speaks German; we may need that later. I will explain that you are from British Intelligence. Under no circumstances must you say anything about your relationship with her. You must remain silent. You are here as an observer. You understand? You have the photographs, André?'

André nodded and turned to Owen. 'Don't worry. We know what we are doing.'

'Let's go.' Gaston signalled to the guard, who unlocked the door nearest to them.

The room was about twenty feet by twenty feet, harshly lit and windowless. Behind a metal table that was fixed to the stone floor sat a well-built man with slicked-back fair hair. A guard was standing to the side of him. In front of the table were three chairs. There was nothing on the table apart from an empty ashtray.

The man stood up as they filed into the room. He was on the short side, and was wearing the same grey uniform they had seen the other prisoners wearing. The guards left the room, leaving just the three of them facing Georg Lange.

André took a packet of cigarettes out of his pocket and tossed them onto the table, gesturing for Lange to help himself. He took out three, placed one in his mouth and two in his top pocket. Then he smiled. André held a lit match for him, and lit a cigarette for himself.

'We are from French Intelligence,' said Gaston, pointing at himself and André. 'Our colleague here is from British Intelligence.' Lange's eyebrows raised, part surprised, part interested.

'We are interested in finding about some of your agents. We are going to show you some photographs of Abwehr agents that we have arrested. We need to establish their true identities. We believe you may have been connected with them. It would be in your interests if you could tell us what you know about them.'

Lange leaned back, so that his wooden chair was resting on its two back legs. One arm was folded across his middle, the other holding the cigarette in front of him, the elbow resting on the folded arm. His eyes narrowed, before he replied in what to Owen sounded like immaculate French.

'What do you mean by in *my* interests?'

'I mean,' said Gaston, 'that if you co-operate then your chances of an early release will be greatly improved. If you fail to co-operate, then you may find that you are a guest of the French Government for many years to come.'

Lange laughed and shrugged his shoulders. 'My understanding is that the Allies play by the rules.' He smiled directly at Owen as André quietly translated. 'I am a prisoner of war, gentlemen. I am covered by the Geneva Convention. I am not obliged to answer any questions. I only have to give my name, my rank, and my serial number. I have done nothing wrong. There are no conceivable grounds for detaining me any longer than necessary once this war is over.'

'You are an Abwehr officer, though.'

'If you look at my file, gentlemen, which I am sure you have, you will see that I am a Wehrmacht officer. I was arrested in Paris on the 25th of August wearing a Wehrmacht uniform. In my file is an affidavit I have signed testifying that I am not a member of the Nazi Party, neither have I ever been a member of it. You will find no record of my being a member of the Nazi Party. I have done nothing wrong. I am very confident I will be released along with all the other Wehrmacht soldiers, because I know that there will never be any evidence that I ever did anything improper. You should not be wasting your energies on me, gentlemen. There are plenty of Nazis who you should be chasing after. Certainly, I worked in the field of military intelligence, but I do not think that is a war crime, is it? You may not choose to believe me, but I was never a Nazi. Sure, I was a loyal German, but never a Nazi. You will find no evidence that I was. I am sorry; I am aware that I may be repeating myself, but what more can I say – other than the truth?' He inhaled deeply, folded his arms, leaned back in his chair and smiled politely.

André took an envelope out of the small briefcase he had brought with him and removed some photographs.

'I am going to show you some photographs,' said André. 'They are of people we have arrested who we believe are Abwehr agents. We believe they are giving false names. We want you to tell us their real names. As we say, if you co-operate it will be in your interests.'

André placed five photographs in front of Lange, as if he was dealing from a pack of cards. They were upside down from Owen's point of view, but he could clearly see that they were of three women and two men. Nathalie's photograph was on Lange's far right.

Lange studied them carefully, picking each one up and tilting it in the light. His face showed no hint of recognition whatsoever. When he had finished he placed them all down again and laid his hands flat on the table, his fingers spread out as he looked once more up and down the photographs.

'No. I am sorry, gentlemen. I do not recognise any of these people. You understand that in military intelligence we had very little contact with French citizens. There was some, of course, but "agents",' he was waving his hand with the cigarette in a dismissive manner, 'agents appear in books. Military intelligence is all about maps, codes and radio intercepts – as I'm sure you know. Very boring, actually. So, I don't think I can help you. If you are looking for spies, then I suggest you try a library.' He smiled at each of them in turn, anxious to convey the impression that he was genuinely sorry.

Lange helped himself to more cigarettes, this time brazenly removing four from the packet and placing three of them in his top pocket. André lit the one in his mouth for him.

Gaston hesitated as if he was not sure what to do next. He had clearly not expected Lange to stonewall them quite so effectively. 'We have different levels of interest in these people. There is one in particular that we want to know about, more than the others.'

'And I imagine that it is this one, am I right?' Owen's heart leaped and he fought to control his excitement. Lange was holding up the photograph of Nathalie. It had been taken in Hyde Park, so she was smiling and clearly out of doors. 'Shall I tell you why? Because the other four have had their photographs taken in a police station. Mug shots. This one, I suspect, is not in custody, as otherwise you would have a custody photograph of her. She is the odd one out. Am I right? Please do not treat me as if I am a fool.'

Gaston appeared to sigh. 'What can you tell us about her then, Lange?'

It was impossible to calibrate, but the pause that followed felt just a fraction too long. It was enough to convince Owen that Lange was hesitating. His face was very still; if anything he was trying just too hard to show no flicker of emotion. He was allowing himself an extra split second to compose an appropriate response.

'Nothing. I have never seen her before, have I? I thought I had told you that.'

'Are you sure, Lange? If we find out that you are lying to us, that will put you in a very difficult position.'

'I cannot see how. If I don't know someone, then I don't know them, do I? Is there anything else that I can help you with?'

There was nothing. They left the prison disconsolate. The idea of placing Nathalie's photograph among a selection of others had seemed a good idea at the time, but it had backfired. Their debrief in the car felt desperate. Lange was smart, they agreed. He might well know Nathalie, but he was clearly not going to admit to it. The rest of the journey back to Paris was conducted in silence. Every time Owen looked up he could see Émile's eyes darting around in the mirror. Owen was devastated. Lange had seemed to be their best bet for finding Nathalie, but he was not going to co-operate. He knew that they had no proof of the connection, so could easily block them. Owen could feel Nathalie slipping from his grasp, after seeming to be so close.

They were dropped off in the Rue Taitbout and André and Owen trooped miserably up the stairs, with the concierge's beady eyes following them from the entrance hall.

For a while, nothing was said. Owen sank into the sofa and helped himself to one of André's strong cigarettes. André paced up and down, at one stage kneeling down by the box containing photographs and glancing at one or two.

Then he seemed to have an idea, turned to Owen and said 'Wait here,' and disappeared.

It was an hour before he came back. When he did, Owen was none the wiser. 'I rang Gaston. He liked my idea. He is going back to the prison to collect something. Then I'll take you into the sewers of Paris.'

Chapter 33

Strasbourg, January 1945

For the first time in five years, the bells of the Notre Dame were able to summon the New Year into a free city. The city had been occupied by the Nazis for nearly four and a half years, longer than almost any other city in France. The bells sounded muted.

There was some shouting in the street, but her mother was asleep and the baby was settling in her arms. She stood at the window, inside the drawn curtains, gently rocking. Over the rooftops, she could just make out the main spire of the cathedral, lit up for the first time in years. In a nearby street she could hear a crowd singing *La Marseillaise*. After the years of silence, you could hardly turn a street corner without hearing that music, she thought. On the table behind her was a half-full glass of white Alsatian wine, its chill long gone. Her mother had insisted on opening a bottle, but she did not feel like celebrating.

–

Her son had been born on an unusually warm Tuesday afternoon at the end of October. It was an easy birth and she had been well looked after by the doctor and the women at the farm. Even the four boys seemed to respond to the baby, spending hours crowding round him, fascinated by every feature. Once the baby was born, the doctor said, the boys began to recover.

Although he had her eyes, when she looked at the baby, she could only see Owen. For most of the time, this gave her great comfort, and she felt an overwhelming love for the baby and its father. When no one was listening, she would talk softly to the baby in English. 'Everything will be all right,' she would assure him.

At other times, she looked at the little one and the enormity of what she had done would hit her. Then she felt distant from the baby and for a few hours would just go through the motions of motherhood, before her mood changed again.

Everyone at the farm had been unsettled by the three men who had appeared near the entrance the night before the birth, but they soon reassured themselves that it was nothing. Only she and the doctor guessed they were Germans, and only she had heard what they said. Their presence haunted the farm for the remainder of her stay there.

She wanted to move on soon after the birth, but the doctor persuaded her to rest. The four boys had repaired enough of the house to make it habitable and, more importantly, warm. To the east, parts of Alsace were still at war. Fighting was raging over the Vosges Mountains and every night the sky was streaked with Allied aircraft.

On the last Saturday of November, the priest from the village came to visit them.

'I have two pieces of news for you. The first good. The second bad.'

They had all gathered around the table in the farmhouse. The priest was enjoying being the centre of attention on a day other than Sunday. He poured a second glass of the rough *vin de table* that was being passed round and continued.

'The good news is that Strasbourg has been liberated. It was two days ago, on Thursday.'

The doctor translated into Polish, German and Yiddish, which she now knew was the language he communicated to Rachel in. The Roma women understood Polish. It was a long process. There were polite nods of approval around the table. They were pleased that Strasbourg had been liberated, of course but, after what they had been through, good news would have to be much more profound.

'Yes. There was a real battle. The Americans and the Free French broke through the Saverne Gap on Wednesday and the French Second Armoured Division entered the city at eleven in the morning on Thursday. General Philippe Leclerc was the commander who liberated the city!'

The others looked at the priest who appeared to be overcome with emotion. They all raised a glass to General Leclerc, of whom none of them had ever heard.

'The second item of news is not so good,' said the priest, deploying his most funereal voice.

'Last Monday a whole family was killed at a farm not far from here, just the other side of the hill behind us. I say last Monday. In fact, that is when their bodies were discovered. They were probably killed some days before.'

The doctor was hesitating before translating. When he started to speak, he kept it very short. He knew that there was only so much bad news the people around the table could take.

'All of them had their throats cut. Mother, father, two sons and daughter.'

The priest shook his head. The doctor did not translate.

'Apparently there are reports of small bands of renegade German troops operating in the area. Probably ones who became detached from their units and have nowhere to go. Usually SS. You had better take care.'

When the priest left, they agreed it was time to leave the farm. The doctor was going to take them all to Nancy, where a proper refugee centre had been set up. She said she was going to head south to join her family in Lyon.

–

She had waited at the farm for just an hour after they left, and then she and the baby headed east. The fighting had only just ceased in Alsace and there were reports of pockets of German resistance, but a mother carrying a baby proved irresistible to the first American truck they saw, and they were in Strasbourg by lunchtime.

It was hardly recognisable as the city she had left four years previously. The damage, she had expected, along with the other physical aftermaths of war. The air of resignation and the exhaustion etched on the faces of the people, she hadn't expected. The city was teeming with French and American troops, and seemingly thousands of German prisoners of war, slowly marching in long lines, enduring the pent-up resentment of a long-occupied population.

It did not feel like she had come home, but she had nowhere else to go. Ever since her son had been born she had understood what was driving her back to Strasbourg: if Owen was ever going to find her, it would be here.

The area where her mother lived was unscathed compared to the centre and some of the outskirts. A neighbour who she didn't recognise helped her lift her bags up the stairs to the apartment while she carried the baby.

Her mother had said nothing when she opened the door. Her lips trembled and she reached out a hand to cup the baby's face before hurrying her into the apartment.

'Do you want to tell me your story now or later, or shall we pretend that nothing has happened?'

She sat down in the familiar armchair. Her son was awake and feeding from her breast.

'Do we have hot water?'

'Is that your explanation?'

'If I can have a hot bath, then I will tell you everything.'

Her account to her mother had been so well rehearsed, so tightly edited and refined, that it did not take long. It had been prefaced with an instruction that there were to be no questions.

'I left in May 1940 because I was afraid. You had already been evacuated, so I couldn't contact you. I thought I would return, but I went to Paris. I came across the identity card of a woman my age. She looked similar to me too, so I assumed her identity. She also had the permit and papers that allowed her to live in Paris, so it was all so easy. I still thought I would return, but life there was not bad. You have to believe that, in many ways, it was normal. I found work in one of the big hospitals. I thought many times of contacting you, but I was afraid that would compromise my identity. If I came back or even risked contacting you, it would all be too complicated. I was worried it could unravel everything. I had a comfortable life in Paris. I was selfish, I am sorry. I am ashamed of that. But I am back now.'

Her mother raised her eyebrows; she appeared unconvinced and certainly surprised at the brevity of her daughter's account of the past four years.

'Not even a letter?'

'I'm sorry.'

'And the baby?'

'The baby was born a month ago in Paris. As soon as I heard that Strasbourg had been liberated, I came home. Here I am!'

She laughed, but her mother remained stony-faced.

'The father?'

She had the script ready. 'A good man. A doctor at the hospital where I worked. But he helped treat injured resistance fighters and had to leave in a hurry. That was at the end of April. I have not heard from him since. I don't know. He did buy me this ring though. If it makes you feel better, you can tell people that I was married to him.'

Her eyes filled with tears for her baby's absent father. Her mother softened and reached over to pick up the baby.

'It all sounds very innocent to me, Ginette.' She was clearly not convinced. 'A few days before I was evacuated, two men came round asking for you. They frightened me. I told them that you were at work, which you were. I never said anything to you at the time. I was going to mention it, but then I was evacuated.'

'Probably from the hospital here.'

Her mother shook her head firmly. 'Probably not, Ginette. If they were, they would have been aware you were at work. The one who did the speaking, he was from Alsace. The other was German, I'm sure of it.'

'I thought you said only one spoke?'

'Ginette, don't argue with me. I know Germans, and the other man was German. I know it. What were you mixed up with? Was it the reason for your disappearance? What about the strange political views you used to have?'

She got up and went to draw the curtains.

'Whatever my views were, four years of the war have changed them. In any case, they had nothing to do with me leaving. I'm home now. Do you want me to stay – *us* to stay?'

She had noticed that her mother had been cuddling the baby, pressing her cheek against his.

'Of course. Where else are you going to go, anyway?'

'If we stay, it is on the understanding that we discuss these matters no more.'

'Is there something important you have to tell me? Like, his name?'

'I was waiting. I thought I would wait until I got home. I wanted you to have a say.'

They agreed on Philippe, after the general who had liberated the city the previous week.

'And what will you do now, Ginette?'

'I'll get a job, mother. The hospital may take me back.'

The room was dark apart from a dim lamp in the corner. Philippe was fast asleep in his grandmother's arms. She knew that her mother did not believe her, but she knew that she would not pry any further.

So life would go on as normal and she would wait.

And wait.

-

The bells of the Notre Dame had finished pealing and Strasbourg was surprisingly quiet. In the next room, she could hear her son begin to stir.

Chapter 34

Gaston returned to André's flat in the early evening and handed a package over to him. Only then did André explain his plan. Up until then, Owen had imagined that they might actually be spending the night in the sewers.

André's idea, he had to admit, was an inspired one. It was risky and could go badly wrong, but he could not think of a better alternative. His real worry was that Lange would be released soon and would then disappear.

'We'll walk,' André said as they turned left out of his apartment block and headed north.

It was a damp night and it was a while before either of them spoke.

'This is Pigalle we are entering. Have you heard of it?' André asked.

'The red light district?'

'If it was only the red light district that would be fine. This is where everything that shouldn't happen does happen. It is where the underworld of Paris gathers. Anything you want, you can buy here. Anything. Even the Germans couldn't tame it in the whole time they were here. You see that guy over there?' They were on the Rue Pigalle, walking past a small bar at the corner of an alley. André was waving at a friendly-looking man in his early forties leaning against the door. Despite the cold, he was in shirtsleeves.

'When he last came out of prison he discovered that his wife had been having an affair with a friend of his. He cut his wife's ears off and made her eat them. I will leave it to your imagination what he did to the friend.'

'And what happened to him?'

André laughed. 'Nothing. Lack of evidence. There is very little evidence here in Pigalle.'

A short man in a full-length cashmere coat was shepherding a young girl out of a long Citroën which was blocking another alley. 'If you have specialist tastes, this is where you come. That is Claude over there. He specialises in young girls, sometimes for himself, but mostly for clients. He did a lot of business with German officers. He was able to pick up a lot of intelligence that way, I am told. Boys you get in another street. Any age you want. The Germans had a taste for fourteen-year-olds, I'm told.'

They darted across the road as an argument started in the alley: a delivery truck was objecting to Claude's Citroën blocking the road.

'Right, we're going into the side streets now, just be careful. If we keep moving fast we will be all right. The pickpockets don't like a moving target. I'm known here anyway, but you look like what you are.'

'Which is?'

'A stranger.'

They had crossed Place Pigalle and turned into a long, narrow alley. At first Owen thought it was covered, but the buildings on either side were no more than feet apart, and the sky was obscured by overhanging balconies that appeared to touch each other. Halfway along, André turned up a small flight of partially concealed steps and then they cut back into another alley, which had no street lighting, relying on the occasional dim light thrown out from the gathering buildings. The alley appeared to come to a dead end, but André opened a creaky wrought iron gate and they found themselves in a tiny courtyard. A statue of a naked lady stood in the middle of the courtyard, surrounded by plants. A spout that had once turned it into a fountain was sticking out of the top of her head. The ground was bathed by low level lights. André knocked on one of three doors opening onto the courtyard.

Owen heard André mumble something, and mumbling in turn from the other side of the door. Then a delay as a series of locks, bolts and chains were noisily unfastened. The door was unusually high and the man who had opened it was unusually short. He stood behind the door, holding it open just far enough for André and Owen to squeeze in, then hastily shut it, putting all the locks, bolts and chains carefully back into position.

Owen had never seen anything quite like it before. The whole of the ground floor and first floor appeared to have been excavated to form one large room. It was just one large space, with no floors other than the ground floor and no dividing walls. The roof beams were exposed and a small bird was flying between the rafters. Owen could not work out what was keeping the building standing if all the supporting walls and joists had been removed. It felt like an urban cave. There were desks, printing presses, drawing boards, shelves of pencils and inks and a door in a side wall that opened into a dark room. On the opposite wall there were three sinks, side-by-side. One was stained black with ink. There was a small table next to another sink, with food and drink on it. The middle sink had a syringe on the side. The back wall had a ladder propped against it, leading to more shelves. A black and white cat stared down at them from one of the shelves, wedged in between volumes of large, torn, leather ledgers.

'Owen. Welcome to the den of the best forger in Pigalle, which also means the best forger in Paris and, of course, in France – if you don't count Marseilles, of course. We tend not to count Marseilles. Makes life easier. What are you calling yourself this week, Louis?'

'This week?' The short man was jumpy and needed to think about the question. 'This week you can call me Bertrand, André. You can still call me Louis, but Bertrand may be safer.' Bertrand could not have been more than five foot tall and had a nervous tick. Every few seconds his head jerked towards his right shoulder in an involuntary movement. Not good for a forger, Owen thought.

'Now then. Bertrand is a genius, aren't you, Bertrand?'

Bertrand nodded.

'If Bertrand can't copy it then no one can. A clever man. But he has also been a naughty boy, haven't you Bertrand?'

Bertrand now spoke fast, in a surprisingly deep voice.

'That is unfair, André. I explained to the FFI and they understand. If I hadn't done what they asked, the Germans would have killed me. It was the tiniest of favours. And I promise you, I didn't do a good job, did I?'

He sounded nervous. André walked over and put his arm round Bertrand's shoulders.

'Bertrand's mistake – Louis, you don't look like a Bertrand, you know – was to forge some documents for an SS officer. All through the war he was so helpful to the resistance and then he goes and spoils it all in the last few days.'

'André, I promise you. I had no alternative. But I made a deliberate mistake. He was caught, wasn't he?'

'So now the FFI have agreed that as long as Bertrand continues to help us, he will keep his balls, won't you, Bertrand? Not that I think you have much use for them, but they are nice to have anyway, eh?'

Bertrand calmed down when he realised he was not in more trouble. He made a big play of shaking Owen's hand and thanking the British. The British passport was the hardest to copy, he wanted Owen to know that. For him, this was clearly the greatest compliment he could pay. The British passport and the Greek passport, but who wanted a Greek passport? A bottle of Absinthe appeared from a shelf and they all sat round a table in the middle of the room while André carefully explained what Bertrand was to do. Owen toyed with his glass but avoided drinking any. He noticed André did likewise. Bertrand made notes of what was being said and asked a few questions, refilling his glass as he wrote. He understood. Once he slipped into the role of forger, he was no longer the nervous little man with the jerking head. He was now calm and sounded authoritative. Owen could see why he was a master.

'And when do you want all of this by, André?'

'Tuesday?'

'Impossible. Some of these documents you want will be very difficult. One of them I have never attempted before. Thursday at the earliest.'

'Wednesday morning?' asked André.

'How about Wednesday evening?'

'No, Bertrand. I'll be here Wednesday lunchtime. If they're ready, you get to keep your balls. For me, that would be a very good incentive.'

Bertrand nodded. There was no need for André to add that the work had better be good. That was taken for granted.

-

He arrived in Paris while his prey was in the forger's den.

He had been seething when he found out that morning that Quinn had slipped the net and had been spotted in Boulogne, getting on a train for Paris. There would be time for recriminations later, Edgar reassured himself as the RAF plane began its descent into Paris. It was simply appalling. He had put enough measures in place to ensure that if Quinn so much as bent down to tie his shoelace, he would know about it. And what had happened? Quinn had booked a week's leave, which, of course, he knew about. He'd even paid for the hotel in St Andrews, they had checked on that. But he'd fooled those bloody idiots by leaving early, and it was more than twelve hours before they could pick up any trace of him.

Now the priority was to find Quinn. He would not lose him this time. He could not begin to contemplate the possibility of Quinn actually finding his wife, and what the consequences would be of that. It really did not bear thinking about. Edgar reached into the pocket of his greatcoat and felt the reassuring shape of his service revolver. That would not happen.

The last time, it had been simply unacceptable that the French police had been so tardy in supplying the hotel registration cards. He bet that they had been far more accommodating to the Germans. Now he had a promise that he would have help from the Embassy. He may have to stay up all night, but he'd be most surprised if he had not found Quinn by the end of Sunday. Then it would just be a matter of keeping a careful eye on Quinn and letting him do all the work.

–

André went on his own to collect the documents on the Wednesday and was back in the apartment by two that afternoon. Gaston was coming to collect them at five. Owen stayed in the apartment as much as possible. He had no doubt that by now, Edgar would be searching for him in Paris. The hotel registration cards would be of no help, so he did not want to give him the satisfaction of finding himself in the same queue for the Eiffel Tower. He felt safe in the apartment.

Émile drove them south of Paris, the journey to the prison taking a bit longer than it had early on the Saturday morning. He had not acknowledged them as they entered the car, but throughout the journey Owen noticed that he kept glancing at them. Gaston's contact had warned them not to arrive before six, when the governor would still be on duty. After seven would be better. All the prisoners would be back in their cells by then.

They arrived at seven thirty and Gaston's friend made a couple of calls while they waited in his office. Ten minutes later the phone rang and they were on their way through the labyrinth of corridors, courtyards and staircases.

Lange was handcuffed to the chair when they went into the same room as they had seen him in on Saturday. He looked confused and a bit dishevelled. His fair hair, which had been carefully slicked back on Saturday, appeared uncombed. He sat behind the table, looking from Gaston to Owen to André, but the look was a nervous, darting one. The air of self-confidence that had been so evident before was absent. André lit a cigarette, making a point of not offering one to Lange, who looked as if he could do with one.

'Is this really necessary?' The German asked, noisily holding up his two hands as far as the chains would allow.

'We'll see, but I think it probably will be,' said Gaston, carefully putting on his reading glasses. 'Do you have family, Lange?'

Lange shrugged his shoulders and gave the slightest of nods, his eyes narrowing.

'According to your file, your wife is Helga. Daughters Charlotte aged... let me see, twelve now? Maria, she'd be fourteen... fifteen?'

Lange eyes blazed at them.

'And what is Mainz like to live in, Georg? I understand it is a historic city. Isn't it where the printing press was invented?'

Lange sat very still, controlling his breathing. Gaston was leafing through a thick file of papers as he spoke.

'And what is sustaining you now, Georg, is the knowledge that in just a matter of months, possibly even weeks, you will be back in Mainz with Helga, Charlotte and Maria, eh? This unfortunate war will be forgotten and you will go back to being a pillar of Mainz society, if there is such a thing. Am I right?'

No reaction from Lange.

'And you did indeed have every reason to believe that. There was no evidence that you were a Nazi or had committed war crimes.'

Silence.

'Your French is excellent, Georg,' continued Gaston, 'so you will have noticed that I used the past tense there. There *was* indeed no evidence that you were a Nazi or had committed war crimes. I have no doubt you spotted that. But now, let me show you the evidence. You will notice that I am now using the present tense. André, please.'

Gaston removed his glasses in a triumphant manner as André got up and walked over to the table. Owen could see why they had asked for Lange to be handcuffed. He spread out the documents on the table and held each one up in turn in front of Lange's face. Lange was shifting uncomfortably in his chair.

'Let me present exhibit A,' said André. 'A Nazi Party membership card. Very good. You didn't join until 1941 by the way, in case you are wondering when you signed up. You left it a bit late, but we thought it best as we only had recent photographs of you. Obviously a wise career move, Lange. Makes sense, it probably stopped you being sent to the Eastern Front. So you are a member of the Nazi Party now, Georg. Congratulations.'

'Bastards.' Lange struggled in his chair.

'Keep still, Georg, the more you struggle the more your handcuffs will hurt. I know that from bitter experience,' said Gaston. There was a pause, before André continued. 'Now then, the Nazi Party card was easy to produce. It is not exactly rare, but these,' he was waving a sheaf of papers in front of Lange, 'we are very proud of. Exhibit B, we will call them. Have a careful look. The first one is dated the 16th of July 1942. You know what date that is, don't you, Georg? Need I remind you? It is the date of the *grand rafle*. The roundup of the Jews in Paris. And before you tell me again that you were not involved in this kind of thing, that you were in military intelligence... Here, we have a series of orders...' André was leafing through the sheets '...signed personally by you, ordering the arrest and deportation of Jews. That is clear evidence of a war crime, would you not agree?'

Lange was shaking his head angrily.

'You know I was not involved in anything like that. This is an outrage, it—' he shouted.

'Shhhhhhh.' André had a finger to his lips. 'Be quiet, Georg, I have not finished yet. And here is exhibit C. We know that you were in Boulogne in June this year. You admitted that yourself in your affidavit, in your very own handwriting. By the way, thank you so much for alerting us to the existence of that affidavit, it was most helpful, as you can see. It is good to have a nice large signature like that. Very useful for a colleague of ours. Anyway, back to Boulogne. You admit you were there in June. A perfectly legitimate place for a Wehrmacht intelligence officer to be based, I am sure. But do you remember what happened on the 7th of June, the day after D-Day in case you have forgotten?'

Lange shook his head.

'Let me remind you then. Two hostages were executed in front of the Hôtel de Ville. In reprisal for the killing of two German soldiers. Do you remember? A mother of two children and a teenage boy. Well, I have news for you, Georg. This document here,' he held it in front of Lange's angry eyes, 'shows who signed the death warrant. Georg Lange.'

André sat down. Owen noticed that he was shaking. It was as if he had come to believe the veracity of Bertrand's forgeries himself, so good were they. Gaston got up and leaned on the table in front of Lange, who had now turned white, perspiration pouring down his face.

'We can do one of three things with this information, Georg. It can go to the authorities and you will face a war crimes trial. I would have thought we are looking at a minimum of ten years before you see Helga, Charlotte, Maria and Mainz again, that is if they'll wait for you that long. Mainz will, of course, but possibly not Helga. And Charlotte and Maria will not remember you in any event. And then that evidence from Boulogne is very damning. They may even seek the death penalty there. There's only one way to find out.

'The second thing we could do would be for you to be transferred from here tonight and your car intercepted on the way by the FFI. Do you want me to describe to you what they would do? No? I can promise you, ten years in prison will be a very attractive alternative, even if it will last a lot longer.'

There was a long pause now, during which Lange lurched forward and vomited down the front of his grey uniform. When he lifted his stained head up, his eyes were red with tears. His mouth was half open, flecks of vomit and saliva dripping down his chin. The cell now had a rank and fetid smell. Lange was trembling violently.

'I can appreciate your discomfort, Georg. Are you ready for me to tell you the third alternative? All of these documents can be destroyed. They would be burned, in your presence, and the minute the war is over you would be released and free to go back to Helga, Charlotte and Maria in Mainz. If it was me, I would see that as the most preferable of the three options. And you want to know how you can get us to do that? It's simple. You tell us everything you know about this woman.' Gaston slapped the photograph of Nathalie down on the table. 'Everything. You have our word that if we find out that you have been telling us the truth, all of this will be destroyed.'

There was a long silence as Lange stared at the photograph and the documents laid out on the table in front of him. He was rocking very slightly in his chair.

'And how can I trust you?' Lange's voice was quavering.

'You can't. It is a gamble,' said André. He waited before continuing. 'But I would have thought the alternatives to not trusting us are far worse. It is a risk you have to take.'

'Do you want some time to think about it, Georg?' asked Gaston.

The German looked up slowly and his gaze took in all three of them. Any pretence at composure was long gone. He was broken. His face betrayed a mixture of fear and hatred. Within the space of less than ten minutes he had gone from a sophisticated and professional officer to a broken man.

'Of course not. I'll tell you everything I know. But I want to tell you something first. It was not difficult to recruit her. She came to us.'

-

There was an air of definite satisfaction in the Renault as it headed back to Paris that night and they discussed everything that Lange had told them. It was in marked contrast to the gloom that had accompanied the journey back the previous Saturday. Owen even noticed that there was some life in Émile's eyes as the driver kept looking at them, taking everything in.

Had they not been so tired, they might have been tempted to stop for a drink in one of the bars around the Avenue des Champs Élysées – and had they done that, they could well have been spotted by the tall Englishman in the long dark greatcoat and wide-brimmed trilby. Some of the bar owners had spotted him more than once over the previous days, peering into the bars, looking around but never buying a drink – which was what bothered them most. One or two had asked him his business and he produced a pocketful of accreditation that quickly persuaded them to mind their own business.

Major Edgar was seething. There was no sign of Quinn. He had established that he had arrived at the Gare du Nord, but since then he had vanished. He could be anywhere, though his instinct told him that he was still in the city. There was no joy with the hotel registration cards. Either Quinn was not in a hotel or the French were just being inefficient.

Had someone told him that at one stage that night, as he crossed the Rue du Colisée, he was probably no more than a couple of hundred yards from Owen Quinn, as his car headed towards Boulevard Haussmann, Edgar would not have been altogether surprised.

It had turned into that kind of chase.

Chapter 35

France, February 1945

They did not leave Paris until the Friday, which was 2nd February.

There was good reason to delay their departure. Paris was a city sustained by rumours, most of which arrived with a clamour one day, only to disappear silently and forgotten the next. But the weekend that Owen had arrived, a rumour emerged that appeared to have more substance to it. By the beginning of the week it was confirmed. On the day after Owen had travelled from London to Paris, the Red Army had entered a concentration camp near Kraków in southern Poland. It was called Auschwitz and was where André and his family and most of the other seventy-five thousand Jews deported from Paris had been taken. André was so desperate to find out if anyone from his extended family or any of his friends had survived that he spent most of the Thursday at a Jewish community centre trying to find out.

But the message was confused. The Russians had found seven thousand survivors in the camp, most barely alive. Many other prisoners had been taken away from the camp in the days and weeks before. It would be some time before they knew the names of who was still alive, if that was the right word to describe them.

Early on the Friday morning they set off. André had borrowed a car from a friend and had managed to get hold of enough petrol to get them to their destination 'We may have to push it for the last few miles.' The car was a snub-nosed Peugeot, more reliable than handsome. They headed north east from Paris, which was a longer route, but there had been reports of some fighting just to the south of where they were heading and André wanted to make sure they kept well away from it. For most of the morning they were in the Champagne region, their progress slowed considerably by long military convoys heading east and long lines of German prisoners of war trudging in the other direction. They were stopped at a few checkpoints, where Owen's Royal Navy identification helped. At one checkpoint, some American troops even allowed them to siphon off some petrol from an abandoned German staff car. It meant that they now had enough fuel to be sure of reaching their destination.

By early afternoon they had dropped down into Lorraine, where there was evidence of more recent fighting. Paris had suffered the deprivations of war, but had emerged unscathed in terms of damage. The same could not be said for Metz and the small towns and villages they drove through. If anything, thought Owen, it was worse than the Pas de Calais.

By the time they had driven through Nancy it was getting dark. They decided to press on: they knew that the roads would be difficult, but neither of them wanted to hang around. There was an air of anarchy in the area. Any time the car stopped it was quickly surrounded by people desperate for food and water. Young children pressed their faces against the windows. When they drove off, people would kick out at the car and some stones were thrown at them. They knew if they did find somewhere to stay the night, it would be too risky to leave the car unattended.

The checkpoints were getting trickier now. So far, Owen's Royal Navy identification had helped them through them. But as they drove, they had been discussing to what lengths Edgar might be going to track him down, which Owen was in no doubt he would be doing. What if he had put out an alert for Owen Quinn? It was perfectly feasible that he could put out a notification that he was a deserter, or worse. So they decided to rely on André's cunning and his FFI identification.

As they entered Alsace, the atmosphere changed. It felt as if they were driving through Germany. The road signs and village and town names were only in German and the buildings were noticeably Germanic in appearance.

'I'll give you a quick history lesson, Owen. Alsace has always been a mixture of German and French. Before 1870, it was part of France. Then there was the Franco-Prussian War, which we lost, and Alsace and parts of Lorraine became part of Germany. After the Great War, they came back to France. In 1940, the Germans returned. This area was not part of occupied France or even Vichy. The Germans made it part of Greater Germany. Now, it has come back to France. So if anyone here who was born in the 1860s and is still alive, they would have lived under German rule twice and French rule three times. When the Germans have run the region, they have discriminated against everything French, and I daresay that when we have ruled the area we have not exactly encouraged the German language and culture, not that you can blame us.' He turned to Owen and laughed. 'But it does explain why this is a rather strange part of the world, and why so many people here are so strange. But then, I think you know that, don't you, Owen?'

They entered Strasbourg just before six o'clock. Their original plan had been to seek somewhere to stay that night and try to find Nathalie in the morning. But nothing prepared them for the devastation. The city had been heavily bombed by the Allies and then there had been bitter fighting before General Leclerc's French troops took the city at the end of November.

Although still identifiable as a city, it was only just functioning as one. The damage was everywhere to be seen. People were still huddled in the ruins of buildings, whose darkened shells were lit by dozens of small fires as they tried to keep warm. Owen realised that you needed to be close to the damage to see that war caused more than physical damage and psychological suffering. There was a smell to it, a fetid taste that stuck to the back of the throat.

Enquiries about hotels were met with confused smiles, so they did what all travellers unsure of their final destination do and headed for the centre. Just off the Place du Temple Neuf they found a small café in a narrow street, where the white walls were pockmarked with bullet holes. They were able to park the Peugeot across the street where they could see it from their table in the window.

Owen was beginning to learn that André always had a plan. He was not complaining. André's forgery plan had worked so well that they were now in Strasbourg armed with Nathalie's apparently real name and an address. Lange had also confirmed that she had indeed been a nurse when the Germans recruited her.

As they sat in the café they agreed that their priority was to go to the address that Lange had given them. He had warned them that the address was from before the war and he could not guarantee she would be there. He was certain, though, about her real name.

The owner of the café just shrugged his shoulders and shook his head when they asked him if he knew the road. He eyed them suspiciously as they left the café. None of the passers-by wanted to know.

People were naturally suspicious and Owen noticed that most of them were speaking French with a distinct German pronunciation. André appeared to be having trouble finding directions as they wandered around the centre of the city.

Eventually a couple walked by who were happy to help. Yes, they did know this area, 'but you must realise it was damaged when the Germans invaded in 1940 and it was bombed last year.' Not many buildings had been left standing. 'Come, we'll show you where it is. We're heading that way ourselves.'

The area was barren. There were indeed just a few buildings left standing in the road where her house was meant to be, and none of them intact. They thanked the couple, who hurried along. On both sides of the road, and for blocks either side, there were piles of rubble, punctuated by the jagged remains of trees, whose top halves had been snapped off by the force of explosions or burned by fire. There was no sign of life, other than some children pulling a wooden trolley, laden with wood and scraps. They went over to talk to them, but the children abandoned their trolley and ran off. They drove around the area and eventually came across an elderly lady dressed all in black, walking a skeletal black Labrador.

No, no one had lived in this area for some time. Most people had moved out in 1940 and the few that remained had left when the Allied bombing started. Her French was slow and difficult to make out. André asked whether she would prefer to speak German. She nodded. They spoke for a couple of minutes and then she merged back into the shadows, pulled along by her dog.

'She thought we were from the authorities. Many people here are worried that they may be called collaborators, so people are going to be suspicious of us. She told me she's lived in this area most of her life and didn't seem to recognise the name, but her memory is not good. Maybe there was a family of that name that lived here ten years ago, she is not sure. But if they did, they would have left long ago.'

'We could go to the police,' said Owen, 'they may have a record of the surname.'

'I am worried about alerting her in some way. We just don't know who to trust around here. I mean look at us,' said André, pointing at the two of them, 'a Jew and an Englishman. We don't exactly blend in, do we? As soon as we walk into a police station or the Hôtel de Ville, people will notice us. We need to be cautious. If someone alerts her then you may never see your child. Jean did give me the name of a contact here, but apparently he will not be back in Strasbourg until Monday. Shall we wait until then?'

Owen thought about it. Perhaps they had no alternative. Then it was his turn to have a plan.

André liked it.

A few hours after André and Owen arrived in Strasbourg that Friday night, Edgar had his first breakthrough.

Since arriving in Paris the previous Saturday, Edgar had used all the influence he could muster to ensure maximum co-operation from the British Embassy. It worked. When he turned up at the British Embassy in the Rue Faubourg St-Honoré that Monday morning, Edgar was able to see the ambassador straight away. By the end of the meeting he had been promised the full co-operation of the British Embassy. 'No question about it. Winston clearly thinks this is important. We'll do what we can to help.'

Edgar commandeered Embassy staff to help monitor all the hotel registration cards. They spoke to police and any other officials they could find. He had scoured the streets and the bars. But there was no trace of Quinn. There was always the possibility that he had left Paris, but Edgar felt that even if he had only stayed in the city for a day or two, there would be some clue here as to where he had headed next.

The breakthrough came late on the Friday afternoon. One of the military attachés at the Embassy had been speaking to a contact in the resistance the previous day about another matter, and that contact had happened to mention that one of his comrades, a man called Gaston, had been assisting a British Royal Navy officer. The attaché did not think to mention it to Edgar until the next day. Edgar kept very calm. It would not help matters if he held this blithering idiot up against a wall and asked him why, precisely, he had waited a whole day to tell him this? That could be dealt with later. He would arrange a transfer to somewhere more unpleasant than Paris. There were plenty of options. Right now, he needed to track this Gaston down.

It took a couple of hours. Edgar was being cautious. If Gaston had been helping Owen then he may well be better-disposed towards him than the British authorities.

They found out where he lived, which was in the rundown Marais quarter on the eastern edge of the city centre. Gaston was in a nearby bar, in an alleyway off the Rue des Rosiers.

'We appreciate you helping Owen,' Edgar told him. 'He was one of my best agents. He has a lot of problems. You will understand. We need to find that woman before he does. For her own protection. Where is Owen now? It is in his interests for you to tell us. And yours.'

Gaston said nothing. He slid his glass across the zinc-topped bar for it to be refilled. The barman understood and reached for his oldest Armagnac. The Englishman was paying. Gaston was not sure whether to believe him. He had only become involved in the first place to help André, and André had been so unsettled since he returned to Paris that maybe this Englishman was telling the truth. But then, he had liked Owen and he had believed him.

So he decided to give the Englishman part of what he wanted. Not the name or any other details, though. Maybe that was the solution. Something, but not too much.

'They left for Alsace this morning.'

'Do you know where in Alsace?'

'No.'

'Strasbourg?'

'Possibly.'

'And can you give me any details about the name and address they may have been given?'

Gaston shook his head. He was regretting this now. He shouldn't have said anything.

'How did he get this information?'

Gaston shrugged. 'I don't know. I only saw him once or twice. He seemed to have a contact. I don't know whom.'

Edgar gestured to the barman to fill up Gaston's glass again. Maybe that would loosen his tongue. But he ought to have known better. Try as he might, he got nowhere. The Frenchman was polite. He would like to help. But he had told him all he knew and repeated it. 'He's headed for Alsace, possibly Strasbourg.'

Edgar thanked Gaston, gave him a piece of paper with the phone number of the British Embassy on it, and in return Gaston promised to contact him if he heard anything. *Of course.* Edgar left enough money with the barman to pay for Gaston to finish what little was left of the bottle and headed back to the Embassy.

It was late now, gone nine o'clock. He had been promised he would have whatever help he needed and right now he needed a good car and a reliable driver who knew the way to Strasbourg.

Gaston stayed in the bar until late. The Englishman's money was going a long way. He was bothered though. He should have relied on his instinct and not trusted the Englishman. Émile joined him at nine o'clock that night and listened silently as Gaston recounted what had happened.

'Should I have trusted the Englishman?' he asked Émile. Émile shook his head, thanked Gaston for the drink and left the bar in a hurry. Gaston realised that it was foolish to ask Émile. He trusted no one these days. After what he had been through, who could blame him?

–

They found the hospital easily enough. The one large hospital in the city was just across the river that surrounded the old centre, just off Rue de la Bourse. Their good fortune continued. The first doctor they stopped to ask in the corridor came from Paris and was happy to help a fellow Parisian. 'Come with me, let me take you to the records department. I hope you find your friend and that she and her baby are healthy.'

The lady in the records department assumed that because the doctor had brought them along, it was in order for her to help. 'Because otherwise,' she said as she slid her chair over to the right filing cabinet, 'it would be quite irregular for us to pass on records to someone else. T... here we are, T... let's see Troppe, I can't see anything... When did you say it was? October or November? Can't see anything here. Troppe...'

Owen was not altogether surprised. They were assuming that she had come back to Strasbourg. If she was running away, then this could well be the last place she would come to. And if she did, she would probably have used another name.

She carried on searching, encouraged by André. She was still muttering 'Troppe... Troppe' under her breath as she worked through the documents when a nurse came in carrying a bunch of files to leave on the desk.

'What were you saying, Thérèse? That name?'

'Troppe. I am looking to see if a baby Troppe was born here last year.'

'The only Troppe I know is Ginette. Ah well.' She turned and walked out.

André and Owen were stunned. They followed the nurse out of the room.

'You know Ginette Troppe?' André was taking care not to appear too desperate.

'Sure, I worked with her here in Strasbourg before the war. She went to work in Paris during the war apparently.'

'Yes, that is where I know her from,' said André. 'I heard she had returned here and as I was in Strasbourg I thought I would look her up. She gave me her address and you know, I lost it. I knew she was expecting a baby, so I thought maybe I could find the details here. I have some gifts for her, you see.'

'I don't think her baby was born here. But why not ask her yourself. She's back working here now.'

—

After that, it was not difficult. Even though it was late at night, the nurse agreed to check – discreetly. 'Of course, I understand, sir,' she had said, pocketing the folded notes. 'Everyone appreciates a surprise.' Ginette Troppe, it seemed, was due in at six o'clock the next morning. Her shift would end at three in the afternoon.

They found a hotel near the railway station and stayed there that night. Owen registered using his cousin Peter's passport, which he had brought with him from England. They were up at five in the morning. André had already found out which side entrance the nurses used, and they parked the car just down that street, giving them a good view of everyone approaching the entrance.

Owen was slumped in the passenger seat wearing a hat, with a scarf wrapped across his face. André was concerned that he looked like a robber, but at least he was not recognisable. At a quarter to six, the morning shift began to arrive, in ones and twos and the occasional threesome. It was a bitterly cold morning, with frost on the ground, and it would be difficult to identify her if she was wearing the hood of her cape up as some of the other nurses were doing. André decided to get out of the car. He had looked at her photograph often enough, and Owen had described her in detail, so he reckoned he would recognise her. He was just opening the driver's door of the car when she appeared. She was walking alone along the side street where the entrance was. Her cape flowed behind her and she had the hood down. As she walked along, she threw her head back in her characteristic fashion so as to gather her long hair together. As she walked closer to them, she tied it back., and Owen caught a glimpse of her face. Her deep black eyes pierced through the mist. Owen was in no doubt whatsoever. He made to open the car door, but André restrained him. 'Later.'

That was André's plan. *Let her do her shift.* It would cause trouble if they approached her first. *Let her do her shift and then we can follow her home. You need to know where she lives, don't you? You want to find your child?*

They went back to the hotel to rest. André fell asleep and Owen stood at the window, looking out over Strasbourg. Somewhere out there is my child, he thought.

He realised that he had not expected to reach this moment. Until today, he had not expected to find her, so he had not given any serious thought to what he would do when he did. Would he kill her? Could he forgive her? Would he take her back to England and hand her over to Edgar? Would he march her to a police station? Hand her over to the FFI? Would he be able to forgive her and stay with her? He had no idea. And then there was the child. Until the nurse last night had mentioned that she had given birth, he had not known for sure that she had even had the baby. Could he possibly allow her to keep the child?

He stood leaning against the window, working his way through a packet of André's cigarettes, his heart pounding away and any kind of rest out of the question.

André woke at one. Naturally, he had a plan. They would eat and return to the hospital. Although the shift ended at three, they would be in position just before two, just in case she left early. They would need to follow her, which was the only way to be sure of finding out where she lived – and where, presumably, the child was. Owen would drive the car so that André could follow her on foot in case she caught a tram.

As they waited outside the nurses' entrance, the drizzle which had been present since they had arrived in Strasbourg had now turned to a downpour, making it difficult to see. Nonetheless, she was not hard to make out as she swept out of the hospital just after three, much the same way as she had entered it: cape flowing and alone. As she climbed down the steps she unclipped her small nurse's hat and untied her hair, shaking her head, her long hair now flowing loose behind her. They waited until she had crossed the street and turned left into the main road. She walked past one long tram queue, and it appeared that she might be walking all the way home. At that moment, a beige tram appeared from the other direction and she ran across the road, raising her hand for it to stop. André had jumped out of the car even before Owen had brought it to a sudden halt.

The plan entailed Owen trying to follow the tram. If he lost them then he would have to rely on André following her on the tram, finding out where she lived. They would meet back at the hotel.

By the time Owen had managed to turn the car round in the road he was already behind a lorry and another three or four cars. A couple of blocks on, the tram stopped, but neither André nor Ginette, as he now knew her to be, got off. He was able to pull up behind the tram, but lost it again at the next set of traffic lights. By now the traffic was getting heavier and he decided to have one last go, turning into the oncoming lane and accelerating past the cars in front of him. The tram had just pulled away from another stop as he caught up with it again. He glanced to his right, but could see neither André nor Ginette on the pavement, so he carried on. The tram was turning left now, crossing a river, moving in a southerly direction away from the city centre. He nosed in behind, as close as he could without driving on the tram-tracks. If he lost it now, it would probably be too late. Soon after the left turn, the tram pulled into another stop. He held back a bit before pulling in near to it. Sure enough, Ginette got off, closely followed by André, who looked around and saw him. He waited while André followed Ginette round a corner and followed slowly in the car. It was a long side street with apartment blocks on either side. It was a straight road, so he could afford to pull in and still see where André was following her. She stopped at a *boulangerie* and André followed her in. They both emerged a minute later carrying large paper bags. As she crossed the road, she looked towards him, straight in the direction of the car. He huddled himself further down the seat, but she had not seen him. She was making sure it was safe to cross.

André was well practised, Owen realised. He knew how to follow someone. He had crossed the road in front of Ginette and was now walking before her, allowing her to pass him after a few paces as he paused to tie up a shoelace.

A hundred yards or so later, Ginette climbed up the stairs of a small apartment block, taking her keys out of her handbag as she did so. She briefly turned round as André walked straight past the entrance.

Owen caught up with him a bit further on, where André had turned into a smaller side street.

'Well done, Owen, that was good. Now we know where she lives. Are you ready for this?'

Owen nodded, although he was not sure that he was ready. His heart was pounding so loud and fast that he was feeling lightheaded.

'And you are sure you want me to come with you?'

They only had to wait five minutes before an elderly man walked slowly up the steps of the apartment block and they were able to time their walk up the steps to coincide with his. He was very grateful as they held the door open for him and doffed his hat as they followed him into the entrance hall.

There was no concierge here, which André muttered was a good thing. There appeared to be six floors, three apartments to each floor. Apartment five on the second floor had 'Troppe' on the board.

They climbed the flight of stairs to the second floor. Owen's breathing was heavy now, and he must have been walking slowly as André paused for him, putting an arm round his shoulders as he did so.

They waited outside apartment five. At first they could hear nothing and then, through the closed door, there was the sound of two people talking, followed by silence. A minute or so later, the sound of a baby crying. André nodded. Owen knew his plan. He would wait around the corner so that when the door was opened, it would only be the unfamiliar face of André that they would see, for long enough to get the door open.

André rapped on the door. From behind the corner Owen could hear footsteps coming to the door.

'Who is it?' It was his wife's voice.

Chapter 36

It was the Sunday afternoon before Edgar found what he was looking for. He had arrived in Strasbourg in the very early hours of the morning and spent most of that day driving around the city, trying to persuade the police to let him see the hotel registration cards. *Come back later*, he was told.

He checked into a small guest house in the city centre, intending to get an hour's rest. When he awoke he realised that he had slept for more than five hours. It was ten o'clock at night.

The next day he went back to the police station. They had checked with Paris and they *were* going to be able to let him see the cards. Later. It was noon before he was taken into a small office and shown them.

No sign of Owen Quinn. The only British passport holder staying at a hotel in the city was a Peter Sinclair. He was from the same town in Surrey as Owen.

The hotel owner was very helpful. He was most impressed by the array of accreditation that Edgar had pointedly spread out on the reception desk in front of him, along with the photograph of Owen.

'There were two of them. The Englishman – yes that's him, sir – and a Frenchman. Paris accent. Probably... you know, Jewish... not that that is a problem, sir. There were many of them here in Strasbourg. Before the war. The men checked out yesterday. I've no idea where they went. They may have been going to visit a friend though. I remember now that they did ask me for the best route to the University Hospital.'

Edgar thanked him very much and asked if he would be so kind as to give him those same directions to the University Hospital.

'It is Pascal from apartment eighteen on the top floor,' said André. 'I have a parcel for you that came to me by mistake.'

'One moment, one moment.' She sounded annoyed. It took a moment for the door to be unlocked and bolts and chains removed.

The door opened. André pushed it open wider and, as he entered, Owen followed him straight in. He was already in the hall with the door closed behind him before she realised who he was.

She made to scream, but no sound came out. The colour had drained from her face and her eyes were wide open, as was her mouth. She took an unsteady step back and leaned against the wall.

'Owen!' she gasped. 'Oh my God!'

Very slowly, she sank to her knees. Her mouth was open and she was trying to speak, but nothing was coming out.

'Who is it, Ginette?' It was an older woman's voice from behind a door, accompanied by the sound of a baby crying.

'It is all right, mother. Someone from work.' Her voice sounded hoarse.

She glared at André.

'This is a friend of mine,' said Owen.

'I have heard so much about you.' André bowed with exaggerated courtesy.

'Can we talk alone, Owen?'

'Yes, as long as it is in this apartment.'

'Why?'

'Because I have come for my child.'

Another gasp. She rubbed her knuckles against her teeth, desperately thinking what to do.

'We can go into the kitchen.'

'I will wait in the corridor outside,' said André.

'Mother,' she said, trying very hard to sound calm, although her voice was now high-pitched. 'There is someone here from work I need to see about changing departments. We will go into the kitchen. Please do not disturb us.'

He followed her into the kitchen and closed the door. She gestured towards an empty chair at the table and she sat opposite him, nervously pulling at her hair.

'How did you find me, Owen?'

He ignored her question. 'What shall I call you? Nathalie? Ginette?'

She shrugged. 'How did you know about the baby? How could you have known? You must tell me that, Owen!'

Owen was breathing heavily now, the tension and fury mounting up in him.

'No, I realise I wasn't meant to know. I was in such a bad state over this whole business that I was drinking too much and sleeping too little, so I went to see Dr Peacock in September. He let slip that you were pregnant. You can imagine how much better I felt after that visit. But what it did do was drive me to find you and my child. Is it mine? I don't even know if it is a boy or a girl!'

She got up and paced around the small kitchen before going over to the sink to get herself a glass of water. When she sat down again her hands were shaking so violently that she had to hold the glass with two hands. He could hear it clattering against her teeth as she took a few sips.

'It's a boy, Owen…' She paused and sank her head into her hands. She stayed like that for a while, the sounds of her quiet sobs filling the room. She tried to compose herself, but when she started speaking again, her voice was weak. 'He looks like you. Of course, you are the father… I am sorry, I never intended… But, you know… it happened. I only found out just before I came back to France, when I went to see Dr Peacock. I was in a panic. I had not intended to get pregnant, but I wanted to keep the baby. If I was not being sent to France, I think I would have told you. Not just about the baby, but everything, Owen. I had decided that much. I promise you.'

'You can tell me now.'

'What are you going to do with him?'

'With whom?'

'Our son.'

'What is his name?'

'He is called Philippe, after the French general who liberated Strasbourg. It was my mother's idea really.'

She tried to drink from the glass again, but her hands were shaking so violently that the water spilled on the tabletop. She bit her forefinger to try to stop herself crying.

'Tell me everything first. Why did you work for the Germans? Did they make you work for them or did you volunteer? I want to know everything.' Owen was doing his best to sound angry, but his overwhelming emotions were sadness and confusion.

She was crying freely, the tears gathering under her eyes before rolling fast down her reddened cheeks. For the first time since he had met her, she looked vulnerable. When the crying subsided and she began to speak, he noticed that her face reminded him of the time when she had emerged out of the fog on Westminster Bridge in the winter of 1943. He had realised then that for the first time, she looked unguarded. As if she'd always worn a mask before. She now looked as if her mask had been discarded, and for the first time he was able to look at her face with all her true emotions exposed on it.

'My family is from Alsace. We are of German origin, like a lot of people in this region. In the Great War my father fought in the German Army – Alsace was part of Germany then. As far as he was concerned, he was German. He never thought of himself as French. He worked for the railways, and when Alsace became part of France again after the war, he was sent to Lyon to work. We all went there. I had no brothers or sisters. My father was treated very badly in Lyon. People regarded him as a traitor. People did not talk to him at work, we had no friends. In the time we were there, I don't think we were ever invited to anyone else's house. I was too young to realise, but I grew up with this atmosphere in the house. By 1921, he couldn't stand it anymore, so he gave up his job and we moved back to Alsace. I was seven then. He couldn't get any work here in Alsace, so he went to Germany, but things were even worse there, there were no jobs and they treated him as if he was French, so he felt that he did not belong anywhere. He came back to Alsace in 1922 and killed himself in 1923. I discovered his body hanging from a landing over the stairs when I got up during the night to go to the bathroom. I was nine.

'My mother was destitute, but a German cultural organisation helped with my education and gave us food each week. As I grew up, I became interested in politics. I felt that a strong Germany was important. So in 1935, I joined the Nazi Party. It was clandestine, of course. Alsace was still in France then. I didn't think too much about it. Most of the people in the organisation that had helped us had joined it; they had helped fund my nursing training. Maybe I was trying to repay their help. The Germans were the only people who helped us, and the Nazi Party were the only people who cared about Germany. I moved to Paris in 1938, and I was recruited as a spy. That's it.'

'Did they recruit you or did you approach them?'

'Does it matter? I wanted to help.'

'You are a Nazi then?'

'I don't know what I was then. I was a young fool. The organisation that helped my mother, it was more political than anything else. Many of those people were involved with the Nazis, so I went to the meetings, and began to feel part of something.'

Silence again in the room. She threw back her long hair in the way that Owen remembered, then harshly brushed it away from her face with shaking hands.

'Owen, please...'

'My friend out there,' said Owen, 'was taken to a camp in Poland with his wife and child and tens of thousands of other French Jews. His wife and son were killed. Millions of people were murdered, they're saying. From all over Europe. When people find out what—'

'Owen, you don't need to tell me. What I have seen since I came back to France...' Ginette hugged her arms tight across her chest. There was a long pause. 'It's terrible. I felt guilty. I have seen such suffering. I had to escape from Lille after an SS officer tried to rape me. I stabbed him. I became a refugee. In Lorraine I was looked after by Jews and Gypsies who had been in one of these camps that you are talking about. A Jewish doctor from Poland, he looked after me. He told me about the terrible things that had happened.'

Until now, she had avoided eye contact with Owen. She would look at the table, at the floor, at the wall around her, or at her hands as she buried her face in them. But now she stared at him, her eyes pleading with him to believe her.

'You have to believe me, Owen!'

'Do I?' With that, he stood up and lashed out. The back of his right hand caught her on the cheekbone, just by the side of her right eye. She did not even flinch. A trickle of blood darted in a surprisingly straight line down her face. She nodded once at Owen, as if to acknowledge what he had done. He had staggered back as if he himself had been hit.

'Ginette. Is everything all right?' It was her mother's voice from the other room.

'It is fine, mother. Please leave us alone for a while.'

He stood up, his knuckles resting down on the table, leaning right over her. His voice was trembling. She was now the more composed of the two of them.

'Why should I believe a word you say? Tell me that! What do I know about you? I know that you are a Nazi spy, that you deceived me, that you married me, became pregnant without telling me, and then disappeared. And now I have tracked you down, you are trying to talk your way out of it. Look at me – I don't even know what I should call you. Nathalie? Ginette? Are there any other names I should be aware of?'

Silence. She sat still, saying nothing.

'Go on, I want to know.'

'When I was in the Pas de Calais I was known as Geraldine. Why do you want to know all this, Owen?'

'And any other names?'

'I also used the name Hélène Blanc for a while, after I left the Pas de Calais.'

'And what should I call you, tell me?'

He was leaning right over her now, his face just inches from hers.

'My real name is Ginette. Ginette Troppe.'

'And so, Ginette Troppe. Give me one very good reason why I don't drag you now to the authorities. You're a Nazi spy. You're on the run and I've caught you.'

'You'll do what you want to do, Owen. I can't stop you. But let me say something. You say I ran away, but that is not true. I came back here, to my home town, to my true identity. I could so easily have disappeared after I left the Pas de Calais. There are so many refugees moving around the country, so much chaos – it would have been easy for me to find another identity and then another one. I could have changed my identity very easily. I could have gone to anywhere in France. This country is twice the size of yours. It would have been very easy for me to make it impossible for you to trace me. Think about that, Owen.'

'What are you saying?'

'That I wanted to be found by you, Owen. That is why I came back here, and that is why I used my original name. Look, I even went back to the hospital that I worked in before the war. I was not hiding from you, Owen, quite the opposite. I was making it possible for you to find me.'

She was staring directly at her husband, her eyes beseeching him to believe her.

'But why… why did you want me to find you?'

'It was not just because of the baby. It was because of you. I don't expect you to believe this, but once I was away from you, when I arrived back in France, I realised that I cared about you. I even started to have those feelings when the British sent me away for training. And since then, I have cared about you more and more. I realised that I love you, Owen.'

'That's a convenient turn of events, isn't it?' he said sarcastically.

'It's the truth, Owen. I was surprised myself at my feelings.'

Owen looked shocked. He started pacing around the small kitchen. As he came close to her he realised that it was not just the sight of her and the sound of her voice that had so unsettled him. It was the smell of her too. He would never be able to describe it, and he had never even realised that she had her own distinctive scent that he had become so familiar with.

'But hang on. You didn't leave a forwarding address, did you? British Intelligence had no idea who you really were. I accept that you may have reverted to your proper name and come back to your home town, but how on earth was I expected to know all that? It was only because of a lot of hard work, and even more luck, that I was able to find you.'

'Exactly.'

'Exactly what?'

'That I thought you would find me. I knew that if you really wanted to find me, you would. There's one other thing, Owen. I left a clue, didn't I?'

He leaned back against the worktop and frowned.

'If you did, it must have been a very well hidden one, because I missed it.'

'The brooch, Owen, the cameo brooch. Did you find that?'

He nodded.

'I knew that I had to leave some message for you. I wanted to leave you something of mine. Did you spot the initials on the back of the brooch?'

'Yes, just. But how would that help me find you? The reason I found you was because I persisted, and because some very decent people stuck their necks out to help me. The brooch didn't help.'

'But it helped you realise that I might have left a message for you? That maybe it was a sign of some affection?'

'Maybe.'

She smiled. It was a smile that he could not recall ever having seen before, and considering that he had committed every smile, every gesture of hers to his memory and then replayed them over and over again – he knew he would have remembered a smile like that.

'But that is the point, Owen! By leaving the brooch for you like that I was sending you a message. You were to understand that it would be worth searching for me. When I left that for you, I wasn't even sure why I was doing it. Deep down, I must have thought it was a way of giving myself an option – that it might help you find me. I'm not sure.'

She spread her arms open, as if to say 'And here I am'. *Voilà*.

'Well, I suppose it worked.' Owen paused. 'Did you ever care for me, when we were together, that is…?' He was sounding hesitant now. 'Or was I only a way of getting information?'

She had composed herself. 'Let me tell you this first, Owen. You asked me whether I approached the Germans, or whether they approached me. I will tell you the truth. I approached them. One of the men I knew in the organisation, he said that because I spoke German and English, I could be of use to the Germans. He made it sound exciting. So I went to Paris to meet a man he knew at the German Embassy—'

'Georg Lange?'

'That's right!' She sounded shocked. 'How did you find him? Did he tell you where I was?'

'Carry on.'

She had gone quiet. Her long fingernails were tracing a haphazard shape on the table. For a moment, their fingertips touched on the shiny surface of it, before they both pulled their hands away in shock.

'So I met Lange. In 1938. I thought I was going to be something like… I don't know… a messenger, nothing much more than that. But it was like when I was a child and I used to go on the slide at the playground. Once you started, you couldn't stop. It was impossible. I was sent to Germany for training and before I realised it properly, I was becoming an agent. I was too involved to do anything about it. I felt like telling them that this was all a mistake; that I was just a nurse. I was even thinking of leaving, but then it became too late. One of the other people being trained with me, a very intelligent lawyer from Poitiers, he announced one evening that he had changed his mind and was leaving. They seemed to let him go, but the next morning they took us to a forest for training and we discovered his body hanging from a tree. They arranged for us to discover his body, of course. To send us a very clear message. It reminded me of my father, the way that the body was perfectly straight, apart from the neck which looked as if it had been rearranged at an unusual angle.'

With the back of her wrist she dabbed at the cut next to her eye. The bleeding had stopped, but a bruise was beginning to appear.

'So, I was caught in a nightmare, but at the same time, I must have been influenced by everything they were telling me. I suppose I could have run away or something, or just disappeared. But at the time, nothing seemed real. I didn't believe that there would be a war and I thought that if there was one, then they would have more important things to remember than me, and that could be my opportunity to disappear.

'When Germany invaded France, it was a terrible shock. Deep down, I must have thought that would never really happen. I knew that I would now have to become involved. So I escaped. Owen, I promise you I did. Ask my mother, she had no idea what had happened to me. Ask Georg Lange. I left Strasbourg and headed west. The French authorities had evacuated much of the civilian population from the city once the war started. I was only allowed to remain because the hospital where I worked remained open. It was the only one that was. I was not sure where to go, so many people were on the roads, sometimes it was hard to move. I made two mistakes. The first was that I headed north, and walked straight into the German invasion. They found me in a town called Abbeville. It's in Picardy. The second mistake was that I used my own identity. That's how the Germans found me. You ask Lange if you don't believe me.'

She was beginning to lose her composure again and started to weep. Owen handed her a handkerchief from his top pocket. Their fingers brushed very slightly again as he handed it over.

'I was trapped, Owen. And I was a coward. When the Germans caught me, I told them a story about how I had to flee Strasbourg because I thought the French police were after me. They must have believed me. It worked out well for them because people were being evacuated from Dunkirk to England at the time, and thousands of French civilians were escaping too. It was not difficult for me to join them. The Abwehr spent a day or two briefing me on my new identity and then I was taken near to Dunkirk. It was not difficult to join the people escaping.'

'What did the Germans ask you to do?'

'My mission was to get to London and do nothing other than establish myself as a nurse. I had nothing incriminating on me. In time, I was to find a job in a military hospital. Then I was to make contact with my radio man. Once I had been cleared in London after my arrival, I thought it was too late. I was a German spy by then. So I just did as I had been instructed. It was purely by chance that I met you, Owen, but when I did... there was nothing I could do. I had my instructions. Please understand, Owen.'

He snorted. 'Do you know that you were used? And so was I, as it happens. British Intelligence knew all about you, long before you came to Calcotte Grange. They found out about you, they discovered that you had requested a transfer to a military hospital, and they set the whole thing up. They even arranged for you to meet me. They even guessed I would fall for you. Of course, I never realised what was going on, so you can imagine how I feel. And all the information that you got through me was deliberately false, although I never realised that. It was intended to mislead the Germans into thinking that the Pas de Calais would be where the main invasion was. That is why you were sent there. You were used.'

'I didn't realise all that. Of course, once the Allies landed in Normandy, I wondered about the information, but—'

'Ask yourself this. Was there an invasion in the Pas de Calais? No. It was only ever going to be Normandy. So, you played your part. You helped the Allies.'

'Owen, if that is true, maybe it is not a bad thing. By the time I left London, I did not want to be a German spy. I was having your baby. I liked people in England. I had developed feelings for you, Owen!'

'Do you know what happened to your group in Boulogne?'

She shook her head vigorously. She held up her hand as if she didn't want to know.

'Françoise escaped. Lucien was tortured but is still alive, although he is crippled. Their children were burned to death along with Françoise's mother by your Nazi friends. Pierre killed himself before they could arrest him and Jean was tortured to death. Lucien was in the cell next to his. He took a whole night to die. Lucien said he even heard him calling out your name that night.'

She was frightened now. Owen noticed that she was trembling.

'You said you had feelings for me,' she said. 'What are those feelings?'

Owen was trembling now. 'I don't know what to say any more, I don't know what to think. I want to see my son now.'

'Of course. I want you to see him. Tell me something. You must have had feelings for me. What has happened to them?'

'You know that I loved you more than anything else in the world. And I will tell you something else that I did not realise until a few minutes ago. I continued to love you. I loved you when I found out that you were a German spy, even though I tried very hard not to. I still loved you when I found out what had happened in the Pas de Calais. I loved you when I saw you walking into the hospital this morning, and I still loved you when I walked into this apartment a few minutes ago. All along, I hoped to reach a point where I could finally stop loving you, but—'

She handed his handkerchief back to him. This time, their brushing of fingers was not accidental.

'I'll ask my mother to go for a walk. Then we can be alone when you meet Philippe. What about your friend?'

'He could do with a walk too.'

'Does your mother know the truth?'

'Of course not. She thinks I was in Paris during the war. She learned from my father that it is best not to ask too many questions.'

Ginette moved into the hall and addressed her mother through the closed door of the back room. Please could she leave her in the apartment for a while? 'Everything is fine, no really. Please, mother. I'll explain later.' Her voice was shaking and she was gripping the side of her nurse's uniform.

Owen spoke quietly to André. He would wait in the car.

When they had both left, she took Owen to his son.

He was a tiny little thing, with Owen's fair hair but his mother's jet-black eyes, which brightened up when they entered the room. Owen sank to his knees and picked him up, holding him close to him. He could feel the baby's warmth against his chest and his own tears rolling down his face. Gently, he pressed the little boy's head under his chin. Nothing had prepared him for this moment. His son's hair felt like silk brushing against his face.

Ginette was sobbing behind him, pacing up and down the room.

'What are you going to do with him, Owen? He is the most precious thing to me. Please, Owen, I will do anything. Don't take him, Owen. Don't take him. I am sorry, I was wrong, I—'

Owen sat down in an armchair, holding the baby in an unsure manner.

'I don't know. I have really no idea. I need to think. What can we do? The British authorities are after you. Don't forget, you're a German spy. We can't pretend that nothing has happened.'

'Maybe they would understand, Owen.'

His son was studying his face, wriggling his tiny fingers as he did so.

He laughed. 'I very much doubt that. Do you know what they do to German spies? They hang them. Even repentant ones. We can't go back to England and think that everything will be sorted out. I can hardly live here, as if nothing happened. We will have to work something out. I'm still not sure what I want to do, to be honest. I don't know what I want to happen to us.'

She came over and knelt by the armchair. The baby was staring into the face of his father, his jet-black eyes darting around to take in every feature. Her arm stroked his and for a while all was silent and serene. Owen was totally captivated by the baby.

The tranquillity was shaken by knocking at the door.

She hauled herself up. 'It will be my mother. I will ask her to go to her sister's for a while so we can be alone for longer.'

He was more at ease cradling his son now. To his amazement, it felt natural. The baby was continuing to gaze into his eyes and Owen was certain that he was smiling at him. He grinned back.

He could hear her unlocking the door and then the sound of a hoarse male voice saying, 'Ginette Troppe?'

After that, his recollection was blurred beyond repair.

There was a noise, certainly. Not too loud – he realised later that the gun must have been held straight against her body – but it was a sharp noise that echoed around the little flat. That was followed almost immediately by the sound of something falling heavily and then a much louder and far clearer gunshot.

There was a commotion on the stairs and he heard André shouting something. From the hall he heard a long groan, that didn't stop. He was frozen in the armchair, the baby's smile now wide and accompanied by a friendly gurgle. His little arms were reaching out.

When he found himself in the hall, the baby was in his arms.

André was kneeling by her side, his hands covered in blood. Her face was grey, her eyes open wide but darting around, having trouble focussing. Her head was moving frantically from side to side.

André was trying to stem the blood flowing from a wound in her stomach, but a dark red patch was spreading fast across her chest.

'Talk to her, Owen, tell her to hang on.'

Neighbours had gathered in the open doorway. 'Ambulance!' shouted André. 'Get an ambulance and a doctor!'

Owen took her hand, which felt like ice. Her breathing was slow and very noisy. She tried hard to focus.

'Tell her to hang on, Owen. Show her the baby. Do something.'

He held Philippe closer to her. Very slowly, she reached out to him, her hand stopping before she could touch him. As the colour drained completely from her face her black eyes stood out in even more contrast against the white skin. A smile began to appear across her face and then froze as a groan came from deep inside her and her body seemed to sink slowly into itself.

André stood up, drenched in blood.

'She's gone, Owen. She's gone.'

–

André was pushing the small Peugeot as hard as it would go as they headed north. They had made good progress since leaving Strasbourg. The lights of Metz were now fading behind them, the road ahead dark and broken only by the occasional passing lights of army convoys. He was not sure about Owen's plan, but he agreed that they needed to leave Strasbourg fast.

Owen was slumped across the backseat, his son fast asleep in his arms.

'You are sure it was him, André?'

'I told you, Owen. I am not certain, but I think it was. I was sitting in the front seat of the car waiting around the corner for you when a large silvery-grey Renault pulled up in front of me. I didn't think anything of it. I was trying to rest, to be honest. A large man got out of the car and walked past. I was a bit unsettled by him, I don't know why. A minute or so later, something clicked in my mind and I got out for a proper look at the Renault. It had those very wide running boards. I am sure it was like the car that drove us to the prison to see Lange. And then I realised who the man was. Émile, the man who drove the Renault to and from the prison. The man whose family was tortured by the Gestapo, you remember? He was wearing a beret too, just like he was when he drove us to the prison. So I ran back to the apartment block. Just as I entered, I heard two shots, definitely two. As I ran up the stairs I collided with him running down. He pushed me out of the way. What more can I say? Revenge is our new religion.'

Edgar arrived at the hospital two hours after Ginette Troppe's body had been taken there. He had expected to find a living person, not a corpse.

He had asked for her by name at the reception and was ushered into a side room by a clearly distressed matron. 'Are you here in connection with her death? How has the news got out so soon?'

Edgar must have looked shocked; the matron was very understanding. He showed her the impressive sheaf of documentation that he had from the British Embassy in Paris and explained that she had done some work for the British during the war. 'She was at Dunkirk, you understand.' He had come to Strasbourg to thank her in person.

The matron tearfully explained what had happened. 'Shot, twice. We thought that kind of thing had stopped with the Germans leaving. There had been reprisals of course, but why would anyone want to shoot a nurse? The police have no idea who it was. And she was such a good nurse. Before the war she was a cold person, if I am honest with you, sir, not someone you could warm to. But when she returned from Paris she was a much nicer person. Maybe becoming a mother had changed her. I had no idea she was at Dunkirk. So many people did things in the war that they do not discuss.'

Edgar asked if he could see the body and was taken to the mortuary. He did not want to stay very long at all, especially as he was aware that his presence was beginning to attract some attention. 'If you don't mind waiting, sir, the police may want to talk with you when they arrive... if you could give us your name.' He wanted to be absolutely certain that it was the woman he had first known as Nathalie Mercier.

The room where the body lay was narrow with a low ceiling and it was dark apart from a light hanging directly over the body. He had not expected her head to be exposed, so as soon as he walked in he knew for sure that it was her. The shroud was gathered across the top of her breasts with the edge of a wound just visible, her skin now a marble white and glinting in the bright light.

He had no idea what had happened, and was going to have some trouble in explaining what had gone on. *Had Owen been responsible for her death? What would he have done if he had got to her first?*

There was a knock on the window that separated the room from the rest of the mortuary. The matron was looking anxious. She had explained on the way down that this was most irregular and really she did not have the authority to...

He held up his hand. 'One minute. Thank you.'

He thought of the past four years, and his role in shaping the life of the woman whose body now lay in front of him. He thought of the lives undoubtedly saved thanks to her unwitting help. He thought of her husband, and of what was going to become of him.

More knocking at the window. *I'm coming.*

Edgar turned to look at the body for one final time. He shook his head and smiled. 'You were the best of our spies,' he muttered, 'and you never even realised it.'

Minutes later, Edgar was on his way back to Paris, accompanied by an enormous sense of relief. What could have been a major problem had gone away. The outcome was messy, but all things considered it could have been far, far worse.

Chapter 37

Aftermath

Less than an hour after Owen Quinn had been to visit Captain John Archibald that day in December 1944, one of Edgar's men had turned up, demanding to know whether Owen Quinn had been to the house. He had pushed his way past Mrs Archibald but, by the time he entered the bedroom, Archibald had secreted under his body the notebook which Georg Lange's name was in.

Captain Archibald feigned sleep and the man had to leave. Later that night Archibald managed to get out of bed and burned the notebook in the fire.

His condition deteriorated significantly in the New Year, and everyone said that it was a relief when he died in March 1945.

They used the word 'peaceful' to describe his passing, as was traditional, but Iris Archibald would have described it as anything but. He was often agitated and usually in pain, but what she noticed more than anything else was that he appeared to be full of regret, as if there were matters he still wanted resolved but could not address. In his last few weeks he often asked her whether Owen Quinn had ever been in touch again and she always had to shake her head.

The day before he died, he told her that he wanted to dictate a letter, which began 'My dear Owen…'

He fell asleep after those words and did not wake up again.

His short obituary in *The Times* concentrated on his role in the Battle of Jutland in 1916. Brief reference was made to how he had delayed his retirement to continue service in the Royal Navy during the current war, in what they described as an 'administrative capacity'.

Following his arrest in July 1944, Admiral Wilhelm Canaris was held by the SS in Berlin.

In February 1945 he was taken to the Flossenbürg concentration camp in Bavaria, not far from the Czech border. He continued to be tortured until the morning of the 9th April 1945 when – along with his former deputy, Generalmajor Hans Oster and some of the 20th July bomb plot conspirators – he was stripped naked and dragged into the courtyard of the camp and slowly hanged by the SS.

Flossenbürg concentration camp was liberated by the Americans just two weeks later.

The two SS officers responsible for Canaris's detention and execution in Flossenbürg, Otto Thorbeck and Walter Huppenkothen, were never punished by the German authorities after the war.

–

Arnold Vermeulen felt elated as the plane sped over the last few miles of the silver sea and he was able to make out the coastline of mainland Europe in the distance. After five years, he would be home soon.

All in all, Arnold Vermeulen could not really complain at the way he had been treated.

Considering that in April 1941 he thought he was about to be executed, anything since then had been a bonus. Above all, he felt a sense of relief. He had never thought that he was cut out to be a spy anyway. The British seemed to understand that. He had become a nervous wreck, to be honest. He was a victim of the war. People would understand that in time. But once he had come through the interrogation and agreed to be a double agent, life became much easier. He no longer had to worry about being caught, because he already had been. He had no problems about betraying Magpie because, if he was frank, he never liked her. She was always condescending, treating him as if he were inferior to her, which he probably was.

So, all in all, he had been happy to play along with the British. After they set him up as a double agent, they always treated him properly. He never had to deal with the tall Englishman again, which was a relief. Contact with Magpie was intermittent, but he did everything he was told.

He had begun to wonder what would happen at the end of the war and had asked his handlers that on more than one occasion. There was an understanding that he would have to be returned to Belgium, but the authorities there would be told how co-operative he had been. Maybe six months in jail, certainly nothing more than that.

Life changed a bit at the end of April 1944. He never saw Magpie again. They moved him from the safe house in Acton to somewhere in North Wales. It was not a prison they told him. Not at all. But the house they kept him in was in a locked compound, and the house itself was locked and guarded. Soon after that, he heard about D-Day, and then it was just a matter of time before it was all over. Allied troops entered Belgium in the September and he was not sure how he felt about that. Not relief, but not a sense of defeat either. He just wanted this whole, dreadful business to be over and done with. To get back to his old life, his flat, his records and familiar surroundings.

After VE Day in May 1945 he was moved to a house somewhere in England. He had no idea where it was. It was in preparation for being sent back to Belgium, they had said. He had begun to worry, but then that was in his nature after all.

He had heard some dreadful things on the radio. In April, the Belgian authorities executed sixteen Belgian citizens for their part in torturing prisoners during the war. The sixteen were all shot in the back. He could not get the image out of his mind.

In the middle of May, the tall Englishman reappeared. 'You are going home,' he told him. 'Tomorrow.' He had asked the Englishman whether all these assurances he had been given – about how he would be well treated, just six months in prison etc. – whether he would have them in writing. The Englishman smiled and left. Arnold was sure that he nodded.

He saw him again the next morning when he arrived at the remote airfield. He asked him again whether he had those assurances in writing, and the Englishman just smiled and patted his coat pocket. There was just one plane there, no RAF markings as far as he could tell, and not much else around them. The tall Englishman boarded the plane first and two of his guards came too.

And now the plane was descending, much sooner than he had expected, actually. He had thought it would be a few minutes more before they arrived in Brussels, but then he had never flown before, so he was not sure. The plane had started to descend before it had reached the coast and it appeared to be landing almost within sight of the coast. He was worrying needlessly again. He realised that he was unsophisticated. What did he know about air travel? As the plane came in to land, there was just countryside around them, no sign of anything else. He was not worried, just confused. Maybe they were using a small airport, not the main one, and that made sense. The main thing was, he was home. Back in Belgium.

After that, it was all far too quick and dreadful to take in. The plane had bounced along the landing strip and then come to a sudden stop. As he looked out of the window, he saw a van pull up alongside the plane. The tall Englishman got out and he heard a brief conversation going on, but could not make out what was being said or even what language it was in.

Then he was bundled down the steps of the plane and manhandled into the back of the van, which was filthy and smelled of soil. Scatterings of earth and gravel littered its floor. A man had put handcuffs on him and another tied a blindfold round his head. He had not expected to be greeted with flowers and the Belgian National Anthem, but nor had he expected this. He began to worry. The van sped off. They seemed to be driving over rough terrain, certainly not on roads.

It came to a halt and he was roughly hauled out of the back and marched along. The blindfold was removed. He was in a large barn, lit by streaks of sunlight breaking in through the gaps in the walls and roof. Large parts of the barn were charred and it looked as if there had been a big fire in it.

He was led in front of a small trestle table, behind which sat three men. The one in the middle spoke to him in French. From his accent, he was French, not Walloon.

'Are you Arnold Vermeulen?'

'Yes, sir.'

'You were recruited as a Nazi agent in Brussels in May 1940?'

He looked round, his head darting from side to side. If the tall Englishman was here, he would be able to explain. There was no sign of him.

'Yes, sir. But I don't think you understand—'

'And subsequently operated as a Nazi agent in England?'

If the two men had not been on either side of him, he would have collapsed by now. He was not in Belgium. These people were French. He had trouble getting the words out to reply.

'There has been a terrible misunderstanding. You see, *I co-operated* with the British. I promise you. They even said—'

'Did you ever operate as Nazi agent in England?' The man to the left was now speaking, repeating his colleague's question.

'Yes, for a while… But only as—'

'Does the name Magpie mean anything to you?'

'Certainly, but again I—'

The man in the middle stood up.

'It is clear that you worked with the enemy against the people of France. Now you will suffer the consequences.' He nodded to the two men on either side of the Belgian.

They dragged him screaming across the rough floor of the barn to where a long rope had been slung over a beam, with a stool under it. The ground around where the stool stood was blackened with soot and scorch marks. Another man came over and attempted to tie his legs together, but he resisted. One of the other men kneed him hard in the groin and Vermeulen collapsed to the ground, doubled up in agony.

His legs were tied together and an oily rag was stuffed into his mouth. The two guards picked him up and hauled him onto the stool.

A blindfold, he thought. *Why can't they blindfold me?*

The taste in his mouth was indescribable and he could feel himself starting to vomit.

They appeared to be in no rush to tie the noose round his neck, holding him carefully in position as they ripped the collar from his shirt so that the thick rope was in contact with his flesh.

He noticed two things just before they kicked the stool away. The first was just how much sunlight was seeping into the vast barn. And the second was the sight of the tall Englishman, silhouetted in the open door of the barn, his long shadow being thrown almost as far as the stool he was standing on. He would help him now.

When the stool was finally kicked away, it was at least twenty choking seconds before he even began to lose consciousness. And during that time he was sure that the barn was consumed in flames.

The last sound he heard was of screaming children.

—

The German agent known as Cognac continued to move around England for a good eighteen months after the war, frequently changing his identity and appearance.

He considered moving back to Germany, but realised it was probably safer in England.

By 1949 he had settled into his identity as a Czech refugee so comfortably that he felt able to put down some roots.

He married a war widow in Derbyshire and became stepfather to her two young children. It was a happy marriage, though both his wife and stepchildren knew to avoid discussing the war or his life before it. They were aware that it was too painful for him. The Germans had done terrible things to his family, he told them.

Whenever he read that the British had caught every single agent that the Abwehr had sent to the United Kingdom it would cause him quiet amusement and satisfaction. It was just a shame that he could never tell anyone his story. He tried not to think too much about the past, because there was too much of it. But from time to time, he did wonder what had become of the beautiful Frenchwoman he had kept an eye on during the war.

His wife died in 1959, but he continued to work as a wages clerk in a local engineering factory, and he stayed close to the children and became very close to their children, his grandchildren.

He only let his guard down once. When he was dying in 1974, his stepson, to whom he was especially close, asked if there was anything he would like to do before it was too late. He replied 'To see Germany once again.' His stepson looked confused, but he attributed this to the heavy doses of morphine he was taking.

Cognac had always attended the Remembrance Day parade at the town's small cenotaph. It would have seemed churlish not to do so and he was anxious to fit in, not to draw attention to himself. But he made sure to stand on the edge of the ceremony. Be part of it, but separate too. There, but not there. He was used to that. It was how he had lived his life since 1939.

When he died, the local branch of the British Legion placed a wreath on his grave.

–

Georg Lange acted like a condemned man throughout February 1945, utterly convinced that he had been tricked and was going to be tried as a war criminal. However, at the end of the month, one of the Frenchmen who had confronted him returned to his cell and told him that his information about Ginette Troppe had been correct. He was there to show that he was keeping his side of the bargain. A disbelieving Lange watched as the Frenchman produced the false documents and burned them in front of him.

Before he left, Gaston shook Lange's hand. Georg found the whole thing hard to believe and decided it was best treated as a bad dream and forgotten. He was determined never to mention it to anyone. Who would believe him anyway?

Georg Lange was released as a prisoner of war in June 1945 and returned to Mainz to be reunited with Helga, Charlotte and Maria.

He had assumed he would return to the legal profession, but his few weeks of contemplating what he believed could be his imminent death had a marked effect on him. He trained as a teacher and specialised in working with blind children.

He and his wife spent a few days' holiday in Alsace one summer in the early 1960s, and when they stopped in Strasbourg he did think about looking up the name Troppe in the telephone directory. Purely out of curiosity – he would not have contacted her. But he thought better of it. Some things were best left as they are.

Georg Lange died in Mainz in 1988.

–

After he had helped Owen, André Koln returned to Paris.

The concentration camps around Europe were being liberated and the few French survivors slowly began to return, but it was no more than a pitiful trickle. André was never under the illusion that either his wife or son had survived, he knew that was not even a remote hope that he could cling to. He hoped that some members of his immediate family would return, but none did. Both of his parents, his brother, his sister and her family, and all of his uncles and aunts and their children were gone. One or two friends returned, a cousin of his wife's who had survived a death march, and a few acquaintances, but to all intents and purposes, he was alone. He knew that he was not alone in being alone. Less than two thousand of the seventy-five thousand Jews deported from Paris returned. In all, more than eighty thousand French Jews were murdered in the Holocaust.

André did not return to the law. He concentrated on his journalism, his writing popular and distinguished by an angry passion. He married again, twice; to a friend of his wife's in 1946, and to a fellow journalist in 1953. Neither marriage lasted more than a year. He had no more children.

André's journalism took him to cover the wars in French Indo-China, and it was there that he was shot in 1959. Despite medical treatment, he died of his wounds a few days later. Just before he died he asked a nurse to pass him a photograph from his wallet. He died clutching the photograph of Daniel, his son. The doctor who had been looking after him in the hospital wrote to his editor and said that André was unusually resigned to his fate for someone of his age.

Owen Quinn attended André's funeral in Paris. Addressing the congregation, André's editor said he did not understand why André was so reckless. 'It was almost as if he had a death wish.' People shook their heads. They too did not understand. Only Owen did not shake his head. He understood.

–

Owen Quinn had been due back at the Admiralty on Monday, 5th February, but there was no sign of him until that Thursday, when he quietly returned to work, seemingly with neither a care nor a concern in the world.

When he was carpeted for being absent without leave, he demanded to see Major Edgar.

It was the first indication Edgar had had that Quinn was back in London. His trail had gone cold in Strasbourg that weekend. All he had been able to ascertain was that the neighbours had seen a large man in a beret escaping from outside the apartment with a pistol in his hands. A man, who matched Quinn's description, was seen weeping over a woman's body. Soon after, he left the apartment with a baby and another man, whom the neighbours described as thin, dark and French. Ginette Troppe's mother had arrived back at the apartment as they were leaving. She had been in a state of shock ever since. Even allowing for this, Edgar realised that she knew next to nothing.

Quinn, the other man and the baby were seen driving away in a small Peugeot. After that, nothing. No sign, no trace, no hint whatsoever. If there had been an inkling before that Quinn had had these abilities that he had demonstrated in France, thought Edgar, then he would have made a most effective SOE agent.

He fully expected never to see Quinn again, so he was most surprised on the Thursday, which was the day after he himself had returned to London to explain himself, to get a call saying Quinn had turned up and wanted to see him. The feeling, thought Edgar as he strode purposefully across Whitehall, was definitely mutual.

Quinn was sitting in an office when Edgar walked in. He stood up and saluted and sat down again without being asked.

Major Edgar made great play of demonstrating his anger. He removed his leather gloves and trilby and threw both down on the desk.

'Are you going to tell me what happened, Quinn?'

'I needed to be on my own, sir. Clear my head, that kind of thing. I realise I ought to have been back at work on Monday, for which I apologise. I will, of course, understand if I am to be punished for that.'

'And where were you, Quinn?'

'Just driving around the country, sir. Walking. That kind of thing.'

'You're going to have to do an awful lot better than that, Quinn. France for a start. When did you get there?'

Quinn looked puzzled. He hadn't been to France. 'Check my passport, sir. What makes you think I've been to France?'

It went on like this for the rest of the morning and well into the afternoon. Edgar could see little prospect of getting Quinn to admit to anything. He was well versed in playing the innocent. The most difficult interrogation that Edgar had ever had to conduct up to this point was with an Italian living in Glasgow, who they were convinced was a spy, and who probably was. But it turned out that the man was also suffering from some kind of mental illness. He was deluded, the psychiatrists told him. It meant that he was so convinced that he was innocent that he was not having to play a part. Without the man admitting to being a spy, they had no evidence. They had to let him go in the end. Quinn was proving to be as frustrating.

He lit a cigarette and allowed a few moments for the tobacco to clear his mind. What is it that I am trying to achieve here? Edgar kept reminding himself. The objective was neither to punish Quinn, nor even to find out exactly what had gone on in France. The objective was ensuring that there would be no trouble. No difficulties. No noise. Silence was what Edgar was after. That no one would ever hear of Nathalie Mercier, or Geraldine Leclerc, or Ginette Troppe, or

415

whoever she really was again. No one would know what happened. The whole business would be forgotten.

'Your wife, Quinn—'

'I have not seen my wife since last April, sir. I have accepted that I shall never see her again. I am anxious to put that part of my life behind me.'

Edgar stared at Quinn for a very long time to see if he believed him, and for some reason, he was convinced that he did.

'I am gratified to hear that, Quinn. Don't forget, whatever you went through – whatever we put you through – your wife was a Nazi spy. A totally committed one, I have no doubt whatsoever about that. Our small operation helped to save many thousands of Allied lives.'

Quinn sat very still and didn't say a word. After a while, Edgar felt uncomfortable and dismissed Quinn. He asked Quinn's superior that no action be taken against him for being AWOL.

Edgar kept an eye on Quinn from a distance for a year or so, but he never met with him again. Quinn was as good as gold. His people at the Admiralty said that he was quieter than normal, but seemed altogether calmer. 'At peace with himself' was a phrase used in connection with Quinn more than once. By 1946 Edgar considered that it was safe to let Quinn go. He received an honourable discharge from the Royal Navy in early 1946 and trained as a teacher. The last that Edgar had heard was that Quinn was teaching at a boys' grammar school somewhere in west London.

By the end of 1947, Major Edgar ceased to exist, not that 'Edgar' had ever been anything other than a *nom de guerre*.

His war had been a long one. It had started in early 1939, months before the official declaration of war, and he had even been involved in a clandestine mission inside Germany itself, which had come close to breaking him.

He stayed in the field of intelligence for a couple of years after the war, but found the Cold War altogether too chilly. He could not find it in himself to return to the world of finance, in which he had worked until 1939, so he put Edgar behind him and went into politics. He had a successful political career, and was much admired for his compassion and pioneering work in the area of social reform. Once, in 1955, he was speaking at an educational conference in London and could have sworn he spotted Quinn sitting towards the back of the hall. He looked around for him afterwards, but there was no sign.

In his later years he often thought about what had happened to Owen Quinn. Of course, he could have found out easily enough, but what would have been the point? He had liked Quinn. But not once, either during the war or after, did he ever have the slightest doubt that everything they had done had been other than totally justified. There was no question of that.

The image of Nathalie Mercier, which was the name he associated with her, rather than that of Ginette Troppe, was never far from his mind. He only had to pass a beautiful young woman with long, dark hair in the street to be reminded of her. But what was most likely to bring her to mind was whenever he thought about the deception operation, and how its part in winning the war could still not really be spoken of.

One day in 1957, or possibly 1958, he bumped into Dr Clarence Leigh in the Central Lobby of the Houses of Parliament. His old sparring partner from the SOE was now Lord Leigh of Leominster, or it could have been Leamington Spa – Edgar couldn't remember, though he was sure it was somewhere beginning with 'L' in that part of the country. His peerage was the consequence of an easily forgotten report he had written for the Government on adult literacy, or lack of it.

Leigh now had the hunched appearance of a very overweight man, aged before his time, shuffling slowly from the House of Lords as Edgar emerged in a more sprightly fashion from the House of Commons. Leigh paused when he saw Edgar, tilting slightly back so as to be able to see him properly. Behind him was a young man, who could have been no more than twenty, carrying a bag and a pile of papers.

'Anton – my assistant,' Leigh said, by way of explanation. 'How are you?'

Edgar said he was well and the two men walked silently towards Westminster Hall and the St Stephen's exit, Anton a few paces behind them. Leigh's walking stick echoed on the tiled floor.

Leigh paused again, catching his breath, holding Edgar gently by the elbow as he turned slowly towards him.

'Tell me. Whatever happened to that French girl we were involved with. What became of her?'

Edgar hesitated. He was not sure how much Leigh knew. He frowned, as if he were having trouble remembering exactly who Leigh was talking about.

'Oh! Do you mean Nathalie… Mercier, was it? Lord knows. She disappeared. Never heard of her again after that July.'

They resumed their slow progress to the St Stephen's exit. Leigh was nodding his head slowly, not sure that he believed Edgar but not surprised that the truth was being kept from him. He would expect little else.

'Often thought about that operation we were involved in with you – and her. I think I probably owe you an apology, shouldn't have been so doubtful about it. She must have been worth a division or two to us, wouldn't you say?'

Edgar raised his eyebrows and nodded his head, as if that thought had never occurred to him. He let Leigh carry on talking.

'And you say she just disappeared? Probably best that way.'

'Probably,' said Edgar, before shaking Leigh by the hand and promising to have lunch one day.

He never saw Leigh again.

Edgar never once discussed with his wife anything that he had done in the war. As far as she was concerned, he had been in the Far East for the duration, while she had been left on her own to bring up the children in Dorset. The marriage only really recovered, after a fashion, when he retired in the late 1960s.

During his retirement in Dorset he took long walks along the coast every day. He preferred them to be solitary, but sometimes his wife insisted on accompanying him. He would often stand just staring across the Channel, sometimes for as long as half an hour at a time. On occasion his wife would notice that his eyes had filled with tears. If he saw that she had noticed, he would brush them away and make a remark about the 'bloody wind'.

He could see the other end of the Channel, where the sea was always stained with blood. He had an absolute conviction that, but for his work and others involved in the great deception, it would have been flowing with far more blood.

He died in 1979.

Chapter 38

June 1960

The rail ferry *The Maid of Kent* was twenty minutes out of Dover when the teachers finally managed to settle the boys and were able to sit down themselves for a cup of tea. It was going to be a busy day.

Mr Atkinson, the Head of French, had organised the trip. He sat alongside Mr Quinn, one of the geography teachers. 'Understand you speak French, Owen? You kept that one quiet. Could have used you when Madame Robinson had her fall.'

'Well, I speak a bit. Haven't really used it for years now. I get by.'

'Spent much time in France?'

Mr Quinn drank slowly from a chipped teacup and nodded. 'A bit. A long time ago though.'

The staff were used to Owen Quinn. A quiet man. Well respected. Absolutely dedicated to the boys, which made up for not having any children of his own. Had never married. First class teacher. But very quiet. Not exactly unfriendly, but kept himself to himself. 'Reserved' was the word that was most frequently used to describe him.

'Was that during the war?'

'Yes. I was over there at the end.'

'D-Day?'

'Something like that.'

'Navy weren't you? No chance of you being seasick today then?'

Quinn nodded and smiled politely. The ferry was pitching and it was turning out to be a choppy crossing.

'Been back since the end of the war?'

'No. I think we'd better go and check on the boys, don't you? Can't have any of them falling overboard.'

Mr Atkinson finally took the hint and went through the schedule one more time. The other teachers rolled their eyes. This trip was over-planned.

Mr Atkinson's plan for the day had allowed two hours' free time in the afternoon. He and the other French teacher would stay around the old town of Boulogne; the others could have a bit of time to themselves.

Owen had reread all the letters just the night before. More than thirty of them. They wrote to him twice a year, at Christmas and the start of the summer holidays. The letters always contained one new photograph, news of how he was getting on, and grateful thanks for the money they received every month. The letters never failed to end without a heartfelt expression of gratitude for what Owen had done for them. 'You can never imagine,' they once said, 'how you gave us a reason to live again.'

Owen checked his map and soon found his way to the school. No one would give him a second glance now. The tall young naval officer of fifteen years ago was now a middle-aged man, slightly hunched, slightly overweight, slightly balding.

'After school, he always plays football with his friends in the park opposite. Sometimes for hours!'

Sure enough, a group of a dozen boys aged fifteen or sixteen were playing football in the park across the road from the school. Owen walked over.

Even without the photographs, he would have picked him out. It was not so much the fair hair, flowing as he ran at least as fast as Owen had done at his age. It was the eyes. His mother's eyes. Even from thirty yards away, they blazed out. Like jet-black pools, just as he remembered them. He felt the hairs standing up on the back of his neck.

At that moment, the ball ran towards him. Owen ambled over to trap it. As he did so, the boy ran over to collect it. Owen trapped it and flicked it up for the boy to catch it neatly. *My son.*

'*Voilà.*'

'*Merci, monsieur!*'

For a moment, just a moment, the two looked at each other. Owen knew it was fanciful to imagine that there was any connection there as far as the boy was concerned. Just curiosity. But he did look him directly in the eye and flash him the broadest of smiles before running back to join his friends.

Owen stayed for another few minutes. He was blinking back the tears now, the first time he had cried in fifteen years. He moved a bit further away from where the boys were playing, towards the safety offered by the lengthening shadow of the trees.

He was not sure what to do now. The journey that had begun fifteen years ago in Strasbourg had finally come to an end.

As he and André had driven away from Strasbourg that February night in 1945 he could not be sure that he was doing the right thing. He realised that he could hardly just turn up in England with his son. Who would believe his story? Edgar was unlikely to come to his aid, probably quite the opposite. What proof did he have? How could he bring him up on his own? What would his parents say? Everyone would probably treat him as if he was mad. Literally mad. When he thought about it, he realised his son would probably be put into care. Another war orphan.

They had argued in the car. Owen told André the plan that was forming in his head. 'He is your son,' André had insisted. 'You cannot abandon him.'

Owen told André that the most important thing that he could give to his son was the chance of a normal life and he knew where he could get that.

For the past fifteen years he had hoped that he had made the right decision. Now he was sure that he had.

He moved around the pitch, still in the safety of the shade thrown by the tall trees in the late afternoon sun. He was aware that he cut a solitary figure but he did not want to draw attention to himself. Mostly, he felt a sense of relief. His son was clearly healthy and happy. But as he watched him playing with his friends, he could not fail to be reminded of himself at that age. The same build, the same turn of speed, and even his own favoured position on the right wing.

But he also thought of how his mind used to wander when he was that age, returning home after a game of football or cricket. He'd pass the families walking through the park and assume that that would be him one day. That was all he wanted then: nothing more than a beautiful wife and a couple of children.

Be careful what you wish for.

A few minutes later Owen noticed a couple moving slowly to the side of the pitch: Françoise and Lucien. Naturally, they looked much older than when he had first met them in 1944, broken and totally bereft in their house near Boulogne. Lucien was walking, although with the aid of a stick.

They had come to collect their son. They were calling out for him to come and join them.

'Philippe!'

Author's Note

Although *The Best of Our Spies* is a work of fiction, many of the events described in it and some of the characters are based on fact.

At the heart of the book is the Allied invasion of northern Europe which began on 6th June 1944 – D-Day. The Battle of Normandy was ultimately successful but in its early stages, all did not go according to plan. Despite having air superiority and many other advantages, it took the Allied armies far longer to break out of Normandy than the original battle-plan envisaged.

There can be little doubt that history would have been very different had the Germans not split their forces in northern France between the Pas de Calais (where their superior Fifteenth Army and most of their Panzer divisions were based) and Normandy (where the Seventh Army was based). This was due in major part to the dramatically successful Allied deception operation known as Operation Fortitude. Details of Operation Fortitude only began to emerge many years after the war, which is why it is never referred to by name in the book.

There is no doubt that Operation Fortitude succeeded in convincing Hitler and many of his generals that the main Allied landings would be to the north east of Normandy, in the Pas de Calais. The deception was ingenious enough to continue to fool the Germans for a few weeks after D-Day, thereby delaying the sending of reinforcements from the Pas de Calais to Normandy. By the time they realised that there were never going to be landings in the Pas de Calais, it was too late. Arguably, this was the critical deciding factor in ultimately determining the Allied victory in Europe.

Fortitude was a complex operation and there were many aspects to it, including the creation of the 'dummy' army called FUSAG (First US Army Group), apparently based in the south east of England (and referred to in Chapter 21), along with the use of inflatable tanks and deliberately misleading radio traffic. Perhaps the most effective aspect of Fortitude was the use of agents sent to Britain by the Germans and whom the Allies turned into double agents so as to send false information back to the Germans. Perhaps the best known of these was a Spaniard called Juan Pujol, who was known as Agent Garbo.

The London Reception Centre at the Royal Victoria Patriotic School in Wandsworth, the Double Cross Committee, the SOE (Special Operations Executive), the London Controlling Section and COSSAC all existed. F Section of the SOE sent some 470 agents into occupied France, many of whom were flown in by Lysanders of 161 Squadron of the RAF. All the BBC broadcasts on and before 5th and 6th June are accurately quoted. HMS *Gloucester* was sunk on 22nd May 1941, during the Battle of Crete.

Neither the hospital at Calcotte Grange nor Lincoln House where Owen Quinn worked are real places, although Duke Street in St James's was at the heart of a number of organisations related to D-Day. The Free French were based in Duke Street and the headquarters of COSSAC were round the corner in St James's Square. The Chequers Tavern is still there in Duke Street, and Geales restaurant in Notting Hill Gate, where Owen and Nathalie went for dinner in Chapter Fifteen, also exists to this day.

The Nazi concentration camp of Natzweiler in the Vosges Mountains, referred to in Chapter Twenty-nine, did exist. Known by its full name of Natzweiler Struthof, this was the only concentration camp on French territory. Its main purpose was to deal with political prisoners and resistance fighters (a number of SOE agents were murdered there). However, Jewish prisoners were transported there from concentration camps in the east to be murdered in its gas chambers so that their bodies could be transported to the nearby University of Strasbourg. Their corpses were then used for racial medical experiments by August Hirt.

The German agent, Cognac, is fictional. It had long been believed that throughout World War Two, no Nazi agents in the United Kingdom evaded capture. However, in 2006 the Public Records Office in London released papers suggesting that an Abwehr spy called Wilhelm Moerz did operate in Britain throughout the war and evaded capture. Cognac is loosely based on Moerz. The FTP – Francs-Tireurs et Partisans – was one of the most active of the French resistance groups. The details of the treatment and fate of Parisian Jewry are based on fact.

Many of the German characters in the book did exist in real life. Admiral Wilhelm Canaris was head of the Abwehr until early 1944. His opposition to Hitler and his increasing anti-Nazi tendencies, along with contacts with Allied Intelligence, are now well known. The extent to which he was aware that the Germans were being deceived into believing that the Pas de Calais was the main destination of the Allies is unknown. What is clear is that he and many others in the German military (including those involved in the July 1944 'Valkyrie' bomb plot) had realised long before D-Day that Germany was beaten and accordingly felt that it was in Germany's interests for the war to end as soon as possible. The circumstances of his execution, along with his deputy, Generalmajor Hans Oster, are accurate. The Abwehr case officer in the story, Georg Lange, is fictional.

Apart from the major historical characters referred to in passing, none of the other characters in the book existed in real life. Any connection between any of these characters and people who may have existed in real life is, of course, purely coincidental.

The true events around D-Day, Operation Fortitude, the occupation and liberation of France, and the opposition to Hitler will always be more dramatic than any work of fiction. Nonetheless, I hope that *The Best of Our Spies* does, in some modest way, shine a well-deserved light on the sheer brilliance and guile of the deception operation that played such a critical, yet still underrated part in the liberation of Nazi-occupied Europe.